PRAISE FOR

Surviving Savannah

"Fans of Christina Baker Kline and Kate Quinn will love this beautiful, richly detailed novel . . . an atmospheric, compelling story of survival, tragedy, the enduring power of myth and memory, and the moments that change one's life."

—Kristin Hannah, #1 *New York Times* bestselling author of *The Great Alone*

"Hidden history rises from the watery depths in all its glittering glory but also in its intimate, human detail. . . . A journey readers and book clubs will treasure."

—Lisa Wingate, #1 *New York Times* bestselling author of *Before We Were Yours*

"Fiercely hopeful . . . Callahan's expertly drawn characters are forced to discover how to live past tragedy, and what matters most in the aftermath. This is exactly the kind of story we need right now."

—Paula McLain, *New York Times* bestselling author of *When the Stars Go Dark*

"[An] enthralling and emotional tale. . . . A story about strength and fate."
—*Woman's World*

"An epic novel that explores the [mettle] of human spirit in crisis."
—New York Journal of Books

"Gripping . . . bringing to life a little-known shipwreck in meticulous detail. . . . [An] engrossing, centuries-spanning tale."
—*Publishers Weekly*

"The stuff of which Oscar-worthy movies are made, *Surviving Savannah* is a masterfully crafted and simply riveting read."

—*Midwest Book Review*

"A poignant exploration of how survivors across centuries cope in the aftermath of tragedy." —Modern Mrs. Darcy

"A luminous novel about bravery, connection, and resilience."

—Signe Pike, author of *The Forgotten Kingdom*

"*Surviving Savannah* is a lyrical homage to this southern city and makes a real contribution to the historical record."

—Stephanie Dray, *New York Times* bestselling author of
The Women of Chateau Lafayette

"Through the interwoven tales of three courageous women, *Surviving Savannah* grips the reader in a spellbinding novel full of mystery, tragedy, sacrifice, and resilience. . . . Superb."

—Kristina McMorris, *New York Times* bestselling author of
Sold on a Monday

"Patti Callahan masterfully weaves a little-known historical tragedy, an enigmatic mystery, and a searing family saga into a mesmerizing tale."

—Pam Jenoff, *New York Times* bestselling author of *The Lost Girls of Paris*

"[S]pellbinding. . . . Beautifully written with a masterfully crafted plot, *Surviving Savannah* leaves the reader breathless and marveling at the manner in which the past and present interweave in ways we almost cannot imagine."

—Marie Benedict, *New York Times* bestselling co-author of
The Personal Librarian

"A rich tale of friendship, heritage, forgiveness, redemption, and the thin, too-fragile line between life and death."

—Kristin Harmel, *New York Times* bestselling author of
The Book of Lost Names

"The astonishing story of the '*Titanic* of the South' is brought to vivid life. . . . This tale of survival, love, and loss, as well as Callahan's epic portrayals of a trio of strong, passionate women, gripped me from the very first page. Simply masterful."

—Fiona Davis, *New York Times* bestselling author of
The Lions of Fifth Avenue

"Riveting . . . a heartfelt exploration of the pain of survival amid incalculable loss, and a mesmerizing character study of three women. . . . [A] memorable and profoundly moving novel."

—Jennifer Robson, internationally bestselling author of *The Gown*

"[A] sweeping, captivating tale of a contemporary woman lost in a fog of grief who finds solace, and finally, redemption, as she uncovers the long-buried secrets of a nearly forgotten shipwreck—and the courageous women who survived to bear witness to history."

—Mary Kay Andrews, *New York Times* bestselling author of *The Newcomer*

"Atmospheric. . . . Emotionally charged. . . . Swimming in telling details. With *Surviving Savannah*, Patti Callahan has become the North Star of historical fiction."

—Mary Alice Monroe, *New York Times* bestselling author of
The Summer of Lost and Found

ALSO BY PATTI CALLAHAN

Becoming Mrs. Lewis
Once Upon a Wardrobe

AS PATTI CALLAHAN HENRY

Losing the Moon
Where the River Runs
When Light Breaks
Between the Tides
The Art of Keeping Secrets
Driftwood Summer
The Perfect Love Song
Coming Up for Air
And Then I Found You
Friend Request
The Stories We Tell
The Idea of Love
The Bookshop at Water's End
The Favorite Daughter

Surviving Savannah

PATTI CALLAHAN

BERKLEY
New York

BERKLEY
An imprint of Penguin Random House LLC
penguinrandomhouse.com

Berkley trade paperback ISBN: 9781984803771

The Library of Congress has cataloged the Berkley hardcover edition of this book as follows:

Names: Henry, Patti Callahan, author.
Title: Surviving Savannah / Patti Callahan.
Description: First edition. | New York: Berkley, 2021.
Identifiers: LCCN 2020031988 (print) | LCCN 2020031989 (ebook) |
ISBN 9781984803757 (hardcover) | ISBN 9781984803764 (ebook)
Classification: LCC PS3608.E578 S87 2021 (print) |
LCC PS3608.E578 (ebook) | DDC 813/.6—dc23
LC record available at https://lccn.loc.gov/2020031988
LC ebook record available at https://lccn.loc.gov/2020031989

Berkley hardcover edition / March 2021
Berkley trade paperback edition / April 2022

Book design by Laura K. Corless

Printed in the United States of America
5   7   9   10   8   6   4

This is a work of fiction inspired by an historical event. All dialogue and all characters
with the exception of some historical or real figures are products of the author's imagination
and are not to be construed as real. Where real-life historical persons appear, the details
of the specific incidents and dialogues concerning those persons are not
intended to change the entirely fictional nature of the work.

To my son
George Rusk Henry,
Captain of the May River
and of our hearts

There is a kind of story, God, that glides along under
everything else that is happening, and this kind of story
only jumps out into the light like a silver fish when it
wants to see where it lives in relation to everything else.

INDIVISIBLE, FANNY HOWE

⚓

The Seal Wife
BY SIGNE PIKE

One night I'll break free,
and hair streaming behind
I'll race for the beach.
The wind, brackish and thick
will soften the air
and cling to my cheek.
I won't be able to hear you
over the sound of my feet
pounding the wood
the roar of the water
the hot lure of sand.
Around me the sea-brush will twist and sing,
sheltering the boardwalk
in a thousand arches:
a tunnel of green
that will carry me away
back to the sea.

OFFICE OF THE ADVERTISER

June 18th, 1838
Wilmington, North Carolina

HEART-RENDING CATASTROPHE!!!

"Thus have we hurriedly sketched the most painful
catastrophe that has ever occurred upon the American
coast. Youth, age, and infancy have been sent off in a
single night, and a common death in the same billow."

1

EVERLY

Present day

I was born in water.

For all of my thirty-two years, my mom, Harriet Winthrop, had told the story over and over to anyone who'd listen. I could recite her words verbatim; I'd been told them since my memory began. *A tale worth telling*, she would say when I rolled my eyes as she launched into the story.

"There I was, my darling, only in the beginning of labor. I decided to take a long, warm bath before your daddy drove me to the hospital." Here Mom would laugh and shake her head, pat her hair in place. "The pain was so mild, I thought sure I had hours to go with you tucked warm inside me."

No matter how many times my young face would cloud with doubt, Mom would continue in her singsong voice.

"But I was so wrong. And you came swimming out while your father hollered for your sister, only two years old, to call 911 and then . . ." She always paused here, and I held my breath even though I knew what came next.

"And then . . . your father caught you."

Everyone who knew our family had suffered through this story, which had been embellished over time. There was the other part of the tale where Father had wanted to name me Selkie, but Mom would have none of that silliness. Her children were named after their ancestors.

This story became part of my mythology, my born-and-bred Savannah family lore.

The Winthrop family, we are *very* big on legends, lore and stories.

But it was my grandfather—Papa, to me and my sister, Allyn— who told the best stories. He regaled us with fantastical tales of a land beneath the water. There lived mermaids and the Kraken; there sailed the great pirates, and the lowly fishermen who found talking fish that offered wishes. There reigned gods and goddesses who ruled the waters with a vengeance, smiting all humans who dared to believe they had more power than the sea itself.

The tales of shipwrecks, of vessels that lay on the bottom of the sea, were the ones that inspired our young minds to dream of breathing underwater and finding treasure. At six and eight years old, we loved stories as much as the hot fudge sundaes we were allowed to have on Saturday nights.

In the evenings, Mom cleaned the kitchen after dinner and then sat on the porch with a cut-glass tumbler filled with the clear liquid we weren't allowed to drink. Meanwhile, we joined Papa in the mahogany-paneled library. Each as blond as the other, me with blue eyes and Allyn with brown, we crossed our legs on the plush carpet and lifted our chins to gaze up at him as he settled in the large leather chair and narrated his stories. Behind him, a limestone fireplace big enough for us both to crawl into gaped wide, and on cold nights such as the one blazing in my memory, a fire roared and consumed the dried logs from a back garden oak that had been felled by lightning years before. Above the fireplace hung an oil painting of a lustrous steamship with its sails spread wide and its wheels churning the water into whipped foam, the sky clear and bluer than the sea as human figures on the deck regarded the vast sea. *The Steamship Pulaski, 1838*, stated a small brass plate on the gilded frame.

Shipwreck tales were Papa's favorite—in particular the shipwreck of the *Pulaski*. Papa chose that legend again as we sat in our matching red fleece pajamas. We'd taken a hot bath, scrubbed our skin to pink and brushed our teeth—all the prerequisites for a nighttime story.

He began reciting the words we'd almost memorized.

"You see, before she took all those lives, she was a beauty, elegance her specialty."

"She looked like a beautiful woman dressed in white robes," Allyn said, meaning the sails.

"Yes," Papa said. "Everything was right with the world on a breezy summer night, off the coast of North Carolina, and then everything changed."

"Everything," I said in a reverential whisper. This was always when our hearts sped up—when *everything changed*.

"The wooden steamship *Pulaski* with her double paddle wheels and twin masts sat low in the water for her fourth voyage. She plowed through the restless waves of the Atlantic Ocean." Papa held out his arms as if they were sails. "Her sleek bow pointed north." He dropped his chin and sent his gaze toward the fireplace. "Her destination was Baltimore where she'd been built. Her passengers slept soundly or walked the deck with summer's expectations ahead of them. First Mate Hibbert was in the wheelhouse overlooking the serene scene, his pride solid beneath his starched blue uniform."

Papa settled back in his chair, lit his pipe slowly, knowing we were leaning into the story just as we were pressing into his legs.

"It was late, eleven at night, and one woman remained on the promenade deck, strolling and then reclining on a settee, and from the wheelhouse, First Mate Hibbert smiled at the sight. The wind picked up, and clouds covered the sky like a diaphanous curtain, blurring the moon and obliterating the stars. Peace reigned, and for this he was grateful. Yet . . ."

"Below," I said.

"Unseen," Allyn said.

Papa laughed and bent his head toward us. "Yet below, unseen, in the belly of the fine steamboat, a boiler emptied and the second engineer poured cold water into its copper belly. Steam was needed to power this ship and sweep it across the ocean into Baltimore. And while the passengers, all flowers of the South, slept in their cabins in the middle of the night . . ." His voice lowered as we held our breath and then fell for it every time, the quiet and then Papa standing and hollering, "BOOM!"

We squealed and grabbed on to his legs; he laughed as he sat down, his weight molding the leather to his shape.

"It blew up," I said.

"Caught on fire," Allyn almost hollered.

"When the engineer poured water into the boiler, its hidden strength erupted with the violence of a lit cannonball. A fierce explosion fragmented the peace—a concussion to the night, a violence to the wooden steamboat. Hull planks popped, lamps were extinguished, children wailed and women screamed. Chamber pots rattled to spill their contents across the floor, and berths rolled to block the exits from cabins. First Mate Hibbert was thrown from the wheelhouse to the wooden deck. China shattered and fire flashed. Steam filled the galleys. The passengers awakened, all of them, and the fight for their lives began."

"Then what?" I asked every single time because the answer changed every single time.

"Then the story gets *really* good." Papa's eyes twinkled and he leaned down, smelling of tobacco and mints. "Because now comes the story of how they survived."

The beginning of the tale was always the same, but his stories of the ship's passengers' survival changed with his moods—each different but as vivid as the next. Some survived by riding a whale to shore; others swam underwater and grew gills. Occasionally, passengers were rescued by great flying birds that swooped down and carried them home. This time, he used his deepest voice. "When the Kraken heard the explosion from the very bottom of the sea, he rose to the sound and found people thrashing in the water—men, women and children."

"Did he eat them?" Allyn was the most afraid of the wild Norse octopus-creature who terrorized sailors.

Papa shook his head as if in despair. "He swooped them up into each of his twenty squishy arms. The little suckers on the inside of his tentacles kept them high above the waters. They screamed in fear and panic because they knew a Kraken was the most evil creature of the sea."

"But not this time," I said. "Right? Not this time."

I needed the evil to become good. I needed the dark to become light. I needed the stories to end in triumph or what was the point? I hated the stories where the sad ending left me feeling an ache in the middle of my tummy, the same place where I felt the emptiness left by losing my father the year before. I wanted—no, I needed—the stories to make sense, for the world to be restored at the end.

"Yes," Papa said. "The Kraken was there to save them. And one woman . . ."

"Lilly Forsyth," I interrupted, eager for more about the woman who according to Papa had survived in a thousand different ways. The story always came back to Lilly Forsyth; she was the heroine in every tale, the woman who had all the adventures while the ship sank to the bottom of the sea.

"Tell us what happened to her." Allyn pulled at Papa's pant leg.

"The Kraken carried her to shore and offered her the treasures of the sea if she would come with him to the far ends of India."

"He took her!" I squealed. "That's what happened to her. She went to India."

At that moment Mom wandered into the library, her bottle-bleach-blonde hair flying and her hands carrying a drink. "Dad, I heard you holler. I take it the *Pulaski* has blown up once again?"

He held his hands up in surrender and tobacco flew from his pipe. "I didn't blow anything up. I'm just telling how it was."

"Dad, you scare them, and then they can't sleep. I'm the one who suffers when they come crawling into my bed and wake me in the middle of the night."

Papa brushed the tobacco from his pants. "It's good for them to have a large imagination. They're smart enough to know what's real and what's not."

"Dad, they are only six and eight."

"The perfect age to learn about the wildest stories that make us who we are."

Every story Papa told brought my imagination to life, vivid and real. And also, yes, he was right—I knew the difference between real and imaginary. A bird couldn't carry a child to safety, and the Kraken didn't swim the Carolina shores. Father wasn't coming back, even in a dream. But these were the most beautiful things I knew: Papa's stories.

I looked up at Mom standing in the library's doorway, her eyes as sad as they'd been since Father left the world. Mom loved the stories as much as we did; I could feel it in her gaze, but she was tired of feeling things, even the goodness of a story.

"Don't be sad, Mommy. Papa's stories don't scare me one bit." I looked back to Papa as I asked him, "What *really* happened to Lilly?"

His face became mysterious and closed. "That's a story for another day."

"Papa!"

"The secrets are lost to the waves. Only the sea knows, my child, and she keeps her secrets well." He paused and puffed his pipe with a secret smile. "And maybe one day she will tell you."

2

EVERLY

Present day

I know this: we're made of stories, legends and myths just as we are made of water, atoms and flesh. Once you know it, you can't un-know it; you can't pretend that everything that happened before you were born doesn't have something to do with who you are today. Still, everything can change in an instant, a flash, a blink of an eye. A story can shift completely with the screech of a car tire, the flash of fire or the words of someone you love. It can all happen as Papa had once said: *"And then everything changed."*

And yet the truth sometimes slipped from me and I forgot for moments and months at a time. The day Oliver asked for my help, I'd come to believe that a day was just something to get through without anxiety winning the hour.

The tall floor-to-ceiling windows of my classroom allowed the midday sunlight to fall so brightly that it formed a spotlight on the dust mites, giving them a place to dance. The building with its ancient bones was one of my very favorites in all of Savannah. Which said a lot because there were buildings in this city I loved so much I'd stand in front of a wrecking ball to protect them. The fact that I was able to teach history in this fortress was more than I'd hoped for during the long years of postgraduate work. But there I was: Dr. Everly Winthrop, professor of history. This was the only school I'd applied to teach at, Savannah College of Art and Design—SCAD for those who loved her.

The students gathered their backpacks and ever-dinging cell phones and began to filter out of the room, calling to one another, planning study groups or a night on the town. They had long hair, dreadlocks, spiked hair, pink hair. They were full of life and a vibrancy I not only missed in myself but thought long gone.

From the corner of my vision, I saw a man leaning against the doorframe as casual as if he were posing for a photo shoot. I took him for another student preparing some excuse why he'd missed this or that or the other. I'd heard it all.

From the scarred wooden desk, I gathered the essays my students had dropped next to the art history textbook with the bright cover of Van Gogh, but the man remained and I felt his presence as if he tapped me on the shoulder with his gaze. I turned with the full expectation of reminding him of my office hours.

My breath first told me it was Oliver as it caught in my chest and didn't move. I'd known that one day I'd see him again—it was inevitable—but I'd imagined it happening much later, long after I'd prepared myself with the correct words and penitent apologies. But here he was. He hadn't changed much since I saw him over a year ago—his sly grin, his dark hair wafting back as if there were a breeze, and eyes so brown they seemed made of earth. But, like me, the unseen parts of his life had been completely altered, I knew.

"Hello, Oliver." I held the pile of paper-clipped essays in front of me like ineffectual armor. The overhead light from the hallway bounced off a neon painting of a woman with a snake around her waist. "How in the world did you get in here?"

He took a step closer but did not enter the room. He shrugged with that grin that usually got him what he wanted. "I followed a student in."

"And what are you doing here?"

"I came to see you." His voice was void of Savannah's accent, the lilt and sway of it—he was a California boy. He straightened in the doorframe and rolled back his shoulders.

He stepped into the classroom. "I wanted to talk to you and if I called, or even texted, you'd ignore me or make some bullshit excuse." He grinned to soften the words we both knew were true.

"So, you decided to trap me in my classroom?" I, too, smiled; it was hard not to.

He sat at a desk as if he were a student eager to learn art history—we were on the madness of Van Gogh this week, moving toward Picasso.

I set the papers on my desk and leaned back against it to face him but aimed my gaze to where a timeline of postimpressionist works hung crooked on the plaster walls. "What's up?" My words echoed in the high-ceilinged room.

"I need your help." He held his hands out in supplication.

"How so?"

"It's a mystery to unravel. An exhibit to build. A collection to curate." He laughed and paused with a wry grin. "In other words, it's another consulting job at the museum."

I moved toward him, sat across from the desk and took him in for a minute. He'd always appeared kind, with warm eyes, a relaxed smile, a square jaw and always with an ear toward me as if he were ready to listen. "You're still at the museum?"

"Why wouldn't I be?" He moved and the chair rocked, uneven on the warped floor. A swath of sunlight shot through the window and landed between us like a sword.

"I just thought that . . . I don't know."

"That I wouldn't be able to stay because of all the reminders?"

"Yes." I'd thought a hundred times, maybe more, exactly what I would say when I saw Oliver again. But those words dissipated. In the silence between us came faint sounds of Savannah's bustle: a siren blared, a woman laughed and a dog yapped.

Finally, Oliver exhaled and rubbed his forehead. "Listen, Everly, I miss Mora. Every single day. Just like you. But I can't quit my job and run from it."

"Like I have?"

"I didn't say that."

"You implied it and it's true. I realize you miss her, too, but she was *my* best friend."

"She was my fiancée."

"It's not the same." I forced myself to look directly at him. I wouldn't turn away as I burrowed deep for a few of my long-practiced words. "I knew her since childhood—I don't remember ever *not* knowing her. She was part of my life in every way, every single day, all my life. Even more so than my sister."

He placed his palms on his knees and leaned forward. The pain that crossed his face was as real as if I'd taken a stiletto and sliced with precision. "This is not a contest of grief, Everly. That isn't why I'm here."

"Then *why* are you here?" My face felt hot and my neck prickled with sweat in the over-air-conditioned room. What if he said the words I believed he kept folded in the unspoken places—*it should have been you*? I found my hands balled into fists and slowly unfolded them. If I held tight, a panic attack would find me, and the last thing I wanted was for Oliver Samford to see me come undone.

"I'm here about work. And, trust me, if I thought I could find someone else, I would."

"Well, thanks for that." I stood. "Nice way to ask, Oliver."

"Please sit. I don't know why I keep saying the wrong damn thing with you. What I meant is that I knew asking might cause you discomfort, and you'd probably say no, but you're the only one who can properly do this job. I need you to be the guest curator. As usual, if you say yes, I'll give you everything you want: You can choose the hall, move partitions, change the color of the walls. You can select the graphic artists and extras. Just let me tell you about this project. I do need you."

"Need?"

"Yes."

I didn't sit but I didn't walk away either. My linen dress was sticking to my spine and my hair to my neck. I nodded for him to continue.

"We're doing a major exhibit of the steamship *Pulaski*."

"The *Pulaski*?" The rich smell of tobacco, Papa's deep voice, and the roar of the library fireplace flashed in my memory. My curiosity flared slightly, like a lit but damp and sputtering match. "Why now?"

He dropped his voice to a deep baritone that surrounded the words with mystery. "Because, Everly,"—he grinned and cocked his head—"they just found her."

"What?" A chill skittered up my arms.

He stood to face me, drew closer. "Thirty miles off the coast of North Carolina, a hundred feet deep. They found her."

"And it's her? For sure?"

"For sure. I have proof if you want to see it."

I reached out my hand. "Let me see."

"You have to come to the museum—I have photos there. And a story to tell you."

I shook my head. "I know you very well, Mr. Oliver Samford. You deliberately didn't bring photos so you could lure me to the museum. You think if I show up there, I'll say yes."

"Maybe."

"What kind of proof?"

He paused, lengthening the suspense in his way. "A candlestick . . . with the name of the ship engraved on the bottom. There's gold and silver and jewelry and . . ." He clapped his hands together. "Do I know how to tempt or what?"

An elevator in the middle of my body dropped; I turned away.

"Everly, you know what I meant. Listen, this is a story worth telling. It's the sudden disaster, the ripping of time into before and after. It's the wasted lives."

He could have been talking about us, about Mora, about life and its brokenness that came without warning. But he wasn't talking about us, or Mora. He was talking about a shipwreck.

"I only have one class left until summer break and I was planning on taking a bit of a rest. The anchor? Have they found that? Or the bell?"

"Not yet. They will. No more excuses from you."

"Okay, then, here it is: This is *not* a good idea. Us working together is *not* a good idea."

"No one else has the expertise or skills you do. You'll find the stories. You'll make it all come alive. I can pay you well."

"I don't want your—"

"I know. But don't say no out of hand. Think about it? Come by the museum in the morning. If you say no tomorrow, in the museum with the pictures in front of you, I will never ask again. But if you don't . . ." He held up his palms and shrugged. "I will pester you to the ends of the earth."

"Oliver . . . there are others who can do this, I am sure."

"Do you need me to tick off the reasons why it should be you?"

I fidgeted from one foot to the other, shook my head.

"I'll do it anyway. You're a fine historian, one of the best I've ever worked with. You're obsessed with stories of the sea. You know the *Pulaski* disaster. You're from Savannah generations back. You know how to dig up obscure documents and construct a narrative from them as if you saw it all right in front of your eyes. You *are* the exact right person for this job and you know it, Everly." He paused. "Maybe we can solve the mystery of what happened to Lilly Forsyth."

"She's a myth. She's a story we all liked to whisper about when we were little kids and believed in ghosts." I shook my hands and made an O form of my mouth as if scared.

"She was quite real," Oliver insisted.

"Maybe she survived the shipwreck but not the aftermath. It could be as simple as that. Why does it matter?"

"It always matters. You know that. If anyone can help me unravel the story of what happened that night, it's you. But if you're sure . . ." He took a few steps toward the door, then stopped and turned back. "I'll see you tomorrow. And Everly, it's really good to see you."

I waved him off without answering. When his footsteps faded down the hallway, I dropped into the wooden desk chair and ran my sneaker back and forth over the warped floorboards. They'd buckled and settled many times through their hundred-year tenure. I waited for a decision inside of me. Since Mora's death, I knew better than to move too quickly in response to unexpected events.

The request from Oliver should have sounded exciting, and that was the problem—I knew what things *should* feel like, yet they merely felt dull, like the dentist poking at my lip and asking, "Is it numb yet?"

It wasn't that I couldn't feel anymore. It was that I felt only a small range of emotions when before I'd had all the world's sensations at my fingertips. Since Mora's death, three emotions dominated: sadness, anxiety and guilt. All else—joy, excitement, sweet melancholy— approached me tentatively and then ran for the hills. And yet now, imagining the artifacts of the shipwreck, I felt the tingle of something more move up my spine. A memory of who Mora and I were together flashed—friends constantly seeking adventure and uncovering hidden stories.

I wanted to ask Mora: would you want me to do this? But, of course, she couldn't answer. Even if she were alive, she wouldn't tell me what to do. She'd ask me all the questions that would lead me to my own answer.

"Do you want to do this?" she might ask. "Do you want to unravel a mystery and find out what happened that night?"

"Yes," I'd answer. "But I don't think it's a very good idea. Not at all."

In my imagination she didn't answer. And that was part of the problem. I'd stopped hearing her.

I'd even stopped hearing myself.

3

LILLY

Wednesday, June 13, 1838

Lilly Forsyth jumped gingerly from the carriage onto the hay-strewn wharf and gazed up at the *Pulaski*, her pulse fluttering like the flags on the steamship's two massive wooden masts. The *Pulaski* in its beguiling beauty was lashed with ropes as thick as trees to the Savannah River's wharf. Carved scrollwork, painted white and shimmering in the sunlight, ran along the ship's railing. The red roof of the wheelhouse shone and the letters in gold leaf on its sides seemed to wink at the waiting passengers. Her furled sails lay in neat white rolls at the base of a complicated spider's web of ropes and pulleys radiating from the two masts. Waves slapped against her hull as she sat broad and low in the water, emanating the luxury and sense of purpose advertised by the Savannah and Charleston Steam Packet Company.

Lilly turned back to the shining dark carriage, flecks of mud splattered on the edge of the wheels, and lifted her arms for her five-month-old child, Madeline, a platinum-haired girl with eyes blue as indigo.

Her Negro nursemaid, Priscilla, eighteen years old, handed Lilly the child and then hiked up her dark skirts to climb from the carriage. Priscilla's height, two inches above Lilly, her warm brown eyes unreadable, often had Lilly staring at her nursemaid as she attempted to dissect Priscilla's beauty, to understand it in its bits and pieces instead of its whole.

Lilly's husband, Adam, came last; he frowned at the mass of people headed toward the gangplank, settled his traveling top hat upon his dark hair and focused his full attention on Lilly. His dark eyes moved in a critical assessment from her bonnet over her blue silk dress to her shoes.

He cut a handsome figure—his dark frock coat, curly black hair and the way he nonchalantly twirled his walking stick. His side whiskers were thicker than any man's she knew. His air of casual formality, of charm and arrogance, had prompted her to say yes to marriage, to what everyone had deemed a perfect match. Two aristocrat families combining not only their names but also their wealth in land and property, including the home they were headed to now in Ballston Spa near Saratoga Springs, New York, escaping the misery of a southern summer. Adam's good looks and impeccable manners had fooled her into believing that by marrying him she would be fulfilling every young woman's dream of a happy life, or the dream of a life someone else had fashioned and then she'd adopted willingly.

How wrong she'd been.

Adam gripped her arm tightly. "Tie your bonnet ribbons and hand the child to your nursemaid. It will do no good to be seen carrying your own child."

Lilly took a deep breath and held tighter to her beautiful baby, the plump feel of her soft on Lilly's hip, her round cheeks damp with heat and her hands clinging in tiny fists to Lilly's gown. Why she so often felt compelled to resist Adam's demands, she had no idea, but it didn't serve her well. Lilly caught Priscilla's gaze, which she read as clearly as if Priscilla had spoken out loud: *Do not provoke him.*

Lilly handed Madeline to Priscilla and waved for a porter to retrieve their trunks and valise. They'd brought what seemed half the household's contents for this summer season—their silver, china, and wardrobes, along with a trunk full of Adam's gold with which to purchase another cotton gin in Philadelphia.

A fluttering breeze set the palmetto leaves to clicking like crickets. Around the wharf, huge stacks of cotton bales appeared like snowy building blocks, and the morning heat carried the aroma of horse manure and sweat.

Lilly had seen steamships like the *Pulaski* from far off, but now that she was so close, its enormity stunned her. Two paddle wheels, glistening with river water, loomed six stories above them. "Look at that," she said to her little girl, who merely cooed and cuddled closer to Priscilla's soft breast.

Lilly hadn't slept well in days, but instead of feeling exhausted, she was eager to board the ship. A bruise on her left ribs ached and her thighs throbbed from the slaps Adam had given her the previous night. Now she would have two days' reprieve from his hands.

She'd gone over and over their itinerary—two days at sea with one night at dock in Charleston and *only* one night at sea. Two nights and two days in her own cabin with her nursemaid Priscilla and Madeline, far from Adam, rooms away from his demands and safe from his never-abating anger.

Gradually the crowd began to move toward the gangplank as men worked to unload the trunks and cases. The shouts of family and friends bidding good-bye echoed across the wharf. Priscilla shifted Madeline on her hip as the child made noises that sounded like the birth of a new language. A flood of love filled Lilly and she laughed. "I bet you're telling me the world's greatest secrets." She kissed her baby's milky cheek.

Priscilla, in a brown flax frock and yellow kerchief, took a step back. She didn't want to board and Lilly assumed it was because of the hellish stories told by her mama, stories of being chained in the hulls of ships that transported human cargo.

"It's going to be fine, Priscilla." Lilly nodded toward the ornate packet, the steam wheel rising above them. "Uncle Lamar helped build it. It's the finest there is and—"

"It's the sickness on the sea. I'm afraid of the sickness."

"We'll be fine. We spend one of the two nights at dock." Lilly refused to admit she also feared becoming sick on board. She wouldn't show weakness ever again—it invited others to take greater advantage of her.

Adam plowed past her, leaving both women at the base of the gangplank as others rushed by them.

"Come along now." Lilly walked up the gangplank, her skirts tangling in the breeze and her hair coming loose from the bun at the back of her neck. She wore the married woman's bonnet with ribbons tied below her chin. When she reached the deck and moved onto the promenade with Priscilla trailing her, she turned back to gaze at the elbow of land at the end of East Bay Street. Her husband's name—now hers also—shone brightly in six-foot letters painted on the warehouses that stretched along the riverfront. FORSYTH WHARF. And next to it, competing warehouses with a familiar name—a family name, her maternal uncle's—LONGSTREET WHARF.

Adam's need to own and possess—his wife, his slaves, his plantation, and his investments—was the twin to his jealousy of those who had more. And the Longstreets were among those who had more. Uncle Lamar owned most of the warehouses along the wharf, was the president of the Bank of Commerce and, most impressively, had helped finance the building of this very steamship. It didn't make Adam happy that Lamar's sister, Augusta, was Lilly's aunt and dearest friend. But not much made Adam happy unless he was in charge. Lilly looked for her dearest Augusta now, needing her kind smile and calm presence.

"Lilly!" a woman's voice called out. Lilly spun slightly to see Daphne Fannin, whose yellow hair and pink dress made her look like a piece of candy.

"Daphne," Lilly greeted her beautiful, cosseted friend with a smile. "I'm so pleased to see you."

Daphne nodded at Priscilla and then leaned forward to kiss the top of Madeline's platinum head. "Oh, look at her growing so fast, Lilly. I've barely seen you at church since she was born. I've missed you so."

Lilly focused on Daphne's bright blue eyes, calming as the sea. There wasn't a more attractive girl in Savannah. But Lilly had never been jealous of her friend. Quite the opposite. Lilly now saw that kind of beauty as a detriment to becoming a woman with her own worth and independence. Beauty faded.

"It's a lot of responsibility, having a new baby, and I don't leave the house on Oglethorpe very often," Lilly answered.

"I'm so happy you're here. Look at us." Daphne took Lilly's hand and squeezed it. "Remember when we were young and we planned to go on a long journey to the other end of the world? When we pretended we could fly."

"Yes, what lovely days. The other end of the world. My, my, we didn't even know what that meant."

"We do now."

"Maybe we do."

"You're so blessed, having a husband and baby. What's it like, Lilly? Is it as we once imagined?"

The hot fear of secrecy lifted in Lilly's throat. "It's quite exhausting." She attempted a smile. "And now I must be moving on to find our cabin." She heard the flat tone to her voice; she'd never been good at dissembling.

Daphne's face clouded with concern. "Is all well, Lilly?"

"All is well."

"You're not nervous about the trip, are you?"

"I do think about the steamship *Home*," Lilly said, leaning toward her friend, pretending that it was a sunken ship that concerned her rather than her husband's proximity. "The way it sank with all those people on it. People we knew . . ."

"This ship is nothing like that one." Daphne fairly bounced on her toes. "Look at those lifeboats." Daphne pointed to two lifeboats covered in white tarp and hanging on davits above the deck and two more upside down, uncovered, on the deck where children scrambled over them as if they had been placed there for their play. "And this ship is meant for passengers. Your family helped finance—"

"I know." Lilly forced a smile and kissed her friend on the cheek in farewell. She made herself walk away slowly, as if her heart weren't beating like a rabbit's.

With Priscilla by her side, Lilly went to the edge of the great ship. The sleek, shining wood felt smooth under her soles, and she leaned over the edge as far as she could, gazing into the muddy, churned-up water, not seeing its bottom but knowing it was there. That was how she felt about her own life. She didn't see it clearly, couldn't find its bottom, but it was there waiting for her. Lilly fervently hoped for that, even as the world had taught her time and again not to hope for too much.

A crash startled the passengers, and Lilly jumped back. The gangplank had dropped to the pier. Then, with precision, sailors in their stiff blue uniforms with brass buttons gleaming untied the ship's ropes and tossed them onto the deck, winding them like coiled snakes on the promenade. Lilly didn't move from her spot. She wanted to watch Savannah slip away—to view the houses, warehouses with her husband's name writ large, the bales of cotton and church steeples until they disappeared.

Priscilla bounced Madeline on her hip with practiced ease. She had four younger sisters and brothers that she also helped care for at the plantation. Lilly wondered, but wouldn't ask, if Priscilla missed them, if she felt the deep and horrible ache that Lilly felt when Madeline was away from her.

Lilly held out her arms for her child. "Check our cabin and put away our things, Priscilla. I will stand here until the city fades from view."

Priscilla complied without a backward glance, her gait as heavy as if she carried a hundred pounds on her back. Her skirts swirled around her, her apron flapping up and out, her bright yellow kerchief tightly bound.

Lilly felt Madeline's warm cheek against her own as the ship plied forward in slow motion. Passengers called good-bye to those crowded on the wharf, their white handkerchiefs waving, their voices cheerful with the expectation of an exciting journey.

Chuffing toward the sea like a floating castle, the *Pulaski* divided the Savannah River in two and trailed a foamy wake behind it. Its steam whistle blasted several short shrieks. The paddle wheels whipped the river into pinnacles of water. Lilly might have been standing in the middle of the sky, freedom and flight all around her.

Within moments Lilly saw her dearest friend Augusta across the promenade deck—tall, shy Augusta Longstreet, who ruffled the hair of one of her many nieces and nephews. "Poor girl," Lilly often heard people call Augusta—a childless woman who had lost her fiancé. Except for the childless part, Lilly envied Augusta's freedom from a husband. Lilly wanted to throw her arms around Augusta, tell her all the thoughts and fears and plans that filled her head. She wanted to be six years old again and curled in the hidey-hole of the magnolia tree with seven-year-old Augusta as they dreamed of the perfect life they would have once they were grown.

All nine members of the Longstreet family presented themselves on deck with every expectation of receiving the deference and honor that were consistently bestowed upon them. Lilly's mother, a Longstreet before marrying, would be proud to see them if she were still here on earth. Lilly missed her mother right then with the ache of a sick young child. Even if one didn't know the Longstreet history, if they didn't know that Lamar Longstreet had helped to finance and build this ship, even if they didn't quite understand the power this family wielded in Savannah society, one could have guessed by their manner and appearance. They were the aristocrats who had helped earn Savannah the title "Little London."

Uncle Lamar, the father; Aunt Melody, the wife; and Lilly's six cousins all stood as if posing for a painting. Among them stood Aunt Augusta. Lilly's mother, who'd passed two years ago, had been the oldest of the three, with Lamar next in line and Augusta the youngest. Lilly and Augusta had grown up together more as sisters than aunt and niece.

Melody spied Lilly first and strolled toward her for a greeting, her amber silk skirts swishing about her like waves, the large bow of her bonnet obscuring the lower half of her face.

Melody knew Lilly as well as Lilly would allow anyone to know her these days, which meant not well at all. Although they worked together on charitable endeavors at First Presbyterian Church, Lilly had mastered the tricks that led her aunt to believe she understood what Lilly's life was like. With a swindle of the eye and word, like a magician revealing only what she wanted others to see, Lilly made Melody believe she was the blessed one.

Melody hugged Lilly, and then stepped back with a smile. "Did your husband not accompany you on this trip?"

"Oh, he's here. I'm not quite sure where he has gone at the moment."

Across the way, Lilly watched Augusta lift her gaze from the youngest Longstreet, Thomas, two years old, to spy Lilly and rush forward, the toddler trailing behind her. "My dearest Lilly, you're here. I was so afraid you'd changed your mind." Augusta's pale yellow frock was gorgeous with its handstitched red flowers along the gigot sleeves. Her broad, smiling face drew the gaze upward.

"I'm here." Lilly took one of Augusta's hands while clinging to Madeline with the other.

Augusta laughed in her free and easy way, as Lilly had once laughed, and leaned down to pick up her charge. "Thomas, say hello to cousin Lilly."

Melody called out to one of her children, who was edging too close to the ship's rail, and moved swiftly to intervene, leaving Augusta and Lilly alone.

"Are you well, my dearest?" Augusta asked.

Lilly nodded but didn't meet her dearest friend's gaze. Augusta held out her arms for Madeline. "Let me hold the beauty."

As Lilly handed over her child, the lace of her sleeve rode up to reveal a purple-brown bruise circling the upper part of her tender wrist. "Oh, Lilly," Augusta said, anguish in her tone.

Lilly yanked down her sleeve to cover it and looked to Augusta with a shushing in her eyes. No, they would not talk about this. Not here. Not now.

Apparently Augusta didn't hear the unspoken words because she leaned close to whisper past Madeline's tiny ear, "What shall we do?"

Priscilla's arrival forestalled Lilly's reply. "Mistress Forsyth, the cabin is ready."

Augusta didn't break her gaze with Lilly even as Melody called from the far side of the promenade, "Augusta dear, come meet First Mate Hibbert."

Lilly smiled wanly, sorrow etched around her mouth. "You're being beckoned, my dear Augusta. You must go. We'll find each other this evening."

Augusta kissed Madeline square on the cheek and placed her back in Lilly's arms with a sheen of unshed tears. Lilly breathed deeply, glanced about for Adam and, not finding him, settled onto a settee.

"Priscilla, it is time for Madeline to nurse."

Priscilla glanced at the calm child, not near to fussing for feeding; she took her from Lilly's arms and drew her close as she headed slowly down the stairs to their shared cabin.

With her head bowed, Lilly adjusted her bonnet, the one Adam said he'd ordered from London because of his great love for her. She would sit here on the wooden settee and watch the land become hazy as the day descended on the horizon.

If she had known Adam's nature, would she have married him? Of course not. There had been other suitors, ones both kinder and gentler, but Adam's charm was a cloak that covered his true character. But she could not dwell on it now; she would allow her thoughts to fade with the city's view—the church spires, the Grecian-columned banks and theaters, the sandy roads and bustling carts—and allow her spirit to separate from her body. It was the only way she knew to survive.

4

EVERLY

Present day

I'd been walking for over an hour, Oliver's request buzzing in my ears. It was only a fifteen-minute hike to Mom's house, but I often detoured up and down the streets of Savannah, wandering through the emerald squares with their statues and benches nestled among green fronds, and zigzagging across the historic district with its beautifully restored brick buildings. Walking kept me from revisiting the would-have, could-have land I inhabited when I was sitting still.

I'd discovered that Savannah couldn't be fully explained to those who hadn't visited it. Photos, no matter how glorious, and movies, no matter how accurate, couldn't convey the way Savannah *felt*—seductive and lazy, busy and slow, modern and ancient. Savannah was a contradiction and a complicated melody that could only be known by walking through it, absorbing its every sensual detail.

I paused when I reached Wright Square, its benches filled with teenagers looking at their phones, unaware of the vibrant beauty around them. A couple—the young woman in cutoff shorts and a neon T-shirt with SpongeBob's wide mouth, and the young man with his arm draped over her—was staring at the towering monument in the middle of the square. Four red granite columns supported a pedestal on which four winged figures with arms outstretched held up an iron globe of the world. At the edge rested a rock edifice, round and low to the ground.

"I think a famous Indian is buried here," the man said in a thick New York accent, looking at his upside-down map.

I approached; I couldn't help it. "It's Tomochichi's remains below that rock; he was Yamacraw, and if it weren't for his assistance, Savannah wouldn't exist. He helped James Oglethorpe, the British trustee who was sent here to start a colony, to survive in the new world. This square was built in 1773 and was originally called Percival . . ."

Their blank faces caused me to shush, and I laughed. "I'm sorry." I held up my hands. "It's a history buff's tic."

The woman smiled. "Thank you," she said. "Honestly, that's so interesting."

"Everything here is interesting, if you look closely." I moved on with a wave.

In the heat of the afternoon, I felt grief begin its slow crawl in my chest and up toward my throat. This feeling was what walking usually helped me avoid, but not today, not with Oliver's visit.

Grief had been coiled quietly inside me since Papa's death ten years ago—an absence that was as much a presence as any ghost. I'd become accustomed to the loss in the same way one does a limp. But Mora's death had awakened that coiled animal, that oily, slithering grief that had hidden beneath the marsh and muck of my life. Mora's absence had joined Papa's and together the loss was more than double; it was exponential.

Everywhere I went in Savannah, I was reminded of Mora. The

landscape had belonged to us and to our youth. I wanted to stay. I wanted to leave. I couldn't decide anything at all. I felt frozen and yet still moving through a life that seemed to have been choreographed long ago. I was dancing by pre-planned steps, living by rote memory.

Mora's death had robbed me of joy, removed my curiosity and stolen my love of life's adventure. I'd experienced those with Mora, and without her I wasn't sure I was capable of feeling much at all.

Sunlight toppled through the oak trees, and the scent of gardenias traveled on the air from behind every garden gate. As I drew near the family home where I grew up, the home where Papa had told his stories and Mom still lived, I was stopped short. Two white horses pulling a red carriage along the cobblestone street were blocking our gate.

Tourists filled the three-seat carriage, too-red plastic flowers draped along its sides. With cameras and cell phones, people snapped pictures as the driver, in a nineteenth-century red-and-gold livery costume, droned on. A teenage boy in an Atlanta Braves cap caught my gaze and flicked me the finger. I laughed.

"This is Jones Street," the guide bellowed across the serene afternoon. "One of the widest and best shaded, with the most elegant homes. In fact, the saying 'keeping up with the Joneses' came from this very street."

Even annoyed, I couldn't blame the tour guide. This was the perfect time of day for these jaunts—a moon rising over Savannah with breezes gently wafting in from the river, gas lanterns flickering just enough that one could imagine it was the early 1800s, when old Savannah was long considered in its heyday. Spanish moss dappled the streetscape; fading light bestowed upon the ancient houses a resilient grace.

"This house right here, built in the 1800s, is one of the oldest and finest in the city. The Winthrop family who now lives here is one of the first families of Savannah, a very fine family surrounded by the ghosts of this city."

Having heard it before, I rolled my eyes. I loved Savannah's legends, but not when my own family became the source of gossip. Our more recent history wouldn't be narrated on any tourist route, but all the locals knew, and frequently repeated, the story of how my father suffered from a heart deformity and died when I was four years old. Mom had stayed in the house after his death, and her widowed father, Papa, had moved in to help. She never found anyone she loved enough to marry again and change this comfortable arrangement.

Our home was in the Georgian style with symmetrical facades and a hipped roof, the kind of august residence tourists stopped to appreciate while attempting to peer through the garden gate into the backyard.

Waiting for the carriage to move, I spied Mom pushing aside the ornate iron gate and waving her hand in a shooing motion. I cringed. I knew what was coming.

"Move on. Go on. This is a private home. There are no ghosts here." The voice Mom used was not the one her friends and family heard—dripping in honey and jasmine. This voice, shrill and high, she called up from the depths exclusively for pesky tourists.

Mom must have been sitting on the piazza waiting for me, watching the street like a hawk nested in the live oak. There she stood, all five feet two of her, in white slacks and a turquoise top, her blond hair wound on top of her head for the fund-raiser luncheon she'd hosted that afternoon. In her right hand, as usual, was the Waterford highball glass half full of vodka and ice—it was, after all, almost five p.m. on a summer afternoon. Cameras snapped and the carriage moved on.

I greeted her with a hug and inhaled the ever-present Chanel No. 5. "You know that doesn't do any good," I said. "Now you'll end up on some woman's Facebook page as a caricature of Old Savannah."

"Hello, darling. And thank you for your kind advice. But I don't want those tour guides talking about us."

From the receding carriage we both heard the parting comment. "If you look closely at night, you might see the ghostly orbs that surround that place."

I'd often thought the same—that Mora's orb hung near to check on us all.

I held up my hand to stop Mom from calling out one more parting shot. She let it go. This time. There would be many other days to holler at carriages.

Tourists had always stopped to gawk at the stately Winthrop house. I looked at my home differently. I saw the ivy growing over the crumbling mortar, the paint peeling on the porch spindles and the chimney that needed brick pointing. Glamour with a patina of age and neglect. As a child, growing up here with Papa, Allyn and Mom, my life sprouting from the petri dish of Papa's extravagant stories and Savannah's dramatic history, I'd believed that if there was royalty in Savannah, I'd have a crown. As soon as middle school hit and I understood that there were other families who could claim the same heritage, I was as disappointed as if someone had staged a coup and swiped the title from me.

Mom and I walked through the gate with the lion's head spindle and along the bluestone pathway that wound like a labyrinth through Mom's prize-winning garden. The original homeowners of 1845 would never have anticipated such a lush landscape in their courtyard. For them it had merely been a place for their cistern, waste and livestock.

Evening-tide, Papa called this time. It used to be my favorite. I loved the way the fading sunlight sat on the waxy leaves and the sky sank slowly into night. Mora and I had known that the flickers of sunlight, the last of the day, were actually fairies dancing on the leaves and grass.

"Do you think they have names?" I once asked, my voice a whisper so as not to scare the fairies away.

We'd sat together in the grass as it itched our thighs and we'd squinted exactly so the light would flicker and dim to confirm our belief. "I'm sure they do," Mora had replied in reverential tones.

My mind worked this way now—jumping from past to present: a Ping-Pong ball, a hummingbird, a firefly caught in a jar.

At the back door, Mom stopped and faced me, picking a piece of Spanish moss from my hair. She wiped at a speck of dirt on my forearm. "Have you been to Bonaventure this evening? Is that why you're late?"

"Not tonight. Not in a while."

Mom nodded and didn't ask more. "Allyn's coming over, too. A drink with me on the piazza before she arrives?"

"Is she bringing the kids?"

"Just us girls for an early dinner."

"I'll meet you in the library, okay?" I slipped the backpack from my shoulder.

Mom tucked her chin in question but walked off with a wave over her shoulder.

I tossed my bag on the back-entry bench and before I could change my mind, I wandered down the hallway, past family photos hung in gold frames, and entered the library. Bookcases covered the walls from floor to ceiling; a ladder tilted against the back wall on a track for grabbing books from the top shelf. Not that anyone had taken any-thing from so high lately.

From the window I could see the brick wall that separated my childhood home from Mora's. Wisteria covered the brick and ancient magnolias shielded everything but the chimney pots from view. Mora's family had moved once we graduated from high school, but I still thought of the house as theirs.

This was my favorite room in the house. I loved the endless shelves of novels and history books; evenings spent here with a blazing fire; days absorbed in reading for hours, until the sun faded and my eyes ached.

I stared at the oil painting of the *Pulaski* over the fireplace the same way I had as a kid, trying to imagine the night when the ship exploded. A brass picture light hung over the gilt frame and spread a glow across the wild waves and intact ship. The sky glowed bright blue and clear, the sails up and the paddle wheels in motion.

"You always loved that painting," Mom said as she entered the library.

"They found her," I told her in a low voice.

"What?"

I turned to Mom standing in the middle of a room she rarely entered. "They found the wreck. Off the coast of North Carolina."

"Oh, my goodness. After all these years? I wonder what can possibly remain of it. How amazing." She handed me a glass of rosé and I took a sip before setting the glass on a marble coaster.

The oil paint wave patterns slapping against the hull brought me back in time. "Papa loved to tell stories about this ship. But never the real ones."

"He never told a real story about anything at all." Pleasure filled her voice, not ridicule.

"Well, they were as real as they were meant to be." I paused and the room filled with memories as quick-flash as lightning. "He loved all shipwrecks—the way they separated the living from the dead in such dramatic ways, the way the beautiful ships slipped to the bottom of the sea with everything the passengers owned, the way they completely altered the future of families, and even entire cities."

"Everly, dear, you have inherited his great flair for making the tragic past seem quite romantic."

It was true and I was proud of it. "Oliver wants me to help with the exhibition of the treasures and artifacts they find."

"Oh." Mom clapped her hand on Papa's desk. "You must."

"Mom, I haven't worked with the museum since . . ."

"I know." She held up one hand. "But maybe it's time."

"Not with Oliver."

Mom sipped her drink and then wiped the lipstick from the glass with her forefinger while staring at me. "You two were once lovely friends and he is such a kind man. Why not work with him?"

"I am quite sure he blames me."

"I am quite sure that's ridiculous."

I almost laughed at Mom's imitation of my voice. "It's not for me. Not at all." I sat in Papa's leather chair, curling my feet under my bottom, and settled back. "All my life I believed Dad's old Irish stories that you told me, how the world that hides behind a veil is on our side, how everything works together for good. But it's not true. Life is *not* like that. There is no fate and nothing is guiding anything, and the sooner we all come to that truth, the sooner we can all get on with our lives."

"You don't know what you're saying."

"Yes, I do."

Mom rubbed at her temples with her pink-painted fingernails, just as she always did when she thought deeply or just before a migraine came on. Silence filled the room and far-off thunder echoed, a prelude to the usual evening summer storm's song. "Now, Everly Winthrop, you listen to me. I know how horrid all of this has been. Losing your best friend is awful, but you have a life to live."

"You can say her name."

"Mora. And you know I loved her as a daughter. But that can't keep you from working on something that might fill you with purpose and joie de vivre again."

"Fill me with what?" I grinned at Mom's terrible accent.

"Joie de vivre. You know, the joy of life. You've always had it. Don't let the past keep you from it. I want . . . my Everly back. The woman who always said, 'I wonder what happens next.'"

"Well, damn, Mom, so do I, but I can't quite seem to find her."

Sweat surfaced on my neck where it always appeared right before the terror reached upward and closed my throat. I shut my eyes, reminding myself that I was *not* drowning; I was *not* choking. This panic would pass. It always did.

"Oh, Everly. Are you having one of those attacks?" Mom's voice came through a long, windless tunnel.

I opened my eyes. "I'm okay." I focused on Papa's pocket watch in a glass case on the bookshelf; on the second hand of the wooden clock on the mantel inching forward; on Mom's hands clasped together, her blue veins crisscrossing under thin skin. "I'm okay," I repeated.

"I'm sorry," Mom said again, clicking on the desk lamp. The bright light made me squint and look away. "Maybe this project is just what you need—something else to think about—and you can work with Oliver. You need each other, you know. Maybe this is meant to be."

"There's no such thing as 'meant to be.' Things just happen. And then other things happen. Some good. Some bad. And some are horrendous."

"Stop that now. You don't really believe that; it's vulgar."

"So is death."

Mom came nearer and placed her hand on my shoulder. "That is your pain talking."

I shrugged her hand off and slouched like a child. "Did you steal that phrase from one of your ladies-who-lunch?"

"No, I didn't. And now you're being cruel."

A scaffolding of false protection collapsed inside. Mom was right. I hated that I even knew *how* to be so cruel.

A rustling sound made me turn to see Allyn standing in the archway. "Come save me from Mom's advice," I said.

Allyn was a brighter image of me—she'd kept our childhood blond hair while mine had turned darker blond. She was as casually elegant as the décor of her renovated Savannah home, which had been featured in a lavish magazine spread. "Oh, please," she said. "I can't save you from such travesty." She entered the library and hugged both Mom and me. "What is meant to be?"

"That nice man, Oliver Samford . . . the one who runs the museum." Mom paused and Allyn looked at me with an upswing of her eyebrows. "He wants Everly to work with him on an exhibit."

"Probably not the best idea," Allyn said.

"My words exactly." I clapped my hands together.

"Well, it's about that ship." Mom pointed at the painting.

"The *Pulaski*? Why are they doing an exhibit?" Allyn stepped closer and craned her neck like a hinge to stare up at it.

"They found the wreckage," I said.

"Whoa." Allyn touched the gilded edge before turning to me. "Remember that woman Papa always talked about? The one with the memorial near the river?"

"Lilly Forsyth," I said. "No one ever knew what happened to her, so he made up a thousand stories." I paused and closed my eyes. "Sometimes he'd take us down to that statue and we'd throw pennies into the fountain around it." I opened my eyes. "Dedicated to the perished of the *Pulaski*. June 14th, 1838," I said from memory.

"And often when we asked him to tell us about what really happened to all the people on the ship . . . he'd say"—Allyn sad-smiled, lowering her voice—"the sea always holds its secrets."

"Well, well," Mom said. "Maybe she wants to tell us now."

5

AUGUSTA

Wednesday, June 13, 1838

Always needed but never wanted. That was how it felt to Augusta, a twenty-two-year-old single woman considered as good as a widow what with her fiancé dying mere weeks before the wedding. Also known as an extension of yet another man—the youngest sister of the renowned plantation owner, banker and financier Lamar Longstreet.

On the promenade deck, Augusta hugged Lilly good-bye and returned to her waiting family.

She'd joined Lamar's family on this journey to help with his children, to be available as the aunt and sister-in-law. Augusta smiled as her entire Longstreet family presented themselves on deck, the six children ranging from her favorite, Thomas, two years old with his blond hair the shade of butter, to the oldest, Charles, fourteen years of age with his red curls springing out from beneath his cap. All of them wore the finest silk dresses and sailor suits and stood close to their mother. Lamar wore a three-piece linen suit, a pocket watch dangling from the vest and a grin reaching his ears. His pride vibrated around him, as if he'd built this ship with his own hands.

That morning, the sun just hinting its arrival in the mango-tinged sky, they'd departed in the carriage from Lamar's house on Broughton Street and headed toward the river via East Bay Street. The chinaberry trees were in full bloom, their violet flowers sending sweet perfume into the air, muting the aroma of cow dung and horse sweat. When the ship had come into view, they'd all gone silent in awe. What a thing her brother had done—after years of research, considerable investment of both money and travel to Baltimore where the ship had been built, and much oversight, he'd been instrumental in the ship's construction. He was one of the few men who had envisioned the prosperity the steam engine would bring to the South.

Once at the wharf, Augusta saw that some of the cotton, wrapped like giant sausages in hemp bags seven feet long by two feet wide, were from her family's upstate cotton plantation. Some bags would ship to the northeast and others to the British midlands. Her brother ginned all his own cotton on site to keep the seeds for himself. He certainly knew how to make money. Now with the *Pulaski* on his list of accomplishments, he was as full of success as his plump bags of cotton.

Another man also stood on the promenade deck: Henry MacMillan, his dark hair riding the wind, his clothes of the finest cotton and his top hat taller than most. Upon his face was a satisfied smile. From New York City, he'd acted as overseer for the construction of the *Pulaski* in a distant Baltimore shipyard and had every reason to be pleased. This would be her fourth journey, and the one he'd chosen to join.

Everyone on the ship knew the Longstreet family and greeted them and Mr. MacMillan with respect as they walked past. Arranged in a single line by age, the children jostled one another, and the littlest,

Augusta's love Thomas, rushed over to her. She picked him up and snuggled him, but her worried thoughts were for Lilly and the bruises that she knew weren't from any domestic labor but from Adam's hand. There wasn't anything they didn't know about each other—secrets and past histories mingled as their blood did. Knowing that Adam hurt Lilly kept Augusta turning in the night, trying to find a way to release Lilly from Adam's hold. Yet Augusta had little power over even her own life, much less her beloved Lilly's. And to talk of it would lead to more injury: Adam would deny the accusation and then hurt Lilly more than he already did, Augusta was sure.

Shaking off the dread, Augusta joined her family near the bow, where Lamar stood slightly apart. Bold and loud, he greeted those nearby while his wife, Melody, smiled, her eyes cast only upon her children—straightening a bonnet, smoothing a stray curl, tying a loose string on a sleeve. She was pretty, that was clear. Her skin had always been shielded from the brutal southern sun under the most elaborate hats.

At five foot seven, Augusta stood taller than some men, her long face as handsome as her brother's. She was as well read and educated as he was, but her status as a woman set them worlds apart.

Striding across the promenade deck was a tall man, his body thick with muscles formed by years working the ropes and boilers at sea. His uniform was as stiff as his posture, but he spoke to Lamar with a deference the older man appreciated.

"Captain Dubois!" Lamar called in a voice that made those nearby turn to stare.

"Mr. Longstreet, an honor to have you on the *Pulaski*."

"She's mighty fine." Augusta's brother swung his arms wide and just missed accidentally striking his wife. This was how Lamar was in the world—taking up too much space, little aware of those around him.

The captain nodded. "She's behaved like a proper lady on every voyage."

The men laughed, the women smiled and the children fidgeted. Thomas clung to a tiny iron Poseidon statue Augusta had given him when he'd seemed frightened of the journey. She placed her hand atop his warm head. "Stay still," she said quietly. "You'll be running about in a moment's time."

The two men bid good day and the captain moved from group to group, shaking hands and assuring everyone of good weather ahead and the prospect of an easy journey.

What ease this trip would entail compared to many days spent in a stagecoach bouncing along dirt roads. Traveling by steamship was a luxury, and Augusta was grateful that part of the long trip to the family estate in Saratoga Springs would be spent in comfort. And her brother had been brilliant to allay any lingering fears by arranging for only one night at sea.

Adam Forsyth's voice startled Augusta, and she looked behind him for Lilly but didn't see her. Adam grasped Lamar's hand and bellowed, "Lamar, my friend, what a journey we have ahead of us."

"Indeed," Lamar answered and returned Adam's handshake, albeit a little less enthusiastically. They were all cautious of the man who had boldly insinuated himself near Lamar but who would never hesitate to take him down in business if he had the chance. Adam greeted Mr. MacMillan in turn.

"Henry, we're so thrilled you're here to observe the South on the rise." Adam tipped his hat. "New York City better keep its eye on us. The Empire City of the South will soon dominate coastal transportation."

"You believe so?" Henry's voice held a hint of contempt and Augusta suppressed a grimace. Firing the embers of Adam's temper would serve no purpose, especially since her beloved Lilly would bear the brunt of it.

"I do think so." Adam lifted his chin to Lamar. "With all credit given to this man." He slapped his thigh. "Lamar and I are both members of the Aquatic Club, and we know the future of steamships and transport."

Augusta felt a shudder of disgust at Adam's false praise. He would take everything he could from her brother. Lamar nodded but a smile did not appear to crease his cheeks.

Henry released a tight laugh and addressed Adam. "I don't think New York is yet worried about the South taking over its industry. But I do agree that the South is a mighty fine place. Your tree-lined lanes and lush squares are seductive indeed." He smiled at Augusta; she knew he was only being kind.

Adam cleared his throat and stood taller, sweat appearing visibly on his forehead and doughy neck. "We are now your mercantile equal—what would we want of your mill towns and industry? Our plantations are thriving." Adam leered and leaned closer. "But otherwise we have so very much in common—there is nothing you can get in New York City that you can't get here. From theater to silk to fine wine."

Henry nodded. "Indeed, Mr. Forsyth."

Lamar fidgeted and addressed Adam. "Would you like to see the boiler room? I'm taking my son down there for a view of the inner workings."

Augusta realized her brother was removing Adam Forsyth from further embarrassing them with his ostentatious bragging. The two men wandered off and Henry moved closer to Augusta. Could he hear her heart beating rapidly and unsteadily while he stood so close?

They'd been in each other's company more times than she could count at her family's city domicile, when Henry visited to attend long business meetings. But they'd never stood a mere hand's width apart. She stared straight ahead so he wouldn't see her nervous gaze.

"Miss Longstreet, are you quite all right?"

She tried to smile at him. "I am."

"You seem a bit nervous."

"Oh, I was just thinking about the Telfair sisters, who were supposed to be here, but Mary told me she had a bad, bad feeling about this journey and they rebooked on another ship. I . . ."

"Augusta, she's sturdy and trustworthy." His grin made her heart take another leap. So completely inappropriate, her feelings. So ridiculous. As if she were some young girl hiding in the leaves of the magnolia tree with Lilly and dreaming of the perfect man.

There was no such thing; they both knew that by now.

She smoothed Thomas's hair, which didn't need smoothing. "I'm quite pleased to be here."

"I hope so. Do tell me what you're reading now."

They'd spent hours in her brother's library talking about the differences between the founding of their distinctly different cities: his New York, her Savannah. But what united them—what was *not* different—was their shared love of books. If he saw her as another intellectual, like her brother, that was better than being dismissed as a silly female without a thought in her head. But how lovely it would be if he actually noticed she was a living, breathing woman.

"I am finally reading Sir Walter Scott's 'The Lady of the Lake,'" she said. "I'm enamored of the imagery of Scotland and—"

"Augusta!" Melody's voice called out and Augusta attempted to ignore her by addressing Henry.

"And you?"

"You are being summoned, I do believe." He tipped his top hat and stared out at the river.

She watched him for a moment. She was not in any way an appropriate match for Henry MacMillan, the handsome man from a thriving northern metropolis who had told her he abhorred slavery and who questioned the wealth her family had accumulated in part because of that institution. He would take their money to build the ship, but turn up his nose at their way of life. To have feelings for him, as she did, was not only inappropriate but also foolish. Yet she had read in Pascal's philosophy that the heart has reason that reason knows nothing of, and nothing about Henry MacMillan brought reason to mind.

She moved slowly toward her sister-in-law. After the shriek of the steam whistle, and the crash of the gangplank on the wharf, they'd set sail. Now Augusta gave one last glance at the outline of Savannah. Horse-drawn carriages lurched away, returning to downtown homes and stables along the winding dusty roads.

Augusta lifted Thomas and thought of her fiancé, Isaac, and how he would have loved this trip. He'd been gone for a year now, their engagement having lasted only two months. She hadn't loved Isaac in the way her other friends talked about their beaus, with blushing cheeks and trembling desire, but she'd admired and respected him. When Isaac had fallen ill with consumption at twenty-five years old, mere weeks after she'd accepted his proposal, the tragic loss had changed her view of life and upended her future.

The last child of three, Augusta wasn't plain but neither was she a beguiling beauty like Lilly. Her parents, both gone now, had left Stonewall, the family's Sea Island cotton plantation, to their only son. Augusta was content to be part of his family, helping her sister-in-law while occasionally occupying the room above the piazza where she'd slept as a child. The city house in downtown Savannah, where her brother worked long days in his office, was where she spent most of her time. The crowds in the squares, and the parlors of extended family and friends, were comfortably familiar to her.

Now on the ship, she bounced Thomas on her hip as the landscape of South Carolina passed by in clumps of green and brown. She spied an osprey overhead, its wings spread wide, soaring effortlessly on the wind. So free.

Thomas's weight grew heavy; she could not imagine loving even her own children more than she did her brother's. She kissed the boy's cheek. "I love you, little one. We have a grand adventure ahead of us."

6

EVERLY

Present day

From my bedroom nestled in the high left corner of my home, two crows outside my window woke me, as they did each morning with their raucous calls. Soon others would join them. I lay still, listening, waking slowly. After Mora had passed, Mom had offered to let me stay at the family home—you know, get my feet back under me in familiar territory. But I loved my rented one-bedroom home that sat on a corner in the historic district behind ivy-covered walls and ancient mortar. I adored the bright blue front door that I'd painted myself and was hidden in an alleyway. I shared the back courtyard with six other people.

I stretched and looked out the window to the left of my bed, which was the reason I'd rented this place—tall and wide, it revealed a striking view of St. John the Baptist's double steeples and the wide sky over my beloved city.

When I'd first moved in, the window had been painted shut, but after hours spent chiseling away with Mora, razor blades and screwdrivers our tools, we'd pried it open and sat on the flat roof to gaze out. "You think we'll ever leave?" she'd asked while the sky turned blood-red with sunset.

"I don't know. I hope not." I'd turned to her. "Or I hope so. I can't decide."

"I get it."

She always got it. She always got me.

Our roots dug as deep as the oldest tree—both of us could tell you what anything in the city was before, and what it was today; we'd both attended Country Day and Sweet Briar College; our families were charter members of the Oglethorpe Club and our mothers Colonial Dames; our fathers and grandfathers had belonged to the St. Andrews Society. We each had family buried in Bonaventure Cemetery. Now Mora was there far ahead of most of us.

Very few of my childhood memories didn't include Mora, with her ginger hair springing wild about her freckled face, her laughter so loud and her sense of adventure so bright that they sometimes blinded me. I had faded behind her light, but I didn't care; even if I was the shadow cast by her sun, at least I was part of the adventure that was life with Mora.

With her memory vivid the morning after Oliver had visited me in the classroom, I slipped from bed and opened that window, stared out at the brightening sky. The world slowly came to life; first the bird calls and then the trees, bushes and brick wall of the garden took shape, emerging from the dusky dawn.

A shipwreck found. An exhibit to curate with the freedom to handle the job as I pleased. History to uncover. These were the siren calls I realized now I would answer even as I'd pretended I might not. As if there were ever another choice. I'd made it—somewhere deep down—the minute Oliver had asked. Because the only thing better than avoiding my own life at the present moment was completely involving myself in the lives of those who came before me.

My backpack slapped against my shoulder blades as I took a left onto Charlton Street and passed its centuries-old homes. I knew the history of many of the families who lived in them. Tourists might hear brief remnants of the tales but they'd never know the full truth—whose son had been lost to drugs and alcohol; whose fortunes had dissolved in gambling losses; whose husbands had philandered their way to divorce and financial ruin. Then there were the beautiful stories—the families that gave their wealth to help the helpless and never asked for recognition; the great love that led to great works of art; renowned parties where lifelong friends met for the first time. Stories at every turn.

In two blocks I reached Bull Street and took a left, passing Monterey Square, and headed toward Forsyth Park.

In the summer morning, Savannah's historic district stood proud, as if daring any city to look better than she did. Passing students from the Savannah College of Art and Design and camera-toting photographers, weaving among business people and shopkeepers, I made my way to the park that had once been surrounded by an iron fence to keep the cows inside.

In Forsyth Park petals fell from the tulip poplars like pink confetti, and the grass was vibrant green. Dandelions persisted stubbornly despite bikes and countless feet running over them. The magnolia trees with their creamy blooms as big as dinner plates would later leave unopened pods on the ground, where they would burst with red seeds that stained the concrete.

I was lost in the beauty of the park's thirty acres, and thinking of the days when this was the promenade where nineteenth-century women of a certain class took their exercise. I was smiling at the image of their big-skirted gowns and elaborate bonnets when a motorcycle gunned its engine at the green light, jangling my every nerve. I froze and then ran a few yards into the park before bending over to catch my breath beside the hundred-and-fifty-year-old fountain that had been dyed green *that* St. Patrick's Day more than a year ago.

And the jarring memory arrived just like that, just like it always did—with a flood of fear, and an asphyxiating sensation where the waters of memory swamped me.

Everything shimmered green that day—the March trees bursting with the neon green of new leaves; the hats and shirts and silly shamrock headbands of the revelers all bright kelly green; the beads thrown from the parade floats all green.

Mora, Oliver and I stood at the granite curb behind yellow tape that screamed *CAUTION*. The drumbeat of a high school band floated down the cobblestone street, the tubas and trumpets discordant as they played an Irish tune that didn't sound quite right when played by brass instruments.

The simple joy of a spring afternoon spent in the city I loved with the people I loved filled me to laughter. After a four-year relationship had shattered six months before, my broken heart had slowly healed, and the sun was warm without the summer blaze we all knew was fast approaching.

With Mora and Oliver, I never felt like a third wheel; I never felt like an intruder. I loved them both. I'd worked with both Oliver and Mora at the Rivers and Seas Museum, and when I wasn't around, they'd fallen in love. Neither had wanted to tell me, thinking I might feel left out and worried about my newfound belief that love wasn't worth the effort, but it wasn't that damn hard to figure out. No one with eyes and a heart could miss what was happening between them.

We stood next to each other, a row of three, at the edge of the sidewalk; Oliver between Mora and me while the sounds of the parade drew closer.

Oliver pointed at a floating leprechaun balloon. "I bet the real St. Patrick never saw that coming."

"When he chased out those snakes and spread the good word," I said, "I doubt he envisioned green beer and people wearing shamrock headbands."

Oliver laughed and bumped me with his shoulder. "You're funny."

I bumped Oliver back, and while laughing, both Mora and Oliver took two steps to the right. That's the simple math. Two to the right because I bumped them, because I gave a little push with my hip. I stepped into the space where Mora had stood only seconds before.

At that moment, the revving of a car engine startled us, and we looked up to see a sleek red vehicle hurtling toward us. It took only a second, maybe less, maybe more, for me to wonder why the lead parade car was going so fast and why in the world it was red instead of green. This inane thought was my last just as the car veered into the crowd, through the ineffectual yellow tape and onto the sidewalk where I stood with my best friend and her fiancé.

Behind the windshield, I saw his face, or more accurately his dead eyes—they were dark brown under thick eyebrows; his long black hair touched his shoulders; his beard scraggly and long. And then in a primal reflex, I ran, my legs taking over all rational thought. I took four steps, or was it five? Later, I went over and over this in my mind. Four or five? Did it matter? Mora took only one before she was hit and thrown sideways into the crowd, her arms and legs bent at angles that still haunt my sleep.

Oliver was also hit sideways, rendered unconscious, but his chest rose and fell with his breath. His arms were splayed and his left leg caught beneath his right in a way that wasn't natural. Someone screamed to call 911 and I froze.

Others had been hit, too, and they moaned and cried out, but not Mora. She was still and silent, her red hair fanned out and mixing with blood on the cracked sidewalk next to Lafayette Square. Her eyes were open—this I will never forget—staring at the cloudless sky. Her left arm twisted over her head. Blood ran from her ears and nose, and a puddle formed behind her head. I vomited onto the sidewalk and then a scream, shrill and foreign, erupted from my throat.

The man with the dead eyes flew from the driver's side and ran through the crowd. No one had the wherewithal to stop him; there were lives to save. He smelled like an outdoor bathroom, stale and damp, as he slammed past me and disappeared around the corner. I retched again at the physical contact, but it unfroze me, set me in motion. I ran to Mora and knelt beside her while sirens wailed toward us. I tried to stop the blood. I screamed her name. A man grabbed me. "Don't move her. Don't touch her. They're coming."

I looked to Oliver, but he lay next to her without moving, breathing but unconscious.

It should have been me.

The memory finished having its way with me, and I sat on a wooden bench in Forsyth Park and breathed slowly—four count in, hold for seven, blow out and hold for eight—over and over using this technique. The driver's dead eyes—if I ever saw them again, I would know him. I would know those eyes in the middle of the night. I looked for them; I ran after men who had the same build and dark hair. Someday, I believed, I would find him.

After another breath, I stood and shakily walked down the long sidewalk to the park's south end. Grief, with its choking reminder, arrived with the guilt of having let myself forget for even a minute that she was gone. It wasn't fair to Mora to be happy.

The idea was, of course, ridiculous. Everyone told me that. The grief books, the psychiatrist Mom had sent me to; Allyn, who cried out that Mora, more full of life than anyone we'd ever known, would want me to be happy.

In a few steps, I found myself in front of the Sentient Bean—it was *our* favorite coffee shop. Out of both honor and habit, I walked there many mornings for coffee to go.

"Everly!" I turned to see Sophie, my dear friend. I missed her. I hadn't seen or talked to her, or anyone else aside from family or co-workers for that matter, in months. Sophie ran to me and engulfed me in a hug. She stepped back, keeping her hands on my shoulders. "I've missed you so. I've been calling and calling."

"I know." I exhaled. "I'm sorry. I've been a terrible friend."

"Are you kidding?" Sophie swatted playfully at my shoulder; her deep brown eyes, eyelashes thick and long, were as comforting as her hug. "I'm the terrible friend. I shouldn't just call and text. I need to show up. I say that all the time to the kids in my classroom, show up for people, and then . . ." Sophie stopped midsentence and hugged me again. "Your usual?"

"Huh?"

Sophie turned to the barista and ordered for me. "Half-caf latte with almond milk," Sophie said. "Now sit," she ordered. "Talk to me for five minutes. Tell me how you're doing."

I sank into an iron chair across the café table from my friend. "I'm okay. I guess."

"What can I do?" Sophie wiped the table with a napkin.

"It's been over a year, Sophie. I can't keep thinking people need to *do* anything. But I'd love to take a long walk with you, or go to a movie, or something. Now tell me about your life."

"It's been crazy but okay. You heard about my brother, right?"

"No."

"He took off for Nashville, seeking fame and fortune as a country singer." Her deep laugh echoed across the tables and others turned. She reached forward, the six bangles she wore on her wrist jangling like wind chimes. "I guess if Darius Rucker can turn from Hootie into a Black country music star, so can my brother."

"He'll make it," I said. "He's that good."

And then we were off, talking about local gossip and discussing friends we both knew. I asked about her students; Sophie's African American heritage led her to study and teach the history at SCAD. When the latte arrived, I stood to go. "Off to the museum."

"Wait. What? Your sister told me you would never work there again."

"When did you start listening to my sister?"

We laughed and said good-bye before I headed the six blocks to the museum, sipping coffee until I reached the last drop and stood in front of the Rivers and Seas Museum of Savannah. I turned my back to the marble stairs and red front door to gaze out at the city. Was there a prettier place? It wasn't that I'd never traveled; I had. I'd been on European vacations as an adolescent with Mom and Papa. Later, for school and work I'd been on trips up and down the East Coast to learn of the nation's history. But not once, except for a brief moment in Ireland, had I thought there was a city more mystical and beautiful than Savannah.

I wouldn't accept this job with Oliver out of some sort of meant-to-be like Mom believed. I didn't put my money on those concepts anymore; those were ideas spouted by people who had never experienced a rupture in their well-planned lives. But this project would absorb my hours and my mind for as long as it took.

The museum's battered but beautiful old building with its brightly lit rooms held as many memories of Mora (and then Oliver) as anywhere else. We'd worked together on every special exhibit they'd done over the past five years—the ships of the Revolutionary War; the pollution of the great rivers of Georgia; the history of the SS *Savannah*—Oliver the director, Mora the head curator while I was the guest curator.

It wasn't that I hadn't wanted to do this work anymore, but simply that I felt unsteady near Oliver. The three of us had known each other as intimately as family. We could read a thought on a face. I knew they would get engaged a week before he asked; a subtle shift in him had told me.

"If one wants to move beyond the past, one must not delve into the past," some out-of-date advice book once told me. But no one, even if they believe they have, moves past the past. It follows; it shadows; it breathes quietly in the dark corners. Ask me, I know.

I set my hand to the brass doorknob and opened it to a dusty dimness. The lights were off and the front desk empty where their most loyal volunteer, Mrs. Farmly, usually sat with her gray bobbed hairdo and cheery greetings for anyone who wandered in from the street.

I walked through the room of ship models and stopped before a five-foot-long, to-scale model of the *Pulaski* steamship. I crouched low and stared through the glass. Two replica lifeboats hung above the decks and two more on the deck. *Only* four. Ropes hung across the double masts and down to the bow. Wooden settees were fixed to the deck along the railings, facing seaward, and the wheelhouse was displayed as a tiny dollhouse in the middle. I'd never paid the model much attention, at least not the minute details. I could rattle off the names of every ship featured in the museum, both models and paintings, but had I really *looked*?

I wandered down the back hallway to climb the creaky stairs, past a display of the family whose home this had been during the Civil War, a family that had watched the Union general, William Tecumseh Sherman, march down the broad street and capture the city. I reached a closed door: *Dr. Oliver Samford—Director* stated the brass label. Hand-carved trim made to resemble a ship's rope surrounded the doorframe. I turned the knob and went in unannounced.

Oliver sat behind a desk, his back straight, staring straight ahead as if someone stood in front of him. The desktop was organized in neat piles of papers and folders.

"Good morning," he said in a too-cheery voice. "Have a seat." He motioned to the empty chair in front of his desk. My favorite yellow lined legal pad and a felt-tip pen lay ready for me. "I assumed you already stopped for coffee so I didn't pour you any."

I looked behind me and then back to Oliver. "Are you expecting someone?"

"You." He removed his black-rimmed reading glasses. "I'm expecting *you*."

"Am I that predictable?"

"No. But one can hope." He flashed the grin that went all the way up to the corners of his eyes.

"What is all this?" I sat and put my hands on the desk, palms down.

"You first. Tell me why you're here."

"If you knew I was coming, you tell me." Irritation scratched at my throat.

"I have no idea what you've decided. I just knew you would come."

I tented my fingers and leaned forward. "Oliver, I will curate this *Pulaski* exhibit. *If* it is the *Pulaski*. If it's not, I'm leaving. That is the deal I've made with myself and the one I will make with you. I want you to pay me well—I want to buy my rental. I have only one more class before summer break, then I can focus on curating an exhibit. And yes, I admit you know me well. A shipwreck. Lost treasure. Unknown stories. They're all my siren calls. You knew what I'd say."

He grinned again. "I do know you. Just the word 'shipwreck' and we're off and running."

"Did you know that Mora is here . . . was here . . . because of a shipwreck?"

"What?" He laughed and stood to come to my side, leaned back with his palms on the desk. "Tell me."

"She was Irish and the Irish arrived here in Savannah because of a shipwreck. An entire ship of indentured Irish servants was headed north when a storm blew it off track and it wrecked off the Georgia coast. Of the hundred passengers, only forty survived. Oglethorpe bought their indentures for five pounds apiece and Mora's ancestors went off to plantations to work. With that one storm, that one wreck, Irish immigration in this region was forever altered." I paused. "Mora and I loved that story. We would pretend to be marooned on the shores of Savannah while handsome British men saved us from sure death by shark attack."

"She never told me that one. You two had quite the imaginations."

"We did."

Oliver and I were silent for longer than was comfortable, Oliver looking down at me and I up at him. I finally glanced away and placed my hand on the folder. "This is the proof?"

"It is indeed."

"Loads of steamships went down in those waters. We know that."

"But the wreck was found where the *Pulaski* exploded and sank." He picked up the folder. "These are the files and photos and information from Endeavor Exploration, the group that does the work with another salvage company called Deep Water Ventures. I have it all here. Now let's get started." A chair screeched across the floor as Oliver slid it over to me, took a seat and opened the first folder. "I'm going to put you in touch with the head of the dive, Maddox Wagner. He can tell you everything they know so far."

I attempted to keep my face placid, but the stories hidden in history, narratives discovered through artifacts and letters, buried beneath the muck and murk of the ocean's silt and sand, were irresistible to me.

Oliver sat back in his chair. "Why don't you take all this home and let me know what you find. There isn't a lot written about this wreck—only a few articles, as far as we know. What does exist is right here in Savannah, at the Georgia Historical Society. I suspect local families have papers you'll want to dig up."

I opened the folder to see a list of names. "What's this?"

"An incomplete manifest. It lists some of the passengers, the workers, the servants, the captain, first mate, et cetera."

I studied the sheet of paper. Female passengers didn't have first names unless they were children; otherwise they were listed as "missus" or "miss" with a last name only. Enslaved people didn't have names at all.

Oliver moved closer, tapped another folder. "These are photos of the remains of the wreck taken by Maddox Wagner."

They were pictures underwater, of a watery place that had enchanted me all my life. A world unseen. The universe viewed only by the bravest divers and sojourners. Mortals had to live with secondary accounts. As a child, I'd pretended to be a mermaid and a Selkie. To be born in a bathtub was one thing, but to be born of the ocean seemed the most mystical of any fate.

Oliver continued as I turned the pages. "Maddox's discoveries will make you want to dive down there with him."

I leafed through the images one by one: coins; a comb; a collection of glass bottles; a candlestick; a luggage tag; a key. I came to the last photo. A hundred feet below the surface, thirty miles off the coast of

North Carolina, inside a wreck a hundred and eighty years old, beneath silt that had flowed up from the camera's lens, rested a tiny, crusty statue of Poseidon, his face covered in algae and the right arm broken off at the elbow, robbing him of his trident.

My breath caught in a moment's remembrance of who I once was—a woman obsessed with the sea's mythology, with its goddesses and gods. The ocean was enigmatic, but this time she was offering me her lost secrets.

Papa had said, "*Only the sea knows, and she keeps her secrets well.*"

I glanced again at the photo of the iron luggage tag. "I wonder if the person this belonged to, who put it in their bag that morning, survived." I looked up. "How many lived?"

He slipped out a piece of paper. "We don't have a full manifest, but this is what we do have. It's only a few names so . . . to discover the rest is part of your job." He stood. "Come with me. I want to tell you a story."

We wandered back to the room of ship models and Oliver stood between *The Steamboat Pulaski* and a model of a slave ship, the *Wanderer*, only a few feet away. He spread his arms wide between the two, almost touching the protective glass surrounding them both.

He cleared his throat and in his best storytelling voice he began. "In June 1838, this steamboat—now known as the Southern *Titanic*—headed out to sea for a quick trip to Baltimore. The advertisement stated: *Only One Night at Sea.* But on its way, it blew up." He pointed at the four replica lifeboats. "With only four lifeboats—the ones hanging are called quarterboats and the boats uncovered on the deck are yawls."

"I know this part."

He ignored me. "And this ship"—he pointed at the *Wanderer*—"set out to sea twenty years later in 1858, under the pretense of being a luxury yacht, flying the pennant of the New York Harbor Yacht Club.

Instead it sailed to Africa and picked up over four hundred Africans as human cargo to be brought back to Georgia to be enslaved."

"It's horrific," I said. "I know that story, too."

"Not the whole story. Not the story behind the story."

I laughed despite my very best attempt to keep a straight face. He knew that the words "the story behind the story" were as good as a drug to me. "And?"

He turned his attention back to the *Pulaski*. "That morning of June 13, 1838, the famous Savannah plantation owner, banker and ship financier Lamar Longstreet boarded with his wife, their six children, his sister, and his niece with her husband, baby and nursemaid. He had helped to both finance and oversee the building of the beautiful ship. He was there to show off his achievement, display his confidence in the ship and take his family north for the summer." Oliver stood silent for a dramatic breath, and I leaned forward, almost touching him.

"Deep in the night, a terrible explosion occurred and within forty-five minutes the ship sank. Passengers were cast into the sea and drowned. Lamar Longstreet's oldest son, Charles, fourteen years old, acted with heroic courage on that horrendous night and during the days surviving at sea that followed. For his actions he was dubbed 'the Noble Boy.'"

"So he survived?"

"Yes, he survived . . . only to become the man they called 'the Red Devil.'" Oliver now turned to the *Wanderer* and set his hand on top of the plexiglass. "Charles Longstreet refitted this pleasure schooner and fooled the country so he could illegally bring to Savannah from the African Congo human cargo of over four hundred men, women and children. He was known to be both relentless and cruel. He was also part of the Fire-Eaters group, rabble-rousers agitating for a civil war."

"Unbelievable," I said. "A young boy survives the sinking of the *Pulaski* as a hero and becomes a terror called the Red Devil?"

"And Lilly Forsyth was his cousin."

"The fabled Lilly is the Red Devil's cousin? This is curiouser and curiouser." Oliver laughed at my quoting *Alice in Wonderland*. "Did anyone else survive from this family?" I counted on my fingers. "This family of what? Twelve from one family, including Lilly, her husband and her baby. Thirteen was her nursemaid. Did anyone survive other than Charles?" I crouched down and stared into the model of the Pulaski, and asked, "What the hell happened that night?"

Oliver's suppressed smile gave away the line he knew would be the final bait. "Go find out for us."

7

LILLY

Thursday, June 14, 1838
11 P.M.

The wooden door of Lilly's cabin gleamed with polish; the hard-wood floors were slick, the berths made up with tight corners, and the pillows plumped. After spending the night docked in Charleston, the *Pulaski* had proceeded northward. Lilly had spent the day on the top deck, avoiding Adam, and begging an excuse to skip dinner because of seasickness so she could retire early. Two days and one night had passed in alternating bouts of mild nausea and flashes of appreciation for the beauty around her. She'd chatted with other passengers she knew.

There had been no chance to be alone with her beloved Augusta, what with the children underfoot and the close quarters, but they'd walked the promenade together and their unspoken words were enough. Between the lines rested concern and love, and her own restless hope. They had made plans for summer get-togethers, entertaining outings and lazy afternoons.

"Melody brought all her silver and china with her," Augusta whispered. "Entertaining must be done properly. And you never know who you'll need to impress."

The two women laughed at the social pretense. Lilly said, "Adam brought a trunk filled with enough gold to buy Saratoga Springs, if he pleases."

"I just want to feel cool breezes and release my corset and sleep without the crowing of roosters waking me at dawn," Augusta said. She sounded weary as she shifted Thomas from hip to hip; he clung to the little Poseidon statue he never put down.

"I don't foresee that in your future." Lilly pretended to gaze ahead, her hand over her eyes as a shield.

"How is Adam . . . doing?" Augusta asked.

Lilly looked at her friend juggling the child. "Adam's thirst for more and more has turned into a desire to have William Jay build him a house on Oglethorpe Street. All he wants is to surpass your brother in every regard."

"Well, that's absurd."

Just then Adam had arrived and Augusta had scurried away to where the Longstreet children chased a wooden ball from one end of the promenade to the other. Lilly's guard had been down, although she should have known better. Adam had sidled up next to her on the wooden seat and taken Madeline from her arms.

"Darling, how romantic this trip is with the rising and falling waters, the pleasant scenery." He hugged Madeline too tightly and she let out a cry. "Where is your nursemaid?"

"Her name is Priscilla."

His eyes flamed. "Where is she?"

Lilly pointed a few feet away to where Priscilla stood at the brass railing. Adam stood, swayed from something more than the ship's movement, and approached Priscilla. Without a word, he handed her the child and returned to Lilly. He stood in front of the settee and blotted her view of the sea. "Come with me." He held out his hand. "Show me your cabin."

"I need to stay up here, dear. I become quite frightfully sick below deck." She knew the excuse wouldn't work, but she had to try. She had viewed this journey as a reprieve. How could he come now and destroy even that? He took her hand and she felt the small bones of her fingers being crushed beneath his, a familiar feeling that brought a rise of nausea. She let out a small cry. "Stop."

"Come with me."

And she had.

The act had been quick and for that she'd been grateful. This time, his need to assert power over her didn't include the violent desire to injure, but merely to dominate. Her left wrist ached from the way he'd held her arms over her head, but otherwise she'd emerged unscathed.

Now, on their last night, in her cabin with Priscilla and Madeline, Lilly stood next to a ceramic basin painted with tiny white flowers and sloshing with clean water, to begin readying for bed. Lilly brushed her long dark hair with the ivory comb, humming a song her mama had taught her as a child: "Washing Day," the silly lyrics sliding up and down the scales. Behind her, in the mirror, Lilly saw Priscilla's reflection smile. Before removing her dress, Lilly glanced out the small porthole at the moving sea: a secret world hidden beneath the dark sky.

Gratitude for her solitude flooded her body just as the milk for her baby had once flooded her breasts—before she was bound and told that Priscilla would be her nursemaid and it was the proper way to do things.

Tonight, she was safe.

Lilly curled up with Madeline at her side, her silver rattle tinkling with the ship's movement, and Priscilla snoring softly in the next berth. Sleep waved toward Lilly with the rocking of the sea.

Her sleep was so deep that when the sound of a gunshot awoke her, reverberating so closely that she was catapulted from her bed and crashed onto the hard floor, clinging to her baby, she was completely disoriented.

Adam.

This was her first thought. It had happened before—his anger bursting forth with firearms; his anger exploding from a barrel to a tree, to an animal, and once at the wall behind Lilly as she held their child.

Lilly's heart bounded as she squeezed Madeline and screamed out Priscilla's name. Madeline burst into a squall. Had it been a bad dream? They were still on the steamboat, luxury surrounding them. Soft linens. Porcelain washbasin. Silver candlesticks. Fine gowns.

Yet something was amiss. The lantern lights wavered from the wrong angle, and the floor listed.

Priscilla called out, "I'm here, missus. I'm here."

Lilly struggled to stand as the ship lurched again and the chamber pot spilled urine, soaking the hem of Lilly's white cotton nightgown.

Then the stench of fire and smoke seeped under the doorway.

"It's a fire," Priscilla said as calmly as if she'd said, "You're late for the captain's dinner."

Priscilla's calm came from something Lilly knew well: a disconnect from reality that allowed her to withstand the situation. She'd done it herself when Adam had been at his worst, and Lilly had seen Priscilla almost empty herself of emotion to do what must be done on the plantation. But Lilly's panic climbed with the smoke. "We must get out." Lilly reached for her silk jewelry bag. She handed her distressed child to Priscilla so she could tie the bag around her wrist—she would not leave without her valuables; they could mean freedom. She knew this even in the depth of fear.

The ship trembled with a terrible force, as if a sea monster below had crashed into the hull, as if a great lightning bolt had ripped into the shining wood. But neither of those things had happened; despite Lilly's vivid imagination, she did understand what was real. She grabbed the beloved silver rattle from the bed and tucked it into the palm of her hand, the tiny jingle bells denting her palm, and then she dropped it into the jewelry bag. "Have we crashed into another boat?"

Priscilla didn't answer as screams reached their ears, wails that came from great pain.

Lilly grabbed her child from Priscilla, the baby's writhing body absorbing their fear. "The boat is built of wood—if it's on fire . . ." Lilly stopped and stared at Priscilla. "We shall not die this way. Do you hear me?"

"I do hear you, mistress," Priscilla said, her voice animated now, rising with energy.

Lilly shuffled in her bare feet to the door of the stateroom when her foot slammed against something hard and splintered. She hollered in pain. "The floorboards. They're popping up."

Lilly's free hand, her small velvet bag dangling from her wrist, found the door handle and turned it. She stepped into the galley and slipped, her foot falling through space. Her body plunged forward to slam onto the wood floor, her child loosening from her grip. A great pain seared through her ankle; her leg had fallen through a hole in the ship's flooring, her precious child with her.

"Mistress!" Priscilla screamed as she grasped Madeline, now stunned to silence.

"I'm okay. I'm okay." Lilly dragged her foot from the hole where her leg had sunk almost to her thigh and she crawled backward. She didn't yet feel the pain; that would come later. Desperation pushed her onward.

"Can you walk?" Priscilla asked.

"Yes."

"This way." Priscilla's voice resonated with something weightier than Lilly's own high-pitched fear. "I see the stars, the sky."

Sure enough, the stairwell was only yards away. Lilly had lost all sense of direction. She stood and moaned as her weight bore down on the ankle. The pain she could bear—losing Madeline she could never withstand.

Lilly pushed past other passengers stumbling from their cabins. They all moved toward the stairwells, hollering out for loved ones.

The wild scene in the galley halls was confusing. Women in night-dresses called for their husbands. Children wailed. Smoke billowed and wafted. The stench of burning flesh filled the air—Lilly remembered this smell; she'd been nearby when the overseer used a brand as punishment to keep his slaves working harder. She retched, her body overcome with horrific memories. One night when she'd refused Adam, he'd threatened to give her a brand all her own.

Just as she neared the stairs, the ship pitched starboard, seawater rushing down the galley an inch or more over their feet. Priscilla was ahead of her holding Madeline as Lilly crawled up the stairs on her hands and knees.

Once on the promenade Lilly and Priscilla at first stood still as the mast, frozen in the midst of madness. Women and men dashing back and forth, children alone and weeping, floorboards popping and water rushing in through the broken places. Smoke rising; clouding the scene in places. Bloody footprints where others had stepped on shattered glass. Men throwing overboard anything they could pry loose in a futile attempt to lighten the ship's load and keep it from sinking.

Lilly focused her sight, took stock—shattered wood. The wheelhouse missing. The bulkhead between the machinery and the stacks was gone. Only a foot away, a man lay unconscious, face down, his limbs askew. This was clear: in the middle of the night, in the middle of the ocean, in the middle of her life, the ship was being torn apart.

"We must find a way to float," Lilly said calmly, with single-minded purpose. "See there?" She pointed to a man and woman running toward the lifeboats. "They know, too. There is nothing to save us but those."

"Can you walk?" Priscilla asked again. Madeline wailed into the night air as Priscilla held her tight.

Lilly bore her full weight and didn't flinch. "I will do what I must." She touched the top of her daughter's matted hair, as a surge of love and protection larger than any wave that could wash upon the deck overcame her. She nearly bent over with its force. "We have to find a way to keep Madeline with us. We must bind her . . ."

Priscilla folded her arms around Madeline as if they were ropes, enough to keep her safe.

"Priscilla, I've seen you and your mama with babies. The way they are wrapped so tightly . . ." The ship moaned, a nearly human sound, and Lilly's hands wrapped about Madeline's waist as she extricated her from Priscilla's grip. "Please show me how."

Priscilla nodded, tears now filling her eyes, her hands trembling as she reached down to the hem of her cotton nightgown, lifting it so her calves and pantaloons were exposed, and then bit into the hem to rip a two-foot swath of material from it. In quick movements, her fingers flying, Priscilla wrapped Madeline to Lilly's chest in an intricate crisscross pattern of cloth and tied it tight as a cocoon around a caterpillar.

"She will be safe," Priscilla said and touched the top of Madeline's head as a priest blessing her, as a prophecy, as a hope.

Lilly took Priscilla's warm hand in hers; the first time she had ever done so, and felt that they were now as bound as Madeline, bound to save each other or die alone. It was clear as the stars in that cloudless sky above them.

A broad man with a beard as white as cotton bolted past carrying his valise and a top hat, bumping past Lilly as if she were a ghost. She lost her balance and Priscilla reached out her hand, steadied Lilly and Madeline. "Mistress, I don't know how to swim."

"Neither do I," Lilly said, her voice as unsteady as the ship.

Priscilla's eyes widened as a voice called out, "Heave!"

Lilly lifted her gaze. The two quarterboats hanging from davits were being lowered, men pulling the tarps from them as the boats swung from the collapsing rail and toward the swell of sea. The other two lifeboats—the yawls that had been upside-down on the deck—were being flipped over, passengers scrambling inside even as the boats remained on the deck.

Lilly and Priscilla made their way toward the lifeboats. With each roll of the ship more water rushed in, but together they clung to handrails slick with seawater and lurched forward as one.

Another gentleman, his suit flecked with ash, strode past them as slowly and regally as if he were headed to the grand theater. He paused, removed his pocket watch and glanced at it before looking directly at Lilly and Priscilla. "It's not yet midnight."

"Help us," Lilly said, her voice choked with tears and pain. "The lifeboats are leaving . . ."

"This ship can't sink. Just wait a bit. The captain will stabilize her."

He'd lost his mind. That was the only thing that made sense. This man had taken the time to get fully dressed, slip on his pocket watch and slide on his best shoes. Another man, tall with a thin face and a gash on his head bleeding down his neck, rushed past. He was dressed in the white officer's clothes, the brass buttons askew, his hat gone, speaking loudly but calmly. "To the lifeboats. Now."

"That's the first mate, Mr. Hibbert," Lilly said to Priscilla. "We must do what he says."

They heard others talking. It was the boiler—it had exploded. It was the engine—it had caught fire. The starboard side shattered. The ship sinking. Prayers flowed from the mouths of women and men as they pleaded with God to find each other, to save their lives, to rescue the ship.

Lilly stepped forward and again slipped under her weak ankle. This time the jewelry bag tilted and the silver rattle rolled out. Lilly reached for the tiny rattle, whose chiming bells had been their lullaby each night, and felt it slip from her fingers. The glint of silver bobbled on the deck, and then rolled, sliding, slipping and then disappearing into the dark waters.

8

EVERLY

Present day

Maddox Wagner made me think of a modern-day pirate. He walked with a swagger. His legs were so long that each measured, deliberate step drew the eye. Had arrogance or years spent riding the rise and fall of the sea produced that distinctive gait? Or was it his rimless glasses, unruly white hair, and full beard flecked with tints of red that made me imagine a benign Bluebeard? His broad smile exuded boundless excitement.

"Well, hey there," he said, approaching me with an outstretched hand.

"Hello." I couldn't match his eagerness but shook his hand as if I could. We stood outside in the museum garden, afternoon rain threatening with far-off rumbles and the breeze damp. A yellow-billed cuckoo warbled in the tree above us, a song of Savannah. Swanlike blooms covered the gardenia bushes.

Maddox leaned over and sniffed a white flower. "My God, that's ambrosia." He grinned at me. "Isn't Mother Nature amazing?"

"Sure." I adjusted my sunglasses, which were slipping down my nose. "You must be Maddox Wagner."

"I am indeed. And you, I know, are Everly Winthrop. I'm pleased to make your acquaintance."

I grinned. "Is it 1838 again and I don't know it?"

As he bellowed with laughter, I thought that everything about him seemed too much: his size, his laugh, the huge canvas bag he carried. "That would be fantastic. Then we could see what really happened. As it is, we must guess and use conjecture. We're piecing it together."

He stepped too close and I backed up. "But piecing it together is the greatest challenge and the best fun." I paused. "Don't you think?"

"Oh, it is. Why else would I sacrifice my health and my money to scrape and ply the bottom of the sea?"

"Well, I'm glad you're here." I took a few steps toward the museum, motioning for him to follow. "Let's go inside and talk."

"Or here?" He patted the concrete bench and sat down; a man who was accustomed to being in charge. "I have everything I need with me. Do you need anything inside?"

"No." I stared at this man who had invested all his money and spare time into treasure hunting. Or, as some called it, salvaging. Not so different from my sister, who scoured every flea market, empty house and abandoned building for treasure to put in her fancy house. But Maddox was looking below, where no one else could see.

I wasn't good at guessing ages, but sixties seemed about right. His face was set with the wrinkles and deep lines of a life spent in the sun. This man hadn't been pampered.

He dropped his bag on the bench between us. "I have so much to tell you."

"That's good because I have so much to ask you. I doubt this can be done in a quick sit in the sun."

"It's a good place to start."

"Yes." I pulled a small recording device from my purse. "Do you mind?"

"Not at all."

"Tell me first—do we know for sure this is the *Pulaski*?"

Maddox's smile was so big it almost looked forced. "Yes, yes, yes. I knew all along but we needed proof. Everyone always wants proof." He leaned closer to me. "You do know that all the best things in life can't be proven, but damn if they don't always want it." He dug around in his bag, pulling out stacks of paper and putting them back until he lifted out a single photo. "Proof!"

He held one of the photos that Oliver had shown me, this one a blown-up version showing the iron rust like grains of sand. "This is a luggage tag with *Pulaski* carved into the iron. I wish you could hold it. Photos never do justice to what we find below."

"What you find below," I repeated and he stared at me for a moment before removing my sunglasses. "What are you doing?" I snatched for them, but he held the glasses out of reach. "Give those to me."

"How am I to know your reaction when I can't see your eyes? You sounded sad when you said that, but looking at you, I can see you aren't." He handed my glasses back to me.

"It doesn't matter what I feel or don't feel. What matters are the facts. Please go on." My voice felt as humid as the air.

"Of course more than facts matter. But that's a conversation for another time."

"If I'm going to curate this project, I have to know the details down to the last jot. Get it right."

"If you're going to curate this project, you also need to *feel*. This tag." He handed the photo to me. "Look closely. One summer afternoon a woman, or a man, or a child boarded the luxurious steamship *Pulaski*. They'd spent the previous days packing their trunks and valises. They rode in a carriage up to the docks right here in Savannah, the galloping horses becoming filthy with the grime of the sandy roads. They said good-bye to family and friends, waving and calling good wishes. Then a porter came and clipped this tag onto a bag." He pressed his forefinger onto the photo as if the luggage tag were something he could feel. I saw the dirt under his fingernails, the cracked lines of hard work and salt water. "Then the bag with this tag was taken to their cabin or the bowels of the ship. It could have been a trunk filled with gold coins or family silver, or just hand-sewn gowns. The passengers expected, each and every one of them, to see it in two days' time on the Baltimore docks. Instead, that bag and that tag have been lying on the bottom of the ocean for one hundred and eighty years. If that doesn't make you feel something, then, ma'am, you might be the curator with the best reputation but you aren't the curator for this wreck."

I slipped my sunglasses back onto my face and made a noise that almost sounded like disgust, although I didn't mean for it to be so.

"Ms. Winthrop, I'm sorry." He shook his head. "My enthusiasm sometimes gets the best of me and I can be insensitive."

"No need for apology. But don't assume you know me."

"Of course I don't. But I did choose you."

"You did?"

"Yes." He sat as still as a hunting dog pointing at a bird in the field.

"Why?"

"Because Oliver told me you have one of the finest reputations in the city. What I'm looking for is an exhibit that will bring to life a wreck that has long been ignored, one that changed the history of Savannah, Georgia, when it claimed some of its finest families, when it took both treasure and fortune down with it. A wreck that completely changed maritime law. A calamity. The Southern *Titanic*. What

I'm looking for is someone who understands that what we bring up from below changes things above. I'm looking for someone who can help me show that the past and its stories are important even now." He stopped abruptly.

I felt the edges of my mouth move up. "That's all you're looking for?"

"A tall order, ain't it?" He leaned forward and I smelled soap, as if he'd just stepped out of the shower. "And that's just the beginning." Then he settled back on the seat as warm, fat drops of rain began to fall. He didn't seem to notice as he reached into his pocket. "I have something I wasn't sure I'd show you. But now I see that I must."

The rain kissed my neck and shoulders.

Maddox withdrew a tight fist from his pocket. I stared at his hand as he slowly opened it. Resting in his palm there appeared to be a crusty circle encased in barnacles and rust: an artifact that brought Papa to mind: a pocket watch.

I touched its edges. "This belonged to someone who boarded that ship." I looked up at Maddox.

"Yes, it did," he confirmed. "And in many ways, it still does."

I paused with the gravity of it, the past alive in this one artifact. "I wonder if they survived the explosion, the person who owned this watch." The raindrops fell onto the watch face in his hand.

Maddox closed his fist around the antique as if to protect it, and the quick spurt of storm passed, leaving electric energy: the watch, the conversation, the very rain felt unreal.

Maddox glanced up at the sky. "That was just the first burst. We should get inside."

We stood and I felt movement under my feet as if I were on the deck of a ship myself. But I wasn't; it was my life in motion. "I promised my mom I'd meet her for lunch, so I need to go. Can we catch up later?"

"This evening?" he asked. "There's more to show you."

"Yes. I'll meet you at four thirty at the office." I nodded to the building behind us.

"No. Let's meet somewhere with food." He grinned. "The river-front, exactly where the *Pulaski* was docked, where our passengers boarded with their watches and their luggage and their hopes and dreams." He stood and slipped the watch into his pocket. "See you soon."

A photo remained on the bench, dimpled with rain, and I picked it up to hand to him: the grainy image of a silver candlestick crusted with algae. What luxury had been on board; what beauty had sunk with a single explosion.

He tucked it into his bag and then left me in the museum garden, my hair and clothes damp, my heart hammering, and a sense of expectation rising like heat I hadn't felt in a long while.

9

AUGUSTA

Thursday, June 14, 1838
11 P.M.

What a lovely two days it had been. The ship's luxury and comfort were everything Augusta's brother had promised. Now, having spent a night docked in Charleston, and with the arrival of dozens of new passengers, the ship sailed like a bird toward Baltimore. Men on the lower deck. Women and children above. The children wouldn't all fit in one cabin and Melody had put the boys with Augusta; Thomas was so attached to his aunt that Melody sent him with Charles to sleep alongside her.

Resting in her berth now, Augusta watched Thomas and her oldest nephew, Charles, with his red curls splayed upon the pillow, asleep in the berths beside her. The sway of the sea felt as sublime as the soft sheets she slept upon.

She rolled onto her side and stared at the boys in the candlelight. Then the flame flickered, beeswax dripping, and a sound, otherworldly, horrific—an explosion—crashed through the night. The silver candlestick crashed to the floor. Augusta shot up from her bed. Her eardrums vibrated and the ship trembled. It wasn't so much terror that swamped her as confusion.

Heat, as searing as if the sun had fallen onto the ship and was radiating through the hallways and under the doorframes, blew into the room like the breath of a beast. She stood frozen in fear. An eerie silence pervaded—the engine had stopped and the great wheels had stilled.

She glanced around to get her bearings. Their room contained three berths—two built in where she and Thomas slept, and a third rolling berth where Charles slumbered.

With a breath that tasted of smoke, she moved quickly, scrambling. She had no idea what was happening to the ship, but it wasn't right. She grabbed Thomas and shook Charles. "Charles! Get up. The ship is in trouble. Something's blown up or caught fire."

He jolted upright. "Auntie?"

"Something is terribly wrong."

Darkness saturated the room, and the berth where Charles lay blocked the doorway exit. Augusta held Thomas, who was just waking, snuffling and confused. "Charles, move the berth so we can get out."

Charles shoved at the bunk, using all his strength, his red hair aflame in the dark. "Auntie, it won't move. It won't. We're trapped." His voice climbed into a wail.

Augusta stood on top of the bunk, leaned toward the door. "Help us!" she screamed, hoping her voice would reach the captain's office a mere twenty feet across the galley.

She then placed Thomas, bleary-eyed and whining, on her berth, and with Charles they pushed again at the rolling bed, but it was jammed. Between them they didn't own enough strength to move it. She turned to the window. Could they crawl out? She vividly imagined the sea filling their room and then their lungs. And with that she froze.

If they were to survive, if they were to live and find their way out, she must be rational. She must be logical. Not merely her own life hung in the balance.

Augusta closed her eyes, drew the boys close, one on either side. "We are going to be brave and smart. We need to get out of this room."

Charles nodded and Thomas whined, pulling at Augusta's nightgown.

Imagine in your mind's eye the ship you walked all day with Lilly; see your path out.

Above them stretched the promenade along the entire length of the ship. Two front and back companionways led to the main deck. Charles, Thomas, and she slept in a stateroom in the midsection of the ship, given to them by the captain who said he never slept on board. The ladies' cabin at the stern and the men's beneath the ladies'. These facts didn't so much come to her one at a time but in images and memories of the past day spent wandering.

Twenty feet across the hallway were two passages with closets that stored the china and glassware, and then the captain's office. Behind the china room, two more staterooms opened on the east side of the ship where her brother, her sister-in-law and the remainder of the family were bunked. Most importantly, outside her stateroom a passageway led to a double stairway where she would exit to the upper deck and promenade. That was the way they must go.

Charles set his feet wide as the boat tilted so steeply starboard that the dark line of the horizon visible through the window slipped lower. "I will save us, Auntie Augusta." His fourteen-year-old voice, halfway between a man's and a child's, cracked.

She took a shaky breath, frightened of not taking another, feeling the pressure to gasp for air. The transom window above the doorway might be big enough to climb out if they could reach it, which they couldn't. Maybe if she put Charles on her shoulders? With a heave she again shoved her weight against the berth, and prayed to the holy God whom she worshiped in the small church at Stonewall. Where was her brother? Her sister-in-law? Lilly and sweet baby Madeline? Had they already found their way out?

"God help us," she whispered as she shoved once more against the berth.

With a groan, the ship careened to the port side, and the berth slid with the movement as the door flew open. The bunk's hard edge crushed her toes as it rolled over, but she felt little, for now a means of escape presented itself.

The sounds that reached her terrified her more than the heat and tilting of the ship. China crashed and shattered in the closet across the hall. Screams from other passengers echoed as if from another world. Augusta grabbed a coat for each child, and they ran into the darkness using her mind's eye to envision the passageways and the stairwells.

The four lifeboats; she'd seen them. She'd touched them. She knew where they were.

With unusual strength she stumbled blindly through the hallways as she carried Thomas and held Charles tightly by the hand. Other human forms stumbled out and past them.

"Melody!" Augusta hollered across the passageway.

"Here. I'm here." Melody appeared at Augusta's side. "You go. Go. Go. I have the others with me."

"Where is Lilly?"

"I haven't seen her . . . now go."

"What is happening?"

"I don't know. God, I don't know. Lamar said it was the safest ship in the waters. He said . . ."

They stood in their white nightgowns like ghosts, the air thick with the rancid smell of burning wood and, yes, flesh. Augusta could taste it in the back of her throat. She threw her arms around Melody as the oldest daughter, twelve-year-old Eliza, pulled at her sleeve. "Mama, help me."

Even in the darkness Augusta saw the forms of Melody's four other children—Eliza, William, Rebecca and Caroline. Melody clung to Augusta's arm for one more moment and in a voice as strong as steel said, "We will save them. Follow me."

They ran forward as a great tearing noise ripped through the hull, the sound of wood separating from itself, its bonds broken. Augusta had heard these sounds one other time in her life—when lightning had struck the great oak outside the plantation house. As it was rent apart, the tree had groaned as the ship was doing now, an animal sound of demise. With that, Eliza fell to the ground and began to crawl. "Stand!" Melody screamed.

Augusta grabbed Eliza's hand as they all stumbled forward through the dark and smoke to where Augusta knew the stairwell would take them to the promenade deck. A single-minded intent to save herself and the children pulsed within her. There was no room for fear.

Not yet.

She ran as fast as she could with Thomas in her arms and Charles and Eliza by her side. Her white cotton gown flowed around her, her hair loose.

They neared the stairway and spied the muted moonlight above; the ship's lights were extinguished now. Augusta moved toward that light, yet in the shadows at the edge of the stairwell, something barely seen sent fresh horror and fear surging through her like electricity: bodies scattered, unconscious, burned or injured. But she couldn't help them—there were six children between her and Melody to save.

An anguished cry tore from her throat. "Oh, Melody, hurry now."

Augusta took the stairs two at a time.

10

EVERLY

Present day

That evening, Savannah's riverfront bustled with activity as if it were a weekend, although it was only the first Tuesday in June. A stretch of cobblestones lined with flickering gas lanterns that cast a diffuse light ran parallel to the river. I turned to Maddox, standing at my side. We were both lost in imagining that June morning in 1838 when the luxurious and beautiful *Pulaski* had been tied to these very docks, the Longstreet buildings tall behind the wharf.

What hadn't existed then, and now dominated the scenery, was the soaring bridge that crossed the Savannah River north into South Carolina, a sailboat of an iron structure that curved like the arched spine of a great sea creature. Just under the bridge on the same bank stood the largest port in the East, where barge ships as big as town squares docked and cranes looked monstrously out of place against the quaint city. Further inland were smokestacks spewing gray smoke from the paper mill.

But when I looked right, the barges, the docks and the dark plumes disappeared and the wild Savannah River curved and swayed past Tybee Lighthouse to the sea. Along the riverfront sat restaurants and bars, tourist shops and candy stores; benches to sit on while gazing at the water. Small children ran about selling handmade flowers fashioned from palm branches; men and women playing instruments with their cases open for money crooned into the evening. Couples and singles, groups of families and hordes of adolescents, strode along the walkway looking for anything from trouble to love.

We'd been silent for a while when I pointed behind us up the bluff to the city. "You need to know a bit about the city and the time period if you're going to know about the passengers and the ship."

"Tell me." His voice sounded sincere, full of interest.

"Savannah was founded in 1733 as a philanthropic trust. You might hear about how the debtors came first, but that's only partly true. Originally we were founded to help the working poor."

"How so?"

"Gardens were planted with mulberry trees to be harvested for silk. Farmland was given to each settler. The policy was meant to encourage the creation of a community of working yeomen. Slavery was outlawed. In fact, the founders knew that if they allowed slavery it would encourage wealthy landowners and that was the opposite of what they wanted."

"So much for what they wanted. Things have changed a bit."

I nodded. "Of course they changed. Their good intentions didn't last. Slavery was legalized by 1755."

"On plantations."

"Not just there. There were house slaves in town and plantation slaves in the country. House slaves did kitchen tasks, housecleaning, laundry and of course there were nursemaids and seamstresses. When the *Pulaski* left in 1838, Matthew Hall McAllister was mayor. The city had already survived the yellow fever epidemic of 1819 and the great fire of 1820. Hopes were high for brighter days to come. Short staple cotton was shipped down from the upcountry and Sea Island cotton from St. Simons brought double the money of short staple. Both were in huge demand in Europe. Money flowed in and the city thrived."

"Except for the enslaved harvesting the cotton."

"Exactly," I said. "All that wealth pouring in was made on the backs of enslaved people."

A grave look crossed Maddox's face. "It's hard to imagine how this was tolerated for so long."

"Rationalization is mighty strong. Humans haven't changed that much."

"Yes." He paused. "Tell me why so many were willing to travel on the *Pulaski*—why so many took chances on steamships that sometimes blew up and sank. It seems a terrible gamble."

"Before the modern day, before air-conditioning, Savannah in summer could be a horror. The summer flies, the stinging gnats—we call them no-see-ums—the heat, the fevers, the malaria. The theaters shut down. The racetrack was closed. No balls and concerts. The city emptied out. Those who could leave, did. The wealthy, and the ones who had places to go and a means to get there."

Maddox closed his eyes as if he could see it. "I've read about that morning. They came to the wharf in buggies and on horseback because trains didn't reach south from Baltimore to Savannah. They could ride the rails north after Baltimore, but they had to get there first."

"Yes," I confirmed. "Water travel was the fastest. To go by land took three or four days; it was arduous and dirty and there weren't many places to stay along the way. There were rumors of robbery, too. So even though everyone knew steam travel wasn't the safest, it was faster. And as a bonus, the *Pulaski* was advertised as 'only one night at sea.' So all bets were taken—what could go wrong in one night? This ship was made for speed and safety and luxury. Though I guess it doesn't much matter what we're made for. It matters what happens when the boiler explodes."

Maddox tipped back his head and let out a bellow of a laugh. "Touché and so true! Now, should we get something to eat? And drink?" He patted a leather satchel flung over his shoulder. "I have some things for us to go over."

"I want to show you something first." I led him to the right, past the World War II monument featuring a world globe split in half and beneath it the names of those from Chatham County who had served and died. A short distance farther on was a five-foot-tall bronze statue of a woman whose skirts ballooned in an unseen wind. She faced the river, her body turned slightly toward the Atlantic. In her arms she held a baby swaddled in a blanket.

Maddox's large presence walking so close unsettled me. I felt the space between us shrinking. I walked faster; he kept up. I wanted to push him a few feet from me, and yet when I looked he wasn't all that near. We reached the statue as I took two steps away from him.

"This is a memorial to Lilly Forsyth and all those who suffered when the *Pulaski* sank. She was rumored to have survived but was never seen again. Since we don't have a list of all those who lived, her survival could be a myth; just one woman to represent the horror of that night." The statue stood surrounded by a small pool where spouts of water shot upward from the edges of a concrete basin and splashed the bottom of her skirt. I reached into my purse and grabbed a loose penny, tossing it into the pool.

"Your wish?" he asked.

I stepped back. I wouldn't tell this stranger my wish—to find Mora's killer—any more than I would tell anyone else. It was the one wish that I carried with me every day. "Can't tell." I shrugged. "Or it won't come true."

"So, what's her story?" He walked to the edge of the statue.

"No one knows. She was part of the Longstreet family and married a man named Adam Forsyth, and they were both on the ship to Baltimore. Honestly, until I saw her name as Lady Forsyth on the manifest yesterday, I wasn't sure she was a real woman. When we were kids, my grandfather would make up stories about where she went." With my palm, I shielded my eyes from the sinking sun beginning to glint off the river. "Hers is one of many stories that was lost along with that sunken ship. She probably drowned. There's always confusion in such situations. Hell, on that manifest, women don't even have first names. But here she stands, representing all that was lost, and all the mystery surrounding the wreck."

Maddox gazed off to the river as if he could see something I could not, as if he knew the answers already. "It's awful."

I paused and then told Maddox how the Noble Boy and the Red Devil were one and the same, how Charles Longstreet sailed on the *Pulaski* and then commandeered the horrific slave ship the *Wanderer*.

"You mean"—he pointed at Lilly—"she was part of the same family? And all of them were on that journey?"

"Yes."

"Wow. Damn."

"I did some more research on Charles. Listen to this—he became the last man to die in the Civil War. Literally the last man in a battle called Wilson's Raid in Columbus, Georgia. Shot through the heart."

"Can we use the word 'karma' here?" Maddox brushed at the air as if to clear it of Charles's memory and then came so close I could see the freckles on his ears. "Let me get this straight. There are six kids. He's the oldest. He survives and is given the moniker Noble Boy. Twenty years later he finances and sends a schooner to pick up over four hundred enslaved people from the Congo. He is never convicted. Then he goes on to fight in the Civil War—most likely to defend this exact way of life—and is shot through the heart, the last Confederate soldier to die in the war."

"You got it." I tucked my hair behind my ear and delivered the punch line. "Six days after Lee surrendered to Grant at Appomattox. The war was over and he died anyway."

"Holy shit."

"Very eloquent." I laughed and he stuck his hands in his back pockets and stared out toward the river.

"And you want to know what happened to him. To that family and to Lilly," he said.

"Yes."

He took a few steps toward the concrete edge of the riverside, the stanchions for the larger ships big as chairs. He placed a foot on one and stood as if posing. Now that Maddox was leaving space between us, I felt I could take in a larger breath. I let him be as he watched a tour riverboat designed to emulate earlier styles, the *Queen of Savannah*, slide into dock. Mates on board were dressed in 1800s costumes, just like on the carriage rides.

I wanted to holler to the passengers holding their sweating wineglasses and cell phones that the pretense didn't come close to the reality of that time period. But I let them be, looking past Tybee Lighthouse toward where the mouth of the river opened to the Atlantic. Maddox stepped back as a mate from the boat jumped out to catch the rope being tossed.

"You know," he said finally, "not everyone who survives trauma becomes a better person. The idea that surviving brings everyone to a new and better place is a lie told by people who need the world to make sense."

My breath caught and I repeated his words as if he'd spoken in another language. "By people who need the world to make sense."

He spun around to face me. "Yes."

I glanced once more at the river moving toward the sea, sloshing against the seawall, and everyone on the riverfront going about their lives as if the water could not take them, as if life could not take them. "Let's go talk," I said. "I want to see what you've got in the bag."

We took a few steps toward the restaurants when a laugh, one I recognized, echoed across the plaza; I turned to it, and there sat Oliver. For a year, I'd not once run into him or seen him—maybe because I'd turned into the slightest bit of a recluse—but there he sat at a table with his back to me. His dark curls and blue T-shirt were familiar, but I didn't recognize the woman who sat with him. My first thought was how pretty she was. Very pretty. Curly blond hair worn loose: it looked alive in the breeze. She wore glasses with purple frames and took a long swig from her large glass of white wine. Oliver set his hands on the table and leaned toward her. I couldn't hear a word they said, but the body language was as clear as if there were tiny cartoon bubbles above their heads that said "We're flirting."

My stomach lurched and tears sprang to my eyes. For what? For proof that life moved on? That Oliver had moved on? I didn't know, but sadness swamped me.

Maddox had moved a few steps ahead and turned back to me. "You coming?"

"Sorry. Yes." I hustled to catch up.

"I asked earlier for an outdoor table with a river view. I think that's important."

He understood, and that pleased me. If we were to talk of the *Pulaski* we must be near the place where the passengers had boarded. I'd always believed that one can't understand the past without visiting the places where events took place. At their best, curated exhibits told stories, and those stories were best understood in the landscape where it all happened. In this case, that was here in Savannah and at the bottom of the sea.

We found a table and Maddox brought our chairs around so we could sit next to each other while facing the river. He moved aside the place settings and dropped papers onto the table. We ordered Prosecco for me and whiskey on the rocks for him and sipped our drinks.

"Let's start with what you need to know." He handed me a data sheet. "You can read this later. It's all about the Baltimore shipyard where the *Pulaski* was built for the Savannah and Charleston Steam Packet Company. Here are measurements, all the brass tacks."

I glanced at the paper scattered with facts and figures: a side-wheeler steamboat with two masts, one promenade deck, and an aft deck. Two lifeboats on the promenade and two hanging on the sides. Two hundred and three feet long. Twenty-five feet wide. Sixty-eight tons. Two hundred and twenty-five horsepower. Two low-pressure boilers.

"Only four lifeboats. I noticed that on the model. My God." I folded the paper and pushed it aside. "Let's talk about the passengers. I've found the best way to make an exhibit interesting is to make sure to follow a story. And this Longstreet family seems to be waiting for their story to be told. What happened to them all? How did a young boy survive such tragedy to become so . . . despicable?"

Maddox leaned forward so I could smell the mixture of whiskey and mint on his breath. The lines near his eyes and mouth had formed around a smile that rarely left his face, but did now. He stared at me long enough for it to become uncomfortable before he spoke again. "There are many reasons we bring up these shipwrecks. Gold, for sure. The thrill of the chase. The pursuit of something intangible and ineffable. But for me, it is this, too—the stories of people long gone and lost to history. I do it for the challenge—for me, there's nothing as exciting as deep-water salvaging. And we literally rewrite history with what we find."

"Rewrite history." I broke eye contact and looked back to the pile of photos and papers. "I wish I could do that."

Our waiter, a young man with a crew cut and a wide smile, arrived at the table. "Have we decided what we'll have to eat tonight?"

Maddox rubbed his eyes as if awakening. "Just bring us the fish of the day blackened and the freshest vegetables you've got." He handed the menus to the young man without once glancing at them. "Another round of these." He pointed at our drinks.

Our waiter walked away and I asked, "Do you always take charge that way?"

"Oh, God. I'm sorry." He paused. "I'm an ass. I just didn't want to stop the conversation and . . . forgive me. Would you like something different?"

"No, keep talking."

"That I can do." He smiled again. "Why would *you* like to rewrite your history?"

"What?" I took a sip of my drink, pretending I didn't know what he was asking.

"See? That's why I rushed him off. I knew it would stop whatever you meant to say." He brushed his hand through the air. "Talking about wrecks allows us to also talk about ourselves. That's the other part I love. How it opens us up to life."

"I don't really know what I meant, so let's get back to the ship's victims and survivors."

"Yes, back to that." He sounded disappointed. "She exploded at eleven at night when most people were already in their rooms, settled down for their one night at sea. Although they were gone two nights, only one night was spent at sea."

"One night . . ."

"That's the hell of it, right? People chose this ship because its owners boasted that it was the fastest and most luxurious, and for those frightened of sea travel, especially after what had happened to the steamship *Home*, only one night at sea seemed a safe bet."

The waiter arrived with our food. I took a bite of the blackened snapper and found myself secretly glad Maddox had ordered it.

"What happened to *Home*?" I asked.

Maddox used a napkin to wipe his face before settling back in his chair. "*Home* plied the water between New York and Charleston. It sank on October 9, 1837, less than a year before the *Pulaski* sailed on its ill-fated journey. She carried a hundred and thirty-five of the who's who of Charleston society. It, too, was a steam-powered side-wheeler. The big difference is that it was originally made for river trade and then converted for seagoing passengers. It sailed directly into a storm called the Racer off the coast of North Carolina. They didn't see it coming."

"We rarely do."

He smiled but kept talking. "*Home* had been outfitted with mahogany and skylights and all the best of everything, but it had only three lifeboats and two life preservers. Ninety-five people lost their lives off Ocracoke Island."

"Almost sounds like you're talking about the same ship."

"Right. So, passengers boarding the *Pulaski* were already leery but willing to place their faith in the new technology."

The second glass of Prosecco was coursing through me. "I think they also trusted the Longstreet family. We don't know about the others yet, but in local lore Lilly is already everything from a ghost to a hero. The Forsyth plantation is a historic site. Some say she never boarded the *Pulaski* at all, or maybe she got off in Charleston and ran away with a lover. I want to find out what happened to her. Maybe she died mid-explosion . . . who knows."

"If she boarded that ship, we might prove it by finding something that belonged to her."

I wiggled my fingers in a swimming motion toward the ground. "I'm going down there with you."

He laughed, but it was deep and kind, not mocking. "No, you're not."

"I'm an expert diver. It's part of the reason Oliver asked me to do this project."

"It's a double-tank technical hundred-foot dive."

"Been there. Done that."

He leaned back and stared at me. "We'll see."

We sat for a long while listening to the cries of sea gulls and a gui-tar player strumming a song about love. Finally I turned back to Mad-dox. "Are you thrilled you finally found this wreck? I mean, there must have been false starts and failures . . ."

"Yes. I'm thrilled. In this business there are countless disappoint-ments. But after years of charting the waters and weather of that night, I knew we had the right spot. We were ten miles farther out than the original estimates and when we found it—I felt both vindicated and ecstatic. The ship sank so quickly, with no time to retrieve possessions, so we know there will be plenty of gold and jewelry. We've been care-ful. We aren't even using a suction dredge to move sand around. We're doing the job by hand and with metal detectors. We want to keep everything intact."

"How long will it take to bring it all up?"

"Years. But we can create an exhibit without having *all* of it. Down so deep, visibility is only about seventy feet and the water is fifty-eight degrees. It's a difficult retrieval to do by hand—without the machines and diving submarines we use in much deeper dives."

"What does it look like?" My heart picked up its pace as I imagined the skeletal remains of the ship under water, its deteriorated body folded into the sand.

"Because wood rots, it now looks like a sixty-foot-by-ninety-foot pile of copper."

"The boilers," I guessed.

"Yes. There are so many things left to find."

"This is going to be so interesting." I flipped through the photos and ate dinner while the present ebbed away and the past took shape before me, as if rising from the water.

11

LILLY

Friday, June 15, 1838
Midnight

Lilly froze at the surreal scene. Steam, injury and chaos made it almost impossible to understand what had happened.

Passengers in varying states of dress, some in evening gowns and suits, many wearing their nightclothes, inundated the deck. They had all finally realized the grand ship was sinking. Women screamed for their husbands while clasping children who were too frightened to cry out, as if they more than anyone knew nothing would save them now. A man stumbled across the deck bleeding from his neck where a scrap of iron poked out. When he fell to the ground, his blood puddling beneath him, passengers stepped neatly over him. There were too many lives to save, Lilly thought. Too many.

Where was the rest of her family? The cousins. Dear Augusta. Melody. Her uncle. Where were they?

While rushing toward the lifeboats, pushing past other passengers, sliding in the cold water, she took stock; the starboard side had been blown open by the explosion, and the boat listed heavily. The acrid smell of burning wood; the metallic odor of blood and flesh; the swooping sensation of fear; the choking thickness of smoke.

The wheelhouse, which she knew had stood on deck above the boilers, was gone. The masts chewed apart and unstable, the smoke-stacks lilting.

"Keep Madeline wrapped tight," Priscilla said. "I can't swim and this will be my fate, to die at God's hand. But you must live. You go now."

Lilly grasped Priscilla's hand. "We will save each other and we will save Madeline."

Lilly's hand slipped from Priscilla's as the ship heaved, seasick from its injury, and Priscilla and Lilly grabbed on to the mast in front of them. They wrapped their arms around the wood, waiting for the ship to settle before they worked their way closer to the lifeboats, the hanging quarterboats slowly being lowered.

They clung to the wood as they watched two men in full evening attire—one older, one younger—fight for space on a settee they'd wrenched from the decking. Finally the younger one, in a rage, grabbed the other man under the arms and with a mighty heave tossed him overboard. Lilly screamed and turned away in shock. Nearby, a Negro man lashed together boards and an empty gin barrel for his fretful master, a man with thick gray side whiskers whose attire in a nightshirt hadn't dimmed his expectation of receiving service at any cost. Lilly knew the Negro man wouldn't be joining his master on the float.

Elsewhere on deck, a woman slid toward the sea without any attempt to save herself, her pink dress sliding over her head, her hands held above her, offering her body to the dark depths. And all the while, the ship groaned like a beast in great pain.

Shrieks filled the air. Cold seawater rushed over their bare feet.

"Where is Master Forsyth?" Priscilla hollered across the chaos.

Lilly didn't answer, wanting to scream out to God to not let Adam find them.

The mast then quivered beneath their hands and Lilly's and Priscilla's gazes met: they instinctively let go of its great heft and moved to the edge of the boat, sliding, holding on to one another, grasping the rails. With a shudder felt deep within the bowels of the ship, the mast let loose and fell like a mighty tree, plunging to the deck with a crash that shook the ship. Passengers ran, and yet one gentleman in his dressing coat had neither room nor time to escape the crushing weight. The crunch of bone and flesh was sickening.

Lilly and Priscilla turned away in horror as four men hauled the man's body from beneath the shattered mast. When Lilly looked back, a priest from Charleston, whom Lilly had met the second day of the voyage, now in pantaloons and a linen shirt stained with blood, leaned over the man. Dipping his fingers in seawater, he drew a cross upon the man's forehead and then together the four men committed the man's body to the sea. His life, snuffed out that quickly, that horribly, sent Lilly's fear rushing into her like the sea onto the deck. She couldn't breathe, her body immovable, her mind screaming and her fingers clutching so tightly around her baby that Madeline wailed in pain.

Priscilla, now shaking with fear, her eyes flickering from one end of the boat to the other, spoke without conviction, but with something like hope. "God is with us."

"No, he is not." Lilly closed her eyes. Everywhere she looked terror reigned. Men and women floating in the sea; children sliding away from their parents; men rushing their wives and children to the life-boats to beg for a spot. The rich. The poor. The indentured servants. The Negroes. The engineers and Captain Dubois and officers—they were all same now. Humans desperate to be saved.

Who was worthy of salvation? Were they? Was she?

"God can't be here," Lilly said as she opened her eyes again, resolute to live. "He doesn't choose that way. We don't get to live because he loves us best, Priscilla. We get to live because we find a way to live."

"Mistress." Priscilla's voice sounded pained at such blasphemy.

"He didn't save us from Adam, and he won't save us from this. We will save ourselves," Lilly insisted.

Priscilla began to recite a prayer in a language that Lilly had heard only when she'd visited the slave cabins and they hadn't yet seen her, a language so melodic and pure that she felt sure if God existed, he heard Priscilla.

12

EVERLY

Present day

Safely ensconced at home an hour after my dinner with Maddox, I wished I hadn't had the second glass of Prosecco. Had I said anything unprofessional to him, the treasure hunter with the searching green eyes? I had to be careful. Much more careful. No way he needed to see the way Mora haunted me. My history of loss wasn't anything I wanted him to know.

Maddox didn't need to know that the hell of it all was this: I knew as deeply as the roots of the grand oak in our side yard that if I hadn't been joshing, if I hadn't given Oliver the little hip shove of laughter about St. Patrick, if I had just stood there quietly that afternoon, then the car driven by the man with the dead eyes would have missed Mora; it would have plowed through the crowd to her right. Any idea that I was "supposed" to live, or that I'd been spared for a reason, a reason that can't quite be named, was absurd. It was chance. It was a step or two. There wasn't a day I didn't think about it—about how I walked about the world alive and well while Mora was gone.

Simple routines now ordered my days. That did not include drinking with an all-too-insightful man old enough to be my father.

I dropped my purse on the red velvet couch I'd found at a flea market and had cleaned to within a thread of its life, and plopped down, setting my feet on the iron coffee table. I lifted the phone to call Allyn, tell her not to come over with the kids as she'd planned, when Oliver's name lit up on the cell screen next to an image of his face. The photo was from an afternoon in Charleston when we'd gone with Mora to visit the aquarium. He was wearing dark sunglasses and a wry grin, his crooked front tooth on full display. His cheeks were red with sunburn and a baseball cap pulled low. The photo was one of my favorites. Or had been. Now I didn't know.

"Hello, Oliver." I used my most serious voice. "How are you?"

"Is this an answering service? May I please speak with Everly Winthrop?"

"You're funny," I said, our usual tag line.

He laughed. "I wanted to see how the meeting with Maddox went."

"I didn't realize I was auditioning. I thought it was a done deal, but I could tell he was testing me."

"I knew you'd pass whatever test he had in mind."

"Tomorrow, I'll go to the Georgia Historical Society and start digging, find out what I can about that night and the Longstreet family."

"I'll stop by and see you there. Okay?"

"No need. Maddox and I've got this."

The hush of the phone line felt unnerving, but I sat with it, staring into the fireplace piled with birch logs. Nature abhors a vacuum, I remembered, but I wouldn't fill this one.

Finally, I heard his exhale. "Okay. Keep me updated."

"Will do."

When we hung up, the air vibrated with his voice. It was easy to slip into our banter, our always-at-ease way of being with each other. The music I'd clicked on when I walked in the door switched to Alison Krauss and John Waite singing the old classic "Missing You." I jumped up and turned off the music, but not soon enough. The memory was already plowing through my Prosecco-soaked mind.

In the weeks following Mora's death, Oliver and I saw each other almost every day. Sometimes we tried to figure out how it could have gone differently. Other days we avoided the subject altogether. We stalked Savannah, Oliver keeping me company as I stared into the eyes of every dark-haired man we passed, knowing I would recognize him if I saw the monster again. We worked with the police. We went to Bonaventure at midnight and sat by her grave with a bottle of whiskey.

One afternoon I realized I'd been checking my cell for a text from Oliver every five minutes for hours; I felt panicked and worried that I hadn't heard from him, that I *wanted* to hear from him. I had slid slowly and inexorably onto dangerous ground. I had passed from needing a friend to needing *him* in a deeper, more complicated way. I could not. I would not. It would be a betrayal of Mora and his commitment to her.

For days after that realization, I ignored him. Then he showed up at my blue front door bearing a bottle of whiskey—Mora's favorite, Writer's Tears—and an invitation to kayak to the sand bar where we'd all spent more hours than could be counted, swimming and dreaming and napping afternoons away until high tide licked our toes.

"I can't go." I stood there in my sweat pants, T-shirt, and fluffy slippers with the backs pushed down from being too lazy to wear them proper (as he would say).

He pushed into the living room without permission and placed the whiskey on the black granite kitchen counter and stared at me with the same pained intensity I'd seen at the hospital when we sat in the hallway on a wooden bench with blood on our hands. I'd wept, "It should have been me. It should have been me." And he'd sat quietly, his body shaking, and said not one word. Of course he knew it. Of course he agreed.

"I won't let you stay here like this, Everly. She wouldn't want it."

"How do you know what she'd want?" I'd almost spat the words. How dare he tell me what my best friend would want.

"No. She wouldn't. And you damn well know it."

"You know what she would want, Oliver?"

He didn't reply.

"I think she'd want to be here. That's what I think she'd want."

"Yes." He leaned against the counter and a tear ran down his cheek. He was always easy with the emotions. "No two people loved her more than we do. Ignoring each other isn't helping this grief. Please go with me to the sandbar. We'll just kayak there, swim, and kayak back. I want . . . no, I need, to do something I did with her. Anything. And you were just as much a part of it."

"You think that's going to help us get over her? Somehow give us closure or some inane idea like that?"

"No. Getting over someone is a myth. Closure is a myth. She'll always be with us. Come with me anyway."

The sandbar was empty late on a Monday afternoon in May, twilight turning the edges of the world supple and pink. We swam in the rich salt water of the river and floated on our backs. Menhaden flickered against our skin; sequins of sunlight on the water formed a pathway back to the sandbar.

I dove first, pointing myself toward the bottom of that tidal river, kicking as hard as I knew how, fighting the outgoing tide, to touch the sand. I stayed down there, my toes wiggling in the muddy sand, a crab skittling away. I held my breath until it burned and then I shot to the surface.

Oliver waited for me up top, paddling to keep from being swept out with the tide. When I swam up we looked at each other and in complete agreement without words, we dove together. He took my hand and we pushed and kicked and exhaled our way to the bottom about ten feet below and touched the sandy bottom, our eyes open as the salt stung them like bees.

He yanked at my hand and we kicked to the surface, a few feet farther down, and kicked our way back. Again and again we descended without a word, and ascended until, out of breath, Oliver began to swim toward shore only a few yards away. "Come," he said. I shook my head and dove again. His voice sounded dull and muffled as he called me back. But I wanted to go down there, over and over and over. Five more times? I don't remember but finally he swam back and grabbed my shoulders. "You're scaring me to death, Everly. Stop! The tide . . . come back . . ."

We kicked and breast stroked our way to the sandbar and fatigue sank into me like a weight heavier than if I had a barbell strapped to my back. I floated the last yard as he dragged me to the sand.

I collapsed and he lay next to me, both of us warm and damp. We rested on our backs and told stories of Mora, alternately taking sips of the whiskey. His words began to feel silky, the sand something that held the world together. My body floated between sky and river, and the grief slid underground. "Tell me one I don't know from child-hood," he said as he sat, tracing his toes in a circle so a spiral formed in the wet, dark sand.

"I think she told you all of them."

"I'm sure she didn't," he said and flopped back to the sand, rolling on his side to face me where I rested on my back absorbing the heat and healing of the earth.

"I don't know." I looked at him and when I did, I cracked open. The safe place I'd built for her memory, guarded by steel doors and padlocks, blew open with the dynamite of his endearing question and kind eyes. And I couldn't tell him a story because once I started crying I couldn't stop.

It was convulsive, those tears that hadn't been spent. My body shook with them.

"Oh, God, Everly. I'm sorry. I'm sorry. I didn't mean to make it worse."

I couldn't answer him because I was past words. There was nothing left to say, only to feel. His reaction was quick and his arms were around me. The sheer weight of his hands, of his body, helped me feel that I was not spinning out of control. He was, it seemed, holding me together.

I curled like a sea snail into the curve of his body and allowed him to hold me there. When I felt his lips on my neck, I lifted my face and let my lips meet his. The kiss was urgent. When his hands slid up my legs to my salt-sticky thighs, I came to my senses. I stood in a rush and flew like a bird across the river in that kayak, leaving him alone on the sandbar with his kayak. And that was the last time I'd seen him until he sauntered into my classroom.

I could have blamed it on the whiskey—I did when I told Allyn the story much later—but I knew I hadn't been drunk, or not drunk enough to allow for the way our bodies had found each other. The desperate and aching need that had been created by Mora's absence had been briefly filled by Oliver's presence.

As I sat on my red couch, shame swallowed me with thick, choking hands. The memory of that evening felt as sullied as the bottom of a bar's dumpster on River Street. What a fool I'd been.

I'd refused to speak to Oliver since that night. I'd told him it was dangerous and that what we'd done was only out of grief and fear and it could never happen again. He tried to explain how we couldn't be blamed and it wouldn't be repeated—he promised. I didn't believe him. Or I didn't believe myself.

I missed him. I missed him *almost* as fiercely as I did Mora but with a different and vibrant tenor and energy because he was alive and well, walking distance away. Grieving Mora opened great swaths of hopelessness and guilt, darker energies. But Mora's death also meant the death of anything to do with Oliver—surviving without her was one kind of betrayal, but possibly making a mistake that would mean falling in love with the fiancé she'd left behind was another disloyalty altogether. I would not allow it.

It didn't matter so much that I had met Oliver first, albeit only minutes before Mora walked into the office to welcome him to the museum, and her light turned me to shadow. The three of us, quick as lightning, formed a trio ready-made for adventure. She and I introduced this California boy to the lush marshes and hidden estuaries of our native landscape, taught him how to cast a shrimp net, how to catch menhaden for bait, how to swim with the tides. He fell in love first with the land and then with Mora. How could he not fall in love with her? She was part of the South, seemed to have been born from its thick mud and hanging moss, from its dirt roads and hidden corners. He seemed to love her just as wildly as I did, even if in a different way.

And love, it wasn't my specialty. For four years I had loved a man without ever seeing that my feelings weren't fully reciprocated. I was not to be trusted in matters of the heart.

I'd been *madly* in love, but the memory was now as distant as the bottom of the sea. I know I'd felt both consumed and entranced with the need for Grant Phillips. Our relationship had guided my days—

when would I see him? When would we get engaged? When would he admit that we were forever? In those days, my thoughts had circled back to him whenever there was a free moment. It was a cycle that went round and round.

When he left me, when he shattered my particular dream with some nonsensical blathering about finding his truth, I was left shaking. Finding his truth? I soon realized, of course, that this was code for "I don't love you." But instead of facing that harsh reality, I'd struggled to understand the exact meaning of "finding my truth." I took apart each word, rearranged them in different order, unraveled and rewove. Of course it never made any sense.

How could I have ever thought Grant mattered enough to lose sleep over? He was a charming but selfish man who loved to conquer but didn't love to stick around.

He left Savannah; I had no idea where he went. For a year I tried to track him down, make him explain. Who was I then that I was so desperate for a man who didn't love me in return?

We'd broken up six months before Oliver and Mora fell in love, which explained their reticence in initially letting me in on their romance. They were afraid of hurting me when I was still reeling from rejection. I got it. But I saw what was happening anyway.

I'd sworn off men, at least until I understood why I chose men who didn't want me.

And then came St. Patrick's Day, and after that, my feelings crawled into hibernation. I was lonely, not for a man in a warm bed, but with the knowledge that in the end, and in the middle and beginning, we are alone. The love that comes and goes in our lives is just a momentary reprieve.

It was dangerous to want to be near Oliver so much. I'd confused love before. I damn sure wasn't going to do it again.

Now, alone in my house, I curled into a ball. If I could cry I might feel better, but my tears had dried long ago.

My cell phone beeped and I looked down.

On our way.

My sister and her kids. I forgot to cancel.

Can we change to tomorrow? Please. Buried in work.

Nope. Almost there.

13

AUGUSTA

Friday, June 15, 1838
Midnight

Augusta, Melody and the children reached the promenade where the lifeboats either were being lowered from davits or sat on the aft deck. Augusta glanced about with frantic fear, her gaze snagging on where the explosion had ripped apart one side of the *Pulaski*; there was no way the ship would stay afloat. There was no salvation on deck any more than there was below. A gentleman in evening attire hollered to all of them, "Please, this way, higher, this way. We must balance the ship." He seemed delusional. The bow was pointing up now, the sleek wood her brother had recently run his hand over splintering apart.

Clinging to each other, they all moved in unison. They slipped sideways with the lilting ship. Augusta's arm burned with the strength needed to keep Thomas tight to her body. The starboard side of the boat appeared to have been bitten in half. She scrambled to keep her footing, slipping and sliding, clinging to the children and striving toward the life boat strapped on the promenade, still covered in canvas. Hadn't she and Lilly remarked on its presence earlier in the day? Hadn't they mentioned that the steamboat *Home* hadn't had enough lifeboats or rafts?

Lilly.

Where was Lilly and her precious child? Augusta would know her even in the chaos, but she didn't see her. And Henry—had he made it out from the men's cabins below? The thought for others was cast away by a grinding sound. Augusta twirled around to see the two quarter-boats being lowered into the water, passengers huddled inside, the ropes hissing as they dropped astern.

God help us all.

At least there were two more lifeboats, the yawls on deck, being prepared. Fourteen-year-old Charles was obedient and quick on his feet. He stood ready to help, his fists balled up at his waist as if he might fight the ship, save them all. Augusta leaned down to him. "You are brave and good, Charles. Stay strong."

He nodded and forced back tears while Thomas squalled and clung to Augusta's nightgown. The sky was bright with stars and the half moon waning, casting an eerie glow across the waves and the battered, collapsing beauty that was once the *Pulaski.* Augusta turned when she heard her name being called.

Lamar ran toward them. He was dressed in his suit without the vest, head-to-toe as dapper as if they were headed to a formal dinner at a fine Savannah home. "Take the children," he hollered to Augusta and Melody. "Get in the lifeboats. Don't delay. I don't see that we have more than five minutes. The hull will go down with the weight of the engines and boilers." He threw off his jacket, dropping it into the inches of water that covered the deck. Augusta witnessed his pocket watch sink below the surface. The ornate heirloom had been her grandfather's, then her father's, and now his. She reached down to seize it, but Lamar pressed her forward.

Melody spoke into the night. "We must save the children, Augusta. Think of nothing else."

Augusta took stock as she ran toward the lifeboats: the bulkhead between the boilers demolished, already being swept away in the waves. The head of the boiler destroyed and its top blown to both the back and the front of the ship.

God help us all.

The mast was a fallen tree, with huge splinters as dangerous as swords poking from its once solid surface. Smoke rose and whirled like a cloud from below and the cries of the injured trapped belowdecks came from hell.

God help us all.

Even in the dark, Augusta saw the blanched terror on her brother's face. "I don't have much hope for any of us," he said.

Then, out of the crowd appeared First Mate Hibbert, blood congealed grotesquely on his face, barking orders to place the yawls into the ocean.

Augusta braved a touch to his shirtsleeve. "Mate Hibbert." He paused to look to her, his face contorted with a bruise the size of an orange on his forehead. A cut on his cheek oozed blood.

"Oh, Miss Longstreet, you must take the children and get in the lifeboat."

"What has happened?" Her voice shook with fear.

"I was in the wheelhouse and that is the last I remember. I awoke to all that you see now. Get in one of the boats. Go now."

Lamar embraced his wife, lifted her face and kissed her. "Let us all get in the boat now." Other men arrived and together with a heave they slid it to the edge of the ship so when the sea lifted, the boat would rise with it. The yawl was a curved wooden structure with seats along both sides, able to hold about twelve passengers. The oars had been washed away and the men yanked up the floorboards, which had buckled below them, and pulled them loose.

"For oars," they told Lamar. "We must have oars or we are no better off than floating on this ship."

God help us all.

At the other end of the deck, through the smoke, Augusta spied Henry helping a woman climb up from the stairwell. She opened her mouth to scream at him; to tell him to save himself, to come to her! But saving the children was all that mattered. Augusta pulled Charles and Thomas along and they climbed into the lifeboat, Melody and the other four children beside her. Sarah MacKay and her two young daughters climbed in as Lamar lifted them and set them on Sarah's lap. Then he settled in and pulled his family close. "The ship will sink and with God's providence, our lifeboat will sink horizontally and float off. Hold tight."

A familiar voice called out and Augusta turned to see her childhood friend Daphne, still in her lovely silk gown. Daphne, whose money and beauty could not save her.

"Daphne!" Augusta called out and reached for her hands, almost clawing at the air to get to her friend. But her efforts were futile as only yards away Daphne thrashed and scrambled with nothing to grab. She disappeared over the edge.

Augusta cried out and squeezed Thomas so tightly that he wailed in pain.

God, she wanted to place her hands over her ears, to shut out the sights and sounds that would haunt her all her days. She looked to her brother, her heart hammering. She took in long, deep breaths in anticipation of having to hold her breath, of having to go long moments, and maybe forever, without the breath she needed as the lifeboat dipped forward.

Charles shivered in fear and held on to her hand. "We will be saved," he said in a voice older than his years, stronger than he could possibly have felt.

They huddled together in the lifeboat, the women and children, waiting for it to be swept into the sea, holding on to one another, crying out for loved ones and God's help. Then there he was: Henry stood above Augusta and handed her a tin cup. "Miss Longstreet. You will need this for bailing, hold on to it."

"Aren't you getting in?" She grasped his wrist. Who would deny his own salvation?

"I must help the others . . . I will find something that floats." He touched the top of Thomas's blond hair. "Save your family."

"Please come with us." Augusta placed the tin cup between her feet, holding the children's hands.

"I will find you," Henry said as he turned to walk into the crowd that pushed forward toward the boats.

A sailor stood nearby, holding out his arms. "They are full. Move aside. They are full."

Augusta waited for whatever the fates would bring when the lifeboat floated into the sea. She watched with horror as passengers fought their way across the deck. Others were pushing past the sailor, clambering into the lifeboat, and they were now squeezed tight, too close together. Hysteria gripped Augusta and she stood to climb out onto the deck, looking down at all those she loved in the lifeboat.

But her brother's voice implored her. "Get back in, Augusta. Now."

"It can't hold." She told the truth, an odd calm descending over her.

"It's your only hope. My family's only hope."

His pleas moved her and she slid back into the seat and placed

Thomas on her lap. She would live for him. He was the only reason she returned to the rickety lifeboat.

Eliza took her arm. "Oh, Auntie Augusta, what shall we do?"

"Look to Jesus. He can save us."

As if in answer to Augusta's futile words, the ship groaned and split, the hull sinking as quick as Lamar had said it would, and the lifeboat was carried with the vertical rise of the stern, waves surging beneath them, sweeping away passengers still on the deck. Augusta turned away from the hideous sight of women and children being washed into the sea. Their screams were otherworldly.

Then a wild wave blew toward them and the lifeboat lifted off the deck beneath the wave and pitched. With a rush, it plunged bow first into a cresting wave.

The boat with twelve in it, Augusta and her family, Sarah MacKay and her two little ones, clinging to one another and to the vessel's cracked sides, bobbed for only a moment before it became clear that the dried-out seams would not hold. Seawater rushed in. Within seconds the vessel pitched forward spilling them all, each and every one, into the sea.

14

EVERLY

Present day

Family had always possessed a gravitational force field, part love, part obligation, mixed with the usual petty irritations and the bonds of an intimately shared history.

Mom's ancestors had arrived on these shores via the sailing ship *Anne*; they were among the first settlers to land with Oglethorpe, sometimes called the First British God of Georgia. He set his feet upon this land and declared it a settlement of the English. True "originals" Mom always called her family, as if they grew from the rich Georgian soil and briny water of the estuaries and rivers that flowed to the Atlantic.

At a young age, I would ask, "But where were we before we were original?"

And Mom would laugh, flick flour from the chocolate chip cookies she was baking and ask, "Does it matter where your family was before

here? Someday you'll have a child and you'll remember your ancestors, too."

My own children had seemed a remote possibility back then, when
I was six or seven years old and sunlight fell through the Spanish moss
onto our garden lawn and honeysuckle filled the air with a scent so
intoxicating I wished I could take it to my pillow (I tried that once and
found the stems wilted and crushed in the morning).

On both sides of the family, there had been a many-times-great-
grandfather in the Revolutionary War, another in the Civil War, men
who found their place among the rice, indigo and cotton fields and
then shed their blood for the South; and women who had survived
crop failure, yellow fever and hurricanes, and still come to one another's aid. Women in my family who had founded the first orphanage
and the Georgia Historical Society.

Our house, named Oaklawn by an unknown ancestor, had been in
Mom's family for four generations, built by enslaved people and then
added on to and updated through the years.

Dad's family—the Irish side—had a more shadowy history. Like
Mora's family, Dad's descended from the shipwrecked Irish immigrants
who went on to survive indentured servitude and war, each generation
improving its circumstances until Dad's great-grandfather distinguished
himself as a brilliant merchant and married a woman from a wealthy
family. By then Mom's family had fallen on hard times and lost Oaklawn, and the Winthrops purchased it.

None of this mattered to anyone but us Winthrops.

My doorbell rang. Allyn stood holding a plate covered in tin foil.
Her kids, Merily and Hudson, six and eight years old, pushed to get
through the door first, laughing as if they'd invented the best game
ever.

I stepped aside to let my sister enter my home, then leaned down
and hugged each child. "Hey, kids," I said. "How's summer going?"

"The greatest in the world," Merily said, bouncing on her toes, her pink dress, in a daisy print, rising with her.

Hudson hovered near his mom, as if Merily's exuberance must be tempered by his reticence. We entered the kitchen.

Allyn held out the plate. "I have cookies. Homemade. Chocolate chip—your favorite." She set the plate on the white kitchen table and pointed at the papers stacked around it. "What's all this?"

I broke off a piece of warm, doughy cookie and popped it in my mouth. "My next project."

"Next?" Allyn smiled. "That means you're doing it." Together we sat at the table. "Are these photos from the wreck?"

"Yes." I felt a surging sense of purpose. My job was to make sense of this pile of documents and photos. I had a puzzle to solve. I had something to investigate and explore. Anticipation fizzed inside me.

"What wreck?" Hudson picked up a photo of a diver underwater facing the camera and holding up a coin between his thumb and forefinger.

"The shipwreck happened a hundred and eighty years ago. And that coin, it's a gold doubloon. There're hundreds more of them hidden under the sand. When families traveled back then, they took all the money they would need on the trip with them. No such thing as credit cards." I tousled Hudson's blond hair.

Merily snatched the photo from her brother's hand. "Treasure? Real treasure like in *Treasure Island*?"

"Well, I'm not sure I'd call it treasure," Allyn said. "It belonged to families that . . ." Her voice trailed off and she looked to me for help.

Hudson's chest puffed with indignation. "Gold at the bottom of the sea is treasure."

"We call it artifacts," I said. "Then again, I'm a dorky historian. So, let's call it treasure. Much more fun."

Merily set the picture down and picked up another. "What's this?"

"A pocket watch. Back then men wore them, and the fancier the pocket watch, the fancier the man."

"What man wants to be fancy?" Merily asked, and set it down.

"Wrong word again." I touched my temples and tapped. "Cool. The pocket watch made them cool. They would attach a gold chain and let it dangle in front of their chests."

"That's really dumb." Hudson checked with his mother. "Why would you wear a clock on your chest?" He rolled his eyes. "What else did they find?"

"They're still looking." I took another cookie and then both kids did the same.

"Right now? They're looking *right now*?" Hudson threw his arms in the air.

"Yes. Treasure hunters are a hundred feet down there, trying to raise it all up."

"A hundred feet!" Merily looked at the photo again. "What happened to the ship and the people on it? Are they down there, too?"

"The people aren't down there anymore . . ." I stopped. How to explain that? "But the things they brought with them still are."

"Where did the people go?" Merily asked.

Allyn answered. "Sweetie, most of them died, but some were rescued."

Hudson chose a third photo. "Can we go see it? Can I dive for treasure? Can I have a gold coin?"

Our shared laughter lightened my mood and Allyn shooed her children upstairs to watch something on the coveted iPad, while we sat on the couch. "Sorry it's a bit late. The kids had a birthday party and I really wanted to see you before we headed home. So, what do you hope to find?" she asked.

"I'm not hoping for *one* thing. I just want to make sense of the night of the explosion so the exhibit is interesting. I'm going to dig up their accounts, find the stories. It's exciting." I leaned closer. "I know it seems far-fetched, but what if we really could find out what happened to Lilly Forsyth?"

"I think Papa would rise from the grave to celebrate." We smiled knowingly at each other. "So . . ." Allyn bit her bottom lip and then asked the question that must have been simmering. "You're ready to be around Oliver more often now?"

"I must be." I crinkled my eyes back at her. "And don't look at me like that. This isn't about Oliver. This is about the *Pulaski*. And I'll be mostly working with the man who's leading the recovery—Maddox Wagner. That's where I was tonight. And Oliver has moved on. I saw him with a date tonight. I doubt our relationship will cast any pall on his thriving life."

"Everly." Allyn shook her head with a half grin.

"I guess he moves on quickly . . ."

"It's been over a year since Mora . . ."

"It's been five minutes. It feels like it just happened."

"Listen, I don't care who you work with; I care that you stop hiding out in this little house."

"That's not . . ." I stopped myself from saying "true" because it was true. Except for work and family, I rarely engaged with other people and I spent far too much time sitting home alone.

Allyn nodded at my truncated declaration. "This is bringing a spark back in your eyes, but I do worry about you being around Oliver. I mean . . ."

"Listen, I'm past it. We can dismiss one weird afternoon in the middle of great grief. We were clinging to whatever remained. Now— I still miss Mora. He misses Mora. The danger is past. I've seen him three times in two days and all is well. We were . . . adrift back then."

Allyn laughed and shot her head back. "Damn, Everly, we are all adrift. Every one of us." She shook her head and scooted closer. Allyn hesitated before asking what must have been bothering her even more than Oliver. "Please tell me you've stopped looking for him."

"The monster who killed Mora?"

"Everly." Allyn glanced up the stairs as if her children had heard me.

"No. I will never stop looking for him." I set my hands on my knees and leaned forward. "If I can uncover two-hundred-year-old mysteries, if I can dig through papers and photos and put together a story, then surely I can find the man who killed my best friend. I won't ever stop looking."

"Everly. Please be careful. With all of this."

"I will. Listen, I know Mora is with me on this. I can feel it. She would love the detective work and the mystery of it all. It's *her* museum even if someone else runs it now. And it's a fact—that afternoon with Oliver was a huge mistake. I should be ashamed, but it won't happen again. All of this"—I spread my hands to indicate the photos and documents—"is about the wreck, not about Oliver. The end."

Allyn smiled and leaned back, rested her arms along the back of the couch. "The end. Yeah. Sure. Anything you say."

I tossed a cookie at her. "If I feel weird about anything, I'll quit. I promise."

Allyn reached over and hugged me. "Never quit, my beautiful sister. That's not your way."

15

LILLY

Friday, June 15, 1838
Midnight

A man sloshed through the water that puddled on the deck, and as he drew closer Lilly recognized him—Mr. Couper from Savannah. She'd met him the first evening, a dapper man in charge of a widowed woman, Nelle March, and her ten-year-old son, Theodore. Yes, they, too, were scrambling toward the larger, hanging quarterboats being lowered from davits.

"Mrs. Forsyth, come with me." Mr. Couper took Lilly's hand. "Do make haste."

They pushed through the crowd of people who were slipping and sliding with the tilt of the failing ship. But with single-minded intent they reached the quarterboat as two sailors finished lowering it into the sea, the ropes hissing beneath their hands and against the rails. The first quarterboat was already in the water, pitching against the wild waves.

"Now, give me your child," Mr. Couper demanded in a voice that did not allow for argument. He spoke as if he stood in full military uniform instead of in a nightshirt and pantaloons, a blue cloak wrapped around his body.

Lilly untied her child but still held tight. "I will die before I let her perish."

"You will not die. Now jump down into the quarterboat and I will hand her to you. Go." Lilly gently handed Madeline to Mr. Couper and looked to the boat. It held six men, two women and one child. There seemed to be no more seats and yet Lilly and Priscilla held hands and jumped, landing with a crack, gasping for breath and waiting for the vessel to settle before sitting up. Lilly's ankle screamed against its second blow but she cared only for her child. Together they glanced toward the deck, Lilly's arms held out for Madeline as the steamship lurched, emitting a great shriek of splintering wood as its bow and aft ascended and the middle section began to sink.

With horror, a scream clogged in her throat, Lilly watched as Mr. Couper slid from the rising deck and tumbled beneath the waves, still holding her child. Lilly flung her body forward, arms outstretched over the side of the quarterboat, but Priscilla held her back. "Wait!"

Lilly's scream then broke loose. "Madeline!" She would jump in the sea; she would dive to the bottom of the deep blue for her daughter. "Madeline!" she called again as Mr. Couper's face emerged above the crest of a silver wave, his cloak floating about him like an ink stain. Directly next to the boat, he held Madeline over his head. He focused on Lilly and tossed the child toward her. With arms already held out, Lilly caught Madeline about the waist and together they fell back onto two other men who held her from behind. With Priscilla by her side, they watched as Mr. Couper used his great arms to heave himself into the quarterboat, gasping for air while Madeline screamed her distress in high-pitched lament.

With a hard seat beneath them, Priscilla and Lilly sat wet and shivering, Lilly rocking Madeline back and forth, uttering her name over and over into her neck. She felt her jewelry pouch still dangling from her wrist where it had been tied tight. If she had slid into the ocean it might have been a hindrance, but now it settled with the weight of the future, if one existed at all.

"The ship is sinking! Grab the oars," Mr. Couper commanded the men. "Row away or we will be sucked into the vortex."

"We must save the others!" a woman cried out. "My family!"

"We will find them if we can. But for now, we must save those here."

Mr. Couper and a bald man with a thick mustache rowed with all their might until a third man, his beard speckled with water glimmering in the moonlight, took the second oar and assisted as they rowed away from the collapsing ship. The second quarterboat with Mate Hibbert also moved away. Only the two lifeboats that had hung outside the ship were safe, and they were in one of them.

Mr. Couper removed the cloak that could have drowned him and spread it out on the bottom. With strong force, the men drew the lifeboat away from the ship and then stopped two hundred yards away. Silence fell and the weight of night was so heavy that Lilly felt as though the starlit sky pressed down on her. She watched as the center section of the ship caved in the middle as both bow and aft shot to the sky.

The promenade deck broke free first, timbers splintering, splitting the sea, sloping and sending passengers into the waves before bobbing up to float like an apple in a barrel. The aft deck disconnected with a startling elegance, also breaking free and sinking only to rise again. Then the screams began, the horrifying cries of passengers echoing across the water.

Mr. Couper closed his eyes as he spoke. "There she goes." His voice broke with emotion.

They all watched in horror as the remainder of the great *Pulaski* sank beneath the waves with an impossibly silent slide, its two ends rising with passengers scrambling onto it and clinging to the edges. Lilly considered what sank with her, and the sum of it all—human and material—was incalculable and infinite.

"Dear God, they shriek in their last mortal struggle." Mr. Couper leaned over the edge of the lifeboat, gasping for breath.

For Lilly, these moments existed as a dream from which she could not awaken. No one spoke a word, each lost in their thoughts of those suffering their last breaths in the arms of an indifferent sea. They had boarded the ship together but they died alone, as everyone must. Minutes passed and the harrowing shrieks changed to the echoing calls of "Helllllloooo. Is anyone out there?"

Lilly shivered in her nightgown, now feeling the physical sensations that had been numbed by shock and fear. Her skin crawled; her stomach lurched; her ankle beat with its own painful pulse; her bones shivered beneath her dimpled skin. She became aware, for the first time, of the absolute state of undress in which they found themselves, of their complete vulnerability. Stripped of social status and pretension, they were—all of them—frightened, humbled, and all too human.

Oh, Lilly thought, the terror of those alone floating on small remnants of wood. How could they leave them? What could be done? Tears poured down her face, over her chin and onto the soft head of baby Madeline, who against all odds slept as peacefully against her bosom as if they were still in the safety of their cabin. Why was she deserving of this seat in the lifeboat? Where was her beloved family? Her Augusta protecting the children?

Those who were in the dark waters grabbed for whatever floating debris they could and in the darkness, they called for other survivors. Lilly tuned her ear for a familiar voice—Augusta; Aunt Melody; Uncle Lamar. She listened until she heard the deepest voice, only feet away, yelling, "Help me. Do not row away; I can pay!" Priscilla grabbed Lilly's hand and squeezed.

Adam.

Lilly's heart leapt into her throat, her body quivering with fear. She could speak up now, tell them all that it was her husband who called only twenty feet away in the dark night, and Mr. Couper would grab him from the waters.

Or she could remain silent and allow Adam to perish.

She didn't hesitate: she allowed his death.

She would never deliberately take his life. But she would merely *allow* it. Here, neither fate nor God existed; only her decision mattered. Her choice. Her life in exchange for his death.

Priscilla and Lilly sat quietly and unmoving, stricken by their guilt but unwilling to alter it.

Mr. Couper spoke over the desperate cries for help and the crashing waves. "Let's reach the other lifeboat and assess our situation. We have twelve on our boat and it is leaking. We can't take anyone else or we will all perish."

Two of the men—Lilly hadn't ascertained most of the names yet—rowed toward the second quarterboat where First Mate Hibbert flagged them with a scrap of white fabric.

Around them, passengers swam to floating pieces of wreckage, to rigging, settees and barrels, to flotsam and luggage, timber and decking. "Please bring in more of them," a woman next to Lilly cried out. "I can't bear to watch them suffer."

Mr. Couper's voice came hard as flint. "All of their hopes rest in finding flotage until we reach shore to send for help."

As the two quarterboats drew near to each other, Mr. Couper and First Mate Hibbert began to discuss the situation. The two yawls on deck had been rotted by exposure to the sun and were of no use. Those who had boarded them were gone, swallowed by the sea. Lilly's boat was full, and yet First Mate Hibbert's carried only five people. He could pick up at least eight more. It was decided that together they would row among the wreckage and pluck whatever souls they found first, making no judgment as to their worthiness, and pull them aboard. To elect by any other means seemed inhumane. They first saved two severely burned Negro firemen, then a judge from New York, a woman from Charleston, and two more men. With Hibbert's boat now full, they had no choice but to row away from the devastating scene.

Lilly held her breath each time they came upon another soul, praying in a way she was certain would send her to hell. *Please don't find Adam.*

"You can't leave," Nelle March cried out as they rowed away from the flotsam. "There are people still floating. There are . . . children and mothers and families." She held close to her young son, who buried his face in her shoulder. Seawater slapped the edges of the boat, splashing into their laps and faces, oblivious to the horror. It was merely doing what the sea does—surging and rising and sinking without mercy.

Mr. Couper sat before Mrs. March, his face pained and his hands bleeding. "Mrs. March, if we put any more on either of these boats, we will sink. We are bailing as it is now."

Lilly looked to the gentleman using his hat to dip water from the bottom of the boat and toss it to the sea.

Mr. Couper continued, "We must save those we can."

Waves crashed against wreckage and bodies, spraying, turning the sea to silver. The *Pulaski* had disappeared and only the light of the waning moon and the diamond glint of stars was reflected on the water.

Mr. Couper spoke to them all in a firm voice. "We must row toward land." He glanced at the sky. "It seems to be about three in the morning and First Mate Hibbert believes we are thirty-five miles east of the North Carolina coast. We will make for land as quickly as we can and send help for the others."

"Where is Captain Dubois?" a man asked.

Mr. Couper shook his head. "We can only pray for his rescue. Meanwhile, Mate Hibbert is as knowledgeable and proficient as Dubois. We will listen to him."

Using the stars for guidance, they began the hard row toward shore.

In a voice saturated with despair, Mr. Couper said, "The young, the beautiful, the wise, and the brave now sink."

With Madeline wrapped close to her body, Lilly covered her ears with both hands, pressing so tightly she felt the air trapped and swirling against her eardrums. Her heart withered inside—leaving a living soul calling for help was anathema to all she knew. But she would save Madeline, whether it meant she went to hell or not. Right now she cared nothing for the afterlife, only for the life after this horror.

16

EVERLY

Present day

Can you imagine living in an old house like this?" Maddox paused
at the bottom of the marble steps leading to the front door of the
Georgia Historical Society.

We'd come to dig through the archives of *Pulaski* documents. "I
can." I shaded my eyes to bring the house into focus. The gothic-style
building, peacock-proud and surrounded by a low iron fence, dominated a corner across from Forsyth Park. A black iron sign mounted in
the yard announced the name and when the society was founded—
1839—a year after the wreck.

"Fun fact for you?" I asked.

"Sure," Maddox boomed. "I have a feeling you're full of them."

"One of the founders of this historical society was the mayor who
handed Savannah over to Sherman near the end of the Civil War."

"There isn't much you don't know about Savannah history, is there?

Which are more interesting, the facts or the legends?" Maddox pulled his baseball cap lower.

"The legends, of course. I mean, even we historians know no one remembers dates. We're captivated by stories."

He agreed with only a nod and together we walked up to the carved wooden front doors. His laughter echoed across the portico. "Wait, you *do* live in an old house like this, don't you? That sly grin tells me. I bet you live in one that was built before the *Pulaski* wreck."

"Not that old, but yes, my family home is even older than this building."

He opened the door and his voice echoed across the marble entryway of the hushed library. "Is your family original to your house?"

Ten faces lifted from long research tables where brass gooseneck lamps cast circles of light onto sheaves of papers and stacks of books, puddling around laptops. Maddox had the good sense to cover his mouth with his hand and shrug as if to say sorry. He glanced at me and whispered, "Libraries have never really been my thing."

Even his whisper seemed to fill the room. I smiled and placed a finger to my lips. "We can talk, but quietly. This is one of my favorite places in the city."

I spied two women behind the circulation desk staring at Maddox. He did look as if a boat had dropped him off at the wrong dock.

I continued in soft tones. "But no, our family isn't original to our house. My dad's family bought it in the mid-1800s from my mom's family, after it had served a few other purposes—an orphanage, a house of ill repute and a hotel. Slowly the Winthrops restored it and added on to it and now Mom will never leave it, even on threat of death. She is the house. The house is her. I don't know any other way to explain it."

"You live there now?"

"No." I motioned for him to approach the research desk. "I have my own place. Come on, enough about me. Let's dig into the archives and see what we find."

After explaining to the librarians we wanted anything they could find on the *Pulaski*, a young woman with flaming red hair and a tattoo of a bird winging up her arm disappeared for several minutes and returned with a file folder jammed with photocopied articles and handwritten notes. "This is what we have. The most informative will be from the 1919 *Georgia Historical Quarterly*. We add to this folder whenever we find anything about the wreck, but there isn't much. There are a few books upstairs on steamboat disasters that may mention the *Pulaski*."

"Nothing on microfiche?"

She shook her head. "Not yet. Ask if you have any questions."

"I do have one more," I said. "Do you have anything about the passenger Lilly Forsyth? There's a statue of her by the riverfront."

"Not much, and what I do have will be in that folder. I think a few articles mention her. I know there is one about the day they put up the monument in the mid 1800s. But I don't have much else."

We took seats, shoulder to shoulder, at a long, empty table and began to sift through the papers, deciphering original documents that were often hard to read and in poor condition, but I was used to that. This was my kind of treasure: letters on thin vellum; old newspaper articles with torn edges and alarming headlines—CALAMITY AT SEA. AWFUL STEAMBOAT ACCIDENT. HEART-RENDING CATASTROPHE. The letters were handwritten in script and would need to be transcribed.

We read in silence, then filled out forms that would allow us to make photocopies of everything in the file.

"Here's a lecture given by the great-grandson of a survivor," Maddox said.

"Here's an article from the *Savannah Georgian*," I added.

"This is an article from a northern newspaper—the *Baltimore Packet*."

We began to catalog what information we had.

I leaned closer to Maddox. "My God, look at this. Savannah didn't even know about the wreck until June twenty-first—a week after it happened. All those families thinking their relatives had arrived safely in Baltimore and were continuing their journey north by rail or carriage. And even then . . . it looks like another week passed before full reports of the disaster came in."

"No telephone. No train. No telegraph. Just a guy on a horse to get the news here." Maddox shook his head. "Hard to believe."

"It's awful."

"That word is used a lot here." He ran his hand across the papers. "Do you see anything about the Longstreet family?"

"Only that he was the investor." I slid a piece of paper toward him. "This article is about the builders and the investors. But nothing else yet."

We separated the documents—newspaper articles, personal accounts and then letters that referenced the tragedy. "Here's a list of secondhand accounts that were published in the paper. There's not much at all and no survivor list; just a partial manifest."

I set my pencil to the yellow legal pad and began to write the names of all the Longstreet family members who had boarded the ship in Savannah. Twelve in total, and Lilly's nursemaid made it thirteen.

I drew a rough family chart. Lamar Longstreet and his sister Augusta. Their niece, Lilly; her husband, Adam; and the baby, Madeline. Then Lamar's wife, Melody, and their six children, including Charles the Red Devil himself. I drew a circle around him. "As far as I can tell, he's the only one who survived."

"There had to have been more."

"Why? Because we think it too cruel that fate would wipe out an entire family in one night?"

Maddox's face softened and he nodded. "Yes, it seems too much to accept."

"Right now, from these papers, it's just one mass of confusion. Survivors couldn't have known about the fate of other passengers; they would have been in their own world trying not to drown. But I'm determined to piece together a full account of that night, which it seems no one has ever done."

"So many of the wrecks we find are already heavily documented. The accounts aren't always consistent, but there are other sources to compare them against. This one is largely a mystery, which is good in one way—less chance we'll be shattering some beloved, long-held mythology associated with the wreck."

I shifted the folder and found another typed account. "Here's a speech given in the 1940s by a man whose great-grandfather was a child survivor." I sat silent for a moment, skimming the paper before I read in a low voice, "'The Pulaski *was born of a shipwreck*.'"

"What does that mean?" Maddox dislodged some papers as he leaned closer.

"It means that after *Home* went down, the *Pulaski* was built with engineering innovations intended to ensure such a tragedy would never happen again. She was the answer to *Home*. She was supposed to be the redemption of steamship travel."

"Well, this was one hell of an answer." Maddox tapped a copy of a lithographic drawing that I also had at home from Oliver's file, a depiction of the moment of explosion with four men in midair and the wheelhouse floating in the sea like a drum.

I said, "Here's an article describing how Adam Forsyth waited and waited for his wife Lilly to return to Savannah, how she was supposed to be with the other survivors and she never showed."

Maddox scanned the article quickly. "It doesn't tell us how but it says he stood at the river's edge for two days. Then he collapsed."

I took a pen and circled Adam's name. "So he survived. My God, this wreck didn't just destroy in the moment it blew up. It continued to ruin lives."

"Yes," Maddox said, "the aftermath is often worse than the event itself."

Aftermath. It was a bloodbath of a word and I let it slip past with a shiver.

"What do you think happened to Lilly?" Maddox asked.

"Papa said the Kraken saved her," I teased, and Maddox let out a loud guffaw that brought dagger-eyed stares from the other patrons.

We shushed each other like guilty schoolkids. "You had quite a papa."

"Yes, I did."

"Really, what do you think happened?"

"I have no idea. Was she never saved at all? Did someone else claim to be her? Did she run off with another man? Did she become lost and disoriented? I'm not sure we'll ever know. When someone doesn't want to be found . . ."

A cold sweat popped out on the nape of my neck as the dark, dead eyes of the driver of the red car came to me. *When someone doesn't want to be found . . .*

"You okay?" Maddox's huge hand reached out to engulf mine. I shifted uneasily and he pulled his hand away.

"Yes. Sorry. Let's read."

We were silent again as we each read snippets about the past. The bookshelves, the puddles of lamplight on long wooden tables, the scratching of pencils on notebook paper and the clicking of computer keys all receded from my awareness until Maddox finally looked up and wiped a hand across his eyes. "Let's get out of here. I can only read so much here."

I stood and arranged the articles together crisscross to separate one pile from the other. During years of grad school, I'd refined my system. I took the time to list each document on a separate paper so I would remember its origin. I knew the drill—you think you'll remember where the article or information originated, but in the chaos of finalizing the curation, it could slip from your memory.

Maddox held a magnifying glass over the miniature print of a newspaper article while I walked to the circulation desk and handed over the forms to have copies made. "You said the other books on steamships are upstairs?" I asked.

"Yes, Section 501." A soft-spoken woman in red glasses pointed to a balcony. She scribbled Dewey decimal numbers on a scrap of paper and handed it to me.

The woman holding my pile of articles said, "Take your time up there. This will take a while to copy. I'll let you know when I'm finished."

I wandered to the back of the room and climbed the stairs to the balcony; behind me were shelves of books arranged according to subject. Looking down, I surveyed the rectangular room lined with books on every wall. Running the length of the room were the long tables where Maddox still sat.

I skipped my fingers across the spines of the books until I spied the section on steamboats and train wrecks. I found *Steamboat Disasters and Railroad Accidents* and yanked it from the shelf, opening it to the chapter on the *Pulaski*. I read a few lines and realized it would provide helpful background information. I tucked it carefully under my arm and was heading back when the sight of Maddox made me pause.

He was leaning over a newspaper article, his rimless glasses perched on the end of a nose weathered by the outdoors. He'd removed his baseball hat, and his thick white hair was as tousled as if he'd just climbed off his salvage boat, and he assumed the posture of someone studying intently until, as if he felt my eyes nudging him between his shoulder blades, he glanced up. I nodded at him and held up the book. And I saw in his eyes a deep sadness that surrounded him like a nimbus.

When I'd lost Mora my world had shrunk as small as the hole one looked through in a child's kaleidoscope. I hadn't been able to find my way into other people's lives or even into my own. Except for this: I could see another's pain. It was as if my trauma had given me a second sight. I'd tried to explain this to the therapist I'd seen, but he'd only nodded and told me, "Yes, trauma does tend to make the inner world shrink down for a while."

I'd sat glaring at the therapist scribbling in his black notebook, as if he'd cursed at me. His placid smile, his cool demeanor—I couldn't take it anymore. Grief was as hot as lava, cold as ice, thick as mortar and thin as vellum; it was everything and nothing. It choked me and brought my life to its knees and he wanted to tell me about how my inner world might shrink?

I'd tossed a frilly throw pillow from his drab couch across the room where it popped against a framed degree from some school that must have never taught him empathy. I'd said words I never hoped to re- member, sentences that scalded my mouth even as they came out. I'd left his office and never returned. I'd known something I couldn't ar- ticulate to him—my body was betraying me, startled by every noise and every touch. I hadn't known what I needed to heal but it wasn't his advice.

If I were to ever talk about Mora again, it would *not* be to a man with a black notebook and platitudes that infuriated. But looking at Maddox I saw that he, too, carried some kind of pain. Our gazes held for a moment or two, long enough for me to know that I was right. I might never speak of Mora to Maddox, and he might never speak of his own loss, but now I knew—he saw me, and I saw him.

17

AUGUSTA

Friday, June 15, 1838
Very early

The yawl nearly disintegrated under the seawater's flood, and all of them found themselves tossed again into the fathomless waters. Augusta screamed even as part of her had known the boat wasn't seaworthy, that she would sink just as the others; her death delayed over and over with slim chance of salvation.

With all her strength she held on to Thomas with a grip of iron, took a deep breath and with it a mouthful of seawater before she sank beneath the surface, and then was buoyed upward toward the pinnacle of a wave. She scissored her legs, her nightgown tangling like seaweed, and with all her strength she pushed to the surface, to light and air. Bursting forth and lifting the child, she gasped for a breath soaked with seawater and reached for anything nearby with her free hand; she found only a handful of a blue vest. She screamed and choked as she realized she had grabbed a drowned body floating facedown, the arm missing and the face bloodied. Kicking back against the sea, she clung to Thomas above the water, terror stealing her breath, her chest squeezing with need for air. Waves rolling over her with a power that she'd never known, primal. Salt water burned her eyes and the inside of her nose.

She couldn't scream; the thick weight of dark water pressed down and took all the strength she had to stay afloat. She surfaced, going dizzy, frantic, she felt her left leg hitch against a large piece of wood—a section of floorboard? A remnant of the mast? Part of her very own stateroom? She had no idea but she could only be grateful for it.

Lifting Thomas on top of the plank, his nightshirt grasped in her fist, she clung to the splintered timber with her other hand and took in gulps of air. Her lungs burned; she coughed, retched and spit until her breath evened out. Smoke rose from the ship, thick and clouding the night sky. Where was westward? Where was land?

Hanging on to the flank of wood, she saw nothing but waves crowding onto other waves, water flowing over and down. Everyone who had been in the yawl with her had disappeared. She screamed against the flinty blackness; cried out for Melody and Eliza, for William, Rebecca, Caroline and Charles. Thomas sat quiet and still, but she heard him breathing. She flailed, held on to the plank and kicked nearer to the sinking ship, fearing the sea had swallowed everyone else.

She and Thomas might be all that remained of the explosion. Could this be true?

The swell and sink of huge waves breathed as the lungs of a monstrous creature whose face she could never see. Wave caps full of froth turning silver and then dark. Then her foot hit something soft and she twisted to see a woman, face up, her nightdress floating around her as a nimbus of white, her dark hair as wild as a sea creature's. Melody. Her beloved sister-in-law gone.

A strangled cry caught in her throat; she could not let Thomas see his mother, who at that moment became swallowed by the next wave and sank, feet first, face lifted to the sky. Images and sounds blurred together; time stretched and collapsed.

Augusta turned away as panic and fear coursing through her body provided a renewed strength. She kicked, her legs pumping and her heart with it. The waves didn't roll as they did on a shore, one after the other, but instead arriving from every direction. Thomas's eyes were wide and glistening; he *was* breathing. In and out. In and out. "I will hold you, Thomas. I will not let go of you."

She glanced around as she rose and fell with the swell and trough of the waves. The water colder than the air, but not as it would have been in winter, she tried to quell her panic, focus on saving Thomas when a voice she knew—Eliza's—called for help, the sound reaching Augusta's ears as surely as if they were in the Broughton Street house and her niece was crying out from a nightmare. Augusta lifted her head from the plank and saw the flash of blond hair, a cloud of white nightdress, and the hand of her niece just above a wave ten feet or less away. Augusta reached out as far as she could, kicked toward Eliza with a bear's roar escaping her throat. If she let go the plank and reached for Eliza, Thomas would sink, and most likely Augusta, too. If she let Eliza drown, she might as well take her own life; she couldn't live with herself. She reached and reached, screaming without words. With the last thrust forward, a kick and an extended hand toward Eliza's disappearing body, Thomas tipped and fell into the waves.

Augusta threw her body over the splintered wood and used both hands to retrieve him. She set him back on the plank as his cries mixed with coughs made of seafoam and fear. "Auntie!" he called and clung to her neck, his lips on her skin.

"Your sister," she said and twisted to see that the form—if it had ever been there at all—was gone. Eliza had disappeared. Melody. All of them.

Unwittingly, she'd made a choice. She'd chosen Thomas without thought, without planning, and with that realization she collapsed over the remnant of the shattered ship next to him. Around her, she spied one or two thrashing passengers, those floating on small pieces of debris and those disappearing with the next wave. Each fought for his own life; none of them could help the other until they found relative safety on something that floated.

Finally, Augusta summoned up the strength to kick until the plank banged against a large piece of the ship, maybe twenty feet by thirty feet, and she gained purchase on an iron stanchion. Others were huddled on its surface and clung to its edges, reaching over to help those who had made their way there.

Dragging Thomas by his arm, she pulled herself halfway onto the wreckage; he screamed in pain as she set him on solid wood. Then her strength failed and she slid slowly back into the sea. She held her breath in preparation for another submersion as she stretched her free hand and found the flesh of another; a muffled voice reached her ears. "Sister, grab my hand."

It was too late. She had saved Thomas so now she could let go, release her life to the sea. No fight in her remained.

A wave swelled and Augusta ascended with it; Lamar grabbed her hair and lifted her high. The ripping pain sent a surge of outrage through her and she grappled with the sharp edges of the wreckage as she was hauled onto it and flopped down next to her brother. Her body shuddered and with great heaves Augusta vomited seawater.

She looked up at Lamar and wailed, "Melody and the children. Oh, Lamar, the children. Lilly. Where are Lilly and Madeline?" She choked on grief that tasted like seawater and vomit.

He clung to his youngest child with both arms and dropped to his knees beside her. There were others around them, but Augusta saw no one except her brother and Thomas. "There's hope, Augusta. Get up, there must be hope."

"Yes." Augusta reached inside herself, to the place where faith and hope had always resided as a surety that God watched over them, that she was loved and cared for. He cared for her, indeed, but he wasn't going to save her. She found courage instead. She'd been granted this moment of life and she must find a way to keep it.

She and Lamar clasped each other, Thomas between them. At last the child found his voice and screamed as loudly as he ever had. This alone brought hope. After many minutes Augusta struggled to her feet and assessed the situation.

Other swimmers were scrambling in the moonlight, pulling themselves up onto the wreckage, and slipping again, reaching out for help. Lamar handed his son to Augusta and instructed her slowly. "This is what remains of the promenade deck. It can stay afloat if it breaks free. Move to its center and hold tight to Thomas."

And with that, Charles appeared, his face rising and falling with a wave, his arms flailing above him as he cried out, "Father!" Lamar reached out his hands and brought his oldest son to the deck even as it shifted and began to rise to an ominous angle.

"My son."

Together, Thomas, Charles, Lamar, and Augusta scrambled to take hold of a broken railing as the splintered promenade began to be lifted higher and higher as the midsection of the ship cracked in half with a sound like lightning and sank. Lamar held Thomas with one arm and the railing with the other. As they lifted, they looked down to see through the windows of a ladies' cabin. A Negro woman was nursing a white baby as they both sank slowly into the sea, the woman's expression serene. Oh, God, Augusta prayed, let that not be Priscilla and Madeline. She lowered her head in fear and defeat.

All around them, lit by starlight and moonglow, they saw floating debris, settees, luggage, drinking glasses, bottles and trunks that bobbed and then sank.

Augusta screamed as, suddenly, the deck cracked and tipped, tossing her again into the sea without Thomas, without Lamar or Charles; she sank alone. This time she would allow fate to have its way with her. And then, just as quickly as she surrendered, an empty trunk floated by and she pulled it closer, flopped across it, and caught her breath.

She could weep later, but for now she must take this one last opportunity and make her way to the deck again. She floated without a sense of time—maybe a few minutes, maybe thirty but not more—when she bumped against the deck she'd been thrown off twice already. Scrambling back onto the promenade deck, she found solid footing beneath six inches of water. She stood soaked and cold, her nightgown clinging to her shivering body.

She couldn't find her family; they were nowhere to be seen. She let out a howling scream.

18

EVERLY

Present day

Darkness pressed on the windowpanes of my little house, the clock ticking toward two a.m. My sight went blurry as I scanned the tight type of a 1924 article in the *Savannah Tribune* about the business dealings of Lamar Longstreet and his son Charles. I sat back with a smile—one more clue discovered, one more person who had survived. This was the thrill I sought with hours of research—a truth that led to the next and the next. I texted Oliver and Maddox—Lamar survived—and continued with my projects.

On poster board, I'd drawn a rough image of the ship, the twin masts and the double wheels. Another poster board held the names of the passengers from the manifest. The few people the newspaper articles had listed as survivors I'd circled in red. I desperately wanted a complete list.

On another board I'd drawn the Longstreet family tree as far as I knew, with a red circle around Charles, and another around his father,

Lamar. Adam Forsyth had also presumably survived, according to the newspaper article about his wife's statue.

My drawings of the ship were rougher than an untalented third grader might make, but the museum would know artists who could decipher my notations. The night of the explosion was taking shape. Accounts in several newspapers from the period had allowed me to write out a timeline on butcher block paper.

I'd told Oliver I'd work from home for a few weeks. I'd handed in the final grades for my students, and settled into the curation. The *Pulaski* consumed me. I didn't have to think about much else—my life, for example—if I was thinking about the ship, the passengers, both Lilly Forsyth and Charles Longstreet, or the night when *"everything changed,"* as Papa would say.

I felt at ease with my simple schedule, the summer now filled with a purpose it'd lacked. I woke early, did a morning run, grabbed my coffee from the Sentient Bean, and then dug through records and archives. I spent evenings with Mom and Allyn and my niece and nephew.

I called everyone I could think of who might know where Longstreet family papers might be stored: the historical society, the Telfair museum, the Oglethorpe Club, the Aquatic Club. The word was out: Everly Winthrop was on the hunt. But so far—complete silence.

As for my drawings of the ship—I'd crudely delineated the 225-horsepower engine pistons, which looked like posts pointing to the sky. Down the middle of the ship, I drew a zigzag line where the ship was broken in two by the blown engines. Then I took a red marker and made an X on the engine that sank to the floor of the sea and another X over the wheelhouse, with an arrow toward the sky to indicate it had been blown apart. Where had the captain been? I'd read that he'd claimed he never slept while the ship plied the sea, yet First Mate Hibbert had manned the wheelhouse that fateful night.

I'd pored over newspaper accounts, one after the other, looking for inconsistencies, for verification. The men's accounts had spoken of surviving, the women's of almost drowning. I read about the children who disappeared beneath the waves, of the inadequate lifeboats. But still I couldn't find anything about the Longstreet family, only that Lamar had invested in the ship and joined its fourth voyage.

I'd walked to the riverfront and done my best to imagine the steamship at port, to envision the families boarding with their humpback trunks and hand-sewn valises, with their well-dressed children and their housemaids in drab uniforms. The enslaved weren't allowed unless they were accompanying the families they cared for; after all, the ship was sailing toward free land. Most enslaved stayed on the wharf during the departure then headed back to in-town homes or plantations miles away. Those same slaves would have packed the trunks, ironed the clothes, organized and packed the silver and china for the journey. Passengers could take what they wanted without giving much thought to how long and arduous the packing and unpacking would be. Nursemaids were allowed on board to feed the children.

I imagined the soft, sandy roads of those days. The city's guards parading up and down the ship looking for stowaways. Then the ship's pistons starting up. The powerful turning of the huge paddle wheels, cascades of water flowing over the glossy red paddles. Black smoke exhaling from its double stacks. The clang of the bell; the blast of the whistle; the crash of the gangplank. High above, on the bluff, the Customs House looming over all of it.

When I felt like I'd slipped into 1838, and the oil lanterns were all there was to light the way, I returned to my house and again worked on the charts, drawings and timeline. With a magnifying glass I read the tiny script of handwritten letters and articles. Then I painstakingly transcribed them into my computer.

A compulsion I hadn't felt in years pushed me harder to understand the events of the night of the explosion, and all that had followed. Why hadn't anyone compiled this information before me? The people on the ship came from families with ties from here to Charleston. Had some unwillingness to gaze at the darker side of life impeded earlier historians? Or was it the unspoken southern assumption, with which I was thoroughly familiar, that we just didn't talk about certain topics?

I didn't know why no historian had thoroughly explored the *Pulaski*. I almost didn't care. I would be the one to reveal the truth.

Using the list of passengers, I wrote their names on Post-it notes. I wanted to place them on rough sketches of the various floats that saved some passengers—lifeboats—two yawls on the deck, two quarterboats covered and hanging on davits; smaller debris; a large swath of promenade deck; another fragment of the aft deck. But I couldn't . . . yet. For most I had merely last names. What inner resources had allowed them to survive those harrowing days and nights? And what happened after they were rescued and were forced to confront the full weight of their loss?

Exhaustion seeping slowly over me, I slipped into a kitchen chair. The crude drawings would appear ridiculous to anyone but Maddox, Oliver and me. For now, they were meant only to help me construct a minute-by-minute account of that fateful night, and the cruel days and nights afterward.

June 13, 8 a.m.—The luxury steamship leaves Savannah and sails toward Charleston, passing Tybee Lighthouse and skirting the South Carolina coast.

June 13—The ship docks for the night in Charleston.

June 14—Charleston passengers board and the ship departs for Baltimore in calm weather at 6 a.m.

June 14, 11:04 p.m.—The starboard boiler explodes approximately thirty-five miles off the North Carolina shore and shatters that side of the ship. The wheelhouse is blown apart. Men are burned and maimed from steam. Water rushes in. Lifeboats are launched holding few people. Passengers fall off. Others jump ship.

June 14, 11:45 p.m.—The ship breaks in half while the aft and promenade decks rise, break off and float.

June 15, 2 a.m.—The two quarterboats head toward the North Carolina shore.

These were the data points, but I felt the weight of the tragedy as heavy as the iron remnants resting at the bottom of the sea.

One hundred and eighty years had passed since then—they meant little to me. The explosion was happening now, again, in my kitchen, on my table, on the poster boards, as miles away Maddox and his crew brought up from the depths combs, silver, medicine bottles and keys.

With a sigh, I ran my finger over the list of Longstreet family members. "Did you find each other again?"

The explosion on that ship had been as unexpected, irreversible and violent as a car being gunned through a parade crowd and taking a young woman's life: a savage interruption of life.

When sleep finally seduced me toward oblivion, I fell onto the couch and closed my eyes to dreams in which I kept looking for something I couldn't find.

"Everly!" A voice woke me, setting my pulse to pounding. I rolled over and tumbled off the couch. Where was I?

Home. The couch. My living room.

"Everly!"

Oliver's voice came from behind the front door. I stood and ran my hands through my hair, swallowed against a dry mouth and groaned. "Hold on. Give me a minute."

I ran upstairs to the bathroom and washed my face, brushed my teeth. No time to deal with my disheveled appearance. And who cared anyway? As I trotted down the stairs, I felt the weight of sleepless days in my fuzzy head and growling stomach.

Oliver stood on the threshold wearing a blue seersucker suit with a white button-down. He appeared well rested, holding in one hand a box containing something that smelled rich and sugary, in the other a cardboard carrier with two steaming coffees.

"You've adopted the traditions of the southern gentleman," I said, flicking the sleeve of his suit jacket.

"You're funny." His wry tone turned bright. "I brought sustenance. I know how you are when you fall into the research rabbit hole and I thought . . ."

I stepped aside and let him in. "You don't need to check on me." But I did reach for the box—donuts and some kind of egg sandwich running with cheese and butter.

"I don't?" His eyes crinkled with amusement.

"I'm a mess but I'm fine." I walked to the kitchen in my drawstring bottoms and pink T-shirt, braless, and thought how I should have changed when I ran upstairs. I set the box down and took out two heirloom flowered china plates I'd inherited from an ancient aunt and arranged the food on them.

"You're awful dressed up. A date?" I asked.

"It's ten a.m. No. I have a meeting with a donor." He brushed off my question. It wasn't any of my business, I knew, just as my love life, or lack thereof, was none of his. But that didn't keep the question from popping out of my mouth like a balloon over the head of a comic strip character.

He made a whistling noise when he saw my work. "Whoa. Look at all this."

I pushed aside a pile of papers and placed the plates on the table. Oliver set down the coffee carrier and I took a long swallow; the coffee burned the roof of my mouth but I said nothing. It was caffeine, after all.

"Yes. I've been working through the night . . . I mean, through the events of *the* night but also through *my* nights." I laughed. "You know what I mean."

He sat down and so did I, for a minute both of us eating as though we hadn't in quite a while.

"Thank you for this," I said, wiping my mouth free of powdered sugar. "All of this—I'm trying to figure out the timeline of the wreck, find out how people survived." I pointed at the crude drawing. "Art isn't my forte, is it?"

Oliver regarded me with concern. Maybe even pity. "When was the last time you really slept?"

"Well, since you just woke me up, I'd say a few minutes ago."

"This is a lot of work."

"Well, Oliver, sometimes things look worse before they look better."

"That's about the truest thing you've said in a long while." He seemed to relax.

Then something that had been whirring around in the recesses of my mind slipped out like breath. "Those flowers you leave Mora. They're beautiful."

"Excuse me?"

"On her grave. The flowers."

"You mean the St. Patrick's ones?" He scratched the side of his face and took another sip of coffee.

"No. I went to Bonaventure last week. The peonies. And the week before, Gerber daisies and . . ."

A micro-shake of his head told me I'd gotten it wrong. He hadn't left the flowers and now I'd done the damn thing I'd promised I wouldn't—I'd opened up a conversation about Mora.

"I don't leave flowers. Or at least not in a long while."

"Must be her mom." I wiped my hands on a paper towel and stood, needing the conversation to be over. "Did you know that the captain of the *Pulaski* died on board? He'd earlier claimed he never slept during any voyage, but he must have been asleep somewhere—First Mate Hibbert stood in the wheelhouse when the explosion occurred."

"Don't change the subject, Everly. No. Mora's mother rarely goes to Bonaventure. She barely leaves her house. Though I suppose maybe she sends someone."

"It doesn't matter." Powdered sugar fell in an arc from the donut I waved.

"It does matter."

I took a few bites in silence and stared over his shoulder. He didn't try to fill the quiet before I asked, "Do you still look for him?" I set down the donut and leaned across the table, my fatigue turning into a release of anger I hadn't known was brewing.

"Him?"

"The monster who killed her." All at once I became acutely aware of my state of disarray. I'd meant to one day have this conversation when I was well dressed and alert. But there I sat, asking him all the things I'd wanted to ask over the past year.

"I do look for him," he admitted. "But not like I once did. I figure he's long gone, on to the next city. He was a vagrant as it was, I've decided. I still can't believe no one grabbed him at the time. That he stood so close and no one even tried to stop him from getting away."

"It's the kind of situation in which, looking back, people wish they'd acted differently."

"What would *you* have done differently?" his gentle voice asked.

I stood up straight, ran my hand through the tangles in my hair and told the truth. "I would have grabbed his shirt, snatched him by the hair, taken him to the ground. But before that moment, if I'd known, I would have switched places with Mora. I would have stood on the other side of you . . ."

"Then it would have been . . ."

"Me."

"Don't say that, Everly."

"I just did."

"Don't say it again."

"Well, I would have at least taken back the little bump, the one that sent you a few steps over."

"Stop!"

"This wreck"—I waved my hand around the room—"is all about destiny. And fate. If there is such a thing. Who made it to the lifeboats, and which lifeboats at that. Two were sturdy; two were cracked. Who found something to cling to. Who lived and who died . . . and then what the survivors did afterward."

The buzzing of my phone interrupted our conversation. We could both see the name: a text from Maddox Wagner.

I read silently and then out loud. *"Forgive if I'm interrupting, we've brought the boat back with a bounty of salvaged artifacts. Maybe you could drive up here today?"*

I texted in return without looking at Oliver. Will leave in 30. Wait for me.

He bent over to read my text. "I'm going with you."

His brown eyes swam with a desire for adventure; I'd seen it more times than I could count. "No. Let me do this alone. Please. You hired me to do this job, and the one reason I almost didn't do it was because of what just happened—talking about Mora as if we could change anything." I brushed my hands together and took a step or two toward the stairs. "I know it was my fault. I brought it up. Looks like you're moving on quickly anyway."

"What are you talking about?"

"Your date. The one at the river."

He exhaled audibly. "You were there?"

"Yes."

"It wasn't . . ."

"It's none of my business. But I will say this. I don't trust a girl who can chug wine like beer."

He almost laughed. "Everly. It wasn't exactly a date."

"What is exactly not a date? A half date? A sort of date? You sure do get over things quickly."

"Over it? You're serious?"

"I am."

"You have no idea, Everly. No idea what I've been through or what I've felt or even what I was doing at the river the other night. You have no idea of the sleepless nights. Or the hours of walking through the city wondering if I should leave Savannah because it will always remind me of Mora. You have opted out of our friendship and my life, and you have no idea . . . none at all . . . what I've been through."

A flush of embarrassment washed over me. "I'm sorry. I . . ."

"That so-called date was a setup. The worst. My friend Harris asked me to meet him for a drink and then left me there with that lovely woman."

I held up my hands. "It's none of my business. Listen, we shouldn't bring up our past just because we're bringing up the past of this ship."

"So eloquently said and such bullshit." He stood and took a few steps toward me. I moved backward one step up the stairs. A prickling dread crawled on the back of my neck. Looking up at me standing taller than him, he said, "She will always be here with us. Always. We *can* talk about her."

"Not now." I placed a hand on my chest. "For now let me do my job. The one you asked me to do." My voice was ice.

He nodded and bowed his head. I could see the whirls of his hair growing into tangled curls. I placed my palm on top of his head as if I were a priest and he were receiving absolution when we both knew it was I who needed to be absolved for bumping Oliver and making them step into the path that the car, minutes later, drove through. I withdrew my hand as if fire bit my palm and ran upstairs. I slammed the door shut, then stripped naked to shower. I waited to hear the opening and closing of my front door, and finally I did.

19

EVERLY

Present day

I threw an overnight bag with a change of clothes into the back seat of my Jeep and set the GPS for Wrightsville Beach, North Carolina. Five hours and five minutes, the robotic voice told me. I'd be there by three in the afternoon.

I'd discovered that music with words posed a danger. A single lyric or verse about friendship or the aching longing of loss became as devastating to me as a punch to the solar plexus. Instead, I lost myself in the sounds of the wheels on asphalt and, for an hour, a rainstorm that cleansed the air and distracted me from my circling thoughts.

Taking the exits and turns when the GPS voice told me to, and grabbing bites from a protein bar I'd brought, the hours passed and I found myself at the water's edge of a marina crowded with boats. I parked and stood for a moment, my eyes adjusting to the bright sunlight glinting off the water.

Cedar shake cottages surrounded the basin, the blue roofs of the village reflected sky and sea, and seagulls cried out as they landed on weathered uprights lining the dock. Boats as sleek as seals and as tall as two-story buildings with complicated poles and fishing gear bristling from the top decks filled every space. I almost wanted to roll my eyes at it all, as if someone had painted a too-perfect scene and wanted me to buy into its story.

People bustled past me, calling out to each other and talking on their phones. The world was moving so fast and furiously toward whatever came next and next and next.

"Everly!"

I turned to see Maddox waving from the end of a long pier. He appeared so wild, so essential a part of the landscape that I could imagine him holding Poseidon's trident. He wore his usual salt-encrusted shorts and worn T-shirt, and he filled the space with kinetic energy, making me feel small and protective of my own space. I walked slowly toward him.

"This way." He bounded out to meet me and drag me toward his boat, *Deep Water Rose*. "How was your drive? Do you need anything?"

"It was fine. Good." I nodded. "Thanks so much for inviting me to see this."

"I figure if you're the one to put the stuff in the museum you should see where it comes from."

"Yes." We'd had good camaraderie in Savannah but here on his home ground, where land met sea, I felt out of place.

When my steps slowed, he frowned in concern. "You okay?"

"I am."

"Right, then."

I followed him down the long, worn pier. The clanging of chains; metal on metal rang like discordant wind chimes. He stopped at a worn red boat with an open deck where four men lounged askew on mismatched lawn chairs. "We're here. Welcome."

As I climbed aboard, I saw that one man was sitting upright and asleep with his mouth open, and the other three were staring at me as if I were an apparition. "Guys," Maddox half shouted. "You never seen a woman before? For God's sake, mind your manners and say hello."

They laughed in unison and nudged the sleeping one with the white beard, who scratched his face and blinked awake. They stood up and introduced themselves.

"Everly here is putting together a knockout exhibit for the Rivers and Seas Museum of Savannah," Maddox explained.

A man named Mark, rugged but clean shaven, stepped forward, his eyes shaded by dark sunglasses, his skin, like all the men's, brown from sun and flecked with salt. He could have been twenty-five or forty-five; I couldn't tell. "You're the one who's gonna turn it into a story?" His deep southern accent made me feel at ease.

"That's the plan."

"It's a mighty fine story down there. A tragedy," he added.

"What's it like?" I asked. "To see what's left of a once beautiful ship?" I glanced at each of the men in turn.

Mark answered. "Humbling. But also thrilling."

Ben, the one who'd been sleeping, was the shortest of them, wearing a Billy Joel T-shirt and stained fishing shorts; he pointed at the stairwell. "We'll show you."

"I've seen some videos of you down there. It looks like an amazing dive."

"You dive?" Sean asked. He was the tallest of the lot; his sunburned lips were covered with white cream.

"I have." I looked toward the diving equipment—tanks and slick black wet suits drying on a rack, masks and breathing apparatus that looked like gas masks, and a jumble of mismatched towels bleached of color.

"It's another world down there," Ben said with reverence.

"How deep is it?" I asked, removing my silver recording device from my bag and setting it on a wobbly table. They all looked at it and fell silent.

"Oh, that's just for me to remember what we talk about. It's not for anyone else. It won't be shared."

They nodded but still no one spoke so I picked it up, turned it off and shoved it into my backpack.

Phil, the last of the men, with a shy smile and golden hair and beard, told me, "It's a hundred feet deep and most of what we find is at least two feet under the sand."

"Why not deeper? I mean, after a hundred and eighty years, wouldn't this stuff be fathoms deep in sand?"

"Sand doesn't go so far. There's only about two to three feet of sand and then it's just shell and bedrock. The hard earth. It's a ghost town down there."

Sean spoke up, coughing first and removing a baseball hat stained with dirt. "Excavation takes time, ma'am."

"Everly, please."

"Everly. It takes time. There's nothing left of the hull because it was made of wood. We look for machinery and boilers but most of it was blown off—who knows how far it spread."

I said, "When I've been below, I thought it surreal, like everything down there is holding a secret. That we're intruders even though we share the same world. The shafts of light disappear and the world closes in . . ."

"Exactly!" Sean moved closer to me. "Here we are in this world and seventy-five percent of it is covered in water and we only know a slice of what it's all about."

"And why these people went on ships that often blew up—I'm not sure I understand that," Maddox chimed in. "It wasn't . . . safe and yet off they went. Each time they built a new ship, its investors promised it would provide safe travel. Who doesn't want to believe a promise?"

He gazed past the marina to something I couldn't see. "But nothing is truly safe."

"Not even staying on land," I said.

"Not even that." Maddox looked back to me.

I nodded at him. He seemed on a roll and the other men grew quiet. Maddox's voice dropped an octave and his gaze sharpened. "Words like 'know the ropes'; 'slush fund'; 'close quarters'; 'batten down the hatches'; to be 'in deep water'; 'high and dry'—we use these phrases without realizing they come from our long and perilous connection with the sea. They came out of our need to conquer what can never be conquered, only respected and discovered."

Sean leaned close. "He used to be a teacher. When he gets like this you gotta let him go."

Ben spoke, "To rock the boat; all hands on deck."

Maddox laughed and his face softened. "Ships and their mystical stories are in our blood. It has never been enough to merely stay safe. Waterways were our first superhighways, and searching for lost things is inherent in the human psyche." He motioned. "Come with us."

Nothing is truly safe. Maddox's words followed me down the stairs. *But it's enough to try*, I wanted to argue. *I am doing it. Trust me, it is enough.*

We climbed belowdecks to a room with a blue ceiling and so much clutter that my eyes immediately went to the one place of order: a table where the artifacts the crew had brought up from the sea floor were carefully arranged in rows and labeled with small yellow signs. I recognized some from the photos but others were new: wide-toothed white combs, rusted metal keys, barnacle-covered coins, cream porcelain dishware, silver candlesticks made almost unrecognizable by encrusted debris, a pocket watch with a shattered face and a gold chain tangled with what appeared to be concrete. A large onyx ring was so encrusted, it might have been an oyster.

"All of this," I said quietly, as if to myself, "has been down there for a hundred and eighty years and now we're looking at it." I surveyed the white porcelain plates, completely whole and unbroken, as if they had settled softly into the sand.

I closed my eyes for a moment and imagined it all at the bottom of the sea, where it had been hidden so long. I wanted to dive down there, to see the place where the sea lay holding its secrets. I felt that crawl of excitement begin somewhere deep down. "This," I said, "is one of the first Wedgwood designs. Creamware made for the queen so they also called it Queensware. Josiah Wedgwood . . ." My voice trailed off and Maddox came to my side, peered over my shoulder.

I didn't look at him, just felt him. I opened my eyes when he said, "And once, it all meant something to someone."

"It means something now." I touched the hair comb and lifted it, ran my fingers along the pointed edges. Some teeth were missing. I then chose a small round piece of iron, a luggage tag like the one I'd seen in the photo. I set it down and eyed the other items. "Tell me about this. How does it work? How do you keep track of this stuff?" I pointed at a snuffbox, a candlestick, an oil lamp.

"We map the floor of the ocean with grids, and then label where each item is found."

I took out my camera, the one I used for all my field research. "Can I take pictures?"

"Sure thing," Maddox said.

I snapped a few photos. "Where do these artifacts go from here, until the museum displays them?"

Ben reached into a small refrigerator and took out a beer, popped the top and took a long swig. "Finding the treasure is the thrilling part. Cataloging and storing it is the boring part. That's up to Maddox here."

"That's me. Boring." He laughed. "We are what the courts call 'substitute custodians.' We are trustees of the property. We are responsible for making sure it is secure and in good condition. The coins and jewelry go to a coin specialist in Sarasota, Florida."

"Why there?" I lifted a coin, tried to imagine whose it had been and what it was needed for. I read the date—1808, a Spanish doubloon. "Whoa!" I turned it over. "Why were there so many doubloons down there?"

"The right term is probably Spanish real. Until 1857 any foreign currency was legal tender in this country. The good ol' USA didn't yet have enough of its own coins."

"So interesting . . . And what is all this gunk, these clumps that look like concrete?"

"Marine algae. A little chemical cleaning and it scrubs off." Maddox took the coin from me and put it carefully back on the table. "After we bring things up, we tag and map and photograph them, and then they go to the conservation facility in Clearwater, Florida. We keep it all in a safe here on board until transport."

"This is beautiful." I lifted the pocket watch. An intricately carved crown adorned the top. A gold chain dangled from the bow. I rolled the chain in my hand.

"That's the Albert."

"Huh?"

"The chain is called an Albert after King Albert, Queen Victoria's husband, who wore his watch on a chain."

"Now there's something I didn't know." I turned it over to see a crest that could best be described as wings without their bird or their angel. Just a set of wings that spread out from the center.

"You know this?" he asked when I held the watch too long.

"It looks familiar. What is it?"

"It's the same watch I showed you in Savannah. I'd love to track down the family it belonged to through the crest. I've cleaned it since the photograph was taken. See the clump there?" He pointed to the marine algae clump with the gold chain poking out. "That's what this looked like until we cleaned it." The watch face glass was clouded and cracked, the black hands stopped at 11:04.

"This is a stunning find," Ben said. "Thanks to me." He took a bow and the men laughed. "This watch stopped when the ship's boiler exploded and life ended without warning for so many." He held out his hands and then slammed them together. "Boom! At eleven o'clock. This watch confirms accounts of the exact time of the explosion."

With a lurch, I felt the salvage boat sway, become unmoored from the dock, roll sideways and head toward the bottom of the sea, my heart sliding with it, my stomach in freefall. The boat hadn't actually moved; the lines held firm. But for one moment, my body had become unmoored as I made the connection between eleven p.m. one hundred and eighty years ago and eleven a.m. over a year ago, when a screeching car stopped time for Mora, and for me.

20

LILLY

Friday, June 15, 1838
Early morning

Lilly's lifeboat, six by eighteen feet, lurched and spun with the power of the sea. The group of twelve huddled together. They learned each other's names. Lilly already knew Mr. Couper and his companions Nelle March and her ten-year-old son, Theodore. The others included Barney, a seaman with white hair and burned hands, his uniform tattered and torn; Solomon, a Negro waiter who wore only pantaloons, his chest bare; Mr. Pooler and his teenage son, Francis, both dressed in dark pants and white shirts; Mr. Harris from New Bedford with a balding pate and a low voice that seemed to demand calm; and Mrs. Bird, who had become so still and quiet, Lilly was half-afraid she had expired and was being held up by the people on either side of her. The night passed, stars bright and moving across the sky as the only indication that time marched on as the men rowed toward the west, grunting with the effort. The waves churning in from north, south, east and west, quilted and stitched with white foam.

The misery of the burned firemen in the second quarterboat became excruciatingly evident as they groaned from their injuries, their cries carrying across the water and night as clear as if they'd been sitting in the same boat. As the morning sky began to glow, the skeletal faces of the two men, their burns radiant in the growing heat of the sun, revealed what night had hidden from them all: the continued horror of the explosion. Lilly turned away. Would it have been better to have saved another?

"Oh, Priscilla," Lilly whispered near to her ear. "Those men won't last a day once the sun rises higher."

Priscilla nodded and she, too, turned her gaze from the sight.

Then Lilly repented for the horrible thought. All human life was worth saving. A stab of guilt for Adam's drowning pierced her. All the hours and days she'd wanted him to suffer, and now she prayed for mercy, that his drowning had been quick, that he was at peace.

Madeline began to fuss, squirming in her wrapping, and Lilly untied the cloth and lifted her baby to her face. She kissed her from cheek to belly button and then handed her to Priscilla. "She's hungry."

Priscilla slipped the strap of her nightdress from her shoulder and her left breast hung pendulous, swollen with milk, her nipple the size of a dessert plate. Madeline latched on immediately and Priscilla used the wrap to cover Madeline's face from the rising sun.

Grief clogged Lilly's throat. She should be nursing her own child, with her own milk. She swallowed her tears and placed her hand on Priscilla's arm. "I am sorry."

"Mistress?"

"Your daughter . . ."

Priscilla looked away, her gaze cast farther to the horizon than Lilly could see herself, to the place where Priscilla's own child, lost at childbirth, must live and move in her mind as a great grief. If Lilly lost Madeline . . . she could not, and would not think of it.

Lilly felt the gazes of everyone in the boat as she leaned close and touched her nursemaid. What would have seemed inappropriate only hours before now seemed as normal as the new day. There could be no pretense now, no vanity or prejudice. In this boat they were not mistress and slave but two women intent on survival. Lilly had never let herself wonder before—was Priscilla's child Adam's?—and she now let herself sink into the question that had always been before her. What could not be considered in her home came to her now with clarity. Hate surged, a heat that began in her breast and spread like fire: hate for Adam, for cruelty, for helplessness.

"Was . . ." Lilly wound her fingers around the small foot of her child, Madeline's toes pearls in her hand. "Was your child . . . ?"

Priscilla looked up, her eyes glazed with fatigue and the fear she kept tamped down so often, a way of being that she had become proficient at maintaining near Lilly. But now, her lips quivered, and she ran her hands along Madeline's covered body. "No, mistress. My little girl, my Anika, she belonged to me, and to a man who loves me, a man I love." She lifted her chin and closed her eyes, a pride and a pain Lilly would not and could not understand yet speared her chest with sorrow.

"I am so very sorry you lost her," Lilly said as the boat swayed and the stars blinked and the rows dipped into the water in a rhythmic dance that hopefully brought them closer to shore. The horizon soon turned orange and the sun climbed the sky like a ball of fire as they considered the appearance of each other on the boat, nearly laughing in comical horror at the sight they made. They would never, at any other time, have seen each other in this condition, wet to the bone and nearly naked. Without the pretense of linen and silk, without the finery of three-piece suits and elaborate bonnets, without the rings and necklaces that told of wealth, they were all equal.

It was easier for the men when they had to urinate, but the women were ashamed, needing to be held over the side of the lifeboat to do what should have been done in private. Everyone helped shield and offer isolation behind capes and shirts and turned faces. Not one of them could get by without exposing their pure humanity, humanity usually hidden behind closed doors and perfumed water.

No one spoke of their servant or their slave. No one talked of their money or their property. They talked of their families; they prayed for safety for those who might be floating on other scraps of wreckage. They sang hymns—"Come, Thou Long Expected Jesus"; "Awake My Soul; Arise to God"—and uttered the names of their loved ones. Lilly did not once let Adam's name pass from her lips even as the memory of his last plea for help haunted her.

When the boat became quiet his memory was thrust into her mind the same way he had once thrust his way into the bedroom.

When she'd first met him, she'd been enchanted. Had he changed or had she not seen the truth of him? She'd been blinded by the sheer immensity of his personality, his ebullient family and yes, his wealth—four hundred acres along the river planted with cotton and indigo. The big rambling home in Savannah with porches that faced the river's breeze and gardens lush with roses, jasmine and gardenia. The security and ease of life he offered.

Soon after their wedding day, she would have easily given them all up in exchange for simple kindness.

Adam's cruelty toward his slaves, his choice of an overseer so wicked that she had begged him more than once to please find another. Both of these should have alerted her to the violence he harbored deep in his soul. Her desires were as nothing to him. A mere woman, she existed equal in his mind to the hunting dogs that he by turns indulged and mistreated.

Their lovemaking became nothing more than him pressing himself into her as he held her to the bed. It didn't matter to him if she was clothed or naked as long as he could pin her arms over her head and enter her hard and fast while telling her how she would never be enough for him. Cruelty aroused him. Hatred became his fuel. At first, she'd begged him to let her participate—but that was when she thought their intimacy was about love. Now she knew better—it was about control. Over her. The household. The servants and slaves. Over all their lives.

After she gave birth to Madeline, she enjoyed a reprieve: a few months of peace and calm when he kept far from her. Lilly knew he turned to the slaves for his hateful pleasure, but she could do nothing to prevent it.

One night she heard whimpers coming from a closet in the spare bedroom and found Priscilla, her arms swollen in the same places Lilly's had been many times. She fell into a despair so enveloping that nothing, not even Madeline's cries, could rouse her from bed. Until Adam told her about this trip, until she realized that there might be a way out. If they traveled up north to Saratoga Springs, and she wasn't surrounded by so many watchful eyes, she might have a chance for escape—maybe far into the northern lands. Or possibly even push a little west. She had planned on figuring it all out once she arrived in New York.

With a lurch of the boat, Lilly returned to her present watery hell. She imagined the other passengers on the *Pulaski*. Were they dead? Were they still fighting for their lives? Where was Augusta? The relief at knowing Adam was gone started to mix with the shame of having listened to his dying pleas and done nothing. Yet she refused to believe she would pay for that decision with her immortal soul.

In that bobbing boat, nausea rising along with thirst, the grunts of the exhausted rowers the only sound louder than the slap of waves, Lilly held her child to her chest and dreamed of a land where crystal-line water fell over boulders, grass grew as thick as a blanket and wild-flowers danced in the breeze.

21

EVERLY

Present day

The salvage boat lurched in the wake of a deep-sea fishing excursion boat heading out to sea. The ropes pulled taut, holding us tight, as I stared at the pocket watch's hands stopped exactly at 11:04. I stood and climbed to the bright sunlight. I needed air. I sank into a red lawn chair and took a few deep breaths. From below came the murmur of men's voices; they were talking about me.

Maddox's face appeared over the ladder as he climbed onto the deck. "You okay?"

"Completely. I've seen what I needed to see."

"What made you reel like that?" He sat next to me and I met his gaze without answering.

Maddox let silence fall and we sat in it until he stood and held out his hand. "Let's take a stroll. Get some fresh air."

"I'd prefer a beer."

By the time we settled at an outside table at the marina restaurant, I'd regained my equilibrium. With sweating glasses of ice water in front of us, Maddox slipped off his sunglasses. "Seasick?"

"The boat was tied up, Maddox."

"Well . . . guess you're a true land lubber. Hate to see what happens when you go out to dive. Maybe you should let go of that idea."

"It wasn't the sea."

"I know." He wouldn't break eye contact with me, looking so directly that I felt hot under his scrutiny.

"Maddox, time stopped on that watch. It stopped for those who didn't survive. It just stopped. And I damn well bet it even stopped for those who *did* survive."

"How do you mean?"

"Aren't we desecrating a tomb? Digging up the past and putting it on display for people to gawk at? Are we eliciting thrills from horrific deaths?"

Maddox leaned back. "Whoa, ma'am. I think you might be running awful fast down the wrong track. Aren't you a museum curator? Isn't it your job to dig up the past and find a way to honor it?"

I looked away, sickened by my own hypocrisy—suggesting that my sudden attack was about anything other than myself. "It's the inability," I said, trying to steady myself, "my complete inability to make meaning out of the meaningless."

"Are we talking about you or the ship now?"

Our beers arrived along with a plate of crab legs and I ignored both, staring off to the boat I'd just run from, and then at the sea and horizon beyond. Sea gulls circled and cried out. A pelican perched on a dock post, his throat working like a piston and his eyes alert. A child trailed his parents, an ice cream cone dripping down his hand and his cheeks red with sunburn. I closed my eyes for a moment and instinctively deflected Maddox's question. "I don't know what we're talking about. I promise to do a kick-ass job curating the exhibit. Don't pay me any mind right now."

"I am paying you *all* my mind right now. We are not talking about the *Pulaski*, are we? We're talking about you and the grief that haunts those turbulent blue eyes of yours."

"I see the same in you. I saw it at the library when I stood looking down from the balcony."

"But we aren't talking about me right now. What did you see, Everly? What did you see just now on that boat that reminded you of whatever it is you're trying to forget?"

"My best friend." I said it simply and easily, as if all along I'd been planning to make this confession. "And I'm not *trying* to forget. I never want to forget. Ever. She died. Mora died. She was killed at eleven a.m. on St. Patrick's Day over a year ago. That watch—it stopped at 11:04 when the ship went down. When so many took their last breaths just like my best friend did." I leaned forward. "The world should have stopped. Time should have stopped. All the watches in all the world should have stopped. But no, I keep breathing in and out. Mostly I spend my time just keeping my shit together. And today? In front of you? I didn't keep it together, and I'm sorry." What a relief, to state the simple truth.

"Everly, don't be sorry. Who could feel anything but the desperate need for relief when reminded of the loss?"

"*The desperate need for relief.*" I repeated his words; the last one I tried to stop with a hand over my mouth. Maddox took my hand in his and squeezed it.

"I know," he said. "Tell me."

"I've tried everything. Everything they've told me to do. I once had a list on a notepad. I called it the 'List of Things to Do to Cope.' Do you believe that? And I tried most of them. Telling the story. Gratitude journaling. Meditation. Affirmations. Talking to Mom's priest. Reading books about death. Books about grief. Books about life. Therapy. Making plans for the future. Being in nature. I've tried all of it. But I stood right there when it happened. I saw my friend crushed and gone. I stood two steps away—it could have been me."

"But it wasn't you."

"Remembering that day derails me at every turn. And the driver ran right by me. I smelled him. I saw him. I had him in my sight, but he escaped through the crowd. I froze. He ran. They never found him."

"I am so sorry."

"Thank you." My shoulders slumped and I propped my cheek on my hand. "Listen, you don't have to stay here with me. I'm fine. I promise."

"I'm not going anywhere."

I kept my gaze on him, taking sips of beer and sitting in the space he held open, in the quiet he offered. Birds sang; lines slapped against masts; a child wailed. "I want it to have meaning."

"Your friend's death or the shipwreck?"

"All of it, Maddox."

"Maybe, Everly Winthrop, we are the ones who make meaning out of the tragedies."

"I don't know how. Tragedy—it can come from anywhere at any time. How do we go through life knowing that? How did we ever *not* know it? And yet we pretend we're safe. It's absurd."

"I think that's true. Very true. We can't unknow the sudden thrust of misfortune that comes out of nowhere. Once it happens, it is an incontrovertible truth."

I almost laughed and instead coughed. "Who are you? A salvage hunting diver who uses words like 'incontrovertible'?"

He grinned beneath his mustache and scratched his beard. "Are you saying us divers are uneducated?"

I felt as if I were free-floating, hollow. The confession I'd made to Maddox had weighed more than I'd calculated. "Nope . . . just trying to bring you into focus. I can't believe I just told you all that. I don't talk about these things. Not ever."

"I wasn't always a shipwreck hunter, you know."

"What happened to you?" I asked, leaning forward.

"I switched jobs."

"No. What happened to you that you can see the grief in me?"

"Right now, it doesn't matter. I am here in this place to hear you."

"Whatever it was—how did you survive it, Maddox? How did you . . . live?"

"I'm not sure what to say, Everly. I don't have the answers."

"Tell me what you mean. Please." I gripped his hand, crushing his fingers together before I let go, realizing I was asking of this man something no one could give me.

He said, "We fight to live. I've done more research than you can imagine on the way people react to calamity. We are our truest selves when life and death walk hand in hand. When crisis comes, and tragedy explodes, our true character comes to the fore. Men throw other men overboard *or* sacrifice their own place in the boat to save a woman and child. Women save themselves *or* a friend. Choices are made. Still, life always propels us toward living. Something in us *wants* to live, if we can tap into that part of our soul."

The sun moved slowly toward the horizon, and I cracked open a crab leg and tugged out the white flesh, dipped it in butter. The taste fired my appetite and we ate in silence, butter dripping onto the plate and my T-shirt.

"I'm tired," I said, as I felt the weight of the past days press between my shoulder blades.

"I have a room at the Marina Inn right there." Maddox pointed at the cedar shake building next to the marina. "I can give you the key. Go get some rest. I have work to do with the boys to prepare the salvage for transport. You won't be disturbed."

"I can't accept that. I can take care of myself."

He laughed and took another swig of beer. "I don't doubt you can take care of yourself but right now, take this key." He pulled it from his back pocket.

I knew he was right. I didn't have one more ounce of strength left in me. To retrieve my bag from the car, find a hotel and book a room seemed as impossible as climbing Mt. Everest in bare feet. I took the key from his hand. "Thank you."

I stood to move toward the inn only a few yards away.

"Everly?"

I glanced over my shoulder. "Yes?"

"You will find your way. I can see that in you."

I didn't believe him, but I was grateful for his assurance.

22

AUGUSTA

Friday, June 15, 1838
Early morning

When Augusta's anguished scream faded, she saw Lamar rushing toward her, water splashing around his feet on the broken promenade deck. Slowly her family had dwindled, one by one, until only she and Lamar remained. She stood unsteadily, up to her calves in seawater.

Was she dreaming under the inky night, the heaving waves rising and falling as the half moon hovered like a wink above them? "Where is our family, Lamar? Where?"

He answered with a sob in his throat. "We must hope. We must."

"It can't be *just* us. It can't." Augusta bent over with anguish. Where was her beloved nephew Thomas?

Lamar took her face in his hands. "Do not give up."

In the darkness a man bumped into Augusta. He wore a full suit and carried a carpetbag as if he had walked across the ocean and couldn't account for his whereabouts. Moonlight reflected off his bald head.

"Mr. Hutchinson," Lamar cried out, and shook the man's hand with a formality so at odds with their circumstance that Augusta stared in wonder.

"Miss Longstreet." Mr. Hutchinson nodded at her. He took a key from his front pocket and opened his carpetbag to hand her a man's shirt. "See if this will keep you warmer."

Augusta accepted it wordlessly and slipped it on over her wet nightgown. How had this man remained afloat this entire time while the rest of them had been tossed into and out of the sea over and over again? She was right—she should never have tried to get in that cracked yawl. If the family had stayed on the deck, they'd all be there together. Lilly. Madeline. Eliza. Thomas . . . the family names floated through her mind like the ship's contents bobbing on the waves.

The men bent their heads together and Mr. Hutchinson said, "Let us grab the floating lumber that is out there and tie it together for flotation. We must do what we can until help arrives."

"If help arrives," Lamar stated.

"When," Mr. Hutchinson answered with vigor.

They began to catalog their salvage. A box that held cables and ropes could be used as a chair. A torn sail could act as a signaling device and a rain catcher if the skies opened up. Augusta barely heard them, scanning the dark waters. Thomas and Charles had been right there, right next to her, and now they were gone.

Darkness pressed against her sight, but she squinted and searched for a small child when a loud voice called out, "Whose child is this?"

Augusta ran to the edge of the floating wreckage as a man treading water held a child over his head. A small blond girl scrambled onto the platform, the water reaching her knees. Augusta's heart sank. She was maybe four years old and wearing only underpants. At the sight of her father a few feet away she called out, "Daddy!" and began to crawl through the water. Her hair had become as tangled as seaweed and her skin was red and puckered.

Her father had been huddled in a crouched position but now he waded toward her, water splashing on those around him as the sea spray from a large rogue wave washed over them. Groans and cries filled the air as the man fell to his knees and took the child in his arms. "Connie. Connie. Connie." Her name became a prayer.

Augusta's heart floundered, her body collapsing, her tongue tasting of sea, her stomach lurching with nausea, her mind confused with darkness and chaos. Oh, dear Thomas, are you gone?

The father approached Augusta with the young Connie, now wrapped in his shirt. His face shimmered with either tears or seawater. "Please hold her while I help some others."

Augusta took the girl in her arms, a sprite as limp as rope, while her father and Mr. Hutchinson turned a box upside-down for a few women to sit upon. The father began to rope together a few pieces of lumber and call into the darkness. "Hellooooo?" He perched on the edge of the decking, ready to save anyone who came within sight.

Another voice, as if echoing the first, called out, "And this child? Whose child is this?"

Augusta's soul leaped within her at the sight of blond hair. She jumped up, handed Connie back to her father, and claimed Thomas from the stranger's arms. His wails combined with coughing, and he fell against his beloved aunt's shoulder as she sat hard on the box before rocking him and muttering his name.

Thomas. Thomas. Thomas.

Lamar joined them, fell to his knees and covered them both in kisses before returning to his work with Mr. Hutchinson. Thomas cried until he became spent and then collapsed into a sleep that seemed too deep. Augusta stroked his hot cheek and whispered her love into his ear. Around her, she watched the bravery and sacrifice of men and women as they tended to those around them. Some slipped back into the sea to assist in raising others to the deck; others threw ropes and removed items of clothing to cover those they rescued. A woman in the water, splayed across a plank of wood, held a child above her head until someone grabbed the baby and then she sank below the waves without a fight, having used the last of her strength. She disappeared without so much as a plea to God.

Cries for help came to them with the incoming sea spray, and yet the wreckage they were on and the remnants of wreckage floating nearby could not be propelled toward each other. Another box was added to the decking, this one higher for survivors to take turns sitting upon to keep their feet out of the water.

Now, as morning sun broke through clouds in colors vibrant and rich, Augusta couldn't help but think how, even amid horror, the world remained undeniably beautiful. Thomas slept deeply on her lap, his limbs heavy with exhaustion.

Her feet were numb from the cold water; she shivered and her teeth slammed against each other. Mr. Hutchinson crouched down beside her. "Miss Longstreet. Let me help you."

She lifted her gaze to the man with the slick mustache, whom she was accustomed to seeing at her brother's bank in a full suit and topcoat, or at the ballroom in a black frock coat. Now he was stripped of all except his kind smile and tear-filled eyes. She asked, "How can you help, Mr. Hutchinson? We're in wretched conditions."

He plopped down to assume a watery seat on the deck, removed a knife from his belt and, his face furrowed with tender concern, removed his wool socks and cut off the top few inches, which were still relatively dry. With the utmost care he slipped the pieces over her feet, holding each foot in his hand before releasing it. His ministrations struck her to the core.

"This should warm you." He placed his hands on his knees to bring himself to stand. He coughed and wiped his brow. "God bless you, Miss Longstreet. You are indeed a woman to cherish."

She couldn't answer, tears catching at the back of her throat. Such acts of kindness, she thought, would save them all. How had they ever spoken so glibly of fate and destiny determining their lives while she'd sat in the lap of luxury? She could cry out for fate to save her now, but only the actions of each soul here would influence the outcome.

From the dark waters, pleas for help were fading. And as light fell upon the broken promenade like a heat-soaked weight, they were able to assess what remained. A body was found in the water, facedown, and when Lamar turned him over he cried out, "Oh, it is Samuel Parkman. Oh, God."

Augusta closed her eyes to the knowledge, but she couldn't close her mind to knowing. Samuel, the dear man of Octagon Plantation in Bluffton who had lost his wife years ago and had boarded with his three daughters for a summer in the north. How much loss could they all take? It would seem eternal now, loss upon loss as wave upon wave washed upon their raft.

Augusta opened her eyes to account for the living: twenty-four souls, crew, men, women, Negroes, and children, in varying states of disarray. They took stock—no food, no water. They had a few pieces of clothing, a box or two to sit upon. They all wore scraps of clothing: shirts, torn vests, pantaloons and nightdresses. Some stood and continued to call out to sea for loved ones; others folded in upon themselves and sat in the inches of water on the decking to weep.

"Brother, your associate Henry, did you see him at all before we sank?"

Lamar looked at her with the kindest eyes; she couldn't hide her regard for Henry from him. "I did. The last I saw of him he was helping women into the other lifeboats. Maybe he made it into one of them."

"Maybe." Augusta mumbled the word into Thomas's warm hair.

"You care for him," Lamar said.

"It matters little now."

Lamar placed his hand on her shoulder. "The people we care for always matter. We can pray he's found refuge."

"If he died saving others, if he drowned while others found their way here . . ." Her throat burned with the thought; if she let go her emotion she would burst into sobs. And that would not do. She must stay strong. If Henry lived, so be it. If he'd died, at least he wasn't suffering as they were. The dream, the foolish, childish dream, that he would feel the same about her, had sunk with the ship.

As the sun climbed the sky, a man hollered that he saw something floating. Everyone stood, their eyes alert. As it came into view, the sun blinding, they spied a woman who sat atop a box, rowing with what appeared to be a stick but making little headway. When a wave brought her closer, a tall man at the far end of the promenade, one who had been leaning all night against another man, cried out in a broken voice, "Clara, my love. Tell me it's you!"

"It is." Her weak voice carried across the water.

Almost naked but for a torn nightdress on her shivering body, Clara was hauled onto the promenade by several men. Her black hair lay matted to her face. She fell into her husband's lap and together they wept; the others stared at them in awe, and with regret that they hadn't been reunited with a loved one they'd been praying for all night. Bargains with God—*I will do anything if you bring back my wife, my husband, my child* . . .

Lamar came to Augusta's side. "See, sister? There is hope. Maybe others have found a way to survive."

Augusta nodded and stroked Thomas's head. As long as she had this child, could she dare ask for more? Where were Henry and Lilly? Baby Madeline? She'd seen the sea swallow Melody and Eliza, but her brother desperately wanted to believe that more of his family lived.

"Sister, I'm grieved I brought you on the ship. That I brought all of you here. If they aren't to live, I must not either."

"Stop that." She took her brother's hand, which was bleeding with a gash across his palm. "You did not blow up the ship. You have saved other lives. You are here. Do not give up on me or on your child. You cannot blame yourself. What we must do now is find a way to survive and help others do the same."

He drew in a long breath and stood. "Yes." He spoke the word as if redemption depended on it.

The day wore on in misery. Children cried out for water. The moans of the sick were steady and slow. Those who died were covered with shirts and pants, and yet wind and wave often exposed them again before the bodies could be consigned to the sea. The waves swelled and surged, the sun rose higher and slowly other pieces of wreckage came bobbing into view, alien remnants of a shattered world.

23

EVERLY

Present day

I bolted upright in bed, my heart rousing with terror. Where was I? A too-hard mattress. Itchy covers. Darkness of a moonless midnight.

I remembered—Maddox's room at the inn. The afternoon pulled at me like a rip tide.

The curtains were open and I lay on top of a quilt covered in tiny anchors and smiling blue fish. A headboard was covered in navy fabric with white piping. I took in these details and grabbed my cell phone to see that it blinked four a.m. The early morning was always the cruelest time when I couldn't fall back asleep and my mind spun with the could-haves and would-haves.

A text from Maddox blinked, and I clicked on it, feeling a swooping surge of regret. I'd told him my story; I'd opened the locked box with him as if my loss and the vestiges of the *Pulaski* had both been brought up from the darkness below.

Maddox had written: I am bunking on the boat. Sleep well and stay as long as you please.

The text had come in at eight p.m. I'd flopped onto the bed at six, which meant I'd been sleeping for ten hours already. The last time I'd slept that long I'd been a teenager.

I needed to leave. I needed to gather myself and get the hell out. I felt naked. Exposed. Cracked like that damn pocket watch with the shattered face.

Standing at the window, I gazed out at the night-lit marina, the boats' silhouettes like cutouts against the dark sky. I clicked on all the lights in the room and entered the bathroom, where I brushed my teeth with a washcloth and Maddox's toothpaste. I'd left my bag in the Jeep and had nothing else with me. I took in his sparse belongings, his dopp kit and backpack from which clothes spilled out onto the only chair.

On the small wooden desk papers lay scattered, all photos of the artifacts, typed documents and legal papers I didn't read. On the bedside table was a book about shipwrecks and a glass of water.

I looked for hints of the man I'd trusted with my story, but found only necessities he'd grabbed for a quick trip. Something on the floor drew my attention—a folded note someone must have slipped under the door. It read: *"Don't leave. Whenever you wake up, don't run. Text me and I'll be there to help in whatever way you need."*

I placed the note on the bed, grabbed my backpack, and closed the door softly behind me. I would text Maddox when I arrived safely home; if I told him now he would try to stop me, the last thing I wanted.

Back on the dock in the dark morning, I took a moment to get my bearings until I remembered where I'd parked.

The return drive to Savannah enveloped me in silence; I felt part of a magical other world I rarely inhabited. Somewhere outside Myrtle Beach, I stopped at an all-night diner and ate my fill of hash browns and buttery scrambled eggs. When I arrived home at ten in the morning, a cup of coffee from the last rest stop half-consumed in the cup holder, I reached for my cell and texted Maddox.

I am home. Thank you for a place to rest; I will pay you for the room!
The artifacts are fascinating and I am ready to curate a fine exhibit.
Back to work. With gratitude, Everly

Yes, he would understand the unspoken message—no more mucking around in my private grief. No more conflating my tragedy with the *Pulaski* tragedy.

Then I called Oliver, but the phone rang until his voice mail answered, not in his voice, but in a robotic voice to leave a message. Until I'd seen him a few days ago, I hadn't given much thought to Oliver's life outside the museum. I'd once known all about that life—he'd spent it with Mora, with me, with the mutual friends we all hung around with.

I clicked the off button and placed the phone on the kitchen table. Did he still hang around with the old crowd? Go to concerts and festivals? Art gallery openings and dinner parties? Most of my friends had given up on inviting me—a solid no for a full year tends to decrease social invites. But Oliver? Did he still go?

It didn't matter. What did it have to do with me? I had work, my family.

As I gathered the charts and graphs for the museum, and stared at a photo of a diver holding a candlestick, a memory swam to the surface of my mind, unbidden and starkly real.

Since Mora had been killed, I hadn't donned a scuba suit or tank;

I hadn't wanted to see the world deeply below. But now, knowing about the wreck, imagining it lying there beneath a hundred feet of water, I woke to the remembrance of my first easy dive with her.

Mora and I had thrown our duffel bags in the car and driven to Key West in search of Hemingway's hangout on the archipelago. We'd just finished reading *To Have and Have Not*, and we wanted to find the very place he sat and drank. After arriving and realizing there wasn't a single hotel room available in town, we retraced our route to a mildew-smelling motel several keys north and dropped off our things to explore. Somehow, within hours, we also found ourselves at a scuba shop signing up for a class and a beginner's dive. It started for me there: the woman who bragged of being born in water began to understand the allure of the world below.

We snorkeled first, to get the feel of breathing underwater, to understand the easy in and out of our breath coming only through the mouth. In shallow reef water, we floated with our masks pressing into the bridge of our noses, leaving a dent on hers and a bruise on mine that would last for a week. We breathed in and out of our snorkels and flapped our fins as if we were the mermaids we'd pretended to be as children. Bright-colored fish, looking as if they'd been imagined by someone on a psychedelic journey, swam past us.

Sea urchins so pink they looked spray painted; the sound of shifting sand like Rice Krispies popping in a milk bowl; an eel slithering from below a piece of neon coral that looked like the brain of an alien dropped into the sea; a sole yellow puffer fish; a school of fish with orange Xs on their tails, as if they'd been marked. I was swimming in an aquarium; I spied what others saw only on TV shows or through panes of thick glass.

I'd been born for this.

Never looking up, we kicked our way past the breaker mark beyond which the instructor had told us not to go. No one had noticed we'd separated from the group. No one stopped us. We'd gone too far, a phrase we joked later we'd been accused of by many adults during our younger years. Finally, Mora grasped my wrist underwater and I raised my head above the surface, floated and removed my snorkel to look at her in question. Without saying anything she pointed toward shore, which had receded much farther than I would have guessed. "Whoops," I said, a tremor of fear catching my breath.

"He said it's harder to swim in than out. I think we should go . . . back."

I nodded even as I felt the tug of the sea pulling in the opposite direction, as if its force had been created for one thing only: to take what it could and keep it. Through the masks, our eyes held. This time we might actually be in trouble, without help close at hand.

"You think they forgot about us?" I spoke around the snorkel, moving my fins slowly to keep afloat. My heart began to pick up its pace, my pulse bounding in my wrists and neck. I grimaced. "We aren't very good at heeding warnings, are we?"

"Appears not. But we've got this."

"Yes. We do."

We dipped our heads again and slowly, slowly, fought the current while swimming back to shore. If we stopped for even a moment we were pulled sideways or back out to sea. I breathed slowly, in and out, wishing I could take a deep breath through my nose—the way I usually calmed myself. How to breathe was out of my control—the only thing I could do was keep going.

It might be the same now, I thought an hour later as I entered the museum—keep going.

It was almost noon, and I carried in the notecards and poster boards from my three-day work binge in a large portfolio. I would do the remainder of the work here. I had an office and an empty room in which to begin mapping out the exhibit. I needed to find a way to dig into the Longstreet family history, find more documents.

As I set the folio on the tabletop, I became aware of sunlight filling the room with warmth. A cleaning crew had obviously come through, and the room with its hardwood floors and white plaster walls smelled like lemon.

My cell buzzed. I didn't recognize the number. "Hello?" I balanced the phone between ear and shoulder, juggling the papers as I set them down.

"Ms. Winthrop?"

"Yes."

"This is Margarite Mulvaney. You left a message with the Aquatic Club asking for information about Longstreet family papers. I am a Longstreet on my mother's side—Lamar would have been my four times great grandfather."

"Oh, so lovely of you to call me back." I hustled toward the window for better service and stared out the bubble glass windows to the garden. June sang as a symphony of color, flowers crowding and blooming with faces lifted high. The green glowed almost neon, so vibrant and full of summer's high light.

"I hear you're looking for papers on the family who boarded the *Pulaski*?"

"Yes." My heart hammered as it always did when I thought a clue was about to be uncovered.

"I don't have any. And no one in my family I've called does either. If any papers exist, they would be almost two hundred years old. I assume you've checked the Georgia Historical Society?"

My heart took a long slide toward disappointment. "I tried there. They don't have anything."

"I am so sorry. There are articles and even chapters in books about that terrible catastrophe. And of course there is the statue at the riverfront."

"But I've found very little about who survived or how."

"Records from that time are so sketchy." She paused. "Listen, I've been working on my family tree for a year now. A project I'm doing for my mother, who is failing. Our family has so many branches I am lost after the fourth generation back. Women died young or in childbirth, and then the men remarried and had a passel more children, it gets dizzying. Do you know about Charles Longstreet?"

"He's the only one I do know about. That story is easy to find. Who can resist a story about a Red Devil who got his due?"

"Isn't it odd how we can find the devastating stories and not the inspiring ones? My daughter calls that trauma porn."

I laughed. "Sorry. It's not funny."

"No, it's human nature. We want to understand. I get it. And I'm so sorry I don't have any more information. I suppose if any papers exist, they're rotting in some attic in Richmond or New York, or were used for fire starters during the Civil War. I am sorry."

"Me, too. Thank you so much for calling."

I hung up. Sometimes a dead end was where things ended and sometimes it was a cul-de-sac where I could turn the inquiry around and look elsewhere. I was determined to keep looking. Past generations had had no idea that I, Everly Winthrop in the twenty-first century, would care about their papers and their journals and their letters, but that just meant I had to try harder.

Sounds coming from the back room alerted me to another presence. "Oliver?" I called.

"Coming." Oliver stepped into the room. "You're back already." He rubbed his hands together in exaggerated expectation. "I need to know every single thing you saw. Was it amazing?"

"More like surreal. Seeing things just as they came from the bottom of the ocean after being there for almost two hundred years . . . I have photos and I'm parking all these charts here."

I opened the huge portfolio and brought out the poster boards cov-

ered in drawings, notes and pictures. I dropped the photos of the artifacts, which I'd printed at home. I set up my laptop and plugged it in
while Oliver glanced through the papers. "This is a month's worth of
work. Now please tell me that the remains you saw are interesting
enough to create a mind-blowing exhibit."

"More than you can imagine." I clicked through the photos on the
computer while Oliver, too close for comfort, peered over my shoulder.
"The artifacts are so personal. A hairbrush, candlesticks, creamware
plates, keys and . . . watches and jewelry. I think we can display the
objects in two ways. One from an omniscient point of view—an over-
arching view of the night with a timeline of events. Then I want to
tell the story through the Longstreet family's eyes. We'll follow them
until the end. I will find out who lived and who died and what happened to them. They are the story inside the story. They are the Savannah family that represents us all."

"Any luck there?"

"Not yet. I just heard from a Longstreet descendant who has done
some searching on her own and found no family papers."

"But that won't stop you."

I took a deep breath. "Sometimes it does feel like a goose chase.
But I think we follow that family onto the ship. That allows us to show
the rooms, the cabins, the way the night unfolded."

"How did Charles survive? Do you know that yet?"

I shook my head. "I'll find out."

Oliver stood silently, his breathing the only sound but for the air
conditioner rattling in the background. As he studied my work I noticed for the first time in a long while everything about him. The way
he held his palms up when he spoke; the way his smile pulled harder
on the left; the way his eyelashes clumped together at the corners. He
radiated such a sense of confidence that I'd always believed he could fix
whatever had gone wrong.

"You know you're making your job twice as hard as it needs to be," he said. "We can create an exhibit around the ship and the night of the explosion, using the objects Maddox has brought up. The story of how the wreck was found can be part of it. You don't need to dig deep enough to find individual stories. The objects are powerful just as they are."

"That's not enough. An exhibit is always better when it's personalized."

He stared at me for a moment. What was he seeing that escaped me? Then he said, "I have a question—speaking of personal. You know that oil painting in your mom's house? The one of the *Pulaski*?"

"You remember that?"

"I do. It's beautiful. Was it handed down by a relative? I mean . . . why did your grandfather have it?" He shrugged. "It's a selfish curiosity. I'm hoping your mother will let us use it in the exhibit."

"How funny that I have never—not once—thought about where it came from until now. It's just always been there. We have loads of oil paintings around the house. Some were handed down; some Mom found in art galleries. I really don't know. But this one has its own special place in the house with a light shining on it. I'll ask her."

Oliver pointed at one of the photos I'd printed. "And this?" He held up the image of the pocket watch. "It gives me chills. This is exactly what we want for our exhibit. Time stood still. This could be our **centerpiece**, the image you see when you walk through those doors. As usual, you deliver the goods. Thank you for doing this."

"Look closely," I said quietly.

Oliver squinted. "The hands stopped at eleven." He glanced up and I saw the man I'd seen on the sandbar. The eyes that had witnessed the death of the woman he loved. The heart that had been caved in by the squeal of tires. We stood there as frozen as we were that day. "Everly."

He'd said my name so softly and gently that I teared up. "Isn't it awful?"

"It is."

He sat down hard on a chair. He stayed bowed over his knees with his head resting on his palms for a few minutes, long enough for me to want to touch him, to try to bring him out of the dark place. But I waited, my heart pounding and my throat tight. Finally he looked up, his eyes damp. "I'm sorry about that. I didn't expect it, that's all."

"We usually don't."

"What are the odds?"

I shrugged. "I mean, one is eleven at night and one at eleven in the morning but still . . ."

Oliver cracked his neck left and right. He rubbed his face and then with his three middle fingers he massaged his forehead before looking to me. "I'll call you soon. Thank you for your hard work. I need to return some calls and . . ."

"I understand." I sat down in the chair he'd deserted and watched him leave.

I intended to answer e-mails and do one more computer search on the *Pulaski*, but instead I typed in *Maddox Wagner* and hit search.

Several articles popped up. Did I want to click? What if someone did the same about me? As public as a search was, it still seemed an invasion of privacy. Yet I kept on.

The headlines blared at me: *Student Dies on Dive Led by Respected Marine Biologist. Maddox Wagner Loses Job over Tragedy. Maddox Wagner, Revered Marine Biologist, Loses Student in Dive. Maddox Wagner Resigns after Tragedy.*

One after the other, the headlines told the story of a research dive led by Maddox Wagner that went horribly wrong. A young female graduate student had died. Had her death been a result of criminal misconduct or an unavoidable freak accident? I held the clicker over another link and hesitated just as a calendar alert popped onto the screen.

Allyn's birthday—don't forget the cake for dinner at Mom's.

I slammed shut the computer. Whatever happened to Maddox was none of my business. None at all. I headed for the door as my phone rang: *Maddox.*

A sudden electric feeling flashed across my ribs. Since Mora's death, I was inept at identifying my feelings and determining why I felt that way. I just knew I was frightened of my own emotions.

I shook them off and headed toward Mom's house. I returned to Oliver's question—where had the oil painting of the *Pulaski* come from? And why did we have it?

24

LILLY

Friday, June 15, 1838

The night seemed to last longer than its actual hours. A weak moon beneath the cloud cover hovered without moving across the sky. Time stood still as if in horror.

"I will never get on a boat again," Mrs. Bird said in a quavering voice. "I will never come near the water again. I will move to the mountains and . . ." She continued in a soft voice that flowed past Lilly like a breeze but failed to calm the fear swooping in and then away like a bird that disappeared behind the clouds. The boat rose and fell with the billows and quiet soon descended. The grunt of the men who rowed toward an unseen shore joined the cries of the scorched Negro firemen in the adjacent boat, which kept pace alongside them like a ghost ship.

Lilly wanted to cover her ears to block out the sounds of agony. Eventually the cries ceased and they all knew why Mr. Couper rowed far ahead—he didn't want them to witness the body being interred in the sea.

A strange sensation came over Lilly of being separate from her body, untethered from the misery. She became a pure presence floating over the water, a woman so free that she couldn't possibly drown. Her body could lift and float; it could fly. Her mind imposed images on the dark canvas of night where the line between sea and sky blurred until they became one. She spied crocuses and daffodils blooming in green fields; the petticoats of her skirt as she climbed the gangplank to the ship; sunlight falling through Spanish moss and onto the rosebushes of her back garden; the fireplace crackling in the library while rain tinkled against the windows.

She faded off and an afternoon years ago appeared before her as surely as if she hid in the woods with Augusta at that very moment. They were six and seven years old, and winter was drawing near. The leaves were lighting themselves from within, turning yellow and red, falling to the ground in a carpet that Lilly and Augusta believed was being rolled out just for them. Through the trees, they watched the slave children play rolly ball—a game where they rolled a ball with sticks and tried to get it into two holes they'd dug into the ground. Lilly and Augusta wanted to join the slave children. Augusta spied Priscilla, whose mother was a seamstress for both Augusta's and Lilly's mothers, and Lilly wanted to roll the ball, too.

But Lilly and Augusta were forbidden to play with them. There they stood behind a tree in their finest frocks decorated with silk ribbons while Lilly noticed that the slave children were wearing simple cotton dresses, dust blowing from beneath their bare feet.

Lilly took Augusta's hand and squeezed it. "Let's go play with them."

"Mama will whoop us," Augusta had replied in earnest, always wanting to be the good girl while Lilly wanted to remove her frock and play in the mud, fly above the tree canopy, swim in the river, lie in her underthings under the stars. Lilly felt as if she spent most of her life trying *not* to do exactly what she wanted to do.

"Lilly, if you go, it's not you who will get the whipping, but them." Augusta pointed at the children, tossing a ball and hollering with joy. "Don't do it."

For the first time, Lilly understood that her actions, her freedom, were inhibited by rules that made no sense, and by adults who couldn't adequately explain them. Lilly had balled her hands into fists and punched the trunk of a live oak, bringing blood to her knuckles.

Augusta's eyes had filled with tears. "We'll make our own rules when we're grown. My Lilly, only when we're grown."

"Yes." Lilly had turned on her heels and run through the shaded woods, as beautiful as anything she'd ever known, the yellow and red and green hinting at something even more resplendent than she could see. She'd felt as if the seen world was conspiring by hiding something greater, and with Augusta by her side they would find it together.

When they'd reached the river, they'd lain in the grass and watched the water flow toward the sea. They hadn't talked, knowing they couldn't change this world but someday they could build their own. They'd rested and held hands until they heard Augusta's mother calling their names.

Now, back in a lifeboat in the middle of the ocean, Lilly jolted awake to her own child's cry, and returned to awareness of her situation. The misery of heat and thirst slammed into her, of her throbbing ankle and depleted child. Soon they would both run out of whatever life remained in them. And maybe then she would see what the world had been hiding all along. Maybe something at the heart of it could only be seen when life ended.

The line between life and death—she had never known it to be so thin. It shimmered like an invisible thread. It existed as one breath—that was all—one breath out and then not taken in.

Lilly watched her darling Madeline—a breath in, a breath out, a breath in, a breath out.

Time passed in the misery of the swell and dip of the seas. The sun reached its zenith, tropical and oppressive, and the heat bore down with such intensity that soon the hope of their survival, the brief belief that they would live, diminished. Mr. Couper tore his cloak and soaked it continually in water, handing it to the ladies and children to press upon their skin. By midday, the thirst seemed to come upon all of them with fierce need, their tongues seeming to grow in their mouths. A coat was made into a sail that caught little wind but made them all feel as if they had taken some action to save themselves. Mr. Couper navigated by the position of the sun and they rowed westward, their eyes straining for land and their lips praying for rain.

They had been at sea now for one night and almost a full day. Not even twenty-four hours since the explosion. And yet time had stretched itself into another shape—much more than twenty-four hours of Lilly's life had passed.

Mrs. Bird, only a few seats over, leaned forward. "May I hold the baby? Offer you a reprieve?"

Lilly held Madeline even closer. "Thank you so much, but Priscilla and I share her care. All is well."

"You two are quite a pair," Mrs. Bird said in a voice that held something of awe. Only days before, such a remark, at a dance or concert hall, would have been unthinkable. Now Lilly heard in it respect for both her and her slave.

A short while later an ear-piercing scream came from the other rowboat. "Shark!"

They pulled in the oars, their progress ceased and their diminished band of twenty-three watched the fin of a shark circle about for what seemed hours. Finally the creature swam away. They floated without moving for a few more moments and took in the countenance of each in turn. The sun had already blistered their arms and faces. Their lips were dry and chapped, some of them bleeding. But they were alive and they all had every intention of staying that way.

Three, four, five times, someone believed they saw land and called out. With hope, they all looked up only to realize it was a mirage. The men's strength faded. The rowing slowed as the hours wore on. Had the ship been farther out than First Mate Hibbert had estimated?

It was now late afternoon, the sun—bloated and fiery—cleaving a line toward the horizon when First Mate Hibbert called from the second boat, "Land ho!"

They all stared at a thin line that appeared to be a curved strip of sand, a horseshoe of land. Behind it, indistinguishable lumps appeared—houses or dunes they couldn't yet know. But yes, it was land.

Hope and vigor returned and the men rowed harder until they drew nearer and nearer to sand-covered hillocks. They all leaned forward, straining with both eyes and body to come closer to salvation.

25

EVERLY

Present day

As I headed toward Jones Street, the coconut cake shifted in its box; most likely the gorgeous icing was crushed. Of course I would screw up the one thing my family had asked me to do—"Just get the cake, darling. That's all you need to bring."

Oh, and show up on time.

Well, I'd do both, sort of.

Mom waited at the garden gate, her eyes scanning the street for the offensive tourist carriages, one of which was even now coming around the bend. "Mom!" I waved my free hand to distract her. But there was no diverting her from her favorite hobby—harassing the carriages. She figured if she kept on, they would eventually find another route. Ignoring me, she stepped toward the curb. The carriage, sadly, reached her before I could.

"Don't believe a word he says," she hollered at tourists snapping photos of the house and garden gate.

"Mom!" I stepped in front of her to block her from the carriage.

With one look at me her countenance changed completely. "Hello, darling." She took the cake box from my hand and turned on her heels, expecting me to follow.

From the carriage a voice carried. "You think she's crazy?"

I turned to see the sweet face of a young girl, maybe ten years old, staring at us. "No, she's not," I called.

The little girl smiled and her mother placed a protective arm around her.

I followed Mom into the house. She placed the cake on the kitchen counter and kissed my cheek. "You think I deterred them from coming this way again?"

"No, but I think you gave the tourists a good story to tell when they get home."

Mom lifted her nose as if she smelled something terrible. "There are so many honorable stories in Savannah. Why must they always talk about ghosts? It's absurd."

"And interesting. It's what I do—disturb those ghosts."

"Oh where, oh where did I go wrong?" Mom smiled and shook her head before lifting the box top to assess the cake. Minimal damage: one side was slightly dented and the Y in "Allyn" was lopsided.

"Mom, how was your day?"

"Quite lovely, dear. And yours? How is your work with the ship going?"

"It's so interesting, and mysterious."

"Which you love."

"And that reminds me—Oliver asked me. Where did we get that painting of the *Pulaski*? I mean, why do we have it?" The edges of the kitchen counter dug into my spine as I leaned against it. Mom stood before me wearing a pair of linen pants so pink they seemed to shimmer. Her crisp white blouse was ironed with a perfection I'd never mastered. I seemed to make things worse when I ironed, not better. How she always looked so put together was a mystery to me.

"Oh, I thought you knew." Mom ran her manicured fingers along the edge of the counter as if she were cleaning up invisible crumbs.

"I don't."

"Mora's grandmother Josephine gave it to Papa. She hated it and was going to sell it. He loved it so she gave it to him. Long before you were born."

The revelation caught me by surprise. Why hadn't I known this? "I had no idea," I said. "Why did she give it to him? Don't tell me there was some kind of—"

"No! Nothing like that. Our families lived next door and she was remodeling and didn't like it. I don't know the whole story, of course. I was your age at the time. We've had it ever since."

"So odd."

Mom headed upstairs. "I need to freshen up for Allyn and the children."

When she was gone, I opened the screen door to the side garden and walked out to get my bearings before my sister arrived. I was thinking about the timeline of the Longstreet family.

By 1838, importing enslaved from outside the country had been outlawed, but slave-trade among the states had not. Cotton was king in the South. The cotton gin had increased production and wealth. Men ruled the world and, except for a few singular cases, women were adornments. How did they tolerate it? And how did they survive a disaster like the *Pulaski*?

I crossed to the bench under the pergola where white hydrangeas were so lush that Mom's garden looked like a bowl of popcorn mixed with flashes of pink and red roses. The day's heat was dissipating and climbing jasmine on the pergola sent out its seductive scent.

Soon, Hudson's and Merily's voices rang out from the front porch, where they were arguing about whose turn it was to push the other on the tire swing. Allyn's laughter joined them.

The children burst through the screen door into the garden. "Aunt Everly!" Hudson galloped toward me like a horse and offered me a hug before veering off to the tire swing with his sister.

Allyn followed, and I gave her a hug. "Happy birthday, sis. Where's Burke?"

"His plane was delayed. How's your project going? Sophie said she saw you at the coffee shop and you seemed . . . a bit more like your old self."

"And that's supposed to mean exactly what?"

Allyn held up her hands. "I'm just repeating. She meant you looked great and seemed . . ."

"Not like such a sad sack of a woman."

"Stop it, Everly. You know what I mean."

I relented. "I do."

We were silent for a few moments, taking in the children's laughter, and then from Mom's kitchen Frank Sinatra singing.

"How's your new project going?"

I set my hand on Allyn's and squeezed. "Thank you for asking. The project is going great. Yesterday I was in North Carolina, to see the artifacts. So forgive my bleary-eyed state. I drove back very early this morning."

"The man you're working with—Maddox, is it?"

"Yes." I flicked a fallen magnolia petal from the bench. "Actually, I did a little Google search and learned he has a bit of a past. I shouldn't have looked him up. It's not fair to do that to people but I couldn't help it."

"A past? Like prison? Or . . ."

"No. Nothing like that. It appears he was a professor and one of his students died on a research dive."

"How awful!"

A firefly flickered past and Hudson jumped from the swing to catch it. Allyn watched with a smile before turning back to me. "Well, this is a professional relationship. I wouldn't worry about it."

I groaned and bowed my head. "Well, I blew that up."

"How?"

"I made a huge mistake."

"Oh, God, Everly, did you sleep with him?" Allyn whispered.

"Of course not!"

Allyn let out a breath. "Well, you need to sleep with someone." She jostled me and laughed.

"No kidding," I said, laughing back.

"So what did you do to blow up your professional relationship?"

"I told him about Mora. I told him how hard it's been since her death. Telling him was a mistake even though it felt right at the time." I rolled my eyes. "How many people have said that about something they've done that was completely inappropriate?"

"A billion or more." Allyn touched my arm. "You keep your grief so bottled up; so closed inside. I think it's good that you told him; sometimes it's easier to tell a stranger, someone who doesn't know anything but what you choose to tell them."

"But this is a man who might have done something horrible to be pushed out of his job when he was obviously highly respected. And now he knows personal information about me. I chose the wrong guy to confide in."

"You're blowing things way out of proportion. Oliver wouldn't be working with him if he were truly dishonorable."

"But now I have to pretend I don't know what happened."

"We all have a past that haunts us, Everly. I for one am glad you talked to him. Can I ask why you did?"

"There was this pocket watch they brought up from the bottom of the sea—its hands were stopped at eleven and . . . that's the time . . . you know."

"I'm sorry, sis. I am so, so sorry." Allyn leaned over and hugged me.

We sat silent for a few moments before I said, "I need to get in and help Mom before I get the look."

"I know the look."

"You stay here and let us spoil you on your birthday." I kissed my sister's cheek and entered the kitchen where Mom stood cutting tomatoes and humming along to the music. She turned as I entered. "By the by, Everly, you look beautiful tonight."

I shook my head. "Your standard for me has lowered for sure."

"And I do love that your cutting sense of humor is returning." Mom laughed and wiped her hands on her apron, where her name was embroidered in script. We each had one—Christmas presents from Aunt Joan four years ago. I had never worn mine.

"Now will you be a dear and set the table? I don't want your sister to lift a finger tonight. She works so hard with those rambunctious children."

The china and linens were stored in the dining room hutch. I chose Waterford stemware and the Irish linen. If I knew one thing from etiquette classes and debutante training, it was how to set a pretty table. I moved the vase of hydrangeas to the center and arranged the candles. Reaching beneath the mahogany table, I untaped the hidden key to the silver closet and went to retrieve the water pitcher and silver—the same things in our closet that the passengers carried to Baltimore. My thoughts wandered back to the women of the *Pulaski*.

How different were their lives from mine? No electricity. No photos. Handheld fans. Enslaved people to tend to their every need. No railway. No air-conditioning, only the breezes on the piazza and through open windows.

Same houses. Same roads. Same loves and wants and needs.

As I carried the pitcher and box of flatware into the dining room, Hudson bolted through the room and careened into me. Everything slipped from my arms and fell onto the Persian carpet. Mom called from the kitchen, "Is everything okay?"

"All good. Just clumsy me," I called out and winked at Hudson, who stood stock-still waiting for a rebuke I didn't intend to give. Finally he smiled and helped pick up the silver flatware before running off.

The passengers on the *Pulaski* had packed up all their silver, all their china, to take on this trip. It was important to them, not only for its monetary value but for the status it conferred. Now it rested below the waves.

While I set the table, I idly thought about the silver Maddox found, that watch with the silver wings; it was there to tell us something. The watch, stuck at 11:04 and forever timeless at the bottom of the sea.

Suddenly I wanted to call Oliver—a primal reaction. I wanted to tell him what I'd been thinking and how we needed to investigate the crest on the watch and find out who it belonged to. But then I remembered him sitting at the riverfront with the blonde. I remembered him saying I had no idea about his life. All true. I needed to keep it straight-up professional between us. I would talk to him about it when I saw him at the museum. Maybe my family knew where that design had been seen before.

When I finished the table, I wandered into the kitchen where Burke had just arrived in khakis and a white button-down shirt; he was loosening his tie and hugging the children. I nodded vaguely as I opened my photo app to pull up the photo of the watch to show Mom.

"Well, that was rude," Allyn said with a laugh.

I paused to hug Burke. "I'm sorry. Hello, dear Burke. Honestly, I'm so glad you're here. I was completely preoccupied."

"Research, no doubt." His smile let me off the hook, acknowledging that when I was down the research rabbit hole all was forgiven. He was no different when submerged in his own software designs.

"Y'all, look at this." I held up the photo. One by one each family member looked closely. "This," I said, "is a pocket watch that was found on the bottom of the ocean. And I know I've seen that design or crest before."

"Mom, do you have any idea?" Allyn asked.

Mom glanced up to the ceiling as if it held the answer. "I have seen it. Where?"

Burke was making himself a vodka and tonic when he chimed in, "You have to admit this is fascinating, Harriet. You can't blame your girl for wanting to know more."

"Everly, darling." Mom said. "I don't know. It does seem familiar but . . . I do know our family is not tied to the *Pulaski*. Thank God. The Winthrops suffered enough tragedy over the generations, from yellow fever to that damn fire of 1820 that burned down our house on Oglethorpe Square, to war—how many men did we all lose? We deserve a reprieve from that one doomed ship."

Merily burst into the kitchen, one pigtail undone and her face smeared with dirt. She looked around at the adults. "When are we having cake?"

Allyn hugged her wild daughter and lifted her to a bar stool. "Right now."

"Before dinner?" Hudson asked as he climbed up next to his sister.

"Yes, indeed." Mom placed the cake on a pedestal cake stand. "Tonight, I do believe we should all have cake first."

The kids let out whoops of joy and I took in the room—my mom, sister and brother-in-law, niece and nephew. Mom lifted the knife to cut into the coconut cake with its dented side and thick icing. I couldn't imagine the devastation of losing an entire family. Perhaps Charles Longstreet had been the sole survivor of his siblings. How might that terrible loss have warped him, until he was capable of buying and selling human cargo?

"I love y'all," I said.

My family went suddenly still and silent until Merily said, "I love you to the deepest sea and back."

We laughed in unison at the phrase I'd taught her to say instead of "to the moon and back."

"To the very deepest," I said and hugged her as she shoved a piece of cake in her mouth.

After dinner had been gobbled down and Allyn had hustled her family toward home, I stood at the sink washing dishes with Mom. Outside, the lanterns on the back porch spread puddles of light on the grass, moths flickering in and out.

"How are you feeling, Everly? This project seems to be bringing you some . . . happiness?"

"I'm just doing my job, Mom." I dried a dish and reached to put it away. "You know I think it's fascinating, bringing things up from the bottom of the ocean."

"Papa would have been thrilled—knowing they found the *Pulaski* and that you're involved. Have you thought about diving down there? You used to love it."

"I did love it."

"Not anymore?"

"The last time I went was with Oliver and Mora in the Keys. I want to dive again. I'm not quite ready, but I want to, and I told Maddox and Oliver."

"That's good, sweetie."

"I think I might go visit Mora's grandmother and ask her about the painting. I want to know where it came from and why she didn't want it."

"That's a good idea. Maybe she has a story to tell about it."

Mom began to hum with her hands in the soapy water and I watched her for a few moments before asking, "Mom, I know this might seem like a crazy question, but did you feel . . . unsafe after Dad died? Like any minute the whole world could implode?"

Mom leaned against the sink and closed her eyes. "It was a long time ago, darling. Almost thirty years now. But I don't so much recall being worried about my safety as wanting to feel alive again." She opened her eyes. "Yes, I was worried I would never feel alive again."

"But you did."

"It took a while."

"But you never . . . fell in love again."

"How do you know that, Everly?" She wiped her hands across her apron.

"Because you never married again." I realized as soon as I said the words that they were absurd. Love didn't always equal marriage. I held up my hands. "Okay, that was stupid. I just meant . . . I never saw you with anyone else. There wasn't another man."

"You and Allyn were my priority. I never again found a man who made me want to leave my ship for his dinghy." She grinned and winked. "But that doesn't mean there weren't men."

"Mom!"

She grinned again. "Feeling alive, vibrant. You will again. Mora was as much a part of you as your family, I know that. Her absence will feel raw for a long time."

"Do you . . . ever get over it?"

"If getting over her death is your goal, you'll be miserable, darling.

You'll carry the loss with you, but in new ways. Your dad and Papa are with me always. And with you, too, I expect."

I sank into myself. There I was trying to get over something that I would forever carry. Now the question was: How could I carry it? And what would that mean?

26

LILLY

Friday, June 15, 1838
Afternoon .

By three in the afternoon, green hillocks and a sandy white beach lay visible before Lilly and the other passengers. The beach curved along the shore and then tapered to dunes and grasses that moved restlessly in the breeze. The bulky images beyond were either small houses or fishing shacks, no one really knew, not yet.

Even while remaining in the lifeboat, Lilly could almost feel the sand beneath her feet, taste cool water on her tongue, and sense the solid, unmoving earth. And yet a barrier as substantial as a hundred miles of open sea kept them from their goal.

A solid line of surf breakers, six feet high and more, beautiful when viewed from land, she was sure, but treacherous to the exhausted, half-naked passengers of their frail craft. It was the last of mighty nature they must overcome to reach land: a fortress of water. Pointing their bows away from the breakers so as not to become caught up in them, the two quarterboats were brought together to discuss a plan.

"We can't last much longer," the judge from New York in First Mate Hibbert's boat said. "We must take the chance."

"Many of us don't know how to swim," said another.

And the chorus of voices lifted.

"We must row farther down and find calmer water."

"We need a safe inlet, not this."

None could agree and Lilly slumped against Priscilla, who had begun to hum the songs of her mama, songs of salvation, Jesus and heaven, soothing herself and Madeline with strength that Lilly herself wished she possessed.

Mr. Couper looked to them and Lilly spoke the truth. "Neither of us knows how to swim, sir."

He seemed to sink into his body, his shoulders dropping so low that Lilly was afraid she had struck the final blow.

First Mate Hibbert was being pressed by the desperation of all those in the second boat and he succumbed, telling Mr. Couper and the other survivors, "We shall go first. You watch. If it is too danger- ous, we will go for help while you stay where you are."

It was agreed and despite her thirst and fear, Lilly nodded along with the others.

They watched, all of them, as Hibbert and the judge rowed toward the breakers. Lilly wanted to turn away from the twelve passengers clinging to the sides, from the skeletal face of the fireman, from the old judge from New York who leaned forward, his bald pate blistered. In- stead, she prayed for them and lifted her hand in an odd good-bye as they rowed away.

The quarterboat crested the first wave, Lilly's heart and breath ris- ing as if she were with them, a bird taking flight. The boat seemed to sit on top of the crest and then just as suddenly it plummeted from view. Priscilla grabbed for Lilly's hand and together they held their breath and waited for the boat and the passengers to return to view.

Time felt suspended, yet it was only a moment before they saw the hull of the quarterboat; it was upside down, its passengers scattered in the sea. Arms, legs and faces were obscured and blurred through the white foam as they fought for solid ground.

"Swim!" Lilly screamed, although she knew they couldn't hear her, and there was no way she could save anyone.

No one spoke, but together their breath synchronized and they were as one watching the others fight for their lives. First one figure stumbled onto shore, and then another.

"I cannot see," Mrs. Bird said with a break in her voice. "Who is alive?"

No one answered her.

They watched as the two on shore bent to breathe but did not collapse. They immediately bolted back toward the water and dragged two more people to shore. Those two bodies walked and then fell to the sand. Mrs. Bird began to cry and pray.

Our father

She leaned over the boat, listing it as she retched and then began again.

Who art in heaven

Lilly reached inside herself for the strength she knew she had, for the emotional iron forged during her husband's abuse, and with the resolve that had put valuable jewelry in her wrist bag, she looked to Priscilla. "We shall put our feet on that sand. Do you hear me?"

"Yes, mistress. I hear you."

The sun had burned the thin skin around Lilly's eyes and the swelling clouded her vision. She covered her baby, lethargic and in a state past sleep, but still breathing steadily. Returning her attention to the beach, she spied two figures prostrate on the sand and two others beginning to stride in opposite directions, surveying the water. Soon two more were dragged to shore, half stumbling, half walking. Six in total.

Finally, after some time, as the sun moved closer to the horizon, a man, assumed by all to be Hibbert, dragged the quarterboat from the sea and onto shore. They knew then—six of the eleven had lived through the breakers. Five had not, including the judge from New York, the man who had begged them to row for shore.

Mr. Couper, his face blistered and his hands swelling to purple, touched the top of Madeline's head. "We cannot make it through those breakers."

Mr. Harris, his hair plastered to his face and a wound on his thigh now beginning to fester with pus and blood, stood up and spoke for the first time. "We must try. It is the only way to save our lives. We have no strength to row another hundred yards farther down the beach. We will go into those waves and right the boat to keep afloat."

Lilly forced herself to speak. "Can we wait a little while to see if they find help? Two of them have gone off." She pointed toward the shapes they believed were buildings.

"We will die if we're forced to spend another night at sea." The man leaned toward her. "We will help you get to shore."

Mr. Couper spoke up. "It will take all your strength to save yourself from those hellish waves. They are six feet high with an undertow and a force that only the strongest swimmers can withstand."

Madeline let out a cry and Lilly soothed her with a singsong voice and again handed her to Priscilla for feeding. "Mistress, I'm drying up.

I must have something to drink." Priscilla's voice cracked as she again exposed her breast and took Madeline toward her.

"Let us pray for rescue," Lilly said, fear engulfing her. She could not even save her own child from starving; she'd given to Priscilla the job of providing life-giving sustenance. Her own powerlessness was unthinkable, unbearable.

Priscilla's bare right shoulder revealed a wound that had likely been only a scrape when they'd climbed into this boat. Now it had begun to fester. Lilly cringed at the sight and tore a piece of fabric from the edge of her nightshirt. While her child nursed, her sucking becoming ever more frantic, Lilly placed the torn fabric over Priscilla's wound.

Priscilla looked up at Lilly and her eyes filled with tears. "Thank you, missus."

Lilly pressed her hand to the fabric and held it there while her child received the nourishment that Lilly could not give. Priscilla was saving her child's life, if there was life to be saved. Lilly felt the eyes of the other passengers on the three of them; they represented all that might be spared if they bonded together.

Barney cleared his throat and adjusted the scrap of fabric he had placed over his thick white hair. "If only a few of us survive, will someone please tell my wife that my thoughts were with her and I most certainly wanted to return to my beloved family?"

And then each one told what they would want their family to know and the others nodded that they would pass the message along if they could. When it came to Lilly, she held her hand over Madeline's head. "All that matters to me is here. I have no need to pass word along. We shall all live. We shall fight for life and for each other."

The passengers nodded and Mrs. March began to cry quietly, the palms of her hands held over her face. Mr. Couper spoke softly, his voice fading, but still with more conviction than any of the others could muster. "It is approximately four hours until dark. We will wait for help until sunset. If it doesn't arrive, we shall row toward shore. We don't know how far away another inlet or river might be and the men have no more strength. This is our only hope."

Solomon set his hands on the edges of the boat. "No one is coming to save us. We know the dangers we face."

The others agreed and then grew silent as the sun sank inexorably toward the horizon.

27

EVERLY

Present day

In the empty museum's vaulted room I worked alone. It was late afternoon and the outside world hummed with weekend activity, the sounds dulled by the thick plaster wall and music I played. I was waiting on Oliver.

A shift in the air and I looked up to see Oliver standing before me with a pile of folders in his arms. "Good morning. How was Allyn's birthday bash?"

"Not so much a bash as a coconut-cake-eating binge, but nice. Thanks for asking."

"Anything new from Maddox or the team?"

Oliver drew close enough to touch and I stepped back. "Just more photos of silver and china. He did show me a photo of a silver teapot they found and it has the same crest made of wings that's on the pocket watch . . . I really want to figure out who that belongs to. So far it is the only real hint of ownership. The passengers took so much with them. I barely remember to pack a toothbrush when I go somewhere."

The familiar sound of his laughter filled the room. I felt a lift of my chest as if light and air were finally entering. "Any luck with the Long-street family?"

"None. I have a call in to the historical society to see if they have the Longstreet ancestry tree. I still hope to track down a descendant, but damn, the *Pulaski* was six generations back. Why did they only write down what happened to Charles? It's frustrating—as if by choos-ing evil he got to be recorded for posterity." I shook my head. "And I did ask Mom about the painting. You'll never guess where it came from."

"Your papa stole it." Oliver paused. "From bootleggers. From the trash. From—"

"Stop." I laughed. "It's from Mora's family. Josephine gave it to Papa. No one knows why."

"Mora's Mee-maw? The woman who can drink more than a sailor in 1700? That grandmother?"

"The very one."

"So Josephine actually gave something away. Now, there is an un-expected turn of events."

I shut my laptop. "Will you go with me to ask her about it? I mean, I can do it, but I don't want to go alone. We're sure to run into Mora's mom, and I haven't seen her since the funeral. She's refused guests. She never goes anywhere. But if we go together maybe she'll let us talk to Josephine."

Oliver shifted back and forth on his brown loafers. His smile faded. "I don't know, Everly. The last time I tried to talk to Laurel, it was very uncomfortable. In her pain, she lashed out at me."

"But that was over a year ago. She didn't mean what she said."

"Everly, she told me that if Mora hadn't been with me that day she'd still be alive. She—"

"I know. She said it to me, too."

"Can't someone else—like your mom—ask Josephine why she gave the painting to your grandfather?"

"Let's just try?"

Oliver dug his hands into his back pockets. "Why the hell not? If you're up for an adventure then so am I."

The house at the edge of historic Monterey Square, where the Casimir Pulaski monument stood tall and proud, was deeply shaded by a live oak that had survived Hurricane Irma, the only tree on the property that hadn't succumbed to the saturated earth and beating winds. The house was a stately Georgian painted a faded cream color with moss growing in patches along the walls. Pale blue shutters hung crooked on a few windows. Ivy grew along the garden wall and only the left gas lantern beside the door flickered, the right one dead and dark.

Oliver stood next to me on the brick sidewalk in the sweltering heat, beads of sweat on his forehead and the underarms of his white shirt darkening. I held a bouquet of pink roses entwined with ivy. "You ready?" I asked.

"Not really, but let's go."

The stone steps leading up to the front door were well worn, the middle scooped out from the slide of feet for over a hundred years. The street-level entrance one flight down was hidden behind an iron gate, the apartment it led to rented out to a student most likely. The ground-floor rooms would have once included the kitchen and the servants' quarters. The front door at the top of the stairs was painted a dark red.

We climbed and Oliver rang the bell. From the recesses of the house we heard its melody, and then silence. Oliver looked at me and I shrugged. "Maybe we should have called ahead?"

Mora had never actually lived in this house. Laurel Dunmore had bought it for herself and her own mother when Mora graduated from high school. Laurel's divorce from Mora's wealthy, philandering father had left her with money and bitterness—never a good combination.

I lifted the lion's-claw knocker and banged it three times.

Oliver laughed. "You don't give up, do you?"

"Nope."

This time we heard shuffling and then the click of a lock. The door opened and there stood Laurel Dunmore. She wore a white dress, loose and unbelted, that made her look like a nurse. Startled to see us, she took a step back. "My, my. What brings you two here?"

"Hello, Mrs. Dunmore." I held out the flowers and tried my best smile.

Laurel took the flowers and smiled wanly, as if it was something she was not accustomed to doing. She stood her ground. "Thank you for the unnecessary flowers. May I ask why you are here?"

"We wanted to ask you a quick question, and we thought it would be better to do so in person."

"And what would that question be?" Laurel didn't move an inch while Oliver and I stood on her front stoop as if we were selling her something she didn't need.

"It's about the *Pulaski* painting hanging in my family's home. I was wondering where it came from. Mom told me that your mother gave it to Papa. And I wanted to ask about it."

"What do you need to know? Seems you have all the facts you need."

"But I don't. You see . . ." I paused, feeling sweat running down my back. "Do you mind if we come in? It's so hot out here and I promise it won't take long."

Laurel looked at me just as she had when Mora and I were children—she didn't trust me. She thought any trouble we found ourselves in was my fault entirely. Her eyes slanted and then she looked at Oliver. "You're still in Savannah?"

"Yes, ma'am, I am. I still work at the museum."

"I'd thought you might leave." She stepped inside and motioned for us to come in.

The air conditioners, closed windows, and dark rooms kept the house a cold crypt of dark antiques and oriental rugs. We followed Laurel down a long hallway and into a sitting room I'd been in on a few occasions through the years, the last time for the reception following Mora's funeral. I'd sat there so stupefied with anti-anxiety meds that I barely remembered it. I didn't glance around the room, where I knew there were photos and an oil painting of Mora, and instead focused on Laurel. "Can you tell us why your mother gave the painting to Papa? Was it a family heirloom?"

"Why do you need to know?" Laurel laid the paper-wrapped flowers on a mahogany side table.

"Oliver and I are curating an exhibit of the *Pulaski*. Its wreck was recently found off the coast of North Carolina."

"Oliver and you?" Laurel narrowed her dark brown eyes at us. "Together? Are you two together?"

An invisible hand began to clench my throat. No words came out even as I opened my mouth.

Oliver spoke for me, softly and calmly. "We're working together. If there's any way you could help us, we'd be grateful."

Laurel looked back and forth between us, and then she walked to the far end of the room, picked up a cut-glass decanter and poured herself an inch of dark liquid. She downed it in one gulp. She didn't offer any to us. "I knew one day I would see you both again. I wanted more warning."

Oliver stepped forward and for a moment I thought he might bow, he seemed so deferential. "Mrs. Dunmore. I am so very sorry to bother you. Please know that we miss Mora as profoundly as you do."

"I doubt that very much, Oliver."

"I'm sorry. I didn't mean to presume. I just . . ." Oliver faltered and then found his footing again. "The flowers you leave on her grave are beautiful. Both Everly and I have seen them when we visit her."

Oliver's words were having the opposite of their intended effect. Laurel was not only growing redder and more agitated, but also angrier. She took a step toward him. "I don't leave flowers. She isn't there, at her grave. She is here with me. She is everywhere. That stone is in my ex-husband's plot and her spirit is nowhere near there. Do you understand me? Those are not my flowers."

"I understand," Oliver almost whispered.

Coming here had been a terrible idea, I realized. It came back to me then—like a flash—how Laurel had begged that Mora not be buried in Bonaventure, that her ashes be scattered in her beloved Savannah River. Moon River, as it was called in the lyrics by Savannah's own Johnny Mercer.

"I'm sorry we bothered you." I took two steps backward and nearly tripped on the edge of the carpet, grabbed Oliver's arm for support.

Laurel glared at us. "That painting. I don't know why anyone would want it, honestly. But if you want to know why Mother gave it away, you'll have to ask her. She never told me."

"May we?" I asked. "May we ask her?"

"Mother!" Laurel called out in a screech so loud and high-pitched that both Oliver and I startled.

In a few moments, Josephine stood before us. She was now eighty-six years old but in the dim light she almost looked younger than her daughter. She wore a pink frock with ruffles and carried a cane with a gold tip shaped like a lion's head with an open mouth. "Well, hello there, Everly!" She took limping steps toward me and kissed my cheek. "I am so very happy to see you."

She turned to Oliver and did the same to him, leaving a red lipstick mark on his cheek, which he didn't move to wipe away.

"Hello, Josephine," he said. "It's lovely to see you."

Laurel made a noise somewhere between a snort and a laugh and exited the room without a good-bye, leaving the flowers I'd brought to wilt on the side table.

"Forgive my daughter. She's not done well since we lost Mora. Anger consumes her."

"I understand," I said. "We're so sorry to bother you, but I just wanted to ask you a quick question about the oil painting you once gave Papa."

Josephine poured herself a drink of the dark liquid, took a long swallow and then settled herself painfully in a spindle chair. She adjusted behind her a pillow cross-stitched with the letter D. Laurel might renounce her husband but she damn sure hadn't renounced his name or his family heirlooms. "My poor legs seem to be giving out on me, so please do sit with me. And Oliver, dear, if you could please open the drapes. I don't know why my daughter insists on such darkness on a beautiful day like this."

Oliver pulled the thick red damask curtains aside with a swish and sunlight burst into the room, changing everything it touched.

"The painting," Josephine said. "It's not so complicated. I gave it to your papa because I didn't want it in my house. It was a doomed ship and I had many other paintings I liked much better. Your papa was fascinated with ships, and he always admired it. I was quite enamored of him, you know. He barely noticed me, but I do believe I might have been a bit in love with him. He was completely devoted to your grandmother, even years after she was gone. But posh, that's not what you asked." Josephine brushed the air with her hand. "Where was I?"

"The painting."

"Yes. Your grandfather was always off to that Aquatic Club and reading about sailing adventures, and I thought he should have it. So I sold it to him for a pittance."

"Was it a family piece?" Oliver asked.

"Yes, it was. But I married into the family. It came from my husband Perceval's side, and he was gone by then. What did I want with a ship that took so many lives?" She leaned forward. "You do know entire families were lost, don't you? The Parkmans of Octagon Plantation lost the father and three of their children, the MacKays lost the mother and children, the McLains and Coles went down with three generations at once."

"I know a little bit." My heart sped up. Did she know more than I did? "I've read a few newspaper articles. I'm trying to find out more."

While I was talking, Oliver walked to the fireplace, glanced up at the oil painting I'd been avoiding—Mora at sixteen years old in an all-white dress holding a bouquet of white roses. Her red hair, muted in the painting, fell over her shoulder in soft waves. She smiled with the mischievous look I knew so well, one that the painter had caught in a flash. I looked back to Josephine, who said, "I wish I could give you more information, but honestly, all I know is that the painting belonged to my husband's family and when he was gone, I didn't want anything to do with a ship associated with such a horrible story. Life is hard enough."

"Was your husband's family on the ship? Is that why they had it?"

"No, dear. My husband was merely obsessed with Savannah maritime history. He was a member of the Aquatic Club like your Papa George, and he believed he'd been born into the wrong era. He always wanted to be a sculler and conquer the world." She laughed but the sound held some darkness.

"Well, thank you for trying to help." Oliver gently touched my shoulder and nodded toward the door as Josephine's chin bobbed to her chest. She didn't answer our good-byes and we exited as quietly as we could.

On Bull Street, the sun high and thunder rumbling far off, we stood and faced each other. "What do you make of that?" I asked.

"That was gothic and bizarre." He shook his head and pressed his fingers into the sides of his eyes. "Mora would hate to see her mother this way."

"Laurel was nearly always that way. Angry and looking for error all the time. I think it's worse, but still . . ."

We walked into Monterey Square in search of shade, always a pressing need. I stopped stock-still at a bench—a lump of a man covered in a cardboard box lay sleeping, his head on a black garbage bag. His long greasy black hair was spread out and one of his arms was flung wide and left to hang over the edge. Before I realized what I was doing, a pure need overcoming me, I ran to the bench and shook him.

"You."

He startled and rolled over, groaning. "What the hell . . ." His breath was rancid and dank, his body potent with urine. He opened his eyes and stared at me—blue eyes.

"Sorry. Sorry." I tripped backward into Oliver, who took me by the shoulders and turned me to face him.

"Everly."

"I know. I can't help it. I keep thinking . . ."

I slumped and then dropped my head onto his shoulder. He placed one hand on the nape of my neck and I felt the comfort of his touch. The feel of him, so solid, soothed me. "I get it," he said. "You don't have to explain it to me." His words fell warm into my ear.

How I wanted him to take both arms and wrap them around me, sway to the breeze, hold me until my heart stopped hammering and the sick feeling in my stomach settled. But that wasn't going to happen. Trouble began with that very idea. I eased away.

"I keep thinking I'll find him . . ."

"I know." He nodded and looked at the bench before returning his gaze to me. "So do you think Josephine isn't telling us something?" he asked.

"I have no idea. But let's find out."

28

AUGUSTA

Friday, June 15, 1838

Augusta felt thirst like a wild beast inside, an animal's need that could cause harm. Her stomach, as well as those of the others, cramped with hunger. The sun burned through the clouds with oppressive intensity and seemed to bring her closer to the center of Dante's fabled inferno. She glanced about her for what remained of their life raft—another piece of the decking had broken off and they were now crowded on a wooden section of about twenty feet by ten feet. Their bodies had collapsed in various states of exhaustion. They'd lost four souls during the day; nineteen remained. Seawater flowed over their wrinkled and bleeding feet. Some huddled together and others kept apart, curled into protective postures.

The immense and never-ending sea brought them to silence; there wasn't energy enough for talk without food or water. The prayers were plentiful. The cries to the heavens reached out in both song and wails.

Those who had never prayed before found themselves in a bargain with God—*if you will save me, I promise to* . . .

Augusta focused on Thomas; his whimpers were fading and his body trembling. He needed what she could not give him—water, food, shelter. She shook with the agony of it, appalled by her helplessness. She could close her eyes and see and hear the market on Ellis Square— men and women selling eggs and fresh vegetables, milk and cheese, fresh fish and rice. Such a simple routine—going to the market—that she would give all she owned to experience now. The slaves and the freed Negroes with their baskets and the fresh food. Her mouth watered at the memory and a groan escaped her lips.

Remnants of the ship floated around them, jagged broken pieces that appeared and disappeared from view, revealed and obscured by the ever rising and falling waves.

Far off it seemed there was a shape—could it be a larger piece of the ship? It was too hazy to know. Coming into view, only a porch distance away, a man lay flung across one wooden log, his arms draped over it, the top half of his body facing the water while the rest floated below. His dark hair was all she could see. Was he unconscious or dead? "Brother, look!" she said to Lamar.

Lamar leaned toward the edge of the decking. "You!" he called at the inert form. "Are you awake?"

The man lifted his head only slightly, but enough to show Augusta that the man lived. Lamar uncoiled a salvaged rope. He held it up. "Catch this," he called out. "Try to catch this and I'll pull you in." A few others rose slowly to help, and Augusta knew that each of them silently prayed as she did that it was someone they knew and loved.

Lamar tossed the rope and the man's hand lifted slowly, as if it were weighted with something unseen. He missed the rope and it sank, but Lamar pulled it back and tossed it again. Four times Lamar tried until

Augusta was sure the stranger would give up and sink into the sea. But the fifth time, his hand closed around the rope. Lamar pulled slowly, careful not to dislodge the man's grip or tip their own source of support. It only took a few minutes before the man's form reached them, and he looked up with gray eyes.

"Henry!" Augusta exclaimed, her voice hoarse.

He didn't answer. He lifted his left hand to grasp the splintered decking, and then tossed off the log he'd clung to, reaching his right hand up. Lamar bent to grab him.

"Don't," Henry said. "You'll tip off. Let me climb on."

"You don't have the strength."

Behind Henry, sunlight cast him in gold. Lamar grasped the hand he held out. Somehow, together, despite Henry's diminished strength, he was half pulled, half dragged onto the decking. He crawled and collapsed near Augusta.

"Henry." Augusta said his name in an exhale. He immediately passed out and Lamar set him upright against the box on which Augusta sat. She set one hand on his head and wound her fingers around his wrist to feel the beating pulse.

Henry wore pantaloons and a torn undershirt. The skin on his arms was puckered and almost purple from having spent a night in the sea. His feet were blue, swollen almost beyond recognition. She stroked his head and whispered prayers she'd never before uttered, ones she'd heard in church while her mind wandered down frivolous paths.

Had their former lives mattered at all? All the energy and time they had spent to maintain their particular way of living—why had they bothered? The teacups and bric-a-brac, the fine lace and silk gowns. It was all a mirage. Now their silver and linens, their hand-painted table service, their hand-sewn gowns all lay at the bottom of the ocean.

Corsets—what silly garments; she would never wear another. Her finely wrought shoes were gone, too. All ridiculous. All vanity.

The buying and selling of human "property," which she had questioned only superficially, now seemed both horrific and inexcusable. All to maintain that lifestyle?

She ran her fingers through Henry's hair, and understood her past life was a complete fuss and muss about absolutely nothing. Absurdity in the face of life and death. Now only living mattered and she *would* live. Even if tragedy brought the decimation of her life as it had been, it would not take her life itself.

She remembered her conversations with Henry in the library. She'd agreed with him that slavery was an abominable institution, but now she saw how easy it had been to agree with him when she'd had no power to change it. She could nod her head while also enjoying the tea her house slave brought, the beautiful river plantation situated along the curve of the flowing Altamaha River. How could that life exist without the "abominable institution"?

Once, she'd argued that her way of life was better than the squalor created by the northern mill towns, but Henry had strenuously disagreed. Deadlocked, they'd turned back to discussing books. For hours, they'd studied the pages, trading ideas across a table that made touch impossible. Now that same strong man lay half-naked and slumped against her. His body quivered every few minutes and a groan escaped his parched lips. She said his name over and over, softly, wanting him to wake and survive with her. She had much time to study his face, the contours of his cheekbones, his square chin. His eyes sloped slightly down at the corners. His full lips were now cracked and dry. Yet still his hair was so thick she could bury her fingers in it.

How many times she'd tucked herself into bed, stared at the canopy above her, and imagined what it would be like to be this close to him.

Augusta startled as a rogue wave washed over the wreckage. The sound of vomiting joined the groans of the seasick. Breezes came intermittently and the sun seemed to have become stuck in the sky—

burning and burning. How could they have ever thought they'd built a life of safety and comfort? Now they were all at the mercy of the waves' billows and the wind's blasts. Nature was there to remind them all—they were not in charge.

As the day advanced, Henry finally stirred and then jolted upright too quickly. At the sudden movement, he leaned over and spat viscous spittle into the water. He shivered with revulsion and then narrowed his eyes in the bright sunlight, looked to Augusta. "You saved my life."

"Let's not jump to conclusions," she said with a half smile. "It was my brother who pulled you from the sea. And we aren't saved yet."

She took in the crust of salt water on his eyelashes as he shook his head and said, "If we made it this far, we can find a way to shore."

"How?"

He glanced about them and swiped a palm over his mouth. "There are others here." He noticed Lamar huddled over the broken yawl that had washed onto the raft with the four other men who'd helped him pull it onto the deck. They were stuffing torn clothing into the holes and separated joints, and tying together the loose boards with rope, in an effort to make it seaworthy.

Henry tried to stand and stumbled, fell back down next to Augusta. "There is a lifeboat."

"Yes. But it is . . . useless." Augusta felt the stiffness in her neck and back as an ache deep inside her bones. "It was the very yawl I was on with the family. It just floated up . . . but it's . . . useless."

Henry touched Thomas's cheek and tears sprang to his eyes. "Is he all that remains of the family?"

"For now, yes, my brother and Thomas. But I have hope. Look, you just arrived. I had been hoping you would and . . ." She stopped her words quickly, swallowing them whole.

He took her free hand in his. "You are brave and righteous, Miss Longstreet. We'll survive."

"Augusta. My name is Augusta."

Sea salt cracked on his smiling cheeks. "I have known your name since the moment I entered your brother's house."

"You must not recognize me now."

"I recognize the fire I saw in your eyes when I first spied you across the library listening to our conversations."

"You noticed me?"

He chuckled. "Must I admit now that I had no need for as many meetings with your brother as I took pains to arrange?"

"Well, Mr. MacMillan, is that a delirious admission to a woman whose brother just saved your life?"

He didn't laugh as she expected but instead kissed the palm of her hand. "Fate is a funny old thing, isn't it?"

"Let's hope it saves us."

"That part we must do together."

"Then let's," Augusta said. "This was meant to be a holiday, a one-night-at-sea celebration of summer's arrival and it has now become a test of fate, luck, fortitude and God's providence. How could we have ever . . . imagined." She kissed Thomas's forehead and a tear fell, just when she believed she had not nearly enough moisture to cry.

Henry dug his fingers into his temples. "Water." He absorbed the misery around him, the woman folded in on herself groaning, the old man face up in the water staring blankly at the sky, the young woman trembling in her husband's lap. "It's everywhere and yet nothing we can drink. Such misery. God help us. The sea has *no* mercy."

Augusta glanced down at Thomas, fear strangling her throat. They wouldn't last much longer without water. And she wouldn't be able to swim if she was tossed in—not again. The waves swelled and fell, the earth continued to spin, and Augusta was of no concern to any of it.

29

EVERLY

Present day

The museum's morning hours were my favorite—a hushed quiet that seemed to absorb every sound like water, and allowed me to work with concentrated focus. I arranged photos of artifacts by category—personal effects; ship's contents; ship parts; gold and silver. The workroom was locked off from the rest of the museum but I heard guests coming and going. I listened to children bickering and parents calling out; to couples saying, "Look at this," or "Did you have any idea?"

That day in mid-June, lost in my work, I heard the click-snap of the door as someone entered. Expecting Oliver, I looked up.

"Maddox." I dropped the pen I held; it rolled across the floor toward a dusty corner.

In shorts and a T-shirt he seemed to have just stepped off his boat. "Sorry if I'm interrupting you."

"I was so deep in my work, I didn't hear you." I shifted the papers and tucked my hair behind my ears, feeling unsteady.

"Everly, I've been calling you." He took a tentative step or two into the room.

"I know. I've been buried in work." I spread my palms over the piles and pointed at the two other long tables covered in maps and photos and drawings.

"I have new photos for you." He picked up the fallen pen and set it on the table. "We brought in another haul two days ago, and I wanted you to see it."

"Show me what you've got." My steady voice hid my nervousness. This was the important moment—I had to maintain complete professional control or I would ruin a working relationship I would need in the long months ahead.

He looked at me as if assessing the damage caused by our last visit. "You doing okay?"

"I'm doing perfectly well. Thank you for asking. How are you?"

He took a step back and squinted through sunlight arrowing into the room. "Did someone come in and replace you with a robot?"

"I'm sorry. I'm just focused right now. I get that way . . ."

He set his palms on the table and bent over to look at my work. "Holy moly, you've done a lot."

"Holy moly?" I laughed.

He leafed through the papers and then pulled up a folding chair.

"Can I see the new artifacts?" I asked.

"Hmmm . . . yes." He didn't rise but instead shifted things around on the table, moving them to different spots.

"Hey." I placed my hand on top of his. "Don't move it around; it's in a certain order."

"Sorry." He held up his hands. "These articles." He picked up the copy of the *Charleston Courier*—AWFUL STEAMBOAT ACCIDENT. "The way the explosion was reported is fascinating." He took a magnifying glass from the table and read out loud. *"I'm induced to assume the painful duty of communicating to you the awful calamity which has befallen her."*

"Could you imagine?" I paused. "Close your eyes. You're in your in-town house in Savannah, or on your piazza, or in your garden, and you don't know anything terrible has happened because there is no phone or telegram. And you have a daughter or son or friend you thought had arrived safely in Baltimore days ago, and you read this?"

"My God." He shook his head, scratched his beard.

I pushed aside an article to show him another. "This poor city."

I glanced out the window at the city where I'd lived all my life—except during college. All the turning points and emotional ups and downs had taken place here. My heart beat with Savannah's.

"And during that time Savannah was looked down upon by Charleston." I paused and laughed. "Maybe it still is. Because Savannah was founded by England's debtors and Charleston by its highest-born." I held out my hands. "As my mom often says, you'd have to be dead inside not to love this place. She might be biased but still . . ."

Maddox said, "And now we can find anything we need with a click of a button on a computer or phone. No waiting a week for news."

"Not everything can be found in a computer. I haven't learned about anyone in the Longstreet family except for Charles and his father, Lamar, who both lived. Everyone else seems to have vanished that night."

"We've been lulled into thinking that we can find anything on the Internet, but it's not true. And half the time even the Internet tells only half the real story."

I turned away, as if he'd seen me Google his name.

"You can ask me about it anytime, Everly."

"About what?"

"Whatever questions you have about my past. No matter what, you need to know you can trust me."

"I do trust you. I just want to keep it professional, make sure we do an amazing job with this exhibit."

"I get it," he said, but I heard the sadness in his voice. Part of me wanted to explain to him that my reluctance to share about Mora had nothing to do with what had happened on the dive that had left his student dead.

Maddox walked back to the first table, reached into the bag he'd placed on the far chair and withdrew his laptop. He clicked open some photos. "These are new."

I moved my chair closer as he slid the computer in front of me. "You can go through them if you want."

"A lot of coins." I scrolled through the photos to see some repeats of what had already been found. "Why are some dark and some gold?"

"The gold stays bright under water, but the silver oxidizes, so the crusty ones are silver coins. I'm not sure why there's so much treasure yet but . . ."

"Because," I said, "when people traveled for the summer they took with them everything they might possibly need—money, silver, clothes, dishware—so they could replicate their lives in their second home. And they weren't exactly worried about packing light. They had enslaved people to do the work." I scrolled as Maddox watched over my shoulder.

"Why take so much silver and gold?" he asked.

"Who knows? It's part of my job to find out. Maybe someone had sold some land and was returning with their cache. Or someone was moving . . ."

"Fascinating." He reached over me. "That's a snuffbox and a jewelry case. That's a woman's ring with a black onyx stone, probably the most valuable thing its owner possessed."

"Except her life."

"Yes, except her life," Maddox confirmed.

I sat and clicked again on a photo. Maddox pointed. "This is what I came here to show you. We've found a cache of a family's silver that's engraved. I'd love to find out who it belonged to."

I leaned closer and enlarged the image—it was grainy but I recognized a soup spoon and a mustard spoon. The handles had two different monograms—BCM and LKM. "Do you have photos of the underside? On the underside of real silver there are hallmarks that should tell us where the piece was forged, the maker, the date, the silver composition. Families took it all very seriously."

"Yeah, I've never owned silver pitchers and silver coffeepots like these people did." He leaned back, spreading his arms across the chair back and laughing. "Not on my bucket list."

"Such possessions were definitely a sign of prestige. These"—I pointed at the monogrammed spoons—"must have belonged to families with the last name starting with M. Sometimes the family last name is in the middle and sometimes it's at the end."

He grabbed a folder titled "Manifest" and scanned it quickly as I watched him. "There's no one with a last name that begins with M."

"It's not a complete manifest. So, let's find out where this silver came from. "I have a friend," I said and stood. "Maureen Fordham at the museum."

"Of course you do." He grabbed his satchel and nodded toward the door. "Lead the way."

30

LILLY

Friday, June 15, 1838
Late afternoon

Lilly imagined endless land, somewhere far from her own water-soaked world. Back in Savannah, there had been so many times she'd wished she could run away. She'd kept her jewelry pouch on her wrist at all times in the hope that someday she'd be given a chance to escape and would have something to sell to pay for her passage. Adam believed she was attached to the gifts he gave her in a sentimental way. How little he knew her.

The fantasies had been, of course, folly—Adam's reach was long and powerful—but the dream had sustained her. During the cruelest moments she would picture the new place where she would live free of him, free of his ever-policed plantation and of his cruel hands. She and Priscilla would raise Madeline in a small cabin in the woods; in an oceanside shack; in a tent in the Midwest. The dreams assumed different shapes but the desire remained an unquenched fire.

If she'd ever run, the price for being discovered would have been harsh—anyone caught helping a slave escape could be sentenced to twenty years in prison. The slave would not be so lucky, returned to his master at best and at worst brought to the marshes and forced to dig his own grave, then ruthlessly hanged. Now with Adam gone there would be no need to run once they survived this burning hell. They could return to her beloved Savannah and start new lives. She would find a way to free Priscilla, to live a different kind of life. What that was she had no idea, but the thought was a balm.

Lilly closed her eyes and imagined a place so cold her fingers would turn blue if she stayed outside long enough. A place where icy water rushed and she could dip a cup into it and drink as long as she pleased.

The sea reached for the sun as it sank, leaving only a pale light that shimmered on the horizon. Lilly and her mates watched with dread. No help had arrived; the two men who'd run off from the beach hadn't returned and the four who remained were visible as prone figures far up on the hillock.

Mr. Couper sat up in the bottom of the boat. He'd taken a brief rest, and had demanded the other men also take naps before they attempted to row to shore. Now, in a deep voice he proclaimed, "It's time."

The men stirred and opened their eyes to the horror they had hoped to avoid—the flashing white foam of the breakers. "Here is what we shall do." Mr. Couper's voice was firm and calm. "We are twelve souls—six men, four women, and two children. Who can swim?"

All the men said they could, as did Mrs. Bird. Priscilla, Mrs. March, and Lilly turned their faces in shame. Why had Lilly never learned? Why had she been content to float in the river shallows and rely on others to keep her safe? This would be the death of her and her child, of her beloved Priscilla.

"Barney, you must not swim to shore without Mrs. Bird. Solomon, you must not swim to shore without Mrs. March and her child Theodore. Mr. Harris, you are to stay with Priscilla. Mr. Pooler, you and your son Francis will protect each other. I will help Mrs. Forsyth." He wiped his brow. "If we are toppled, you must kick forward until you find solid ground. The waves and surf are strong, the rip tide intense. If we are thrown to the other side of the breakers, you must dig your feet deeply into the sand or be drawn backward into the surf again. You walk with the forward wave and stand firm when it retreats." He rubbed his hands across his red face, cleared his eyes. "And do not grab the neck or waist of anyone who's trying to save you or you will both perish."

They all nodded; their lives were truly at stake. Lilly felt a dagger in the center of her abdomen, ice-cold fear that pierced her. "My child." Her voice released in a wail she didn't know she was capable of making.

Priscilla took Madeline from Lilly's arms and again wrapped Madeline against Lilly's chest with an intricate pattern of folds and knots. Lilly was filled with such regret and love. "This will hold, mistress. It can't move one inch. If you rise, so will she. And you *will* rise." Priscilla kissed the top of sleeping Madeline's head, and tears ran down her cheeks.

Without speaking, the men began to row. The slap of the oars against the waves, the deafening roar of the breakers, and a sea gull squawking a warning overhead might be the last sounds Lilly heard. The breakers were now in front of them, a six-foot-high wall that surged higher and fell. The men drew a collective breath and plowed straight into the newly rising breaker that rushed toward shore, the white foam above them, the blue water below and the land obliterated.

With a sickening rise, Lilly's stomach lifted with the climbing boat; Madeline let out a weak cry as if she knew what it meant. Then with a dip, the boat fell and fell, its nose pointed straight down. With a thump as jolting as if they'd hit rock, the boat miraculously landed upright, one oar flying off. Mrs. March screamed and then a hush fell as they realized they had survived the first wave.

A second billow surged high behind them. The passengers turned to watch as the white crest moved over their heads and the quarterboat was drawn back into the curve of the wave. For a moment it seemed they would be safely carried toward shore in its rounded arm.

Then the wave broke—the water folding in on itself and over the lifeboat. With a sickening lurch, they were all cast into the water as if an invisible hand scooped them up and spilled them out. Lilly closed her eyes as the shock of seawater folded over her and Madeline. With the roar of the water in her ears, her body tumbled at the complete mercy of the powerful waves. Her head slammed against something hard—the boat. She grasped at it but it was upside down, the hull smooth and slippery. Mr. Couper's words of instruction meant little against the pure power of the ocean. She would be able to gasp for a breath only if the wave allowed it, and pushed her to the surface.

Her breath held, she concentrated on finding sand beneath her feet. Using the force of her focus and the dwindling strength in her legs, she pressed her feet into the solid ground and attempted to stand. Her head and chest rose above the water and she gasped for air—one breath, two—and then she and Madeline were thrown again. Three times she was thrown down until her strength diminished, allowing the more powerful sea to win its game of cat and mouse.

With the next thrust, she was standing again and around her she spied the others also fighting for their lives. She stumbled and fell forward, the retreating suction stronger by far than the strength in her legs. She lifted herself to make sure Madeline's head was above water but was drawn down again, salt stinging her eyes. She held her breath, her feet searching once more for the earth, but this time she couldn't find it.

Her lungs burned with need, and her thoughts began to blur—she was unsure whether life meant surrendering to death or struggling again for the surface. She wrapped her arms around her child, knowing there was no way Madeline could have survived this repeated immersion—Lilly would die with her child. She could not—ever—live without her.

A sudden pain ripped through her scalp and an unknown force pulled her to the surface. Mr. Couper's face appeared and Lilly took in a long breath, coughing, sputtering.

"Stand now, Mrs. Forsyth. Stand."

His voice demanded complete obedience and she found the strength within her legs to do what he commanded.

"Do not move while this wave passes, and then we will walk forward. Do *not* fall; I cannot pick you up again." His arms shook around her—he, too, had reached his limit.

Lilly had little mind for anything but looking down at her child's face. Madeline was limp in the bundle of cloth that Priscilla had wound around her. And yet . . . yes, her eyes blinked and looked at Lilly, her mouth open to breathe in the sea mist around them. She coughed and then wailed, her tiny hands struggling against the cloth to reach for her mother.

"Madeline," Lilly cried out in relief and attempted to untie the knots, to release her child from the constricting bundle.

"Not yet, Mrs. Forsyth. Not yet." Mr. Couper clung to her arm with a strength that seemed impossible after what they'd endured. "Now walk."

Lilly took a step forward with the momentum of the wave coming behind them; she stumbled but he held her up. "Walk."

Six more steps and then the wave retreated in its evil attempt to take them both with it. But it wasn't evil, was it? No, it was being exactly what it was meant to be—a powerful wave.

She merely had to survive it.

"Stand firm. It will pass. Stand firm."

Lilly dug her feet into the shifting sand and gazed into Madeline's eyes. *I will hold on for you. I will hold on for you. I will hold on for you.*

And then the power of the retreating wave diminished and with the aid of Mr. Couper, Lilly took more steps to the shoreline. Two men from the first boat ran toward them and dragged Lilly and Mr. Couper to the beach. Together they collapsed on solid ground, Lilly on her back to protect Madeline. Above her, the sky was obscured by clouds thin and flat, wide and watchful, surrounding her like a dome.

"The others?" Lilly asked the man who stood over her.

"They are all here. All safe."

"All?"

"Yes," he said.

She turned to where Mr. Couper rested alongside her, his left side turned toward her. Such an absurd situation—lying next to a half-naked man while wearing her nightdress. His eyes were closed in exhaustion, his breath ragged.

Lilly's heart raced, bounding in a dangerous rhythm as she called out, "Priscilla."

"Over here!"

Lilly rolled onto all fours and spied Priscilla leaning on Mr. Harris; they dragged themselves to hillocks a few yards up the beach. Lilly crawled toward the shoal with Madeline strapped to her chest, where sea oats and grasses grew long and wild, swaying in the wind. She fell at Priscilla's feet.

"Madeline?" Priscilla asked, her voice breaking the name into two.

"You saved her life. You bound her to me and you saved her. I will forever be in your debt."

"Mistress, I did nothing but what I know to do. You saved yourself, and your blessed child. We live. And Mr. Harris saved me. He dragged me and would not let go." She shivered and pointed toward the sea, the white foam silver in the moonlight, the water darker than the sky. "Mr. Barney collapsed and didn't go save Mrs. Bird. Mr. Couper saved them right before he dragged you in. He is indeed a man of God."

There wasn't strength for more to be said, but the two women clung to each other, Madeline between them. It wasn't long before the men became busy sheltering the women and children from the wind by digging holes in the sand. Even Mr. Couper roused himself to cover them with sand as they waited for help to arrive.

The young boy, Theodore, had collapsed. "He is breathing," Solomon said to no one in particular, as if to convince the sky and sand that they had not claimed this one child.

The women huddled together, their wet bodies slick with water and sticky with salt and fear as the men gathered shells, the largest they could find, and began to dig a hole next to the hillock. Soon the dent of sand filled with brackish water and they used the shells as cups. They all greedily drank of it in turns. Lilly grasped the white shell as if it were a communion cup. She drank and gagged on its salty taste, but beneath the brine was the hint of fresh, cold water. "Drink," Barney said. "Help is coming."

Lilly forced the water down her throat with pure will. If she were to survive, she must drink. Soon, she faded off as images in the liminal space between rest and delirium floated through her mind—Adam coming after her as she hid in the bedroom closet; Mother dying on her sweat-stained bed. She dreamed that the dining room table was set with silver candlesticks and red napkins, water flowing from every pitcher and glass, water pouring from the chandelier—cold and wet as Lilly lifted her face to it and drank with the eagerness of a child.

When she awoke with a start, she lay very still. Sated with as much water as she could drink, Priscilla was curled into a comma, her back nestled against Lilly, Madeline at her breast. Lilly's back rounded into a curve of sand that Mr. Couper had carved out for her. A few yards away, like logs, the men were arranged back to back, keeping each other warm.

Night covered them. The sea roared and pounded as breakers continued their murderous thunder. The moon hung midway up the sky—Lilly guessed it was ten or a bit later. Almost twenty-four hours had passed since the ship had exploded and shattered their lives. Had anyone made it beyond the other eleven from her boat and the six from the other?

Her mind raced as she listed the others—Captain Dubois; her Longstreet family; the young girl Daphne giggling at dinner while she flirted with a man from Philadelphia; the preacher from Savannah and his wife. Most of all she thought of Augusta and her beloved Thomas . . .

Adam was gone, his body cast to a place where he could do no more harm. Maybe there was justice. Maybe there was a caring God who watched out for her.

An hour later, Lilly lifted her ear to hear a voice call out, "Hallooo." Lost in the disconnected thoughts of exhaustion, Lilly sat. Priscilla stirred, and Madeline let out a weak cry.

31

EVERLY

Present day

Maddox and I walked through Savannah and I talked about the things we passed as if I were giving a tour: those iron posts were imported from England; that statue memorializes John Wesley and that one Casimir Pulaski—the Polish maritime genius who came to Savannah's aid during the Revolutionary War and was killed in the Battle of Savannah *and* whom the ship was named after; that house is where the events of the bestselling book *Midnight in the Garden of Good and Evil* unfolded; that's the first home with electricity. The fire of 1820 had started on Ellis Square. I kept up a continuous stream of chatter.

Finally, we reached a garden wall fashioned of gray brick. "This is one of my favorite features of the exteriors in Savannah; the bricks are called Savannah Greys. They were made by enslaved people, fashioned from the river's gray-colored clay. So, I love the brick but not how it was made." I paused. "Savannah is complicated."

He grunted in agreement and I continued, "The mortar between the bricks is made of limestone. They would mix it at the river's edge. Now these bricks are worth up to four dollars each. They're two hundred years old."

Maddox shook his head. "And yet it's a disturbing and harrowing legacy."

"Well, if you believe the ghost tours, the ones Mom loathes, the spirits of the enslaved people who made them reside in these bricks."

"You and your stories."

Maddox carried a large leather satchel and finally I stopped and pointed at it. "Did you bring the silver and watch?"

"I did." He patted the bag. "I brought the teapot, the pocket watch and the silver. Anything else, ma'am?"

"Stop." My smile wavered. "I just know Maureen might be able to help, and real things are better than photos."

We continued, only a block from the museum when a man in khaki shorts and an orange T-shirt approached. Lumbering beside him was his giant tortoise, four feet long and two feet wide, his reptilian feet clicking along the sidewalk.

"What the hell?" Maddox stopped midstep and stared.

"Hello, Frank." I greeted the pet owner, who also happened to be my neighbor, and then bent over to greet the tortoise. "Hello, Benjamin, I hope you're having a lovely walk today."

"Hello, Ms. Winthrop. Lovely to see you." Frank lifted his baseball cap and then replaced it without another word.

Maddox clasped his hands behind his back and leaned down to the tortoise. "This is your . . . pet?"

"Indeed it is." Frank narrowed his eyes at Maddox and continued walking as if he were a nuisance. "Good day."

Maddox erupted in laughter. "This city. It's quite something, ain't it?"

We paused in the center of the square, where oak trees spread their shade. The summer heat pressed on us like a wool blanket. "How the hell did they survive without air-conditioning?" Maddox asked as he wiped his forehead with the back of his hand.

"It's almost impossible to imagine, isn't it? That's why the passengers boarded that steamship—to escape the summer heat. And mosquitoes. And illness."

"All good reasons."

I pointed at the Telfair Square sign. "This square is named after the Telfair family, who came from Scotland. Last night I read that two of the sisters were meant to be on the *Pulaski*, but Mary, the oldest, had a terrible foreboding and they rebooked on another ship."

"Wow!"

"In a letter to her best friend she vowed her premonition was proof of some connection between the visible and invisible worlds."

"You believe that?"

"On my best days." I took a few steps away and then asked, "Do you?"

"On all my days."

I began to walk faster. "Ah, to be so sure."

Maddox caught up with me. "I don't know what the connection is, or how it works, or what it means—I'm just absolutely sure there is one. You can't dive to the bottom of the sea or look at the stars or hear a story like you just told me and *not* believe there is some hidden and unseen force we don't understand."

"It damn sure wasn't working for the families who ended up at the bottom of the sea that fateful night," I mused.

"Or maybe it was and we just don't know . . . why."

"True . . . But those poor people. The poor Longstreets. You know, it's astounding to think that anyone from that family could have walked this way also, paused right here. It always astonishes me to think about that."

"This city," he said, "has suffered so much, hasn't it?"

"Yep. Yet those who first arrived here considered it a chance to build a new life in a new land. Come on." I pointed. "We have a few more blocks to go."

The Owens-Thomas House and Slave Quarters Museum sat on the corner of Abercorn and East State Street, a lion-colored plaster structure with curved stairs leading to an arched doorway. The iron fence surrounding it was only as tall as a five-year-old child. "Here," I said. "Maureen works here."

Maddox craned his neck and looked up. "It's imposing, isn't it?"

"Two hundred years old. The Telfair Museum foundation saved it, restored it and conserved the most fragile pieces in the house. It has a very complicated history."

We entered the back way through gardens where livestock were once kept, past the slave quarters and horse stable now converted to a welcome center. As we entered the house, I had to prod Maddox along when he stopped to read the signs describing the original cistern, sinks and woodwork. "I'm coming back here without you." He poked at me. "Can't even stop to smell the dust."

"I've been here lots of times before. It's fascinating but . . . the silver—let's go see if we can find some clues. The man who originally built this house for his family was also a shipping merchant, just like Lamar Longstreet."

"It's all tangled together, isn't it?" He followed me up the stairs and across an arched bridge in the middle of the upstairs hallway, which connected the two wings of the house. "A bridge?"

"Yep. In the house."

After a few more steps over red carpet we reached an enclosed area. "This used to be an open piazza. They closed it in for offices."

He walked quietly, taking smaller steps than usual I noticed, as we entered the office where Maureen Fordham sat at a desk in the back-right corner.

She stood to greet us: a tall woman with bright white hair. The very idea of silver found at the bottom of the sea lit a fire in her eyes. She was ready for us with printed photos I'd e-mailed to her only an hour before. Books about silver identification were spread out on her desk.

Maureen motioned for us to sit across from her. After greetings and introductions, Maddox reached into his bag and removed the teapot, the pocket watch and four spoons with initials carved on the handles. Maureen gazed at the artifacts with something near awe. "These have been on the bottom of the ocean for a hundred and eighty years?"

"Yes. We've cleaned them, of course. And I need to take them right back for conservation. But Everly here thought you might be able to help us figure out who they belonged to, or what era they were from."

Maureen gazed closer at the cracked glass of the pocket watch. "It's stopped at the time the ship exploded, isn't it?"

"Yes," I told her.

"I wonder," she said almost under her breath, "if the owner . . . survived."

I shrugged and leaned forward, feeling the desk's edge dig into my ribs. "That's part of what I want to find out."

Maddox slid a spoon across the desk and Maureen lifted it. "This is a mustard spoon."

"They needed a spoon for just mustard?" He laughed into his question and Maureen and I gave each other a knowing look. It was absurd—a mustard spoon being packed and carried to a summer home. Southerners and their manners.

Maureen flipped it over and ran her fingers along the markings—four indentations of different designs, including a lion's body that appeared to be dancing on one leg.

"These are called hallmarks," she said. "I already looked them up from the photos you sent and these are pseudo-hallmarks, which means the pieces aren't from England. This silver was cast in Rhode Island. Not that the silver is pseudo, but that the hallmarks are made to look as if it was from England unless you know your markings. It's like an impostor but only for those who know. I see you have two different initials—BCM and LKM—my one guess is that the monograms are for sisters. Was this all found together?"

Maddox nodded. "When artifacts are found in one big pile, it usually indicates they were packed together in a trunk that dissolved. But there isn't a last name on the manifest that begins with M, and those that begin with K or C don't have those first names; it seems obvious that M is the last name as the artifacts were found together. But in ship salvaging, nothing is obvious honestly."

Maureen smiled. "What a lovely mystery. Maybe it's a married woman and this is her maiden name. There are loads of possibilities. Maybe someone was transporting it for a family up north."

Maddox then placed the teapot on the desk. "And this is a teapot we found with the same crest as the pocket watch. It isn't imperative but I know Everly would like to attach some artifacts to passengers for the exhibit."

"Have you seen it before?" I asked Maureen.

She looked at it with a squint. "I have. But I don't recall where or what it means. Maybe it was a blank crest that families could use to put their own design inside. Common, really."

Maureen stood up and ran her hand across books on her shelf while she spoke. Her finger paused and she pulled down a thick volume. "You can take this if you'd like and bring it back when you're finished. It has the names and hallmarks of various makers, along with family crests of the seventeenth century. That winged pattern could also indicate a family line. Crests were the way families set themselves apart. They would hire designers and carvers and place it on everything they owned. The practice spread from family to family. This winged design doesn't have a letter, so it's difficult to know. Are you trying to track down all the families?"

"That would take a lifetime," I said with a wry grin. "So, I am focusing on one family—the man who invested in the ship and took most of his family with him. Twelve in all, including spouses and a nursemaid."

"Whoa." Maureen settled back into her seat. "Do you think these belong to that family?"

"No. Probably not. But I wanted to find out what the engravings might mean. And I knew you would know."

"What family?" she asked.

"Longstreet. I'm trying to find some descendants to interview."

She nodded quietly and then tucked a stray hair into her bun. "Remember," she said, "sometimes people don't like to talk about the past. Sometimes people don't like to be reminded of certain unsavory parts of their history."

"What do you mean?" Maddox placed his hands on the desk. "Savannah is such a beautiful place and . . ."

"Take this house, for example." Maureen said. "We can't talk about the families who owned it and their lavish way of life, which some people still find romantic and appealing, without also mentioning the practice of slavery that made it possible. But you need to realize as you poke around in these family's ancestors that most have chosen to put it aside—they don't want to talk about it or admit their ancestors' part in it."

"I see." Maddox nodded.

"Thank you so much for helping us." I tucked the book into my backpack and stood to hug her good-bye.

"I hope you find what you're looking for, Everly. I really do."

What I was looking for—I wasn't even sure myself, but I damn sure wasn't going to stop trying.

After our good-byes and expressions of gratitude, Maddox and I made our way outside to the square. He stopped me in the garden near a pomegranate tree in full bloom.

"Everly, you know we often discover loads of treasure, but only rarely do we discover who it belonged to."

"I get it. But maybe if I follow one crumb it leads to another."

"You don't have to convince me."

As I took in a deep breath the aroma of sweet roses made me dizzy. "Maddox, thank you so much for coming with me."

"You're welcome, Everly." He nodded. "I'll keep digging, too. We'll find some connections."

"Now I need to go get some work done. I'm sure I'll see you soon." I sidled past him and bumped into another patron. "I'll be in touch," I called over my shoulder.

I rushed past the gurgling fountain, around the rosebushes and through the exit gates onto Abercorn Street. Maddox didn't come after me and for that I was grateful. As an ambulance roared by and a man with a cowboy hat walked past me with his tiny white dog on a leash, I stood on the corner and took in a few deep, damp breaths.

I damn well knew how difficult it was to find someone who didn't want to be found: the dead-eyed man who killed Mora, a family and a woman who disappeared one hundred and eighty years ago and my former carefree self who couldn't wait to find out what would happen next.

But I wasn't going to stop looking.

I glanced back to see if Maddox had emerged. He hadn't. He knew his way back to the museum, so I began to walk and was half a mile before I realized where I was headed.

Bonaventure Cemetery, three miles away on the Wilmington River. I grabbed my cell from my back pocket and called a cab.

The family plot had been a morbid concept to me as a child. I'd asked Mom, "Why would you choose a burial place when you're still alive? It's horrible."

"Because," Mom had explained in a sad voice, "our bodies will have to go somewhere someday and we want to stay together, don't we?"

As a child, fear had rushed into me, forcing a quick headache like one caused by drinking a milkshake too fast. How old had I been when that conversation had taken place? I couldn't remember; I could only recall that it was the first time I had understood that everything—my life, my family, the spring evenings with their scent of jasmine and the grand feeling that life was an adventure—would not last. Nothing did. I had wandered through the landscape and read the tombstones with wonder and run my fingers over the carved headstones: the lambs, angels and willows. I'd looked with new eyes at the cracked slate, the newer granite stones, the tall statues and the shorter ones at the dirt roads that led to a fence along the river.

Now Bonaventure was the place of Mora's eternal rest. God, how I hated that phrase. Eternal rest? Mora would laugh at the idea of rest.

I reached the cemetery and jogged through intricate iron gates, my backpack seeming heavier with each step. The gates had been left open, and I went down dusty roads to the wet grass that produced a squishing noise of soaked earth beneath my sandals. The wind communicated with the oaks and palmettos before it touched me, and I lifted my face to its cool breath with the hint of a coming storm.

As I neared the river, I slowed down to read the engravings of the gravestones, something I did every time I came to visit Mora, Papa, Grandmother, and Father. It had become a routine, a way of remembering that death was part of everyone's experience. Other parents and siblings and lovers and friends were buried here also. Loved ones had been left behind to choose gravestones and stand in front of the gaping earth as their lost beloved was lowered into the ground. I wasn't the only one.

I was a few yards from the family plot, and the eerie headstone that already stood next to Father's grave; Mom's name was already engraved on it, her birth date and a space for the final date to be carved into the marble. I shivered. I should have eaten something; I felt dizzy and sick.

Rain began to fall and I wound my way around the other graves to Mora's. When I reached her, I sat on the ground, not caring a lick for the wet that soaked through my white linen pants.

"I miss you," I said to the white marble with its carving of a wild rose—Mora's favorite. "Do you believe they found the *Pulaski*? You'd love this treasure hunt."

As I brushed a leaf from the base of the marble, a flash of bright red caught my gaze. Behind Mora's tombstone lay a bouquet of dahlias. These were the flowers I'd always assumed came from Oliver or Laurel. But both had said they never left them.

I picked up the flowers and turned them over for a hint of the giver. Petals fell off in the rain, a scattering of red on the wet ground. I replaced the bouquet and shielded it with a broad leaf. The rain pelted harder now, the soft earth freckled with raindrops.

I wasn't so sure what I believed about the afterlife, but I did know that we were all connected—my father and Papa, Mora and her family, the passengers on the *Pulaski* and the rain and the shattered ship at the bottom of the sea; the wild oak trees and the rushing river—we were all part of something bigger that I couldn't understand.

One empty boiler. One drunk man in an out-of-control car. These were the things that altered the world.

I leaned against a magnolia tree at the edge of the plot. The fluttering remembrance of a paper I had once nailed to its bark rushed back to me: a flyer I'd made and posted all over Savannah and then brought here to the graveyard. In all capital letters I'd posted—*Anyone who was at the accident site on St. Patrick's Day, please contact Everly Winthrop.* I'd pasted a colored photo from the newspaper that showed the carnage at the square. I'd put my number in little tear-off tags. Hundreds of these had been posted and hundreds of phone calls had poured in without a single bit of information that led the police to find the dead-eyed man.

The police repeated the only information they had over and over to me—he'd stolen the car that morning from a bar on Bull Street, driven it erratically for a mile, hitting both a street sign and a fire hydrant before bursting through a side-street barricade ahead of the parade's lead car. He'd pushed the vehicle to its limit on the empty streets. Once he'd driven into the crowd, he'd jumped out and run. He'd moved too fast; run so quickly that no one had time to stop him. No one could identify him. He was gone.

Some witnesses said he had blond hair. Others dark. Some said he was wearing all black and others said he wore a red T-shirt. So many false leads had come through that the police began to ignore my calls. "We've got this," they would say. "You're only making our job harder," they would say. But they didn't have it, and I didn't give a damn if I made their job harder.

I stood and exhaled with frustration and lifted my face to the rain, letting it cool me. My cotton shirt stuck to my skin and I wiped the hair from my face. I wandered on the soft earth past Papa's grave and touched its edges, and then to Father's before turning to leave.

An older woman stood twenty feet away, her hand on top of a fresh grave and tears pouring as the rain fell. Over her curled, gray hairdo she wore a plastic cap with a string tied tightly beneath her chin. I cut a wide swath to prevent disturbing her when something made me stop; my breath caught and my eyes flickered across Mora's grandfather's grave. How had I never seen it before? Never noticed?

Perceval Washington Powell—A Life of Love and Service: Mora's grandfather. The dates of his life and death, indelible, surrounded by a crest of wings taking flight. The exact crest on the pocket watch and on the teapot. The one I'd been searching for—here, at Mora's family's plot.

Here.

I knew where to go next.

32

LILLY

Friday, June 15, 1838
Late evening

Despite the dark, the sand felt warm where Lilly, Priscilla, and Madeline had lain curled like nesting baby birds. The earth held the summer sun's heat. Brought to awareness by voices calling in the night, they now sat.

"Hello?"

"Help has arrived."

"Where are you?"

The ragged survivors came to their feet, waving their arms and scraps of clothing as bulky human forms took shape beyond the crest of a sand dune. The next moments were a blur to Lilly. Their rescuers brought cornbread, fried bacon, coffee and jugs of cold water; there were warm blankets and soft clothes. Someone counted out loud—eighteen survivors huddled in the sand. They grasped at the food and drink. The women took shelter behind blankets held high, slipped out of their tattered garments and donned dresses that were either too big or too small.

"Slowly," said a deep voice in the dark. "Don't drink too fast. You don't want to get sick."

"Where are we?" Mr. Couper's disembodied voice asked over the wind and waves. He sounded strong again.

"I'm Mr. Redd. You are in Onslow County, North Carolina, on a tiny spit of land we call the Bermudas." A disembodied lantern light swung across the ground and up to sunburned, distorted faces. "When you are revived, we will take you in rowboats across Stump Sound—safe as can be—and there you will find warm beds and welcome hospitality. The town is preparing for you even now."

"The other passengers?" The question came from Lilly's lips between tiny bites of cornbread and sips of water. She could hardly stop herself from stuffing herself to the point of nausea.

"We know of no other survivors." Another voice came from a man whose long, stern face was lit with the light and shadows of the lantern he held. "And there is a great squall coming our way. We pray, the whole town prays, for more who might come to shore."

Lilly was adept at reading tones of voice—over the past two years it had meant her survival. And this man, his eyes flickering in the fire, held no hope for the remaining passengers.

They ate and drank in silence for a few moments, the moon hidden like a discarded flower in the milky sky. Lilly thought of the gardenia bush behind the kitchen house. It was a part of home she'd loved before Adam tainted it. And now he was gone: the thought curled around her warm and rich as the coffee in her belly.

For the first time in their lives Lilly threw her arms around her nursemaid. Here taboos fell away. A relief as immense as the waves that had flipped their boat overcame Lilly.

Half an hour later, they stumbled toward rowboats that waited for them. Priscilla and Lilly held hands as Madeline slept in a warm, dry blanket like the ones Priscilla had also wrapped around Lilly and herself. They followed the silent group, their feet sinking into the sand. Lilly dug her toes down to feel the solid earth, to convince herself that they were safe. She would never get on a steamboat again.

The beach spread before them, bleached as white as the linen sheets Priscilla hung from the laundry line. Grasses and hillock swelled and fell in shadow. The Sound, a sliver of sea, separated them from town— they would need to cross water again.

Lilly knew that each survivor was alone with thoughts of who and what was lost. It was too much to calculate, too great a devastation to allow for speech.

"You, Negro," a deep voice called out. "Come this way."

They were separating them, the Negroes from the whites: Solomon, his burns even now shimmering in the dark; and Priscilla, her slave yes, but now also her irreplaceable companion. They had survived the darkest day and night; they had allowed Adam to perish and they had saved Madeline.

"No!" Lilly's voice rang strong, echoing across the spit of sand and the silver ribbon of water they must cross to Onslow County. "She stays with me. She goes where I go."

33

EVERLY

Present day

Oliver and I stood on the front steps of the Dunmore house and rang that same bell. Once again, we were arriving unannounced. I'd called Oliver from Bonaventure and he'd met me at the cemetery gates in his car. On the way over, I'd used a towel from Oliver's sports bag to dry off; now my hair and clothes were merely damp.

"Now there's no need to rifle through that book Maureen gave me—I found the crest at Bonaventure, not in a book."

"The book?"

"Maureen gave me a book." I patted my backpack. "Full of family crests to see if I could find the wings. But what we want to know is in there." I pointed at the house. "With those women."

"I don't think they'll tell us what we want to know. It's just a winged design. Laurel doesn't seem to care about much that goes on beyond these walls."

"Today I'll make her care."

The door opened and there we were again face to face with Laurel's scowl. "For God's sake, what do you want now?"

Oliver armed his face with a smile, ammunition against her attack. "We want to talk to you about some really interesting things we've discovered while working on the *Pulaski* exhibit. We thought you might want to know them, too."

We stepped into the foyer. The ornate chandelier sparkled. The burlwood entry table was covered completely in silver-framed family photos. Laurel blocked the view farther into the house. "I don't want to see anything unless it's an arrest report for the maniac who killed my daughter."

I set my hands on my hips, drew back my shoulders. "I want the same, Laurel. I do. But please give us five minutes. We want to show you something."

"What happened to you? You look like you were attacked in a mud pit."

"I was at Bonaventure, and it started . . ."

I was interrupted by Josephine's cane tapping down the halls. She wore the exact same caftan as the last time, and her hair in the same knot on her head. "Hello, Everly and Oliver. How lovely to see you twice in the same week. How may we help you?" She motioned for us to enter the drawing room where we'd sat before. This time, the curtains were already open, sunlight flooding the dusty room.

"Look at you," Josephine said. "You're wet and disheveled. Are you quite all right?"

"I am. Josephine, I was at Bonaventure and I saw something . . ."

"For God's sake Almighty," Laurel exclaimed and stalked off, leaving the three of us.

"What did you see?" Josephine's voice sounded less warm and she knitted her hands together in front of her waist as if for protection.

"This." I pulled out my phone and showed her a photo of the wing crest on her husband's grave.

"Oh, my dearest Perceval." Josephine pressed her fingers into the corners of her eyes. "And?"

"This same design is on a pocket watch and a teapot found among the wreckage. This exact same design. I believe your husband's family was on the *Pulaski*."

"Does that matter?"

"Yes, it does. I asked you about it, about the painting, and you said it had nothing to do with you. Or with Mora."

"Why do you care so much about who was on that ship?" Josephine stepped forward and the sunlight fell on her face. I saw the rheumy redness around her eyes, the thin skin: her fragility.

I made my voice softer now. "Because it matters. If your family was on that ship, it's part of your story."

Josephine sat down and we two took seats as well. "I never understood your fascination with the past. You and Mora both. You, too, Oliver. You set up these exhibits and tell stories about the despicable things people did to survive, and you think you're telling the truth. But you don't know the half of it. And none of it bears looking at. The past can't be changed, and it's better not to know."

The fragile Windsor chair creaked beneath Oliver's weight as he bent forward and took her hands in his. "We can't change the past, but it has the power to shape who we are today. We are who we are because of the past, not in spite of it. How can we understand ourselves unless we understand where we came from? And now the wreckage of the *Pulaski* has been discovered. Everly and I believe the ship's artifacts deserve to be featured in a well-curated exhibit. That exhibit can come to life with one family. I loved your granddaughter with all my heart. I want to know if she was descended from people on that ship."

Josephine's tight lips told me she was clearly unconvinced. "If you really loved Mora, you'd leave this alone. Curate your exhibit if you must, but don't drag my family into it, putting my husband's ancestors on display for all of Savannah to gawk at and titter over."

"We won't be putting anyone on display," I protested. "We'll be presenting only verifiable facts with respect and without judgment. I believe Mora would want this."

"You have no idea what Mora would want." Josephine stood up. "You were always so impertinent. Always getting Mora into trouble." She turned to Oliver. "And you. I knew it was only a matter of time before you took her back to where you came from, to California, away from all she loved here."

Oliver and I sat stunned by Josephine's accusation. Had she always believed this, or was her grief getting the upper hand? Suddenly I thought I knew.

"Josephine, your husband's mother was a Longstreet, wasn't she? And she was descended from Charles Longstreet, the Red Devil. Somehow you know that, and you don't want anyone else to know."

"I know no such thing."

"Do you have family papers?" I asked, but she turned her head away and refused to answer. I made my final argument. "Josephine, my intention isn't to sully the Longstreet family name. I want to highlight an illustrious family of Savannah that was instrumental in the growth of its businesses and institutions. I especially want to give voice to the women of the family, because throughout history women have been denied a part in the historical record. On the ship's manifest they're listed as wives, sisters and servants; they're identified by their role with no indication of their individual identities. I want to find out who the Longstreet women were and give them the recognition they deserve. Don't you want that, too?"

Josephine closed her eyes. "I'm tired. I'd like you both to leave and not return."

I had to try once more. I felt so close to understanding something that whispered from far off. "Please just tell me—do you have any family papers? Letters? Journals?"

Josephine's eyes flew open as if I had poked her. "No, it's Perceval's sister who was obsessed with such things. The minute he died, I gave it all to her and got rid of that god-awful painting."

Her admission kindled my determination. "You know, you can't rewrite history by ignoring it."

"Sure you can. People do it all the time."

Oliver stood and took my hand as if to steady me; his calm seeped into my skin. I took a deep breath and squeezed his fingers in gratitude. "Josephine," he said, "would you mind telling me Perceval's sister's name and where she lives?"

"Ingrid Morgan. She passed two years ago. Her house on Bull Street was handed down to her ungrateful daughter, Francine, who sold it last month to some family from Pittsburgh. They're renovating it now. They want it to look like it did in 1840 when it was first built. Fools spending money they don't know what to do with. Why anyone glamorizes the past is beyond me."

Oliver opened his mouth as if to offer a further defense, but instead he tugged on my hand and we exited with thank-yous and good-byes that weren't returned.

Outside, Oliver faced me, still holding my hand, keeping me steady as I shook as surely as if a wind had blown us out the front door of the Dunmore house.

"Mora's ancestors were on that ship," he reiterated.

I felt the pulse in my neck pound as the puzzle began to come together. "If there are family papers, we need to find them. They might mention Augusta, or even Lilly. Or something about the other family members."

"Long shot."

"Mora is helping us, can't you see?"

"Everly." He released my hand and I felt a cold chill pass through me. I hadn't realized he'd been keeping me warm.

"You think I'm crazy, I know." I took a step back, stumbled on a broken branch in the road and righted myself. Wind blowing through the palmettos made the leaves click with secret messages. The smiles of a young couple wandering past suggested they thought we were having a lover's spat and they understood.

Oliver drew closer, lowered his voice. "I don't think you're crazy. I just want you to be careful with your heart. It's tender, and this isn't about Mora. This is about the *Pulaski*." He trailed off and dropped his gaze to the ground where the pink petals of a wild rosebush had fallen during the rain. He squashed a few beneath his shoe.

"You think I'm making it too personal?" I took a step back, my chin lifted in some misplaced righteous anger. "Isn't that what you've wanted? To make it personal? To get the story so everyone could ooohhh and aaahhh about the treasure from the bottom of the sea? Oliver, if no one in that family had survived, Mora would not have been born."

He lifted his gaze to the house. "There you were calling all around the city for Longstreet family papers . . . and part of the answer lay right here with Mora's family . . ." he said.

"It's often that way—we don't see what's right in front of us."

He stared at me for a minute and then seemed to swallow the words he really wanted to say and instead said, "So let's go to the house on Bull Street."

34

AUGUSTA

Saturday, June 16, 1838

Sometime during the third night, Augusta had taken Thomas and moved near Mauma, a slave woman whose master and mistress had perished. Mauma was shorter than any woman Augusta had ever known and she'd seen her often in the market, laughing and conversing with everyone and anyone who crossed her path. Her accent had a singsong quality that Augusta hadn't heard before or since; the straw basket had swung from her arm, roped with muscle. Now, just like the rest of the shipwrecked, she appeared exhausted in body, her forehead dripping sweat over her hooded eyes as she rocked back and forth. Her hair damp and clinging to her neck. Did she know she was singing?

Augusta crawled near Mauma, set her back against the woman and took her hand. Mauma squeezed Augusta's hand in return and her singing paused for a moment. "The waters took my baby," she said softly as a breeze.

"Today?" Augusta asked, misery tempering her voice.

"Not today. Years ago. She walked right into the Savannah River, and it wasn't on no accident. And I wonder now if she's here, wandering these waters with us."

"Oh, Mauma. I don't . . . know. I am so terribly sorry."

Mauma offered a sound between a grunt and a sigh and again began her song, as if singing to that daughter who walked into the waters, the daughter to whom she probably sang this song all her early years. Such devastation humanity bore. Augusta didn't know, wasn't sure at all, that if she survived this she would survive feeling the anguish that would be part of her life, that would reach into her soul over and over. And then again and again.

Mauma continued to chant and sing. The language wasn't Augusta's but the pain expressed was everyone's. Augusta rocked back and forth to the rhythm.

Henry was hard at work with several other men to make the yawl seaworthy—they would die if someone didn't go find help. No one had come looking for them—two days without salvation in sight.

Augusta's battered mind wandered to a woman named Fannie Kemble, whom she had met a few years before, a woman married to a friend of her father's. She'd come to the Longstreet house in Savannah for a visit. Over the tea table, her eyes had flamed with righteous anger that Augusta hadn't understood. Didn't this woman from England with the beautiful lyrical accent have everything any woman could want? A handsome husband. A downtown house and a plantation on the Altamaha River that provoked jealousy in others. Yet she had burned with a critical assessment of the South: "Your devotion to conformity is like nothing I've ever seen. Despite being the most politically free people in the world, you are the least socially free I've ever encountered."

Augusta had both bristled and been enchanted by this woman who had traveled by ship and train and buggy to be with the man she loved.

Of the slaves, Fannie had said they were in perpetual degradation. "All this 'massa' and 'missus' is quite disturbing."

Now floating in the godforsaken sea, her back against Mauma's, Augusta saw her life through a lens that had been clouded with creature comforts and willful blindness. Only despair could allow her to hear what Fannie had said—owning another human being was inhumane.

A cry interrupted the chanting and Augusta looked up to see what the men were hollering about—white sails on the horizon.

"A ship!" Lamar cried out. "There."

Thomas lolled against Augusta's chest. "Thomas, darling. We are saved," she murmured into his ear. He stirred but did not open his eyes. Soon they would be in warm homes, drinking cold water, their feet out of the salt water and their bodies out of the sun. Their cramped stomachs would be filled with food; their parched tongues quenched by water.

Voices that had been silent now ceaselessly and desperately called out to the white sails. The men stood and waved white shirts over their heads; the women wailed. But the sounds were swallowed by the sea. The sails moved away, incrementally, taking hope with them.

What now? If there was to be no salvation by another, were they to wither under the sun? Die of thirst? Augusta believed this the cruelest fate she could imagine. She was briefly envious of those who had died quickly, sucking sea into their lungs and drifting to the bottom. At least they were at peace.

A desperate silence fell over the deck. If that ship hadn't been looking for them, was anyone at all? Had the outside world given up on them? Were they to die this way without even a soul searching for them? Were they already being mourned?

The hours passed. Twice Henry stopped by to check on Augusta, smoothing the hair from her cheek, murmuring reassurance. His touch was as tender as she'd imagined and yet there was nothing for them now.

"Did you see any of Melody's children when you were floating?" she asked him when he sat beside her for a moment.

He touched Thomas's cheek. "I didn't. The last I saw any of you until the moment I arrived here was when you climbed onto the yawl that took on water and tipped you into the sea. I thought all of you were gone. I grieved for you. I chastised myself for waiting to tell you how I felt, for trying my own patience by coming near to you without declaring myself. Of what use was that to me? What did propriety matter? It seemed all nonsense as I floated on the waves and imagined you gone."

"Henry . . ."

He touched her cheek and she leaned into his hand, and then shivered with the memory. "I did see Charles for a moment but then he was gone again," she said. "The waves—they obliterate everything. And Melody . . ." Augusta paused at the horror. "Was gone. I saw her floating facedown, her gown around her like a ghost . . . and then sinking. And Eliza—I tried to save her, but it would have meant letting go of Thomas. I prayed to God. I chose, but not on purpose. I realized it afterward: I chose Thomas, God save my soul."

"You did the best you could. You cannot save everyone. You could barely save the two of you. Do not chide yourself, Augusta. This is a watery hell and we must cling to hope."

Augusta nodded and touched Henry's bruised forearm. "We can try."

The day slipped by in unremitting thirst and half consciousness as she dozed, then was jolted back to awareness. Once when she was almost asleep—blessed absence from the horrors—she was awakened by a man hollering.

"Look there." Wearing a torn evening shirt and pants, a scrap of sail tied around his head to protect it from the sun, Mr. Henderson from Charleston stumbled toward a bit of flotsam that floated near the deck. Augusta focused until she could make out what it was—a wicker basket riding the waves as pleasurably as a child in a lake. Several others rushed to help drag the basket to the deck. Mr. Henderson raised the lid so slowly that Augusta almost screamed at him to hurry.

He lifted the contents one by one and identified them as if they were passengers he'd saved.

"Two bottles of wine. Two vials—one of peppermint and one of laudanum for pain."

"Oh, mercy," another man cried out. Augusta recognized him—Pastor Woart from Savannah. His wife, still dressed in an evening gown, lay next to him, blinking at the wide blue sky without a sound. "Put our trust in the Almighty to do what is best for us."

"Best for us?" a man screamed from the edge of the timber. An engineer, his watch cap still on his head, his face blistered with boils from the steam that had exploded from the engine. "Put our trust in the Almighty for what is best for us?" He approached the pastor with fire in his eyes, anger burning red as his face.

"Yes," Pastor Woart said in the assurance Augusta could not understand. The simple answer sent the engineer to his knees and he began to weep, holding his hands over the injuries to protect them from the glaring sun.

Augusta felt that the air around her was like mud; she moved so slowly, fading and then becoming bright again. Behind the basket another piece of large, splintered wood floated into view, and she wondered if she was dreaming, events not so much happening one after the other as overlapping in time.

On this wreckage, two men sat waving their arms like flags. The flotage listed and a hoarse voice called out, "We've been rowing all day and night. We won't hold together much longer. Please say you have room for us."

"Swim to us. We'll save you," Lamar shouted.

One man jumped into the sea, swimming with the strong strokes of one trying to save his own life. A rope was thrown, Augusta couldn't see by whom, and the man was dragged onto the wreckage.

"Your name?" Lamar asked.

"Mr. Robert Worthington."

"Mrs. Worthington!" Lamar shouted with a strength Augusta didn't believe he still possessed. "Your husband is saved."

The man, muscled and broad, had so little energy that he crawled across the watery deck until he fell into his wife's lap and together they wept.

Lamar tossed the rope to the man who remained on the sinking flotage and pulled him to the edge of the decking. Augusta had never seen him before, but his ripped and burned uniform indicated he was a sailor from the ship. She could not move her gaze from his pink face and swollen eyes. His hands bled and his bare feet were raw. A gash about six inches long was open on his arm, exposing the underbelly of the muscle. She turned away.

Lamar pointed toward the men who were attempting to repair the wrecked yawl and explained, "Over there is a leaking boat. We are attempting to fix it and go row for help."

The sailor's accent told of his Danish roots as he took a few shaky steps toward it. "I can help."

How could she help? Augusta wondered, looking at her own clothing. Could she rip off any more to stuff into the holes of the yawl? No, none that wouldn't sacrifice the covering for poor Thomas. Salvation, she thought slowly, becoming more muddled by the moment, wouldn't come with a parting of the clouds and a great trumpet call, but from the flotsam that floated all around them, and from the men and women who worked for their survival.

By evening, the sun had blistered all their exposed skin. Their gazes weren't so much on each other as on the waves; each crest and fall brought new hope of more survivors, loved ones or protection.

And still all along, Mauma sang, her chants providing the only solace. Lamar, now shed of all but his undergarments, helped string cables and ropes to hold the yawl together; he found a tablecloth to lift as a sail.

Augusta rocked the nearly unconscious Thomas and looked to her brother. "I have lost hope for the rest of the family. It is only you, Thomas and me, the last of us. Oh, God, Lamar. Have you thought of the fact that the very boat you are trying to mend is the boat that tossed us into the waves—the boat that could not hold your family? It is the same one . . ."

Lamar closed his eyes and bent at the waist as if he might be sick and then stood with fierce determination and gritted teeth, his lips blistered and raw. "I had not thought of that. My God, sister. My God, what horrors. How do we survive this?"

"We will." Augusta took Lamar's hand and placed it on Thomas's cheek. "For your son."

As that second day dragged toward night, some sank into unconsciousness. Talk focused on finishing repairs to the yawl so it could hold a few men who would row to shore and seek help. The vessel, some argued, wouldn't hold. Others lamented that it would flip in the breakers off North Carolina's notorious shoals—only the strongest rowers and swimmers should go.

Lamar refused to leave his family, believing they would die without him, as the talk grew more adamant about who should stay and who must attempt deliverance for them all.

The discussion reached a crescendo just as someone sighted another piece of wreckage with two people on it, the waves pushing it toward the deck, hands waving. As the flotsam drew near, the man and a woman upon it seemed to melt into the sea mist like a mirage.

Lamar threw a rope toward them, and as he hauled them in, he cried out in a strong voice. "My son! My son!"

Augusta lifted her gaze. Oh, God, she prayed in her wild thoughts, don't let it be a mirage. Grant us this small mercy.

"Father!"

It *was* Charles, ragged, frightfully sunburned, his lips swollen and his eyes crusted, but he was alive.

"Oh, God's mercy," Augusta cried out. "Charles lives," she told Thomas in his seashell ear. But he didn't stir, his pink sunburn swelling his cheeks as if he had stuffed them with cotton. "It is a miracle, Thomas. Stay with me . . ."

With Charles was a woman still fully dressed, her hair matted to her head and her pale skin pink. They both stumbled onto the wreckage, the woman falling on her back in the six inches of water, and staring up, mumbling thanks to no one and everyone.

Charles was immediately in his father's arms. "Mother? The children?" He was a young man of fourteen, yet still a child.

Lamar pointed at Augusta and Thomas. "So far only . . ." His voice trailed off and Charles dropped his chin, defeated. He slumped into the seawater that flooded the deck.

Augusta lifted her face to her nephew and reached for his hand. "You are a miracle."

Charles's face, crusted with salt and sunburn, wrinkled against emotions Augusta couldn't read. "This is not a miracle, Auntie. This is hell, a desert made of water. And I saw you—I saw you save Thomas while Eliza drowned." His voice was deeper, no longer that of the child who had just cried out to his father. He fell against the wooden box and closed his eyes.

Augusta took in a sharp breath and looked up to her brother. "I tried, Lamar. I tried . . ."

"My sister. You did everything you knew how." Lamar stood over his son. "Rise up, Charles. We must help the others."

Relief and grief braided together inside Augusta's heart. Where was her beloved Lilly? The thought of her drowning, of her lungs filling, of her life departing, was more than Augusta could bear. She must imagine Lilly and Madeline on the sturdy quarterboat or another piece of wreckage, imagine her on one of the boats whose sails they'd seen in the distance.

Charles stood tall, the water lapping against his bare shins where he'd folded up the hems of his pants. Augusta turned her attention to the woman who'd arrived with him and collapsed. Charles bent and touched her hand. "She's twenty-five and from Charleston. Her name is Olivia Barnsby. We survived together. We saved each other."

"The peppermint," Augusta called out. "For Olivia!"

Mr. Henderson brought the basket over. "Augusta, here. You must be in charge of giving out dosages of wine, peppermint and laudanum."

Charles shuddered for a moment and then he spoke: "What can I do now to help?"

Lamar took his son's face in his hands and then hugged him close. "Help us fix this lifeboat so we may go for help."

Charles dropped to his knees and began to stuff the holes with the other men.

Augusta kept watch over the found wine, peppermint and laudanum. It was agreed that the wine would be kept for the children; it was at least some kind of hydration to keep death slightly at bay. Augusta reached into the basket and withdrew the vial of peppermint, placed a few drops upon Olivia Barnsby's lips. She revived and opened her glazed eyes, mumbled, "Thank you."

"Water, Auntie," Thomas whispered with his eyes closed.

Augusta took a drop of wine on her finger and touched it to Thomas's lips before he closed his eyes again.

God, do not allow him to die. Please. No.

The thought of his expiring here, in this hell, was so abhorrent, so horrific, she could barely lift her gaze from his face. She would have to remember the contours of his countenance by heart.

Passengers began to huddle together, to form a circle in the middle of the wreckage while several men moved the bodies of those who had recently perished to the far end, where the waves would wash them away without anyone having to watch. It was then that Pastor Woart screamed out in a wordless and animalistic sound, and they all knew that his wife, too, had passed. She'd been saved only to say good-bye to her beloved.

Augusta handed Thomas to Charles and stumbled toward the pastor and his wife lying deceased in his lap, pale and still. Augusta lifted her hand to see the blue beneath her nail beds. "I'm so sorry," she said, the vial of peppermint now useless in her hand.

As she bent down, she noticed that no one had undone the woman's corset; it dug into her ribs and bound her waist. If Mrs. Woart could have taken in a deep breath, would she have endured for a few more minutes? Should Augusta herself have done it for her? The thoughts circled like wolves stalking prey.

She turned away from the sight just as a wave larger than any before raised the wreckage with a sickening lurch and then plunged it to a stomach-dropping depth. People cried out and grabbed on to cables and ropes to stay aboard. Augusta dropped to a crouch, her legs wide, and allowed the water to wash over her while using what little strength she still had to keep her footing. Her hands found no purchase, but her legs held firm.

Others in the circle clung to each other, allowed the cold water to engulf them. Charles held on to a rope and tight to his brother. With dull eyes Augusta watched the pastor, still clinging to his wife, allow the wave to take them both out to sea. His eyes were closed as they both vanished.

He would not live without her.

Augusta let out a cry, reaching for what was already gone, and then stumbled back to Thomas and Charles. Would they soon all return to the sea? Would it be as simple as letting go?

A woman on the far end of the raft who had been lying listless against a box now stood and began to wail, ripping at her hair and nightdress. "Our gold. All our gold was on this ship. It's gone. Where is my husband? Where is my silver? My gowns?" She glanced about the disaster and her eyes rolled back in her head; she slumped forward to land on the wreckage, her head smashing against the corner of the box where she'd sat. Blood ran from the side of her face and she lay facedown in the water.

Lamar ran to her and lifted her from the water, brushed back her hair and then looked up with such despair that Augusta believed this might be the final death that would render him incapable. But he closed her eyes and uttered a prayer that no one but God could hear. Augusta turned away, not wanting to watch the woman's interment. She had seen enough.

Augusta took Thomas from Charles's arms and sat to cradle him. His body shook now, his every muscle convulsed in spasms until he cried out and then collapsed—again and again this was repeated. Night crept over them and Augusta faded in and out while sitting upright, her arms burning from holding the child's weight.

Henry arrived at her side and knelt next to her. "Your nephew. He lives," he reminded her.

"Yes." Augusta felt the deep need to weep but she couldn't cry— there seemed nothing in her that would ever do so again, so dry and cracked was she. But she touched Henry's dear sunburned face with tenderness. "There is hope for others. For my dear friend Lilly. For baby Madeline." She paused and stared at the place where the woman had just slumped in her death. "Did you hear her, Henry? Did you hear what she lamented as she died before us?"

"Yes. Her gold."

"We will lose ours also, but what does that matter now?" She leaned down and kissed Thomas's cheek, felt a fear so vivid she shook. "He cannot die. Not Thomas."

Henry held her close and then whispered low, "Just as you do not want to live in a world without Thomas, I do not want to think of never seeing you again. Why do any of us wait to say what matters? I will not waste another moment. I want to be near you. It is all I have thought about for months. I will not let you die, Augusta Longstreet."

Augusta smiled sadly. "Don't make promises you can't keep, dear Henry."

"*This* is a promise I can keep."

She leaned against his body, feeling his strong chest and shoulders that in their previous life had been hidden beneath suits and stiff shirts. "Do you think the other lifeboats made it to shore?"

"I don't know. I can only hope."

"Please let that be true." Augusta closed her eyes. "Lord God, see us," she prayed as the night fell dark around them.

35

EVERLY

Present day

The corner house stood three stories high, made of tawny-colored stone and gray Savannah brick. Its tall, wooden, double front door faced Bull Street. Green shutters flanked each window and the transoms above peeled brown paint. Planted behind an iron fence that surrounded the property, climbing rosebushes wound their stems through the rusted filigree. Dumpsters sat on a once-green lawn now parched and filled with lumber and loose bricks. Two men in hard hats carrying construction debris trudged in and out of the front door.

Oliver and I watched. "I've always loved this house," I said, "but I never knew the family who lived here."

"I thought you knew everyone."

"Not even close. Savannah has changed so much . . . I can tell you more about the past than I can the present. Not sure that's a good thing."

He pointed at the open gate. "I think we can just go in."

"I don't think so. It's under construction and . . ." My voice trailed off as Oliver headed up the front stairs onto the portico. A man as round as he was tall, in a painter's white coveralls and a mask, stopped him.

They spoke and I heard a laugh, and then Oliver motioned for me to join him. That man could smooth-talk his way into anything. I took the steps two at a time, half afraid the painter would change his mind, and followed Oliver inside.

Dust clogged the air. Every surface was being stripped of wallpaper and paint to reveal the pearly plaster and fine wood beneath. Years of updates had hidden the true beauty of the house. A formal parlor spread the length of the house on the left with a dining room to the right. All the rooms were bare except for light fixtures covered in white cloth. The wide hall led back to a dark wood banister with a pineapple spindle. "There's nothing here," I said. "We're going to have to call the daughter or ask the new owner if she removed boxes belonging to the family."

"Where would *you* keep family papers?" Oliver asked, heading toward the stairwell. "If you didn't care about them, but you didn't want to throw them away, where would you put them?"

"The attic."

"Right." Light from the crystal chandelier caught the excitement in his eyes. It was contagious. I ran past and bumped him before climbing the stairs to the second floor.

His laughter followed me as we reached the landing. I glanced around at four closed doors. "Looks like four bedrooms and the stairwell to the attic would be at the far end."

We walked on a brown paper runner taped to the herringbone-patterned hardwood floor and reached a stairwell that ran along a back wall. I clicked on the flashlight of my cell phone and we crept up the stairs until we reached a dusty attic full of boxes, discarded furniture and moth-eaten curtains that looked straight out of a 1986 hunter green/burgundy color palette.

I ran the flashlight beam over the jumble. "Looks like they haven't made it up here yet. Look at this furniture. I bet it's worth a fortune." I ran my hand over a Windsor chair with a crocheted flower seat. "I hope they know what they've got."

"I'm sure they do. Stay focused." He laughed and picked up an alligator skull. "Don't get lost in all these beautiful heirlooms."

I recoiled in mock horror and ran my hand over a burlwood dresser. "You keep the skulls. I'll take the furniture."

"No," he said with a laugh. "You look in those boxes." He pointed at a pile of mildewed cardboard boxes. "I'll check these." He set his hand on top of a gray metal filing cabinet, rusted at the edges. "It's a long shot but we can try, right?"

"Right." I shuffled to the far end of the attic, pushing aside cobwebs and dead palmetto bugs that cracked under my shoes. I felt a bit like the Everly of old who would take the dare and dig through dirt to find a clue to the past. The Everly who might burst into laughter at any minute.

The boxes looked as if they would disintegrate under my hands and I lifted a lid to see folders containing yellowed papers, a book with a fabric cover splotched with green mildew, and a pile of letters tied with a faded pink ribbon. I lifted a folder and opened it. Dust flew out and a dead spider fell to the floor. The papers were legal documents I didn't quite understand except for the name at the top: *Longstreet*.

"Here!" I hollered out to Oliver. "Longstreet papers. There are piles of letter-books." I pulled out another of the ancient leather books that had once been used to hold the dealings of families and businesses. This one held certificates of birth, baptism and confirmation; deeds for burial plots and marriage licenses. "Someone was meticulous with their filing. I don't even have all my things in one place like this."

"Josephine said her sister-in-law was obsessed." Oliver drew near. "That filing cabinet is empty." He stood behind me and read over my shoulder. "But it looks like this box is a full-on bingo."

"Bingo?" I looked over my shoulder at him. "Been hanging out in the old folks' home lately?"

"You're funny," he said.

I kicked two boxes below the one I had opened. "How are we going to go through all these and find what we're looking for? We can't stay up here." The heat was pressing down now, the dusty air filling our nostrils. Sweat ran down my spine and into the band of my linen pants already ruined from the cemetery's mud.

"Then we take them." Oliver lifted a box and motioned for me to get another. "Let's go."

"We can't just take them."

"Why not?"

"Because they're not ours."

"We won't keep them, just look through them and put them back. Listen, the woman who left them doesn't want them. They're trash to her. She sold the house without bothering to remove them. We're just helping her."

"This is totally and completely illegal." I patted the top of the box he carried. "This is—"

"Something Mora would do," he said with a closed-lipped smile. "That's what you were going to say."

He was right. "Then let's go." I tried to smile but my lips shook.

We carried six boxes down the stairs and set them in the front foyer where the round man in the white coveralls approached us with his hands on his hips. "You can't be taking things from the house." His southern accent was lazy and rich, and the dip in his cheek poked out like a golf ball.

"Oh, no." Oliver held up his hands. "*We* aren't taking them. They're for the museum. These family papers will be filed with the Georgia Historical Society. We can't allow them to be damaged any more than they already have been in the heat and dust."

The man spit into a Coke can and wiped his face with a white cloth. "Why y'all want to save such musty things I will never understand." He waved us off.

I widened my eyes at Oliver and mouthed, "You are so bad."

"So bad," he mouthed back.

We carted the boxes to the sidewalk where Oliver's car was parked. As we paused in the late-afternoon sun, Oliver brushed dirt from his forearms. "Thanks for taking me along on your adventure. I'd forgotten how fun it is."

I lifted the hair off my sticky neck. "What are you talking about?"

"You. Always finding something wild."

"You're mixing me up with Mora."

"I don't think I could do that."

"She was the one full of adventure. She was the wild one. I was just along for the ride."

"I never saw it that way. Neither did she." His voice trailed off as we loaded the boxes in his trunk and settled in the front seat without saying a word.

The six decaying boxes sat on ragged towels I'd brought in from the laundry room. The tops were off the containers and papers were spread around the room on every surface. I sneezed, and Oliver laughed.

"I need to eat," I said. "I just realized I haven't had food since before I met Maddox this morning."

"Maddox is in town?" Oliver set a pile of newspaper articles on the dining room table.

"Yes. I nearly forgot." I cringed. "I ran off and left him at the

Owens-Thomas House where we went to ask about the silver flatware his guys found. We took the teapot and the pocket watch, along with the silver. I was hoping for some . . . clarification. But so far—none. I have a book about family crests to leaf through. But . . . he implied I was a bit too obsessed with finding out about Lilly, and well, I left him there."

Oliver spread his hands to encompass the mass of papers and boxes and said dryly, "Gee, I wonder why he thinks you're obsessed."

I gave a light punch to his shoulder. "I know. I know. But it's all connected. One thing always leads to another and even though I might not find out who that particular silver belonged to or what crest is on it or anything in these papers, we always find something . . . and you just never know . . ."

"What's going to happen next," he finished for me.

"Exactly." I plopped down on the couch. "My God, I haven't said that in over a year."

"You say it all the time. All. The. Time."

"I haven't, though. That's the point. Not since . . . Mora died. I haven't really cared what happened next because what happens next might be just as horrible as that."

Oliver sat next to me and twisted to face me although I stared straight ahead, toward the kitchen with my coffee press, herbs and teas in glass jars, out the window to the oak tree that shaded the back brick patio. I felt his gaze rest on me and I turned back to him.

"Have you thought about diving to the salvage site?" he asked. "You used to love that."

"I have. Why? Have you?"

"Yes. I'm going to visit the site next week and I thought I might go down."

"You're going to the site? With Maddox?"

"Yes. You sound annoyed."

"Not at all. I just didn't realize you two were . . . friends."

"We have lots to talk about."

A shiver of something like envy ran through me. They were talking, hanging out, living a life while I sifted through papers and photos and made charts and graphs and . . . I shook off the stupid thought while Oliver lifted a photo from the side table. It was a group shot of friends taken at an arts festival two years earlier. "Do you still think about that guy? That ass who broke your heart?"

He meant Grant, my old boyfriend. I'd forgotten he was in the photo. "Oh . . . My heart's not broken anymore. Maybe I miss the idea of him. I shudder with the realization that I gave so much of my life to him. That I wept for someone who wasn't worthy. I was over him long ago. In fact, he changed me for the better." I took the photo from Oliver and noticed he was in it, too. I'd forgotten . . .

"How did he change you for the better?" Oliver asked.

"I will never again—I hope—confuse love with need or obsession."

"Ah." Oliver settled back and ran his hands over a box. "I think this is what qualifies as near-obsession."

"Most likely."

What I didn't tell Oliver was what I did miss about not having Grant around—touch: gentle touch, wild touch, tangled-sheets touch. That was not something to talk about with Oliver.

And yet, why had I avoided him all these months? Who else would understand how I felt? Without saying a word, he sat quietly as if he were holding open a door for me to walk through whenever I was ready. I suddenly felt completely emptied out. I slumped against the back of the couch and picked up my cell. "I'm ordering pizza before we start."

"This isn't a one-night job. What you have here is weeks of work."

"I know. No time to waste." I returned my attention to ordering a pizza while Oliver picked up a few papers. His voice wafted past me as he read. "'When I last had the pleasure of seeing you in England your demeanor was one of melancholy.'" He laughed. "Between their language and their tight script, these letters could take years to decipher."

"I know. I can't wait."

"The things they wrote about; the things they cared about." Oliver flipped through a few more pages. "Seems so archaic. And look how many words they fit on one piece of paper. If I copied this one page in my handwriting, it would take up six."

"At first glance, I don't see anything here that has to do with Lilly or is personal about the family," I said. "This is all about business. Shipping cotton; selling the enslaved; arguing politics; spreading rumors of war. These are letters about a family trying to run a business, keep a legacy alive."

"Here's another letter-book," Oliver said, picking up a leather binder with another lot of papers. "These books were the hard drives of their day. Look at this—they copied every letter they sent into this letter-book. They wrote two copies and filed one here for safekeeping," he said, leafing through it quickly.

I peered over his shoulder. "It was their way of keeping everything on one subject in one place . . ." I paused. "I'm going to run up and change. I'll be right back."

"You just want me to pay for the pizza," he said, his voice light although he kept his gaze on the papers.

I hustled upstairs, showered and slipped into clean clothes even as I heard the doorbell ring, Oliver talking and the door shutting. I came back down in jeans and a T-shirt, my hair wet. What I looked like to him was inconsequential to finding what we were looking for in this pile. The hunt was on.

We chomped on greasy pizza until it disappeared and we were clean enough to touch the documents.

Oliver asked, "Where is that family list?"

I rummaged through a pile of papers on the side desk until I found one listing the Longstreet family. "Here are their names. The father, Lamar, is of French descent. His grandfather settled in Maryland and they ended up here in Savannah in the early 1800s. Lamar was a cotton merchant, banker and as you know, a pioneer in bringing steamboats to the South." I pointed at another name. "His wife, Melody, was also from Savannah but of Irish descent."

"And those circles around Charles and Lamar?"

"I know for sure that they lived. But I don't know about the others. His wife definitely passed because Lamar remarried only a year later."

"A year?"

"Men seem to get over things fairly quickly, *non*?"

Oliver rolled his eyes. "Low blow, Everly."

"Sorry." I cringed. "I didn't mean—"

"Adam Forsyth has a red circle also."

"He is in newspaper articles building a statue for his wife, so . . ."

"Got it. Well, keep reading." Oliver lifted another letter, purely business-related, and filed it back into the letter-book. "I don't see his name anywhere yet . . ."

Oliver's phone dinged and he smiled at the text. "Maddox is worried about you."

"Tell him I am totally fine."

He exhaled and nodded. "Okay. Listen, it's getting late. If I leave you with this, do you promise to get some sleep and we'll keep digging later this week?"

"You have plans tonight?" The question came unbidden.

He didn't answer but instead gathered his backpack and headed to the door. "You need anything else?"

"No. You go on home and I'll spend the evening with the dust of the Longstreet files. Go on. I've got this. If there's anything here that matters, I'll find it."

"I know you will." He dropped his hands on my shoulders and then angled his head forward, kissed me on the forehead in the same gentle way Papa used to. That was who we were now—friendly and warm—and it was good. My heart slowed. "See you in a bit."

When the door clicked shut, I fell back against the cushions. After all my excitement at finding the papers, and the day's insanity that had started with Maddox at the museum, I had nothing left to do but close my eyes.

I vaguely wondered if Oliver was headed to the river for another date. I brushed the image away and thought of the exhaustion and hunger of those who had washed ashore on the North Carolina beach more than a century and a half ago.

I shivered with the knowledge, and a growing desire to dive to the bottom of the sea, to the place where all their ghosts rested with their belongings.

Memories of diving with Mora, of the freedom of breathing in water, of the primal sensation of being part of something so much bigger than myself, flooded me. The multicolored fish that nudged by, the smooth kick of my fin that propelled me forward, the soft hush of my own breath in and out, in and out.

I'd seen aquatic grass that danced its own rhythm. I'd brushed against a parrot fish and watched a barracuda take another fish in one bite. I'd passed through the sunlit area of water to the twilight and swam until my tank was low on oxygen. I wanted to go there again.

The world below was alive; it was teeming with life and mystery. When I dove with Mora, I was able to see a place so foreign that we could almost believe we were the only ones who knew about it. Our ancestors, who couldn't dive this way, had fashioned tales of gods and goddesses of the sea—it was too majestic not to contain divinity. Science believed they'd debunked the gods, but diving always restored my belief.

It had been two years since I last dove with Mora and Oliver, two years since I'd had my gear certified, two years since I'd gone over the safety rules. I'd been taught that diving without a refresher was dangerous, but only slightly dangerous and I'd been enough times. Maybe I'd go again, to the place where Mora and I went together—below.

36

AUGUSTA

Sunday, June 17, 1838

By Sunday night, four nights now on the sea that didn't seem to count hours or days, time meaning nothing to its vast expanse, Augusta didn't so much sleep as fade in and out of consciousness, holding Thomas until her arms burned and her shoulders were painfully cramped. When the ragged group of survivors needed to relieve themselves, the rest turned away to give them privacy. They were all the same now—crew, slaves, men, women and children—trying to live, needing to eat and drink and sleep and relieve themselves. These acts, these simple acts of living that usually took place in the privacy of their homes, now unfolded under the wide starry sky, under the brutal sun, on top of a heaving sea.

The silence was as deep as she'd ever experienced, shattered only when a wave broke upon the wreckage or a survivor moaned. Thomas had ceased speaking by then, and he cried out only at intervals. She stroked his head and wrapped him in her driest garments; she sang lullabies and rocked him against her chest. She perched upon the box, understanding that if she slipped off, there was the chance Thomas, now listless, would fall facedown and drown in those few inches.

From her perch, she spied a young boy slumped over, lashed to another box.

"Why is he tied?" she asked, but no one answered. She cried out louder, "Why is he tied?"

A man, his face drawn, spit his words at her. "That is my son, and I don't want a wave to take him when I'm not holding him."

Augusta dropped her head. Such sheer horror everywhere she looked. If this was what it meant to be alive, it was wretched beyond compare and maybe she should let go as easily as the pastor who had floated off with his wife, as brutally as the woman who had bashed her head on the box.

Paradise with God would be her reward.

Augusta burned with fever. She'd never felt heat as she did now. The waves lashed the small raft and seasickness was her constant companion. Her head felt as if it floated above her, and death sat next to her.

If she allowed herself to fall into the sea, there would only be a few minutes of misery before she walked through the golden gates, or so she'd been taught. But if she fought to stay alive, she would experience hours or even days of misery. She closed her eyes and thought of all that hung in the balance. Instead of waiting for the fates, she could decide. This could be *her* choice.

But something persistent inside Augusta longed for life. A spark quickened as she'd once imagined a child growing inside her would feel. There were Henry and Thomas. There were Charles and Lamar. There were spring afternoons. Cooling rain showers. Flowers that burst from the soil of the riverbanks. There was love.

"Let it be me," a deep voice called out.

Augusta turned to see where the voice came from and saw a man and woman standing face to face. "No," the woman cried. "Not you."

"What are they talking about?" Augusta demanded.

Henry said, "That man believes we can get to shore if we cast lots and toss some people from the raft."

"Is he mad?"

"Likely, but also quite serious."

Henry held up his cut and bleeding hands in a placating gesture. He approached the man, water splashing around his bare ankles. He spoke calmly. "Stop this now. We are Christians and there will be no lots cast. We will not toss anyone to the sea. We will all survive."

Murmurs spread and soon voices became clear and words began to separate themselves and become a true conversation. In the faint light of sunrise, the men talked of who would go find help in the small yawl, which they'd patched together with rope and torn garments. Who were the strongest swimmers? Augusta lightly shook Charles, who sat in the water, his head lolling against her legs. "Will you please hold your brother?"

Charles jolted fully awake and cried out, as many did when they awoke and realized where they were. He came to himself quickly and stretched his limbs, lifted one foot at a time to see his pruned and flaking feet and then sat on the box to take Thomas. Augusta moved toward the men to listen more closely.

Two sailors spoke, the Dane who had been rescued and one other tall one Augusta didn't recognize. Lamar, Henry and a few more able-bodied men. Their arguments went in circles.

The taller gentleman with a seared arm spoke. "If the quarterboats made it to shore, then surely they've sent for help."

Lamar disagreed. "It's been three days. They believe we perished or they would have come for us by now. We must save ourselves. There's no choice."

The Dane argued that Lamar must go in the lifeboat. He was the only one with family on the wreckage, thus he had the greatest incentive to survive the rough landing and return with help.

At first Lamar refused. "I must stay and protect my sons and my sister."

Augusta touched his shoulder. "You must go," she said.

"I can't leave all I love alone here in this hell."

The Dane stepped near with his broad and bleeding hands held out to Henry now. "We need your strength. We need you to row."

Henry replied, "I will not leave Augusta. I made a promise and I would never forgive myself if I broke it." He clapped his hand on the Dane's shoulder. "You have men strong enough. I must stay to protect them."

Lamar agreed with his head bowed. He took Augusta in his arms. "I love you, sister. Watch over my sons. I will see you on land."

Augusta's tears came with one gulping cry and she held tightly to him. "Please return for us."

He nodded into her hair. "Sister, I promise."

With that final agreement, the six men—Lamar, the Dane, Peter Lawson of the crew, Mr. Hubbard of Charleston, Mr. Davis and Harmon Eldridge, strong in body to row—fashioned a sail out of a tablecloth and gathered to say good-bye. Mr. Hutchinson gave Lamar his spectacles and watch. He had already lost his three daughters and only son, and now he decided that if he didn't live, those possessions should go via Lamar to the rest of his family. The Dane suggested they each take one draw of the wine, for sustenance, and then they lowered the rickety yawl into the sea and boarded it. As they rowed away, Lamar reached out his hand and cried out, "Thomas . . ."

As Henry sat next to her, Augusta collapsed back onto the seat and took her nephew in her arms. Even his father's voice had not stirred him.

"There has been so much I have wanted to say to you," she told Henry. "So many things to talk about and now . . . I am too weak."

"We will have our whole lives to do so." He kissed her cheek with a tenderness so overwhelming that her tears started and she touched his face.

Silence stretched, punctuated by Mauma's singing. The foreign words echoed over the waves and across the miserable lot of them.

A tall man approached Augusta. "Can you give me just one drop of wine? Just one. My tongue shall fall out and my body . . ."

"You know we are saving it for the women and children," she said weakly. "It's what my brother has demanded."

The man stuck out his tongue and Augusta spied a grotesque sight—a tongue that looked as rough and brown as a cow's dried hide. "I will die of it," he said in a voice soaked with shame.

Charles touched his aunt's arm. "He can have mine."

Augusta held out the bottle and the man, she never learned his name, put only a drop or two on his tongue and then looked to Charles. "You are a noble boy."

A noble boy he was, Augusta thought, and kissed his cheek. "It is a miracle you are here. God has saved you."

Charles's eyes were dull by then, the spark gone from them, and it made Augusta's heart leap into her throat as he spoke. "There are no miracles, Auntie. I saved myself. No one is coming to save us, and God isn't here."

"He is, Charles. He is here in each of us helping the other."

"No one helped me. And no one is saving us. Father will get help or we will die."

"Charles, my beloved nephew, you don't know what you say." She took his hand and drew him closer. "Do not give up, Charles. Pray for your family. Pray for your brother."

Sorrow broke across his face before he looked away.

Some sang. Others prayed. Twice they spied sails in the distance
that disappeared again. Toward evening the wind changed and this
revived some hope—wasn't their pitiful wreckage now being pushed
toward shore?

But even if they sighted land, in their pitiful weakness wouldn't
they die in the struggle against the breakers that lined the land like
castle walls? Augusta told Thomas, "If we come near shore I will tie us
both to a plank of wood."

He seemed to hear her but remained listless against her chest.
Night drew near with the pinks and purples of the sun settling at the
horizon, so beautiful that for one moment she might believe the world
could not be so cruel as to let any more of them die in such misery.

Soon thunder rumbled and rain began to fall—blessed rain.

They opened their parched mouths to the sky, taking what little
water they could, letting it soak their blistered skin and their cracked
tongues. They used torn sails to gather the water into cups and empty
cans, and drink it in desperate gulps even though it tasted of the sea.

Augusta cupped her hands and waited for them to fill before gulping the water and putting the wetness to Thomas's lips, trying to pour
water upon his tongue and down his throat. Henry did the same and
then offered a full palm to Augusta. When the rain ceased an hour
later, they were chilled and drenched but somewhat revived, enough
for hope to take another breath.

The following morning, the skies cleared but the storm's aftermath
brought tossing winds and high waves that threatened to tear the raft
apart. The wreckage began to groan and the makeshift sails to flap.
Augusta's arms burned and her body ached as if she were made of pain,
and yet she wrapped Thomas closer as the warm sun moved higher and
steam rose from their bodies. "Thomas, Thomas," she murmured.

When he didn't answer, she shook him lightly.

"Ow, Auntie, don't."

She took his hands in hers and saw his nail beds blue, his hands shriveled. She began to rub his hands, but it did no good.

"Thomas!" she cried, but he'd lost consciousness, limp in her arms.

Charles crawled through the water and sat beside her. He wrapped his arms around her shoulders and together they rocked Thomas back and forth, calling out his name while Mauma sang.

When Thomas began to writhe on her lap, Augusta sank into a despair she hadn't known existed. The helplessness, the hopelessness, the complete inability to save the person she loved most ripped open a deeper anguish. Again and again he writhed and Augusta clung to him and cried out his name.

Thomas took his last breath that morning, and Augusta held to his body as if her very touch could bring him to life, a Lazarus of her own miracle even as sobs broke free in wails of agony.

With Augusta's cries filling the air, Charles collapsed, crying out, "Auntie, look—Boatswain is dying. He is drowning." Hallucinations brought to him visions of his pet dog and he reached out his hands for his precious mutt, who rested surely on a rug at Stonewall on Sea Island, a world away. Spent, Charles collapsed on the decking, his head in his aunt's lap.

Augusta pressed her body against Henry's, the four of them, one gone, huddled together as hopeless silence descended on the entire raft.

37

LILLY

Monday, June 18, 1838

The third day of Lilly's recovery was spent in the home of a kind, well-off family named the Benedicts, of Onslow, North Carolina. Lilly luxuriated on sheets as fine as she'd ever known. The room in which she lay glimmered with a pale yellow paint, muted sunlight. Dark wood furniture glowed with polish. Lilly held the soft blanket close to her face, where a sticky salve covered her sunburn. Mrs. Benedict had brought them soup and tea, washed their bodies, and summoned a doctor who'd checked all three of them—Lilly, Priscilla and Madeline.

"Have other survivors been found?" Lilly had asked first thing when she woke on Saturday morning with a bright light slicing through cream-colored curtains. She spoke in a low voice so as not to wake Priscilla, sleeping deeply in the adjacent bed.

"No," Mrs. Benedict had told her. "Not yet."

"Have they sent out ships to search? There were others, many others floating on fragments of the ship. They must send someone. So many were alive when we rowed away. We left them there . . . someone must go find them."

"Did you have other relatives on board?"

"I did. My aunts, my cousins, my uncle . . ."

"Was your husband on the journey?"

"Yes. I fear he's gone." Lilly turned her face away and allowed Mrs. Benedict to believe she was grieved by the thought.

In a bassinet next to Lilly's bed, Madeline let out a small whimper.

"Shhh . . . darling. Shhh . . ." Mrs. Benedict soothed. "A squall is out to sea and the men can't launch the ships . . . not yet. It has been assumed that all who were left could not have survived this long. God rest their souls."

"But they might have. Augusta and—"

"The men know what to do. Don't you worry. You rest now."

Mrs. Benedict closed the door quietly behind her as she slipped from the room.

The men know what to do. Did they?

Lilly's thoughts were a bitter brew.

Adam.

Now, lying in a stranger's bed with Priscilla's soft snores close by, Lilly felt a relief she'd anticipated feeling only once she escaped Savannah and had traveled far away. Now the possibility of freedom, and a new life, lay before her like a tantalizing dream. Mrs. Benedict had allowed Priscilla in her house without a word about slaves or Negroes not allowed in her home. Though not an abolitionist, it seemed her role as the wife of a clergyman, her role as the savior of the shipwrecked, had sent all thoughts of what was inappropriate in this manner to the bottom of the sea with the hull and the sails.

Lilly's thoughts faded in and out like this—clouds that passed and reappeared. She was awake yet saw the sea beneath her. Rising swells seemed to lift the bed the same as they had the lifeboat. She imagined the other passengers on the *Pulaski*. Were they dead, their last breaths taken, or were they still fighting for their lives, burning beneath the sun, thirsty and wet, hungry and injured?

She was one of the lucky ones. The blessed ones, her pastor would tell her.

Lilly rose from the bed, her legs still unsteady. She held fast to the bedpost and took a few long breaths, but she didn't yet have the strength to stand for long, and fell back onto the soft sheets. Madeline stirred in the wicker cradle.

"Priscilla, are you awake? I think Madeline is hungry."

Priscilla sat up on the edge of the bed, the nightdress she wore so large on her that it appeared she had wrapped herself in the sheets. She lifted Madeline and then leaned against the soft pillows as the baby nursed to contentment.

"Tell me about your family, Priscilla. Tell me their story." With her eyes closed, and Priscilla nourishing her child, Lilly needed to know all there was to know about the woman who had saved her child's life.

"Mistress?"

"Tell me their story. For if it is yours, I want to know."

Priscilla took in a long breath. "I don't know much but what my mama has whispered to me in the night. The ledger in Master's office can tell you more than I can."

"I am sorry." Lilly bowed her head, shame becoming a wash of prickling needles along her ribs. What she wouldn't tell Priscilla was that the ledger held nothing but sex, age and color—nothing more. Not even the names of the slaves Adam owned. "It is . . ." Lilly's words, inadequate and lost, fell away.

Priscilla lifted her gaze to look directly at Lilly, an acknowledgment of the power of her request, and she told Lilly what little she did know—of how in the early 1700s her great-grandmother from her mother's side had been brought over on a ship called the *Aurore*, one of the very first ships to bring them to southern shores. They'd been brought to Louisiana and eventually sold to the owner of the Ogeechee River plantation near Savannah.

"We weren't always in-town domestics like we are for your family," Priscilla said softly. "My grandmama died in the fields."

"I have never asked you any of this. I'm sorry I've never asked. I'm sorry for so very much." The world they'd lived in, so cruel, appeared in bas-relief to the ways in which they had worked together to survive the past days.

"Your father?"

"I never knew him. Master sold him when he found him dancing with Mama. Said he didn't like distractions. Mama ain't been the same since. She's been whipped a few times for being insolent. She's still sewing for the family, but she's tired . . ."

"Oh, Priscilla. This is so heartbreaking. How did I not know all of these things?" Lilly paused. "And what is the name given to you by your mama?"

"It is Chike. Mama says it means 'the power of God.' I ain't seen much of my power, but that's my name."

"I see it, Chike. I see it."

"Mistress, we . . ." She paused here at the joined word, at the "we" that had never been used before. "We have survived."

Lilly rolled back on the pillow as the sounds of Madeline's nursing faded and footsteps approached their door. Twilight falling against the window, washing the room in eventide, told them it was time for dinner. It was now the end of day three without word of any other survivors.

"I think we are the only ones who made it to shore, Chike."

"Don't be giving up hope."

"My husband's plantation will be passed to his brother. We shall begin again with a different kind of life."

Chike didn't answer as the door opened and Mrs. Benedict carried in a tray laden with soup, bread and tea.

38

EVERLY

Present day

It didn't take long to drive to Mom's house and somehow, without alerting her, sneak in and out of the storage shed and grab my dive gear. Inside an Evo Mesh duffel bag that Mora and I had chosen together—and bought matching ones—rested all my gear: my BCD vest, mask, regulator, wrist dive computer, and wet suit. It hadn't been touched in two years, but it was clean and ready. I tossed it all into my trunk and drove off in the predawn hours like a thief.

Two weeks had passed since Oliver and I had retrieved the Longstreet papers and I'd spent much of that time examining them. I'd also meticulously gone through the manifest, gathering names from sources with varied names and conflicting lists, eager to find someone with a last name beginning with M. I wanted to solve that one mystery, give the silver an owner.

With a complete accounting, I finally found one name that began with M—a G. McLain. I ran fast down the rabbit hole into archives from 1838 with the search "G. McLain Pulaski" and discovered a man named George McLain in an out-of-print book about the lineage of prominent Rhode Island families. Then a few quick strokes at the Find A Grave website, and I found a photo of his grave marker—he'd perished on the *Pulaski* with his daughter Beatrice Caroline McLain Cunnion, married to Franklin Marshall Cunnion, and their daughter Beatrice. His wife, Louise Kathryn, had passed years before. There was my BCM and my LKM. There they were, right there, stories hidden with merely the hint of a monogram.

The thrill of discovery ran through me, combined with the deep sadness of such tragedy. It was as if from far off, a hundred and eighty years in the past, a thirty-six-year-old woman whispered to me, proved to me that she'd existed and mattered, that she'd drowned on that ship with her father, her husband, and her child. These were not mere names. These were people with lives and families and dreams. They had loaded their silver to bring to the north, loaded their families and their dreams, and all of it—every bit of it—rested miles deep.

I'd held both my hands over my heart. "Beatrice Caroline McLain, your silver is on land. It's now part of something that will honor that night, and the horror you went through."

It might be ridiculous speaking out loud to a woman long gone, a woman whose silver the men had found buried in the sand. Ridiculous, yet oddly necessary.

I'd needed to share the discovery, a milestone that felt monumental, a gift or affirmation from the past. I'd wanted Maddox to know: I'd called him.

"I figured it out. The silverware. It belonged to a woman named Beatrice, who died that night with her father and husband and daughter, and to her mother, Louise Kathryn, who had passed long before this journey."

"Oh, Everly. What a find. How in the world . . ."

"I finally found a passenger list that had the name G. McLain—it wasn't on the first list. I dug . . ."

"Of course you did." His laughter could fill any empty space and here it had across the line.

I'd blurted out what I immediately knew, what Beatrice's silver showed me. The artifacts were calling to me. It was my duty and honor to give them their due. "Maddox, I want to see it. I want to see what lies down there. I want to see what remains. I'm coming to dive with you."

"No need, Everly. I will show you everything that is brought up."

"I'm coming to North Carolina," I'd said and hung up before he could argue with me. His emphatic declarations that I should not come had had the opposite effect—instead of keeping me from the sea, it had fired a desire that I'd thought extinguished, but one Oliver had also lit—a need to go down and see it all.

I couldn't stay on the surface any longer. It felt as if a crack had opened in time and I was able to slip through easily, a ghost running between centuries, both connected to the survivors and untethered from the present.

Now, on the way to North Carolina, I spent those sun-rising hours thinking about the dive, about the artifacts. It had been two years, but I'd been confident in the water, sure of myself in ways that the other students found envious. I could be that way again. Yes, the rules said the gear must be certified once a year, but it had been perfect on the last trip and had since been stored, protected and sure in Mom's shed.

When I arrived at the marina in late morning, I grabbed my gear bag from the back seat and hurried toward the *Deep Water Rose* only to stop in my tracks. Oliver and Maddox stood together at the far end of the dock. Two women stood next to them, both wearing bikinis and sun hats. The four were engaged in an animated discussion until Oliver turned to see me. A smile broke across his face. "Everly!" he called out. "Over here."

I walked slowly toward them as the women wandered a few feet away and climbed onto a sailboat. I reached Maddox and Oliver, my duffel bag falling off my shoulder. I dropped it to the deck. "Did I miss something?"

Maddox and Oliver looked at each other and answered in unison, "No."

I turned to Maddox. "You didn't tell me Oliver would be here."

Oliver laughed. "You do know I'm standing right here?"

"I see you. You were here a week or so ago. You didn't tell me you were coming again . . ." I said.

Maddox shot Oliver a sly grin. "Did you forget to ask her permission?"

"Stop. You know what I mean. I just thought . . ."

"Today we're diving," Oliver said. "We'll go see what the boys have been exploring. I came last week but a rainstorm muddied the waters—now we can go."

The sun moved from behind a cloud and a man on another boat called out Oliver's name. He turned and waved before returning his attention to me. "How do you know all these people?" I asked. "I'm so confused right now." I was more than confused. Something akin to irritation ascended from my belly. Oliver and Maddox hanging out? Planning a dive? Oliver friends with the local boat owners?

"There was a marina party last night. A bluegrass band came to play," Oliver said, pointing at what I now saw was a tent a hundred yards or more away on the grassy edge near the inn.

"I'm the hired help. Obviously," I shot back with gritted teeth. My irritation had turned to bitterness and I regretted the words the moment they fell from my mouth.

Oliver took a step toward me and spoke softly. "Would you have come if we'd invited you?"

I couldn't answer honestly either way, but decided on the reply that might make them feel bad. "Yes, I would have."

Maddox held up his hands. "I'm sorry, Everly. I called Oliver to invite him to the concert and since he'd been wanting to dive . . ."

I looked between them. "Clearly I'm superfluous here."

Maddox pointed at my bag. "What is this?"

"I *am* diving today. With you. That's my gear."

I lifted my bag and headed toward the marina restaurant, anger moving in waves under my lungs, squeezing them so I had to take short, quick breaths. Tears, maddening tears, worked their way up my throat and into my eyes. I would not let them see me like this—not in control of my feelings.

"Everly!" Oliver called after me.

Ignoring him, I hustled toward the inn, my heart hammering. In seconds, he was at my side. "Stop. I'm sorry. I am really sorry. I got defensive. I didn't mean it. But for God's sake, don't be angry because we went to a concert."

I whirled around, my hair catching in my mouth. "I'm not angry you went to a concert." The tears had their say then—nothing I could do about it.

Oliver wiped my cheek with his thumb. "Let's dive down there together, Everly. Let's go see what's left of the *Pulaski*. Let's . . ."

Maddox's voice boomed into the conversation before I saw him. "No way. Everly is not diving."

"What?" I looked at him.

"Only employees," he said.

"That is absurd and I can't believe you just said it out loud." I shook my head. "Damn, Maddox. What the hell . . . you're letting Oliver go. He's not an employee."

"My ship. My dive. My rules." Maddox looked between us and walked toward the boat without another comment.

"No," I said to Oliver, "I'm definitely going. No way is he stopping me. You can go and I can't? Oh, hell no."

"Let me talk to him." Oliver placed a hand on my arm. "Stay here for a minute."

Thirty minutes later the three of us sat at a table overlooking the marina. I narrowed my eyes at Maddox, moving past the discomfort. "So, you tell me—why don't you want me to go?"

"Everly." Maddox exhaled my name and Oliver shot me a look, a warning look of furrowed brow and slight shake of the head. "I've had a bad experience taking a diver down who . . ."

"I know." I closed my eyes for a moment, found my words and opened them to Maddox staring at me. "But I'm not that student. And this isn't that day. I promise."

"You can't promise anything, Everly."

"I can promise you it won't be the same. I know what I'm doing. I brought my own equipment."

Oliver chimed in. "She's a good diver. I've been with her. She doesn't panic. She's experienced. She's calm."

Maddox glanced between us. "I'm outnumbered here. I see that. But I need you to know—I don't feel good about this." He folded his hands together and pointed them at me. "You're certified? Your gear is certified? You're up to date on everything, right?"

"Yes." I swallowed the confession that all of that was true but might have been a bit longer than recommended. Because really that part didn't matter so much. I was certified for sixty feet, not a hundred, but there wasn't enough difference to matter. "Can't you understand why I want to go?"

Maddox took a long swallow of his water and stared at me with a blank look.

"Come on," I said. "Tell me why *you* want to go down there?"

"It's my job." The wrinkles around his eyes deepened as he focused on me. "We've talked about this. Why are you asking?"

"No. You can't answer a question with a question."

He threw back his head and laughed. "You know how people are so fascinated by outer space? Well, I'm fascinated by what my hero, Sylvia Earle, calls 'inner space.'"

"I know who she is: the first woman to walk solo on the bottom of the ocean. They call her a fish whisperer." I grinned. "I watched a documentary about her."

"Only five percent of the ocean has ever been explored," Maddox said. "No matter how long I live I won't be able to see even another five percent. It's a mystery. And it's in trouble. I have no idea why anyone can't see what the sea means to us, what its depths contain, and how we're abusing it." He shook his head. "But that's not what you asked me." He gazed out to the marina. "I dive because I fell in love with the sea as a child. Maybe it's the same feeling other people have about finding the secrets of the universe—of the galaxies and black holes and stars. There is a universe right here on earth. Right around us and below us. It is a mystery and it is magical and it is life itself. Our primordial ancestors came from this place, this deep sea, and I have always wanted to know it."

I settled quietly in myself; his words were so true.

"It's what Walt Whitman called the world below the brine." Maddox continued, "It's not the treasure that motivates me or a desire to resurrect history. But it's what I do now. Just as you haven't always been a museum curator, I haven't always been a shipwreck diver. Life brings us to new places all the time."

"Yes." My heart rate picked up. "See? That's why I want to dive with you."

"It's a complicated dive, Everly. It's a hundred feet and that means two tanks of mixed gas; with thirty-two percent nitrox you'll only have twenty minutes or less. I know Oliver is trained and has done it before. Have you?" His eyebrows lifted with the question.

"Yes. And I have my wrist computer with me." I paused and teased, "Besides, I was born in water."

He tilted his head in question and set his elbows on the table to lean forward.

"Mom told the story a thousand times. There I came, swishing out, swimming like a fish in the bathtub where she spent her labor. So, don't you worry about me."

"Worrying. That's my job."

"I *am* going." I removed a card from my wallet and showed him my certification. "I've been on over twenty dives. I'm not some inexperienced diver who learned in a resort swimming pool."

"Cute, Everly, but I take this seriously. There are . . ."

"I know. There are dangers. Oxygen toxicity, the bends, narking."

"Okay." He nodded toward his boat. "They're waiting to go out. The weather has broken and we have a small window. If you go with us, you have to come now and you might have to spend the night out there, on a cot, with all the men."

"Maddox, a branch of Mora's family was on the *Pulaski*. Some lived. Some perished. I want you to show it to me."

Oliver cringed at the mention of Mora's name and I caught his eye. He nodded at me.

Maddox rubbed his face and exhaled in defeat. "You are going to have to sign all kinds of waivers and you might change your mind when you get out there."

"If I change my mind, okay. But I'm going with you. Unless you want me to make a scene here on the dock." I picked up my bag and stood.

"Why do you *really* want to do this?" Maddox asked.

"I want to be a hundred feet closer to the heart of the mystery. I want to see the wreckage. Diving was one of the things Mora and I learned to do together, and I haven't done it since she died. Her ancestors perished down there. I'm doing an exhibit of everything you bring up. If you need more reasons than that, I can make some up."

Maddox shook his head; he knew when he was defeated, and he nodded toward the boat before striding off. I followed with a smile.

The crew stood on the *Deep Water Rose* deck, pacing impatiently as the three of us approached. They wore bathing suits, dirty T-shirts and almost identical sunglasses. They waved. Oliver stopped me a few steps back and whispered in my ear. "His rule has to do with the student he lost."

"I know. I get it but I'm still going."

"We see that."

We reached the boat and Oliver's smile was broad as he held out his hand to help me onto the boat. I tossed my gear aboard and climbed in without assistance. I didn't want them treating me like a fragile woman.

Maddox cleared his throat. "Guys, Everly and Oliver are going out with us on this one."

The crew nodded and went about their work in a boat as cluttered as a dorm room full of frat boys. Wet suits hanging tangled with scuba gear, regulators, BCD vests, masks and nets sent out the salty-sour smell of sea and sweat. I placed my feet wide and smiled as the shortest of the men, Ben I recalled, untied the ropes and the boat swung out from the dock.

"You coming to take photos?" he asked, and shifted the boat into higher gear. It lurched and I grabbed on to a post.

"No. I'm diving."

No one said a word, but I felt their concern, eyeing Maddox to check for his signal. He stared blankly out to sea. The men settled into lawn chairs and built-in seats, as Oliver kept his gaze on the water. Nets hanging from hooks swayed like spiders' webs. The breeze caught and clanged the metal rings of the diving flag against the pole over and over again.

"How long is the ride out?" I asked.

"Two hours," Maddox answered without looking at me.

I sat down on a slick wet chair. "Anything Oliver and I can do to help in the meantime?"

"Nope. Just relax. I'm going to push her pretty hard to get out there so we can get back before dark. There's a storm about two days off that we want to beat."

"Got it."

The boat's hum and the splash of water against the hull lulled me to near-sleep until I jolted awake to the sound of chains screeching and clattering, the anchor being lowered. I sat upright, my neck aching where my head had fallen sideways. I stood and shook the fog from my mind.

I glanced out to sea and saw nothing but water—exactly what Augusta, Lilly and all the passengers of the *Pulaski* would have seen that night. A heaving sea and not even a distant land to spur them on. My heart jumped into my throat. There was absolutely nothing safe about what I was doing. Maybe I should yield to Maddox's concern, but something in me, something larger than logic, pushed me forward.

I was going down there.

"This is it," Maddox said when we reached the coordinates marked by buoys. "Give us some time to set up. Suit up."

I slipped off my shorts and T-shirt, and stood on deck in my black swimsuit, slick and shiny, while the guys found their personal gear, sliding on suits and BCD vests and chatting with the camaraderie of men who live together in tight quarters and work together side by side, their lives literally in each other's hands every day.

I snapped on my wet suit and mentally ticked through the motions of diving. Donning the tanks, testing the air, snapping the mask into place. It came back to me easily, these motions that could mean life or death.

Maddox, geared up, faced me, and Oliver stood by my side.

"Question," Maddox said. "You're not taking any meds, right?"

"None."

"Absolutely none? No pseudoephedrine?"

"Whatever that is, no."

"Sudafed and the like."

"Nope."

"Okay, let's talk through the particulars of this dive."

"Go." I strapped the wrist computer on and looked up to him.

"It is a hundred feet, and the field is scattered on a grid. My men will have metal detectors, but you and Oliver and me—we'll just be watching. If you see something, show me. I have a bag for retrieval." He patted a bag hanging from the side of his wet suit.

"We are buddies and you do not leave me. You know the signs of narking, right?"

"Of course."

"Then tell me, because, Everly, it's not a joke. What follows that is confusion and then going too deep, or too low on your gas mix, and then you've got oxygen toxicity, which is equal to . . ."

"Death." I interrupted him. "I know. There's no coming back from that one. I get it." I took a breath. "Narking—confusion, giddiness, dizziness, hallucinations. Then all I have to do is come up about ten feet and regain my breath, and my composure. I know."

He nodded in agreement. "And listen to me, one more time. You must signal me if you experience tunnel vision, ringing ears, nausea or any kind of dizziness. If you feel your muscles twitching or a strange sense of euphoria, you must signal me."

"Yes, sir."

"Let's set our computers."

I tapped on my wrist computer and for a few breaths too long I couldn't remember how to set it, how to punch in the nitrox level and the depth. I stared at it. If Maddox figured out I was rusty, he wouldn't let me go.

"You okay there?" He tilted his head toward the water where the other men were already descending, the blue dive flag bobbing on the surface. The dread in his eyes was the same I'd seen in my own—an emotion born not of the moment but of past moments; from when he'd stood in full dive gear and a student insisted she go down. When the instructor didn't feel good about this particular dive but let her go anyway because it might keep the project on time and budget.

"I am okay," I said with a confidence that wasn't nearly close to what I felt. I glanced at Oliver and he lifted his eyebrows in question. And just like that, I remembered. I saw us—in Key West, setting our wrist dive computers, clicking off our times and levels. I bowed my head to my wrist and entered the numbers so that my oxygen clock would be correct.

Maddox sat on the edge of the boat and twisted around to face us. "You descend and ascend at my pace," he said and then toppled backward into the swelling sea with a splash.

Oliver and I glanced at each other and he stepped closer. "Are you sure?"

I gave him a look and did the same as Maddox, sitting, twisting and splashing into the water as my answer.

The sea sloshed over my face, a cold slap. I took a few beats to float and acclimate, the fins on my feet moving to keep myself afloat. I adjusted my BCD vest and dipped my mask into the water, rinsed it out so it wouldn't fog before pressing it to my face and snapping it in place. The sea world was now visible through its clear glass. I bobbed next to Maddox and Oliver, double tanks on our backs.

As I waited and paddled, only my face above water, I realized this view was nothing like what I'd imagined for the survivors at sea. I'd pictured their perspective as if they stood on the ship with a bird's-eye view of the wreckage. But they would have only seen what was right in front of them: waves and more waves: a breathing sea.

When the explosion had ripped the *Pulaski* in two, the two women I'd been following had seen what I was now looking at—the waves hiding and revealing. They couldn't have known what other pieces of the ship were floating, or even who had survived, not unless they were right upon them. If they'd had a child in their arms, or had clung to a loved one, they could have lost sight of them easier than I'd imagined.

I shivered.

Maddox swam next to me. "You okay?"

I nodded.

The sea had ripped children from their parents' arms, it had cast loved ones too far to be found. It all made sense now. The sea was in charge.

I placed the regulator in my mouth and took a few slow breaths before nodding at Maddox. I adjusted the shoulder straps that held the tanks behind me and took in a long, slow breath—the slower and easier I breathed, the longer my oxygen would last.

The murky water stirred around me. My face under the waves, I took in a long breath. Down. Down. When needed, I stopped to clear my ears by pinching my nose and blowing out.

Like a dream, I was underwater and breathing, in and out, in and out, the whoosh of my breath loud in my ears. This was the allure of the sea, of dipping beneath its surface—an unseen world nestled within the seen world. This sea universe existed within its own right, and if the biologists were correct, it was where all life had started—the sea as the birthplace for all creation.

We descended. Fish I couldn't name darted past—bright and dull, gnarled and sleek. My breath was background noise as I followed every cue from Maddox and we descended deeper and deeper, stopping to clear our ears when needed as the sunlight diminished little by little. Soon, in less than ten minutes or so, from out of the murky depths, Maddox flicked on his flashlight. He pointed the cone of light toward the bottom, and I spied the remnants of the wreck among mounds of sand. Fish swam in and out of what appeared to be pipes and piles of steel, curiosity seeming to draw them near to Maddox and me.

A few feet away, Ben held out a long pole with a circle at one end: a metal detector. He wiggled his gloved hand to sift the sand and then lifted a coin between his thumb and forefinger to show me. His smile pushed up his mask, which pressed down on the top of his lips.

Sounds filtered through in magnified warped echoes—my own breath, the soft scrape of sand when I touched the bottom with my hand, the movement of water as a blue fish with a curved mouth and pointed bill swam near.

Comfortable and confident, I watched Maddox and the others unearth artifacts—coins, a ring, a candlestick, a comb—and slip them into drawstring bags, then resume their search. I wanted to find something new and solid; I desired treasure of my own to bring back from the dive.

I dug my hands deeper into the sand and then watched it sift, rise and separate like smoke. I could manipulate this world—how astonishing! I ran my hand through the rising sand and brought my fingers down to a solid oblong object. A key. What had it once unlocked? I glanced to Maddox on my left and touched his arm lightly. He turned toward me. I held out the key and he smiled, took it from my hand to slip into his bag.

I glanced at my wrist computer: 102 feet with eleven minutes remaining. I then lifted my gaze to follow the beam of the flashlight—down again, then left and right as the light passed over the bottom. A flash, and I swam toward it. My earlier nervousness was as distant as the moon. I was one with the sea. I was at ease because this was my world—the one below.

I sensed that all around me were the ghosts of the *Pulaski*, men, women and children who'd perished. I felt them as if their stories echoed in hidden words through the deep blue. It was beautiful, mesmerizing and so peaceful beyond explanation. I'd felt this way only once before. I searched for the memory as my hand reached for the shining object. When was it?

The day the doctor had given me a shot in the emergency room after the accident; within minutes the terror of remembering Mora's bloody body had settled down into something benign. The knowledge had remained, but its electric charge, the mind-blowing grief, had become something dull, hardly recognizable. And along with that had come a feeling of being able to float off without a care. I'd become one with all that was and had been.

It had never been something I could explain to anyone. And I hadn't tried. But I'd also never allowed myself to use more meds. I never wanted to not feel Mora's absence. I hadn't deserved the peace that came with that shot. I hadn't deserved the forgetting and the calm.

Now I welcomed the peace, the knowledge that down here I could drift my hand over the sand and reveal the past as surely as a sea god. I lifted a glimmering object and there was a baby rattle: two small balls on either end of a stick with a pearl handle and a circular engraved disc with tiny bells hanging from it.

I closed my hand around it, felt its form through the glove.

Tranquility reigned down here where the rattle had landed, long outliving the child who had shaken it. I hovered, feeling the halcyon sense of forgetting, aware that the rattle had made the better choice: to sink and stay, to exist beneath the tumultuous world, to settle into the sand.

To rest.

It was clear as sunlight: the events of the past months had brought me to this place at the bottom of the ocean, to tranquility, to where I'd been dreaming about all my life—this was the world for me. Here I was part of something unseen, just as Mora was now. There was such a thin veil between the seen and unseen, between the living and the dead. Who was I to know where that line existed or where she was now? Who was I to understand death or life? They were a mystery.

Perhaps we weren't so far apart after all, Mora and me. Death had taken her but it hadn't taken who we were together, or our memories, or how she had shaped the woman I was right here under the waves, picking up remnants of a disaster hidden from sight for all those years. We were, all of us, hidden in different ways, under different waves. The broken parts, the remnants of our own explosions, kept secret from others.

Those bits and pieces of myself, of everyone, could be retrieved and examined; their stories could be told. If I took the time, if I looked closely enough, if I dove deep enough, I could find my own wreckage and honor it.

I dropped the rattle and watched it settle into a cloud of sand; the cloud of it lifted and twisted, formed a shape that slowly became Mora. She floated there as real as the day she stood by my side at the parade, as real as if time and space had folded in on itself for me. "Mora!" I called her name around my regulator, the sound warbled and dim. I swam closer, reaching my hands for her.

She smiled at me, her red hair rising with the water like seaweed, like a cloud of fire. She twisted, a pirouette of sorts, and transformed, becoming translucent as gossamer, disappearing even as I tried to reach her. She morphed, the form of a woman changing again, and this time she wore a nightdress and carried a child. Above her a bonnet floated and a rattle fell from the child's hand, falling and falling.

Beatrice and her daughter.

I lifted my fingers to touch her arm, to explain by touch that I'd found her silver, and all would be well. We would all be well. This serenity had been worth the horrific moments beforehand. This untroubled place was free of grief and guilt and loss. Free of the background noise of sorrow and loneliness.

I fell into the soft consolations of my mind, moving closer to Beatrice, and to Mora who had faded from sight.

I needed to find Mora again.

Then a hand on my shoulder brought me back, a jolt through my arm: Maddox grabbing me. He tapped his wrist and motioned for me to look at mine, but I didn't need to. I knew all was well.

He gave me the "okay?" sign.

I didn't answer him, although I meant to. I was more than okay. But my arms and hands tingled, dissolving into the seawater to become one with everything.

Oliver swam up holding a candlestick, and through his mask, his kind eyes widened. He, too, held up the "okay?" sign. I nodded or thought I did. He dropped the candlestick and swam closer.

Maddox jerked my arm again with a motion for us to ascend. I shook my head and turned for Mora, and Beatrice and whoever else I could find. I reached to the sand again for the rattle, a long-gone child's toy, but found no purchase. I kicked against Maddox, tossing my head forward to dive deeper.

Oliver grasped me by the shoulders and his gaze locked with mine and he motioned upward. He took my hand and kicked us both toward the surface.

No.

No.

I let my arms float and my head drop, breaking free from his sight. In my mind, images floated by, broken pieces of a fragile life.

What *really* mattered?

Minutes or years passed as I searched for the answer. Finally my heart called out: *Everything. Everything matters.*

We ascended ten feet: enough for the oxygen to begin to fill my mind and clear my thoughts, for the ghosts to disappear. Still aware that there was more than water around me, more than fish and salt water and a ship's artifacts, I waited. There existed a great life force, a presence that could only be called love. Alongside me, inside me, around me, I sensed the waves of something larger than the ocean itself.

Love, where I would eventually go.

But not now.

Not yet.

And even so, love would be there when I arrived. It wasn't something I could see, nothing as solid as the baby rattle or the tanks on my back. It was unseen and it held everything together.

I was in it and I was of it.

Floating there with Maddox and Oliver, breathing in and out, I intuited that Mora would always be with me; we were connected by the same force. She'd left me and she remained with me. This paradox was as true as anything I'd ever known.

My body inhaled deeper and we kicked slowly toward the surface. Oliver and Maddox were blurry, my sight unclear and my mask fogging—my tears had coated the inside glass. With a bright explosion in my lungs and then my chest, I chose life.

It wasn't a slow crawl toward the surface of the living, but a blaze of deep knowing: I chose life, whatever that meant in whatever form it took. Without Mora, but with my family and my passions and my curiosity and with love.

A few more feet up, Maddox had us pause for a minute while we acclimated to offload gases and Oliver took me by the shoulders. Our eyes locked and stayed. This was life. This was love. I placed my hands on his shoulders and nodded yes. Then I moved one hand and pointed up with my thumb, toward the surface, and toward life.

39

AUGUSTA

Tuesday, June 19, 1838

Augusta awoke not to consciousness but to hallucination.

Confusion colored her mind and in it she spied a misty drawing room that was both unfamiliar and dreamy, the windows of the fine home dimpled with rain. She was so cold. But even so how wonderful to be at a party in Montgomery, Alabama, visiting dear friends before she boarded a coach to Savannah for the steamboat trip to Baltimore that her brother had talked her into going upon. The drawing room wavered and thick damask curtains flapped like wings. Cold air seeped into her gown, but wasn't it June in Alabama? Why was it so cold?

Augusta glanced down to check her silk frock only to see she wore a wet nightgown and her feet were bare. Yet there were so many people around her. Horror and embarrassment flooded her mind—how had she left her room in such a state of undress? Had she been walking in her sleep? Forgotten to dress?

She wrapped her hands around her waist as protection, as hiding, and backed away from the beautifully dressed crowd, tripping on something she couldn't see, and landing in water. Water?

She looked down. My God, there was a small child at her feet, purple and cold. Augusta's fear tasted like bile; she screamed and pointed. "Why are there dead bodies here? What is happening?"

Her thoughts spun and wound around themselves like snakes as her body collapsed. Unconnected images flashed through her mind. None made sense. Was she in a dream that felt as real and solid as splintered wood? Where was Isaac? He would take her by the arm and return her to her room. But what room?

She looked up and recognized Mr. Hutchinson. When had he arrived in Montgomery? Why were they so shabbily dressed? She grabbed his arm. "Help me. When is the coach arriving to take us to Savannah?"

"Soon," he said softly, and pulled her close to cover her nightdress. He was embarrassed for her; he would help her. She closed her eyes and collapsed against him, his solid body and soft words.

Time collapsed and soon she awakened to a loud voice. Mr. Hutchinson again, rousing her. "Wake, Miss Longstreet. Wake." She forced her thoughts from their stagnant lethargy and focused. "Look."

She lifted her swollen eyelids to spy white sails on the horizon, spread like birds' wings and growing larger. She came to her feet, shaking with weakness, water dripping, her body aching. She shielded her eyes from the sun and stared at the endless water she'd seen for five nights and five days.

As the ship drew near, they realized it was a schooner. On its deck a man bellowed through a horn, "Be of good cheer. Salvation is at hand."

"Oh, how beautiful!" Augusta cried out and fell again, tipping into Mr. Hutchinson's arms and lapsing into an unconscious state deeper than sleep, yet more shallow than death.

※

The aroma of wet wool and sweat overwhelmed Augusta and she was startled awake to find herself lying on a cot covered in clean sheets. She was on another ship, in another cabin. She struggled upright, dizziness forcing her to take a moment to regain her bearings. From her berth, she spied Charles on a similar berth across from her. Also, Mr. Hutchinson lying on a cot.

She wore the scratchy wool clothes of a sailor, and her feet were dressed in white bandages, throbbing like a heartbeat. She reached across the space to Charles. Was he asleep or dead? Lamar, her brother—where was he? Where was Thomas, her beloved nephew?

"Thomas!" Augusta straightened in shocked remembrance.

A ship's mate appeared from the shadows and knelt at her bedside in his crisp blue uniform. "Here, take some water."

She swallowed with an eagerness that disregarded all propriety. This, this was what she'd been waiting for. A hint of vinegar in the water, but she didn't care. The man reclaimed the flask after she'd taken only a few sips. "You'll be sick. Drink it slowly. Now, tell me, who is Thomas? Describe him and I shall try to find him for you. There are approximately thirty of you here. Only eight remained on your piece of wreckage, but there was also another." His low voice was a comfort, but she knew that this man would never find Thomas.

"Do not look for him. He has joined the angels." She fell back upon the bunk. She did not want to live without Thomas; she would have traded her life for his, and yet here she was. She glanced at Mr. Hutchinson, who lay still and quiet in his berths; at Charles, who seemed utterly spent. Was he breathing? Yes. "Tell me how we came to be saved."

The gentleman told the story as he continued to give her sips of water tinged with vinegar. "You have been saved by the most noble man at sea, Captain Eli Davis of the *Henry Camerdon*, which plies the waters between Philadelphia and Wilmington. We had already saved twenty-two people from the *Pulaski* who had found refuge on the aft portion of the ship. When they boarded us, Mr. Pearson, the sailing master of the *Pulaski*, told us that he believed there were more passengers floating at sea. He noticed something within view that didn't move, that stayed put, rising and falling with the waves and surge of the sea. He begged Captain Davis to sail toward it."

"It was us," Augusta said. "Thanks to God and to Mr. Pearson for alerting you."

"Our Captain Davis searched and could not find you. He was unsure whether Pearson's sight could be trusted. He doubted more people could have survived after all these days without food and water, but he was not willing to give up. He tacked about three times and when he realized he had discovered more survivors, he fell to his knees, right on our deck, and thanked God for using him to save souls that would have otherwise perished."

"We would not have lasted any longer," Augusta said. "Not another moment, I believe." She tried to imagine how she came to be in a bed in a stranger's woolen clothes when she had no memory of having regained consciousness. "How did I get onto the ship?"

"You were carried by our men and then dressed in our woolen uniform. I'm happy to see you wake."

From the berth next to her, Charles groaned and sat up, his head brushing the top locker. "There are sails," he called out loudly. "Do you see them?"

Augusta reached across the space and took his hand. "We are saved, Charles. We are saved."

He collapsed again.

"My brother, Lamar Longstreet?" she asked the sailor. "He and five other men set out rowing toward shore in a separate boat. I fear it didn't make it—the boat was leaking and rotted. I fear . . ." Her voice was stayed on the last words.

"I'm sorry, I know only of those on this ship."

"Do you know if there is a Lilly Forsyth on board?" she asked. "Or a Henry MacMillan, or any other Longstreet . . . ?"

"There is a Forsyth, and a MacMillan. I can't remember the first names. And no, ma'am, there are no Longstreets except you and Charles here. But don't lose hope. There are those who made it on lifeboats. We shall find out more when we dock."

"Where will that be?"

"Wilmington, ma'am."

Augusta closed her eyes. "Wherever you take me, please make sure Charles stays with me." She paused. "Sir, what day is it?"

"It is Tuesday, June nineteenth."

Which meant they had been floating on the sea for five nights and into the fifth day. And if there was a Forsyth on this ship, it was possible that her beloved Lilly was alive, saved by floating on the aft deck wreckage.

40

EVERLY

Present day

The colors of sunset, golds and pinks, streaked the sky like finger-paintings. I sensed the rocking of the boat, the hum of the engine, the slip-slap of water against the hull.

The men had been treating me as gently as they did the treasure they'd brought up that afternoon. Nitrogen narcosis it was called—narking. It hits when and how it will. No one could have predicted it would strike me; no one could have avoided it. To me, it was as if I'd burst through a veil into another world.

Through my sleep I'd heard phrases and words that didn't hold together but I understood they were about me. *Hallucination. Narked. Ignored her wrist computer. Thank God. Safe. Scared.*

Now awake, I faced Maddox on the scuffed bench, his expression blank, his hands gripping the edges of the seat so hard his knuckles blanched. "I could have stopped you."

"No," I said. "This isn't your fault. And I'm fine. In fact, I'm better than ever. Maddox, I saw it down there. In one moment I saw it—I *want* to live."

Writ large in Maddox's eyes I saw the story that had worried him from the very beginning—the story of loss. He'd lost someone who'd insisted on diving and it had almost happened again. He was deeply shaken.

Oliver ascended from the hull of the boat carrying a glass of whiskey and handed it to Maddox. Maddox took it without comment and shot it back.

I leaned forward and patted his leg. "I. Am. Fine."

He shook his head and gazed off to the sea while Ben took special care at the wheel in guiding the boat back to Wrightsville Beach. At Oliver's urging, I slept for a bit and when I awoke the moon was high and the hull clunked against the dock, shifting as the men jumped off and tied the boat to the pier cleats. I stood and stretched, looked about the boat, as unlikely a place for salvation as could be—dirty and wet, its treasure wrapped in towels and blankets.

When we were docked securely, Ben told me, "You know we found our most significant piece today—the anchor; it's a major find. We'll take special equipment out there after the coming storm passes and bring it up." He paused and looked at Oliver. "Did you tell her?"

Maddox addressed Oliver. "You can show her later."

"Now," I said. "What is it?"

Oliver tossed Ben a side-eye glance and then sat next to me. Maddox reached into a bag on the deck and handed a piece of iron to Oliver, who handed it to me. A four-by-five-inch rectangle of iron covered in crustaceans and white barnacles that looked like worms. I ran my fingers over the curves and bumps of the piece. I lifted my gaze to Oliver. "What is this?"

"It is a piece they found today."

I searched my misty mind. Yes. I had grabbed on to a piece of iron that seemed to reach up from the sand. "Oh." I ran my fingers over its edges. "What do you think it is?"

"We have a few others. It's an iron label for a finer trunk or valise. Almost like a luggage tag of today."

"You have others. Why would you not want me to see this?" I glanced up, confused.

"Turn it over," Oliver said softly.

I flipped it over to more of the same. I stared at the barnacles and thick-as-concrete muck for a few breaths until I spied a letter. I focused and ran my finger over the engraving that hid below the hundred and eighty years of sea life that had hardened on its surface.

A. Longstreet.

I gasped. "Oh, my God." Tingles that weren't of cold or fear raced across my arms and legs, up the back of my neck and over my scalp. "This is Augusta Longstreet's luggage tag. This is . . ."

"Yes," Maddox said.

Oliver made a small noise of agreement.

Tears filled my eyes and an expanded feeling of integrity and goodness swelled inside my chest. I stood and noticed the crew confused and staring at me as if I were as delusional as I'd been with the hallucinations below. "I've been researching this woman for months now. I've been researching her family, her life and trying to find her records and story. This is . . ."

"Astonishing," Oliver said.

"Yes." I shivered with recognition and something otherworldly. "Astonishing. As if she's saying 'do not give up.'"

A reverential silence washed over the boat as everyone stood and took turns holding it in their hands. Of all the passengers—the hundred and fifty-five or more of them—it was her luggage tag I had grasped.

With that mystical awareness, I stepped off the boat and said good-bye to the men. "I promise to give the artifacts you've brought up the most beautiful display I am able. What you're doing is important. I'll make sure people hear about it."

Oliver stood at my side. "I'm going to help them clean up, then I'll find you. Go get some rest."

I nodded without answering. Sometimes when there were too many words to say it was best to say none at all.

I walked away, my duffel slung over my shoulder. I'd already booked a room at the inn.

Maddox strode after me and caught my hand as I reached for the door handle of the inn. The two of us looked as if we'd been washed up from a wreck of our own—damp and tangled, me in a bathing suit and coverup and he in a stained T-shirt over his swimming trunks. "Wait."

We stood under the darkening sky: stars sparking one by two.

"I feel like I'm supposed to say something important, but I don't know what," he said, his voice low.

"Me, too."

He took me by the shoulders and looked me square in the eye. I breathed in the aroma of sweat and sea. "You scared me to death, Everly."

"I know. I'm sorry."

"What happened down there?"

"Maddox, I thought I saw Mora, and a passenger and child. I know the truth of it—I was hallucinating—but it felt as real as you standing in front of me now."

"That's the scary part." His lips drew together. "I should have been watching you. Noticed earlier. It was too close a call."

"You were right there! You noticed and I am here. And I realize this now—anyone who is engaged in life *at all* is brave. It's so much easier to stay in the dream, in the hallucination, in the wishing. But today, down there, I chose to live a full life. Or something in me chose it."

He nodded. "Was there ever any other choice to make?"

"Yes. Many. I could do as I have been—living without really living. Nothing is safe, but that's got to be okay. Nothing is certain and the constant trying to make things certain only causes more heartache." I paused. "She's gone, but she's also here with me. I know that now."

He nodded with a look of sorrow furrowing his mouth and cheeks, his gaze falling from mine.

"You know, don't you?" I asked quietly, brushing the tangled hair from my face. "You've had to make the same choice."

"Yes, I have."

Silence echoed and stretched as we faced each other. Then finally he opened the door and motioned for me to enter the small foyer where a young woman sat at the front desk scrolling through her phone and chomping with the vigor of a gum-chewing athlete. We squinted into the fluorescent light.

"I did like it down there, Maddox." I stopped and faced him again. "I thought I might want to stay, but I realize that all that talk from Mom—about being born in water—this time she was right. But this time I was reborn in that water where all the others perished. I . . ."

"You can go back down," he assured me. "We will. But here is where you belong. Up here with the living."

I took his hand and squeezed it. "We carry the same broken pieces inside."

"I do believe so. It's a privilege to share this life with you, Everly Winthrop."

As he left me and I heard the door close, I sent the love I felt for him, for life, for choices made under the waves, out the door with him.

My sleep was deep and dreamless until I awoke to the pressure of a gentle hand on my forehead. *Everly. Everly.* My name uttered so softly as if under water, as if Mora spoke my name.

The bed swayed beneath me as if the sea heaved and fell, as if the waters were still buoying me. My eyes didn't want to open. Some part of me understood that both the peace and wild determination I'd found in the sea would dissipate, and I wanted to hold on to them as long as possible.

Everly.

I opened my eyes to Oliver sitting on the edge of the bed, his eyes and face engraved in concern. I slowly sat, resting against the padded headboard adorned with sailboat fabric.

"I needed to check on you." He scooted a few inches away and gazed at me with soft concern. "I'm sorry I woke you."

"I'm fine." My voice cracked on sleep. I cleared my throat. "Honestly, I'm fine. You didn't have to come." The room fizzled with morning light and I squinted, glanced around. "What time is it?"

"Ten."

"How did you get in here?" I partially smiled with closed lips. "Don't tell me—some smooth talking."

He ran his hands through my hair, gently parting the tangles; my scalp tingled with the touch. "I'm not quite capable of smooth talk right now. You were with Maddox when you checked in and they know him really well so he told them I was your . . . husband." He blushed. Even in the bright light I saw the reddening of his cheeks and around his eyes. "Scoot over," he said.

I did and he settled next to me, leaning against the headboard. "Tell me what happened down there, Everly."

"I was narked. No one did anything wrong."

"I know that part. What happened *to* you?"

"I saw her, Oliver. I saw Mora. She was right there next to me, smiling, her hair wild about her like a mermaid. She was . . . happy. Then she turned into another woman, a ghost and a child . . . they were all so real. And I wanted to be with them, to stay where I didn't feel anything but a kind of detached pleasure." I paused as he dropped his chin to his chest in a motion of defeat. I reached for his hand. "But I didn't. I chose life, Oliver."

"If you had . . . I would not have been able to . . ." His voice held the fear I rarely heard.

I put my fingers over his lips. "Shhh." I paused. "You know, I think I just wanted more from those boxes, and then I thought I'd find it by diving down there."

"Boxes?"

"The dusty boxes still cluttering my house. I wanted them to hold answers. When I discovered the link between Beatrice and the silver . . . I don't know, I thought . . . maybe . . . the treasure would tell me more."

"Ev . . ."

He'd never called me Ev before and I sensed a naming, a particular belonging in the new moniker.

This was ours. This moment. This name. The dive.

I tried again to explain what had happened to me. "It was suddenly as if nothing mattered . . . and everything mattered. Oliver . . . I know that Mora was the adventure of my life."

Oliver shook his head. "The adventure was always in you, Ev. Why do you think it belonged to her?"

"Since we were kids, she was the bright light. I was always and forever along for the ride. And that's okay. I wanted it that way. So did you."

"That's not how I saw it. You were wild and full of life yourself; Mora followed your lead. She might have taken it a step or two further sometimes, but you initiated."

"No."

"Who organized the camping trip to the secluded island on the summer solstice with wish lanterns? Who decided we should dive to the bottom of the haunted lake? Who convinced us to sneak into the graveyard on Halloween? I don't understand how you think it all came from Mora."

"Those were just ideas. She made them adventures."

"So did you. Why are you giving yourself such short shrift?"

I slipped my legs out from beneath the covers. The soft fabric of my silk drawstring pants slipped against my legs. I sat cross-legged and faced Oliver. "I didn't just lose her. I lost part of myself and my zeal. I lost you. I lost the sense of a quest. It would be simpler if I'd just lost her."

"You didn't lose those things. They might be in hiding, but you didn't lose them."

"Down there, where the remnants of the *Pulaski* have sat waiting for a hundred and eighty years, I saw that."

"And you damn sure didn't lose me." He took both my hands in his and squeezed them. He brought me near and dropped his forehead to mine. "You never lost me. I am right here."

A moment passed, a slice of time when I could lean forward into his kiss, into his touch, into comfort. But I wouldn't do it. No. I lifted my head from his and scooted back.

"Ev . . ."

"No. It would be terrible if something happened between us. I am so glad you're here. I need you. But . . . no."

"Nothing is going to happen that you don't want to happen. Our friendship is important. She loved us both."

A bite of disappointment clipped the inside of my heart—*friendship*—and yet I smiled at him. "Yes."

"I have missed you so much. Let's not do that again—stop speaking."

"No, let's not." I paused and reality flooded past the padded feeling of our touch, of the isolation of us in a bed alone. "Oh, my God, I must look such a wreck." My hand went to my tangled hair.

"Not a mess—more like a mermaid."

"Or a Selkie?" I teased.

He laughed and leaned across the space I had created to hug me. "Well, you look like it for sure."

I let him go and slid from the far side of the bed to stand and gaze down at him. He stood to stand in a patch of sunlight on the gold and blue carpet. I watched him and thought of the old stories of the *Pulaski*, of what Papa had told me.

"Oliver, long ago when Papa told me the story of the *Pulaski*, he said, 'Some people didn't die and some people lived.' I've thought about that line so many times through the years, trying to understand all it meant. But down there I understood it. I didn't die that day but I am damn sure not living. I wanted a reason why everything happened as it did. But there isn't one and never will be."

"Yet you have reasons to live." Oliver slid open the curtains and sunlight changed him into a silhouette, his voice strong and sure. "Because there are birds that sail on the wind with two-tone wings. There are dolphins with liquid eyes and permanent smiles. There are mushrooms the size of dinner plates that grow from bark. There are crickets and fireflies and sunlight on waxy leaves. There are wildflowers stubborn enough to grow between cracks in stone." His eyes shone so brightly they might have been ablaze. "And there is wind in the palm leaves, singing a song."

"Oliver," I said. "That was beautiful." My chest swelled and opened and I took in one shaky breath and held it. My thoughts sat in waiting for his next words. Something elemental and true moved toward me like a bird slow in flight, swooping near.

"Once, Mora recited her favorite poem to me," he said.

"'You Reading This, Be Ready.'" I recalled. "William Stafford."

"And there's a line I'll never forget. After she died I tried to memorize the whole poem, but it keeps slipping from me except for this one line: *'What can anyone give you greater than now, starting here, right in this room, when you turn around?'*"

I exhaled a breath I didn't know I held. "Greater than now."

He stepped out of the sunlight, his face alive with something near hope. "I had to find reasons to live, too," he said. "We'll join her soon enough—in whatever way that means—but for now we have to decide: Do we merely survive that horrific morning in Lafayette Square or embrace life with all we've got?" He came to me and pulled me into his arms; he held me there in my ragged pj's and mussed hair.

"With all we've got," I repeated into his shoulder. And in that moment, I might not have felt safe in all the old ways, but I most definitely felt alive.

41

AUGUSTA

Tuesday, June 19, 1838

Through vision blurred by swollen, sunburned eyelids, Augusta spied the large crowd gathered at the Wilmington, North Carolina, wharf below the ship's deck, waving white handkerchiefs in welcome. She held herself up at the rail, shaky and unsure but determined to disembark through her own effort despite her wounded feet. Charles would need to be carried out as he still drifted in and out of consciousness. She hadn't found Henry and didn't see him now on the deck. Beyond the immediate scene, the land curved toward the horizon, dotted with green trees and lovely homes. A sea gull squealed overhead; the sails hissed as they were furled and tied down.

Land.

Blessed land.

Augusta had thought she might never see it again. She scanned the crowd and checked for those she might know. Mr. Hutchinson stood next to her, and his cracked and sunburned face looked as weary as a much older soul. The man had lost his daughter at sea when she slipped into a dehydrated sleep like Thomas, and yet both Augusta and Mr. Hutchinson stood here on deck, alive and deprived of the children they loved. He touched Augusta's elbow. "They are here to provide care for us. Praise be to God."

Augusta took his hand and held it tight in a motion that only a week ago would have been completely inappropriate but was as easy as breathing now.

As the ship bumped into the wharf, Augusta caught from the corner of her eye the familiar dark hair of a man standing far down the rail. She didn't trust herself; the hallucinations she'd experienced on the wreckage haunted her mind. Yet a cry fell from her lips. "Adam Forsyth?" she called out to the tall man. He turned.

Shock darted through her body. It *was* Adam, but he was far from the man she remembered. His beard was tangled and his face scorched and blistered; a wound on his hand was covered in bandages but seeping with blood. "Augusta Longstreet." His voice came as a mere whisper. He took unsteady steps toward her to stand near.

"Is Lilly with you?" Augusta asked, hope rising to the blue sky.

"No." He shuddered and without warning, he bent over and heaved, vomiting water and bile over the deck railing into the harbor water. "I do apologize." He lifted his head as his body shook. "I am not well. Have you seen my wife and child?"

Augusta shook her head and dropped her chin to her chest before asking, "How did you survive?"

"At first, I was clinging to a settee that floated for a day and night, but eventually I broke off a piece to use as an oar and navigated to the aft deck raft where others were huddled. It was . . ."

"Hell." Augusta looked up at him now with the truth.

"Yes. Hell."

Augusta gazed again toward land, where men ran to catch the

ropes and tie the *Henry Camerdon* to the dock. She didn't look to Adam again. The god that would allow him to survive and Lilly to die was not a god Augusta wanted to know.

Much later, Augusta had broken memories of being taken to a house so lovely and a bed so soft that she might have gone to heaven after all. Several ladies attended to her every need and the preacher whose home this was prayed over her. They washed and untangled her hair, rubbed her skin with lotions, and rebandaged her feet with thick white cloth. Charles slept in a bedroom down the hall, and she was told that physicians watched over him all night, as he had been near death. By Thursday morning he'd revived enough that they believed he would live.

In the house of Dr. Armand John DeRosset and his wife, Augusta alternated between taking sips of a cold arrowroot tincture and sleeping. Her sunburn faded under the application of water and vinegar soaks. She slept in another woman's nightdress and time passed unevenly. She often felt the swell of the sea beneath her bed, only to jolt awake and know herself safe. She prayed for her eldest brother, not knowing if it was his eternal rest and soul she prayed for, or his healing. Either way, his name was upon her lips.

On Thursday a knock came to her bedroom door and the mistress of the house informed her that Lamar and five other men had made it safely to shore forty miles north of Wilmington. At that very moment, Lamar was on his way to her. Augusta let the tears flow—tears of gratitude and loss, of grief and thanksgiving.

"Do you know the whereabouts of a man named Henry MacMillan?" she asked the woman. "Who is taking care of him?"

"I don't know, but I can assure you that if he was on the *Henry Camerdon*, he is being well provided for. Dr. Moore is moving from house to house and other doctors have been summoned from neighboring towns. Also, I've received word that the two quarterboats that left the wreck reached shore several days ago."

"Do you have the names of the survivors?"

"I do." Mrs. DeRosset held out a list. "Would you like to read it?"

Augusta accepted the scribbled paper and scanned it quickly. There it was: Mrs. Adam Forsyth, child and servant. "Oh, thank you, God."

"Your brother will be here shortly," the woman said as she slipped the paper from Augusta's hand. "Will you be all right alone for a while?" She touched her shoulder.

"Yes, thank you."

She attempted to stay alert in order to watch Lamar walk through the door, but it was late that night when he burst into Augusta's bedroom and woke her from dreams of breathing under water. "Sister."

Her fever ebbing, Augusta wondered if she was again having visions, but it *was* Lamar.

"You are alive, my dear sister." His eyes filled with tears and he brushed the hair from her face.

"But . . . dear Thomas."

He nodded and his shoulders slumped in anguish. "God have mercy on his soul, and on the souls of all my beloved family. But you saved my oldest son."

"If I could have saved a life, I would have saved Thomas. I tried, Lamar. I tried with all my might and will and prayers. But God took him from us." The grief washed over her once more and she took in the deep aroma of soap and cleanliness that her brother exuded. His face was cut in many places and his hands were nearly the color of eggplant, so disfigured.

"The loss of so many families just like ours, Augusta. I have heard the stories. We are not the only ones. The city grieves. The nation grieves."

"How did you reach safety?"

"We saw land that very day and made it to shore." He paused and hugged her closer. "I had so little strength and the breakers were wild and rough, but we all made it. All six of us."

"Was it you who sent the *Henry Camerdon*?"

"No." He closed his eyes and placed his hand over his chest to tell his story in halting words. "We arrived about two o'clock in the afternoon. The boat came apart in the surf as we knew it would. Exhausted and bleeding, we stumbled to find help; we had no thought of where we were, but we found a little village called New River Inlet. I immediately located the owner of a fishing boat and offered five hundred dollars for each member of my family rescued and a hundred a piece for any others. They didn't intend to go into the storm and I thought money might act as an incentive." Lamar dropped his head, coughed back emotion. "But he refused. He said it was too dangerous. So I offered to pay another man to hurry to Wilmington with word that there are other survivors. Then we were taken in by local families, just as you were. When I awoke . . . Sister, when I awoke I was told that the traitorous fisherman had convinced the messenger not to make the trip to Wilmington as there was no hope of survivors. He had convinced him the mission was folly. Each day that passed, as more vessels came into the inlet, I made the same offer again and again and received the same rejection. My fortune, half of it now at the bottom of the sea, could not save a single person. I believed you had all died."

"Oh, brother. You despaired."

"It is a fact that I begged with all I had. Then we all mourned you as lost. And I wished I'd perished with you. I wanted to die with my family. I had no desire to survive alone."

Augusta fell back against the pillow.

"The *Henry Camerdon* found you not by my direction but by God's providence," Lamar concluded.

"I no longer know what that is." She let a sob break free. "Thomas. I can't believe his death was the work of providence."

She noticed his motions, how small they were without the sweeping arms and grand gestures, as if her brother had been diminished as
they all had. Even he. "Augusta, God's love created the world and we
must create new lives with love. This is not the time to abandon our
beliefs. We have lost most of our family, but not all. My heart doesn't
believe it can survive, but it must. Charles lives. You live. I live. I've
had much time to lie in bed in silence. My wounded feet became in-
fected and I was delirious with fever and pain. And in those lonely
hours I realized that we do live, sister. We *do* live."

"But do we want to?" Augusta turned her face from her brother,
seeing only Thomas, blue and gone, although she had done all she
could. "If love could save, Thomas would be here next to me."

"I bear some responsibility for the tragedy." Lamar's voice broke
and then she felt him straighten with new resolve. "Although we still
don't know why the ship exploded, I must take part in the restoration
of broken lives. You and I can help alleviate the suffering. What will
we do, sister? We will live and we will create and heal and care for others. Through love we will be newly made, as will Charles."

"Melody. Eliza. Thomas . . ." Augusta trailed off as Lamar continued to say the names of each of his children like a prayer.

Augusta let their names rest between them, a silence full of their
absence until she asked, "Do you know what has become of Henry? I
don't even know if he was still alive when the *Henry Camerdon* rescued
us. I never saw him again after I . . . hallucinated and . . ." Her voice
tripped across the memory.

"He was most assuredly saved. But I don't know what happened to
him; I assume he returned to New York. I doubt he will ever want to
see Savannah again."

Had she really believed that by surviving together she and Henry
had found proof they were intended to remain together? The folly of
the love-struck, to believe he was her dove, when the ultimate tragedy

loomed so near. "Oh, Lamar," she said. "How will we survive the surviving?"

Lamar took her in his arms and, in a small bedroom in Wilmington, North Carolina, with his only living child in the next bedroom, they wept.

42

EVERLY

Present day

When I walked in my front door, the living room with its red couch and cream curtains, with its brightly flowered rug found at a garage sale, with its iron coffee table and white-linen-covered lounge chair, was the same as it had always been. And yet everything was different: almost sacred in it ordinariness. My house. My life.

I dropped my duffel bag and walked to the kitchen, took the Brita water pitcher from the fridge and poured a jelly jar glass full. I chugged it down and thought of the ragged survivors floating for five days and nights without water. Everything from my water to the items in my home seemed more vivid and precious than ever.

I thought of Maddox's words, said so long ago on the Savannah riverfront the first day we met. *Not everyone who survives trauma becomes a better person. The idea that surviving brings everyone to a new and better place is a lie told by people who need the world to make sense.*

There was always a choice.

The boxes Oliver and I had taken from the house on Bull Street took up much of my living room. I'd been through all but two letter-books and one file without finding what I was seeking.

Some secrets stayed hidden. I knew that. The unknown couldn't always be discovered just because I wanted it. Although I'd found papers I knew the historical society would want for its archives, none of them had to do with Augusta, Lilly, Melody or the other children. It was as if they had disappeared from record.

I'd thought I'd go straight to bed after the drive back from Wrightsville Beach, but now, instead, I found myself sitting cross-legged on the floor, opening one of the two remaining letter-books. Dust lay on it thick enough to make designs when I dragged my finger through it. Over the last days, I'd examined at least a thousand pages of documents, becoming increasingly bleary-eyed and frustrated.

I opened the app for music on my cell, set it to some Etta James, and began to sing along, my soul feeling quenched by the sea. I could get through the last files and text Oliver that we were ready to donate the boxes, then get the musty things out of my house.

I found papers about Forsyth Merchandising: merchant records with numbers so tightly scribbled I could barely make them out. Letters regarding hemp bags for cotton; a broken cotton gin; an overseer who cheated by hiding weights in the cotton. I'd seen similar papers several times in these boxes and was rapidly, lazily if truth be told, flipping through the last of them when the phrase *Not for Publication* jumped out at me. On the single page was written in all capital letters *THE CALAMITY OF THE PULASKI*. The pulse in my wrist pounded, and I picked up my phone to call Oliver.

"The calamity," I said when he answered.

"You okay?"

"Come over now." I pointed at the handwritten yellowed paper as if he could see it.

"Ev, are you sick?"

"No." I laughed. "I found something." He hung up before I could say more and it wasn't ten minutes before he burst through my unlocked door. From the floor, still cross-legged and covered in dust, I handed him the page, reciting the first sentences. "An account of the disaster to be graphically described in the following paper . . ." He skimmed longer and then read the opening line of a narrative written by Augusta Longstreet. "The steam packet *Pulaski*, with Captain Dubois in charge, sailed from Savannah on Wednesday, June thirteenth, 1838."

He looked at the fragile paper and then at me. "Who wrote this?"

"Augusta Longstreet. Twenty years after the tragedy, she wrote this." Tears blurred my vision. "I had no idea how much I needed to know she survived. How I desperately wanted to find this . . ."

Oliver plopped down on the floor and faced me, our knees touching. "Where's the rest?"

"I don't know."

Oliver read the entire first page while I leafed through the remainder of the papers in the file. "Nothing. All about business. This one page must have gotten separated . . ."

"It says 'not for publication.'"

"Maybe that's why it's hidden in here. Let's start at the beginning of this letter-book, go slower. There have to be more pages." I gently turned the papers to the beginning and went through the file as meticulously as Maddox's divers combing the bottom of the sea, but I found nothing. Oliver had reached for the second leather-bound book and was halfway through it when he grabbed my hand. "Here." He handed the book to me and there, tucked among the business papers with their columns of numbers, letters regarding sales and ships and warehouses, were twelve pages of the same handwriting—Augusta Longstreet's handwriting.

I flipped to the last page where a list of passengers was labeled "Survivors As They Are Known."

"Why did they hide this document?" Oliver asked, drawing closer; we sat shoulder to shoulder, staring at the account, the cursive like the rise and fall of peaked mountains.

"Maybe they weren't so much hiding it as saving it for someone who cared."

"Someone like you."

"Oliver, this is Mora's relative. This is her blood. This is her story. If I'd just looked closer. For weeks, this has been sitting in my home, right here under my nose. I thought—assumed—that because I'd spent hours with the same kinds of papers, I'd find only more of the same."

"But you didn't give up. Somebody did not want this story to be passed on, but you persisted and you found it."

I returned my gaze to the account and flipped to the end, and read out loud, "'If not for the accident, I would not know my love or have my children. I would not know my own resilience and strength. And yet, if not for the accident, Charles might have grown to truly become the Noble Boy he was called during those terrible days at sea. Thomas and Eliza and the others would have lived beyond their short years. If not for . . . if not for . . . if not for . . . but there is no use in lamenting what might have been, for we are here and there is a life after horror. There is tragedy behind, and it trails us and walks alongside us, but still there is the great mystery of life after.'"

I looked up and Oliver's eyes were filled with something I couldn't name, his forehead furrowed. "'If not for the accident . . .'" He repeated Augusta's words.

"If not for . . ." I said.

"But she also wrote, 'the great mystery of life after.' Her loss was unimaginable and still that is what she wrote." He leaned back on his hands, his elbows bent. His hair was wet, I noticed, his thick eyebrows bowed to a V, his arms tan with a small cut on top of his hand. I touched it. "If we tell the story."

He glanced down at my hand touching his wound and smiled. "That's what I get for trying to dig up what I thought was a piece of gold—it was a torn piece of the copper boiler." He shrugged.

"Oliver." I withdrew my hand. "What you just said—if we tell the story. I have an idea for the exhibit. I know what to do now."

"Shoot."

"Tickets."

"Huh?"

I spread my arms wide. "When you first walk in, you are given a ticket to get on the ship. On that ticket is a luggage tag like the one Maddox's crew found. You're given a name and then when you exit the exhibit, you discover your fate."

"I like it so far . . ."

"Now imagine the space divided up: each space will be a different experience from the city at that time, to the ship, to the stories. Treasure and artifacts will be in each space to follow the story. And as you go through you learn about what happened to the Longstreet family. They are our journey through the disaster. You will meet them in the first room and then follow them through each area.

"You also learn more about the ship, the history and the people on it. This personalizes the experience. The stories matter. This makes it more interactive."

Oliver nodded for me to go on, his smile growing. "Now that we have Augusta's account, it might be possible."

"Now that we have her account."

We stood from the floor and sat at my kitchen table, our heads bowed over the pages. When we finished reading I said, "So now we know—only three of the direct family of Longstreets survived. Poor Melody and baby Thomas, poor Eliza and William, Rebecca and Caroline. Most drowned within minutes of the explosion, while Thomas passed only after he'd suffered days at sea without food and water. And still we know nothing about Lilly, except that Augusta was worried about her."

"But Lilly is listed on this survivor list," Oliver pointed out. "As is Adam."

We sat quietly for a moment. Then I said, "Oliver, I feel more sure of my determination to tell the whole story in the exhibit. I'll include Augusta's story—the strength that drove her to survive, the grief she suffered over the loss of her family, and her resilience in rebuilding her life afterward. And I'll include Charles's story—his promise as a fourteen-year-old heir to a powerful man, his kindness during the ordeal that earned him the title Noble Boy, and the resentment and cruelty that turned him into the Red Devil as an adult. Survival doesn't ensure a happy ending, and it isn't the end of the story."

I went on. "Maddox said something to me when we first met that has stayed with me. He said, 'The idea that surviving brings everyone to a new and better place is a lie told by people who need the world to make sense.' For a long time I've been trying to make sense of the world, but now I know that just isn't always possible."

Oliver drew closer and reached for my hand. "And yet surviving a trauma is significant, even a triumph of sorts. It's a second chance. The Red Devil squandered his chance."

And it hit me then, an arrow so sharp I hadn't felt it enter until I saw the damage. If I was to follow the plucky and determined women—Lilly and Augusta both—and claim them for Mora, then I had to acknowledge the Red Devil also. There was no picking and choosing; it was both/and. There were many ways to survive and *many* ways to survive the surviving. The darkness was there, too. Survival wasn't just about the happy story of living. Some didn't survive the living. Some did awful things with the second chance.

I held up my palms as if pleading. "What if Charles had died instead of his baby brother? What if he had been the one to sink? Think of the pain the world would have been spared. Just because we live through something doesn't mean it is for some higher purpose. I don't want to hear that mushy story one more time. I didn't know it when I started out, but I wanted Augusta to save me by example. I wanted her to show me that there is a pattern or reason—a way to live when you're the one who survived."

"I don't understand," Oliver said quietly.

"All this time I've felt guilty because I've been told I was *meant* to live, and I can't find a single reason why that's true. This man—this relative of Mora's blood—survived and then destroyed. There's nothing so special about surviving."

Oliver drew closer. "Everly, yes, there is something special about surviving. But after that, it's up to you. This Red Devil, he squandered his survival. We don't. We won't."

43

EVERLY

Present day

Bonaventure Cemetery was startlingly beautiful. The Wilmington River coursed past with a constant melody that reminded anyone who would listen that life continued. Gray moss hung from rough-barked tree limbs, tangled among waxy green leaves. The iron fences around family plots had rusted yet stood majestic; some gates were locked and others permanently rusted open. I stood by Mora's grave and picked leaves and debris from around the marble stone. A bouquet of fist-sized peonies, pink and slightly drooping in the July heat, lay on the grass next to the marker. I ran my fingers along silky petals, flicked the yellow pollen off my skin.

I'd come straight to Bonaventure after reading Augusta's account of the harrowing five days at sea. If Augusta was Mora's many-times-removed great-grandmother, she was a direct descendant of a woman of grit and determination. If Charles was her relative then she was the direct descendant of a cruel man. Either way, she was descended in some way from both—a living example of the mix of light and dark in each of us.

I allowed the sun-soaked earth to warm my bare legs. The river's hushed current joined with the call of birds I couldn't name.

Shouldn't I have something to say to Mora? Instead I remembered the way her hair curled in corkscrews off her forehead and then fell backward, spiraling toward her shoulders. I saw her deep brown eyes and peppered freckles. If only deep love and purity of memory could entice her spirit across the veil into the land of the living.

I identified another feeling, one that brought guilt. For my unasked-for, unaccustomed feelings for Oliver when he'd sat close beside me on that hotel room bed. It wasn't like the twisted torment I'd experienced with Grant. It wasn't the addiction for recognition and possessiveness. This was far different—more of a desire to give love than to secure it, more of a simple yearning to be near him and to share his life. His voice and his presence, his smile and his touch.

I wanted to deny my desire for him, but such feelings didn't allow dismissal. What I would do was keep my feelings to myself. I would hold them close in secret, until time gradually stole their power over me. Eventually my feelings for Oliver would pass.

Everything did.

A movement made me turn to see a man standing one plot over. He was tall and bald, wearing a red T-shirt, the bright yellow lenses of his sunglasses reflecting the oak leaves. His hollowed cheeks were like those of many of the mourners I'd seen at Bonaventure over the past year. We were like ghosts in the absence of those we loved.

Sympathy washed through me like a rain shower and I lifted my hand to the man, an acknowledgment of shared pain. He began to walk toward me, his hands clasped in front of him as if in prayer. I didn't want to talk to him; I'd just meant to be kind. I turned my face to the gravestone and closed my eyes, hoping he'd take the hint.

"Hello." His voice sounded gruff from disuse.

I glanced up at him, but merely nodded without saying a word. I didn't want to share this moment with anyone but Mora. But he stood there long enough that a slight tremble of fear prickled along my spine, a crawling sensation that made me rise to stand and take a few steps back. We were alone, and he was blocking the way to my car. My phone was on the front seat.

"I'm very sorry." His hands dangled limply at his sides and his fists clenched and unclenched. His cheeks were ruddy and his forehead dotted with sweat.

I yanked my car keys from my back pocket and stumbled a few steps toward my car.

"Don't be afraid." His voice cracked. "I'd never hurt anyone. I never had . . . until that day."

I reached the car and I brought my hand to the driver's-side handle.

The sound of his feet was soft behind me. "Those flowers. They're from me."

Something moved close to me like smoke seeping under a doorway, fire crawling down the hallway. I felt as trapped as if I were in the cabin of a sinking ship.

I thought maybe it would be best to say something, start a conversation as I slid into the car. "Do you bring them often?"

And then he was standing over me holding the car door open with his broad hands. He smelled of earth and sweat. His shaved head shone and sweat formed along his lip line. He removed his glasses and his dark eyes were wet with tears.

Fear slammed into my chest. I tried to scream, to start the car, to move, but I was frozen.

His throat clearing sounded like a man choking. "Don't be scared. I just want to tell you I *am* sorry. I ain't had a drop to drink since that day. I atoned the best way I know how. I bring flowers. I pray." The man dropped his face downward and then covered it with his hands, his next words mumbled. "I'm so, so sorry. I didn't mean to hurt no one. I didn't know there was a parade. I don't remember nothing . . . I don't know how it happened."

Fear evaporated and anger filled my chest. A great cry erupted, searing with rage. I stepped out of the car. "You killed my best friend and you think flowers are going to fix it?" My car engine idling, I lunged toward the man with the dead eyes, my fingers curled into claws. I'd imagined what it would be like to have moved on that terrible day, to have gone after him, stopped him.

Now I knew.

He backed away and a tear tracked down his wrinkled face. I stumbled, caught my hand on the edge of the car door, felt a sharp cut on my palm.

"No," he said. "It ain't enough. But I don't know what else to do." And with that, he ran. His feet dented the earth as he headed toward the rusted chain-link fence and climbed, jumping over it as easily as if he were a cat. The earth bore his weight with a thud. His bald head gleamed in the afternoon sun and his red T-shirt disappeared around a bend.

Speechless and shaky, I dug my cell phone from my bag, dialed 911 as quickly as my trembling fingers allowed.

The police detective, Ray Stuart, fidgeted across a metal desk with two cups of coffee gone cold. I described the man in the cemetery for the fifth time and then bent toward the officer, who had a blond crew cut and pimples along his chin. "You don't believe me."

"I do, ma'am." His southern accent was thick. He pulled his shoulders back, rocked his neck left and right. "I have the file here and I know you've called numerous times about cars you've seen or men who've looked like him. I do believe you. And I am so sorry for your loss."

"You believe me but you aren't going to do anything, are you?" My exhale rattled with anger as my spine ached from the tension of sitting on a folding chair.

"I am. I'm going to alert the cemetery caretaker to call us when anyone comes to leave flowers on your friend's grave. We don't have a photo of him and I can't patrol the city looking for a bald man in sunglasses and a red T-shirt." He tented his hands, his elbows on the desk as he spoke through his fingers. "His fingerprints are in the system from the steering wheel of the accident vehicle. If he commits any violation, no matter how small, he will be apprehended. We won't stop looking."

"Neither will I," I said, my voice hard. "Thank you for your help." I stood with a screech of the chair across the floor.

Once outside, standing on the sidewalk, I raised my face to the twilight sky and breathed out with a groan. I'd been so close to catching him. If I'd been quieter, trailed him, moved more slowly. And once again, he'd gotten away.

44

LILLY

Tuesday, June 19, 1838

Ma'am, I have some news." A quiet voice woke Lilly. She sat up in bed and pulled Madeline closer. She had barely let her go since she'd arrived. How many days had passed since then? Four. Yes, four.

Lilly accepted the cup of tea Mrs. Benedict held out for her. She sipped and then met the other woman's gaze. She was a kind woman, stout and chubby cheeked with an innocence that Lilly would never possess. She'd married a soft-spoken man with a waist as thin as Lilly's. Mrs. Benedict's talk of God and his providence slipped from her lips as easily as air. "What is it?" Lilly asked.

"Thirty more survivors total from both floating pieces of broken ship have been found. They came ashore in Wilmington on a rescue ship this evening. God saved them by his mighty hand."

"Oh, that is wonderful," Lilly said.

By now Priscilla had also come awake and was listening intently.

Mrs. Benedict touched Priscilla's forehead to check for fever. "You are on the mend. And yes, there are other survivors. They are safe in the homes of Wilmington families. Word has been sent to Charleston and Savannah. Passage is being arranged for you three to return to Savannah. It shall mean boarding another ship, but it is the only way home unless someone comes to fetch you by carriage. Our Onslow mayor has arranged for you both to sail tomorrow. If you feel strong enough."

"We do." Lilly wiped a hand through her hair, which had been freshly washed by a young girl just last night. "We've inconvenienced you for four days. We must go tomorrow. I don't know how to thank you for offering us shelter and care."

"God sent you to us, and we are honored to be in his service." Mrs. Benedict smiled as if she'd fulfilled her life's purpose. "And I have saved the very best news for last."

"What is it?" Lilly breathed deeply and lifted the glass of water from the bedside table, took a long swallow.

"Word has been sent that you are among the most blessed. Both your aunt, Augusta Longstreet, and your husband, Adam Forsyth, have survived. They suffered dire injuries and are healing in Wilmington, but they have been saved by God's hand." Mrs. Benedict beamed as if she had carried the news in on a silver platter.

Lilly let out a cry and covered her mouth with her hand. "What kind of injuries?" She regained control of herself, needing information. She had left Adam to perish at sea—how was he alive?

"I wasn't told, only informed that you would want to know they are alive and well and on their way soon to Savannah. I was told that Miss Longstreet and your husband survived on separate pieces of flotage— broken sections of the ship."

"Thank you." Lilly dropped back to the pillow. "I am thankful for their survival." Her voice sounded uneven, as if it were limping across the lies.

"I will allow you privacy for your prayers of thanksgiving." Mrs. Benedict bowed her head and then exited, leaving a washbasin of warm water, some fresh clothes that looked too big, and a tray of warm biscuits and ham. She shut the door quietly behind her.

Priscilla sprang from the bed and stood unsteadily in a nightgown four sizes too big; she folded her hands into a knot. "He's alive."

Lilly posed stiffly at the edge of her bed. Her feet were still healing. Her sunburned skin was flaking off in sheets. Welts still bulged on her lips, though they no longer bled. She eyed the wooden dresser with the small mirror above it and on the polished surface the jewelry bag she'd kept tied to her wrist throughout her ordeal. As she stroked Madeline's cheek, a surge of energy, as if she'd been set aflame from within, blew through her. Her voice lifted with conviction.

"Priscilla, it is time to go."

45

AUGUSTA

July 1838

A month after they returned from Wilmington, on the day of the memorial service for the perished of the *Pulaski*, Charles, Lamar and Augusta stood close together, their health returned but their sanity still precarious. In the echoing halls of the nearly empty Broughton Street house each had heard the other awake crying out from nightmares.

That morning, they walked toward Christ Episcopal Church on Bull Street. Its white Grecian columns glistened in the sunlight; mourners moved slowly up the marble stairs toward double front doors. The cross atop its steeple pierced the sky, an unchanging landmark in town.

Augusta often thought that the world and everything in it should be altered, shifted on its axis, pulled asunder because Savannah had lost so many of its vital inhabitants. But here was this building—as solid and enduring as before the explosion.

The three survivors of the nine Longstreets who had boarded the ship together stopped and stood still, feeling the afternoon heat bear down upon their black-clothed shoulders. Across the huge crowd—all of Savannah seemed to be present, everyone mourning someone—Augusta spied Samuel MacKay, his body slumped, his chin nearly on his chest, and his feet shuffling. His wife and two daughters had been on the same lifeboat she'd first been on, the yawl that toppled them all into the sea. He'd lost his family. Augusta knew this was the first time he'd left his upcountry plantation since he'd received the news.

At the foot of the stairs, glancing left and right, frantic and trembling, stood Adam Forsyth, his cheeks unshaven, his clothes rumpled and his skin seeming to hang from the bones. Purple bags bloated beneath his eyes like bruises. Nevertheless she could conjure up no sympathy for him as he hustled toward the three of them.

"Augusta." His voice was distorted, pulled out of shape by grief.

She didn't answer. His breath smelled of damp, fetid earth, of death. "Do you know?" he asked. "I beg of you—where is my wife? Where is my beloved child?"

Rage exploded inside Augusta. "I don't know and if I did, why would I tell you?"

Her brother took in a sharp breath. "Augusta!"

"There is no room for pretense," she said and spun to face Lamar, anger flaring like a bonfire. "He laid his fists on our beloved Lilly, his own wife, and he deserves no more than my disrespect."

Lamar's brows drew down and he, too, glared at Adam. "Is this true?"

Adam shook his head, his greasy, unkempt hair limp in the heat. "I am going mad with grief. I love Lilly with my whole heart. She is my life. I've donated a huge sum to build a statue in her honor, and for all those who perished. I have lost so much. My gold, my wife, my child . . ."

Augusta uttered a snort of disgust. "Do you hear what you listed first?"

Adam turned away from Augusta, apparently convinced he wouldn't receive any news from her, and pleaded with her brother. "Lamar, we are related now by marriage. You must help me."

Lamar stepped forward and Augusta saw his clenched fists, the quiver of his jawline where he clamped down hard on his teeth. A cut he'd received on the wreck ran from his mid-cheek to the side of his ear. It had healed into a thick scar that blazed red in the heat. "Adam Forsyth, we are no more related than I am to that horse behind you. You are *not* my family."

Lamar took Augusta's elbow and led her and Charles up the church steps as the bell atop the City Exchange across town on the river began to toll. Twelve church bells joined in and they all pealed in unison, a transcendent sound that mirrored the cries of the mourning. Everyone stopped midstep and listened to the lamentation of the chimes. A few cried out and a man nearby dropped to his knees, letting out a wail.

Augusta's memories, like a kaleidoscope that changed with each twist, wandered backward.

When Lamar, Charles, and she had returned to Savannah from Wilmington, they'd found a city in deep mourning. They could hear cries coming from the homes of those who'd lost loved ones. Wives, mothers, children, husbands and grandparents. Not a single person seemed to be left untouched by the outcome of one mistake—it had been discovered that the second engineer had poured cold water into an empty, searingly hot copper boiler and caused an explosion.

As they'd ridden in the carriage toward their home on Broughton Street, they'd spied the black crepe armbands worn by townspeople who stared at them as if they were ghosts: survivors that were not their own. The city's pain was as palpable as if a wicked storm had torn the houses from their tabby foundations.

Augusta had walked with her brother and nephew into the grand entrance of the Longstreet house. Inside, Lamar had fallen to his knees, his head bowed to the mahogany compass design built into the pinewood floor by an artisan from New York. None of it mattered—the home's fine workmanship, the furniture imported from London. Their family silver, which Melody had taken with her for entertaining in Saratoga Springs, now lay at the bottom of the sea. Who cared for any of it now that their family was all gone?

"My beloved wife. My children," Lamar had wailed.

Augusta had taken Charles's hand and he'd placed the other on his father's shoulder. "I am here, Father." But Lamar had ignored him, so caught up was he in his own grief.

The house had once resounded with the cries and laughter of children, of slaves bustling about their duties. In the month since their return, Augusta had heard Charles's and Lamar's every breath and cry. The servants tiptoed past them and spoke in whispers in a house that was beginning to feel like a tomb. What were they to do with their lives now that their family was gone? She understood that her life wasn't as just an individual woman but had been intricately tied together with their relationships, by their absolute devotion and love to each other. What did it matter if she, Lamar and Charles lived and the others—the ones to whom they had been bound—didn't live?

Charles's pain and cruelty burst forth in a sentence that would haunt Augusta for the rest of her life. He turned to her and said in a voice so low it sounded like a threat, "If you had saved Eliza instead of Thomas, we would at least have one more."

Lamar had been shocked out of his grief-filled stupor and slapped Charles across the face. Augusta cried out, "No!"

Lamar stood unbending before his son, who did not move an inch or protect his face. "God's providence has saved us, and we will not speak of such false claims. You must apologize to your aunt."

Charles stared at Augusta and as their gazes held he began to cry, sobbing with uncontrollable shame before he ran from the foyer to his room, where he stayed for at least a week's time, emerging only to eat small amounts and drink gallons of water.

Augusta's heartache had been burdened with additional sorrow and confusion—she didn't know what had happened to make Henry disappear without a word. Had she only dreamed of his love for her? Had she told herself a fairy tale for consolation in the middle of the sea? After all, who would love her, an almost-widow in rags? Henry's love for her had been as much a mirage as the ships they'd thought they'd seen on the horizon, turned to seafoam and mist.

She mourned Henry. She wept for her sister-in-law; she dreamed of Thomas; she awoke every night with an intense thirst that belied all reason and set her to guzzling glasses of water until she could hold no more.

The world was cruel and empty. And maybe Charles was right: she had made the wrong choice when she turned her back on Eliza and grabbed Thomas from the sea instead. But what else could she have done? She played it over and over as her mind bounced between all of these wonderings. Sleep eluded her and sorrow burrowed into her soul.

A horse let out a loud neigh, jolting Augusta's attention back to the afternoon's crowd and a line of horse-drawn conveyances where a worn carriage, the spokes of its wooden wheels covered in mud, its black top dusty, and the gray horse shimmering with sweat, pulled to a standstill. A man emerged from the carriage. His black top hat hid most of his face in shadow, but Augusta knew the cut of his chin, the slant of his lips, the breadth of his chest. "Henry!"

He removed his hat with a swift motion and his eyes scanned the crowd for her. When he saw her, he nearly ran to her side. He grasped both of her hands and tears filled his deep gray eyes. "Augusta."

A great wash of relief and beauty swept over her; a thrill tempered. "You're here. You came." His beloved face so near hers.

"We live together or we die together, my Augusta."

"I thought you'd never return . . . I thought you left me, left us."

"No, my love. No. Never."

She fell against his chest and his hand rested on her back, as solid and sure as she remembered. Their promises had been no mirage. His heartbeat was strong through his dusty shirt and she lifted her gaze to his. "Tell me where you've been. What has happened to you? Why did I never hear from you? I believed . . ."

"I was extremely ill, my love. I developed an infection from the cuts and damage on my feet, and for weeks I was hospitalized. I'm told I was twice given last rites." He laughed a coarse sound that sounded as full of tears as mirth. "The moment I became conscious enough to understand my predicament, I began my journey back to you. I thought, I can reach her before a letter can. Better my words from my mouth than from a piece of torn vellum. It has been a week of trains and carriages. Forgive the delay but I could not bear to board another ship."

"And now you are here." She touched his face, and ran her hands up and down his arm as if ensuring that he was real. His face, it was different now, thinner, and the flesh around his eyes swollen, but the very spirit of him was as pure as the day she'd seen him for the first time in the Broughton Street house's library.

"I *am* here and I will never leave you again." He took her hand, and together with Lamar and Charles they entered the church.

The memorial itself Augusta later recalled in scraps of images: on either side of the aisle, the front rows were reserved for relatives of the deceased, all wearing black, including their handkerchiefs, hats and shoes. My God, how she would have preferred to be sitting in the other pews, those for onlookers, for the judges and officers, for the children and families who knew the passengers but weren't members of their families.

The funeral dirge, the prayers and sermon, the hymns and scripture readings were led by Rev. Raymond Presson. He began with powerful words that brought her heart to its knees. "At the present time, the sympathies of a nation are called forth by an event which has filled hundreds of hearts with agony."

She was not the only one suffering; the city and the nation as well as the individual hearts were all in pain.

When it was over and the sound of bagpipes whirled high in grief, they left the church. Reverend Presson's final words of providence and courage echoed long into the evening. Upon reaching their house they sat stupefied and empty in the drawing room; Darlene, the house slave, brought in a tray of tea and sugar cookies. While Henry attended to his horse and his bags, Augusta and Charles sat across from Lamar as his father told Charles of his fate. "My beloved son, I think it is best if you go to Richmond to live with your aunt Nina. There is a school there that is beyond compare and you will not need to be daily reminded of our loss. I will begin to put to rights our business and our family matters."

Charles's cheeks flamed as red as his hair and he spat the next words with an anger that frightened Augusta. "You . . . wish Thomas had lived and I had died."

"No!" Lamar's words blew from him like the explosion that shattered the ship, the fire that had torn them all apart.

Charles looked to Augusta, rage glowing and then dying in his eyes. She had thought many times that Charles, the boy she knew, had died on that ship, and now a man remained. What would become of that man was still unclear. But the furor in his eyes was a hint.

At his father's reprimand, Charles cast his eyes down now. "No, Father. I want to stay here." His voice grew thick with anger and unshed tears he would never show. "Do not send me away."

"It's a miracle we live, son. And I will not squander your life here in Savannah with the weight of grief. It is time for you to be far from the sea and to gain your balance in a new school."

"It is *not* a miracle." Charles stood up and slammed his hand on the chair. "The reverend, he said that we must adore the God of providence. Not me, Father. I will not adore a god that killed my family. There is no such entity." Far off a horse neighed on the street outside the open windows.

"Charles!" Augusta cried out as if she could stop the blasphemy with just his name alone.

He spun to her. "I lived because I fought to live. No one saved me. No one will ever save me."

"Son!" Lamar stood, twilight slipping into the room, shining on both of them in a glow of orange and red. "How dare you speak such blasphemy."

Augusta stood and faced her nephew. Her love, it could bring him back to life, to his senses. She spoke softly. "Charles, I know your sorrow and pain. I feel it, too. It is a terrible weight. But we have been shown God's providence."

"Was my mother shown providence? My baby brother? My beautiful sisters?"

Tears sprang to Augusta's eyes, her heart knocking against her throat and ribs as it often did when the memory of Thomas dying in her arms returned with a great slam of sorrow. She dropped to the chair and allowed the misery to wash over her while a sob she could not halt tore from her throat in a choking sound. Charles came to her side and placed his hand on her shoulder. "I am sorry, Auntie, but it is the truth. We must save ourselves and Thomas could not. God has nothing to do with any of this."

"He was there." Augusta lifted her face to her nephew. "God was there in the smallest kindnesses—a shirt from a carpetbag; a man who cut off woolen socks to protect my feet; songs sung by a slave, and wine in a basket. There were—"

Charles interrupted in a voice she didn't recognize. "I know nothing of these kindnesses." He turned and strode from the room. His footsteps echoed through the house as they bounded up the hardwood stairs. When a door slammed, Augusta and Lamar startled with its sound.

"Oh, brother," Augusta said.

"Give him time, sister. Give him time."

"Grief is a terrible, gnawing thing. It is eating at him."

"It is eating at all of us," Lamar added.

Only days later, Lamar sent Charles to live with Melody's sister, Nina, believing the new home and landscape would cure the boy's insolence and sorrow.

One month later, in the baking heat of August, Henry and Augusta were married in a small ceremony in the very same church where they had mourned the perished. They forwent a reception afterward and instead moved immediately to New York.

Not long afterward, Lamar left Savannah for Alexandria, Virginia, where he established a new business and a new life. Within the year he married a pretty young woman, Leslie Faust, the daughter of another prominent businessman in town. The house on Broughton Street sat empty until Charles had finished both preparatory school in Pennsylvania and college in Virginia, eventually returning to the city from which he felt he'd been banished. There, he took over many of his father's former businesses.

As for the *Pulaski*, lawsuits were filed, trials conducted, and changes were made to the law. The Act of 1838 was followed by the Steamboat Act of 1852. Now, steam boilers must be inspected on a regular basis, and experienced engineers must be stationed aboard at all times. Now, the masters and owners of all steam vessels were held financially responsible for all damages. Augusta's brother had evaded such responsibility, but no more.

And yet Augusta knew that despite these well-intentioned laws, none of them could keep people truly safe from human error.

46

EVERLY

Three months later

Autumn arrived and the carpet-thick air of summer slid away, the leaves performed their magic with the yellow and red beauty of changing seasons. I'd brought out the box of thin sweaters from beneath my bed. The past week had been drenched in rain, but each day I felt the world open up a bit more, my heart with it.

My students that semester were a creative lot, full of questions and ideas. Returning to the classroom felt astonishing in the simple but wonderful way it brought me back to myself: the students challenged and enlivened me, reminded me of the thrill of learning and discovering. With the bulk of the curation completed over the summer, and with Augusta's detailed account offering a road map, the exhibit was coming together like a puzzle. We had the list of survivors and could— for the most part—make tickets for each passenger. Sadly, and horribly, the enslaved weren't always listed and when they were, it was with only their first names.

I engaged with the world again, in small bits and pieces—practicing yoga and wandering through the riverfront art festival one afternoon with Sophie. I'd felt like the Everly from before, the one who didn't gasp at the sound of every car and believe that the world, at any moment, would crack open and swallow her.

"Do you think," I'd asked Sophie, "that fate has anything to do with anything at all?"

She had stopped in front of a tent of pottery made by a student of hers and removed her sunglasses. Under her wide-brimmed red hat she'd eyed me. "Are you asking me if it is fate that killed Mora? No. A drunk man in a runaway car killed her."

It had been good—no, great—to talk to a friend again, to unload the story of the past months that had altered my view of not only my history but also my life. I'd only talked of it all with Oliver, Allyn and my mom; Sophie was a friend and one who made me feel like I was emerging into life in a larger way, expanding outward.

"And this shipwreck," I'd told her, "you know I'm working on it, and I've found some of the stories. Sometimes it feels like fate is the truth of how someone was saved with something as simple as a floating piece of wood found at the right time. And sometimes fate appears as sheer cruelty—like how some of the enslaved helped the passengers but weren't given aid in return. It's awful." I told her how much I'd read about all of the survivors, of Priscilla and of Lilly, of stories I'd never imagined.

She'd listened as we walked, until we'd come to the statue of Lilly. She'd set her foot on the concrete edge and looked up at the face of a woman carved in bronze a hundred and eighty years ago, and then at me, her skin almost glowing in the afternoon sunlight, but her eyes sad, shadowed even. "Much of that history is awful, Everly. You know that. I know that. Most don't want to know it." She'd stood, right there on the riverfront, as if we watched as enslaved people boarded the *Pu-*

laski and the owners flounced about with their suits and dresses and trunks of gold. She took a breath. "Listen, the enslaved people who survived, the ones who were sold and resold and torn from their families, can't go find their family tree like you and Mora; their ancestry was muddy at best and traumatic at worst. Everything about this sinking is just tragedy built on tragedy."

"I know," I'd said, which was all I knew to say. I'd hugged her, not only grateful but also feeling the weight of a past I thought I'd understood but now realized was only dimly seen.

She squeezed my hand. "You and I both know there's a difference between prejudice and obliviousness but sometimes it can have the same result."

"I hear you." I thought of the times I hadn't given prejudice its due. And the child who'd survived this sinking had wrought such horror.

Was the city past it? Over it? Not any more than I was over the loss of my father or my grandfather or my best friend. That grief was part of who I had become, and yet I was choosing to thrive in the face of it. My city was the same—I would hope they would not ignore the devastation of slavery, or cast it aside, not pretend it never existed or didn't have its echoes. I had no answers but at least I saw the questions I'd never seen before.

"Tell me what to do," I'd said to her.

"Give the enslaved humanity in that curation. Show them suffering and surviving; not just a name on a manifest."

"I am. I will."

And I had done my best to keep that promise.

As with Sophie, I found my pals had been waiting patiently; grief held no real timeline and they knew this. I'd sustained Oliver's friendship not out of obligation or fear but because we enjoyed each other. Too much had been taken from me—why would I reject a friend who saw me, and knew me? Whatever more intimate feelings I harbored in the recesses of my heart would stay secret, a buried treasure of my own. When the need to reach over and touch his arm, or slip my hand along the nape of his neck, or rest my head on his shoulder, arrived, I shut it down. I would not risk losing him altogether.

I'd started to gravitate back to my trademark phrase—*I wonder what happens next?* Now, I knew the answer could hold happiness *or* grief. My belief in the unbroken world was gone, but oddly that revelation made everything more sacred.

Meanwhile, work on the exhibition was in full swing.

I spent hours piecing together a Longstreet family tree, beginning with Lamar and Melody and moving down. It took some digging, but Maureen had shown me how to navigate the ancestry website and search for gravestones and names. It worked—I followed the hints that followed. There I finally found the direct line to Mora: she was Augusta's granddaughter generations back and Charles's niece just as far removed. Shared blood. Shared stories. Shared branches.

That November day, lists of the *Pulaski* passengers, written in calligraphy on huge charts we'd reproduced on Plexiglas, hung on the wall in the room where Maddox and I sat at a long table. We tried out our ideas on computer graphics, jotted ideas on Post-it notes and made careful changes to handwritten cards. Slowly, room by room, it was coming together. With a thunderstorm walloping outside, we huddled over the passenger tickets that would be distributed to visitors as they passed through the front doors.

"The experience will be immersive," I explained. "When visitors walk in they'll receive a ticket with their passenger's name. They walk up the gangplank and onto a deck, and then they learn about the construction of the ship, the weather that day, the city where the person they're pretending to be came from, and the events of that night. When they're finished, they can find out if their ticket belonged to someone who survived or perished. For the Longstreet family, they will receive a story card of what happened to their lives. Some of the enslaved people have a lost history. Something I can't find, and that's devastating to me."

"How so?"

"I asked my friend Sophie, who's a professor of African American studies, and she told me that while Mora and I can trace our heritage to an ancestral tree, while I can argue about who came over on the *Anne* and who might or might not have shipwrecked with Irish indentured servants, and who came from England and when, while I trace my finger over the branches and the links, she can't do any of that. Her history gets lost, muddied, with a trail of nothing but names given by owners that had nothing to do with their real names. It is as appalling as it is true. The story we're telling is about *more* than who survived, it's also about *what* survived: slavery and how the young boy, the Noble Boy, magnified and multiplied the pain by continuing it. Charles survived and he amplified the horrors. How do we possibly explain that except by telling the truth of it? There is no way. There are no words I have to understand it; but we can *show* the truth."

Maddox shifted papers and gestured at the walls labeled for display. "We'll show it, Everly. We will. And its impact will be heightened for its truth. I'm really glad the museum chose to open the exhibition on the anniversary of the ship's original launch in June. We're already free of the conservation process for the pieces you've chosen."

"Look what we've done," I said with a grin. "Do you always get this involved in your . . . projects? I mean . . ."

Maddox shuffled through the story cards I'd been writing—one by one I'd drafted narratives for each of the Longstreet family members. "No. But this one feels personal in a way I haven't felt before. This pile," Maddox said, resting his hand on a thick stack of papers with notes sticking out every few pages. "You read all of this?"

"Yes."

"Wow." Maddox sat back in his chair, exhaled.

"But Augusta's account is my favorite."

"It's amazing you found it . . ."

I opened a satchel and pulled out a rough sketch of a crudely drawn family tree. "And look." I pointed at Mora's name. "Direct line to Augusta."

"My God." He drew his finger up the tree, along the branches to Charles. "And also to him."

"Yes. Mora is related to both of them—Augusta and Charles. It's as if Mora is a living example of all of us—a mix of the light and the dark, a shadowed combination. She is the metaphor for all of us. Nothing all virtuous. Nothing all wicked. This mixture that is life, that is human, that is brokenness and wholeness."

"Yes." He reached for my hand and took it, squeezed it. "She is us. We are her. All of us."

"And cut down in the very moments when all of her life spread in front of her like another adventure."

"Like the rest of the Longstreet family. Like anyone when devastation hits unexpected in the middle of life." He spread his hands wide. "Look what you've done."

"Obsession and persistence might pay off?" I grinned. "If Augusta took the time to write of her experience—if others took the time to write what survivors told them—I want to share it."

"Doesn't writing these cards make you think of how someone might sum up your life? If two hundred years from now someone made a story card of it. What would it say?"

I looked at the man I had once met in the garden outside, when I'd been as closed off and scared as a rabbit. I thought of his kind face when he brought me up from the bottom of the ocean. "I have thought about that. It's sobering."

"I don't know what they would say about me. It would depend on who did the writing, I imagine. Would it be my ex who would malign my name? A student I set off on a successful career path? Or the parents of the student who died at sea? Or you?"

"If I wrote it?" I smiled. "I'd probably make you sound like Neptune, King of the Sea. As if you were born to save my life."

"Aren't you giving me too much credit?" His grin spread to the edges of his eyes.

"Most likely, but that's my prerogative if I'm writing your story card."

He glanced back at the papers but his face, always easy with emotion, showed his gratitude.

I took a breath before asking, "What *would* your ex say, Maddox?" My voice went quiet.

He exhaled and set down the story cards. "Here's the short version. Vivian blamed me for the death of Alison Morgan. I say her name—Alison—in my sleep sometimes. When the investigation was over, and it was proven that her death wasn't due to my negligence, Viv was sorry. She said so again and again. But her lack of faith at the beginning, the corrosive doubt and blame and fear, ate through the foundation of our marriage. It was . . . destructive condemnation."

"I'm sorry."

"So am I. Of course the rejection fed right into my own self-castigation. When it came back that the tank was faulty, the onus still rested on me, heavy as an anchor. It destroyed us." He paused as if his next words were coming from far off. Then he said, "Everly, it doesn't have to be that way for you and Oliver."

"What?"

"I can see the love between you. I can also see the unnecessary guilt that you must let go."

"That isn't why I asked about *you*."

"Yes, it is." His voice was stern.

"Maybe a little. But I also asked because I care."

"I know you do." He smiled and the conversation faded into comfortable silence.

Finally, I stood and stretched. "I'm meeting Oliver at the house to pack up those 'borrowed' boxes." I mocked quotation marks with my fingers. "We're taking them to the Georgia Historical Society. And yes, we did finally get permission from the original owners. They were happy to be rid of what the woman I spoke to called 'the family detritus.' I'll stop back here later."

Maddox waved me off. At the door I turned to watch him for a moment as he continued to read through the cards that had become to me more than just names on a list.

Rain pelted sideways on the windows, overflowing the gutters and cascading down the eaves of my front door. It had been a week of relentless storms, dark skies, trees losing their hold of the soaked earth and trunks toppling to the ground. Flowerbeds drooped and flattened; streets carried leaves and debris in tiny whitecaps; umbrellas blew inside out and heads bowed.

Cozy and dry at home, I opened my door to a knock and Oliver burst in, dripping wet and shaking his head. "Damn, will it ever stop?"

I stepped back, avoiding the spray. "Don't you own an umbrella?"

"About ten of 'em. I never remember to put one in my backpack and then I buy another and I forget that one, too."

He shed his coat and hung it from a hook. I grabbed a pink flowered towel from the kitchen and he used it to rub his hair and face.

"Okay, let's get those boxes out of here for you," he said, glancing into the kitchen where they were packed up and taped shut.

"They've probably left enough mold spores to overtake my house. I'm spraying the kitchen from top to bottom with Lysol after the boxes are gone. I can't believe how many papers I went through before I found what I needed."

"If you'd found everything right off, the hunt would have been boring. And God knows, you hate boring hunts."

I tossed him a look as he walked toward the boxes and then looked out the kitchen window to where the courtyard was in danger of flooding. "Think it will let up?" he asked.

"Weather channel says in an hour or two. Let's wait it out just a bit? I'll make some tea."

"Perfect."

I clicked on the gas under the kettle; the fire leapt up. I slowly chose two tea bags and set them in ceramic mugs I'd bought with Mora at an arts festival. Oliver's quiet presence was something I'd grown accustomed to, grown happy with.

We sat at the kitchen table and listened to the plunking sound of falling rain. "I love weather like this. Is that weird?" I asked, and took a long sip of tea. "It's cozy."

"Maybe because you were born in water?" His laugh was rich. "Ev, remember when we went to the sand bar?"

My insides rose and then faltered in a feeling as thrilling as it was frightening—like the first drop in a roller coaster after reaching the top. "Oliver."

He blushed—honest to God blushed. "Not that part. I was thinking about how many times you dove to the bottom. You scared the shit out of me. I lost count. I mean, you and the water, my God."

"The sea and me." I smiled. "You know, there's a sea myth—one of my favorites—about Selkies. It's mostly a Scottish folktale but as a kid

I wanted that to be my name after Papa told me that Father had wanted that for me. I told Papa over and over to call me that, but he would only do it when Mom wasn't around."

"Tell me."

"A Selkie is a mythical sea creature who can change from seal to human by slipping off her seal skin. But eventually she must return to the water—the sea always calls her home. There are several versions: in one a man steals her skin so she must stay with him. In another he returns the skin. Either way—she's a creature of the sea who is always called back no matter what she must leave behind: love, children or land. She is always longing for her true home, to find her seal skin and return to the sea."

"I wonder if we have one," he said. "A true home."

"I think so, yes. Don't you?"

"I grew up on the opposite coast, so I know what you mean about being near water. But I don't have the connection with a single piece of land as you do here in Savannah."

"There are male Selkies, too. They can shed their skin and not know who they are anymore. I know I belong here, but lately I'm feeling I'd like to get away, find a place where I can be me without Savannah, without the memories." I took a breath and let it go. "Maybe it's time to know who I am without the seal skin of Savannah. SCAD has offered to let me teach for a semester in their abroad program."

Startled, he sat back in his chair and ran his hands across his face. "What? Where?"

"LaCoste or Japan. I can choose . . . both have a history track I can teach."

"France? Japan? Will you go?"

I nodded, lifted my mug to let the steam rise to my face. "Probably France. I think so. Yes."

"You think leaving will help?"

"It can't hurt . . ."

We grew quiet and my cell rang. I ignored it. His rang. He ignored it. We laughed and he stood and placed his mug in the sink. The rain had lessened, trickling in the sound of wind chimes down the gutters. His cell rang again, and this time he lifted it from the kitchen table. He looked at it and then at me. "It's the detective."

I glanced at my phone. "That's who called me, too. Answer!" I jumped up and was at his side, grabbing his arm before I knew it.

Oliver answered and then listened, keeping eye contact with me the entire time. It didn't last long—maybe two minutes. Maybe three. Maybe months.

"Thank you," Oliver said and dropped the cell on my kitchen counter. He looked at me and said, "They caught him."

I dropped into Oliver's arms and he wrapped them around me. His lips were against my ear. "They've been watching the gravesite since you saw him there and he came today. Dropped off more flowers in the pouring rain. Daisies. They took him in; he confessed immediately. He broke down . . . It was like he was waiting for them."

We stood there, Oliver and I, holding each other as the rain pelted the window and our breaths synchronized. Neither of us needed to let go, but neither of us knew what to do next.

Finally, he eased away, only an inch, and kissed my forehead. "The search is over. They found him."

"Thank God they have him."

Oliver let me go, and I almost reached for him again, wanting those arms around me. But instead I wiped my tears and straightened.

He pressed his palms against his closed eyes. "You know"—he opened his eyes—"this is because of you. Because you never give up. Because you're always looking for the connections in life. Because you loved her so . . ." His voice broke, and I felt as if for the first time our shared sadness didn't add up to more, but an easing, a lessening of a load. "Let's get those boxes back where they belong."

The Georgia Historical Society's back room was as dusty as the attic on Bull Street where we'd found the boxes. As we waited for the librarian, I whispered to Oliver, "They'll feel right at home here."

He covered his laugh as Ellen Treadwell entered the room: the sweet librarian with the bird tattoo who'd helped Maddox and me at the very start of our journey. After years of my digging through her archives, she smiled when she saw me. "Hello, Everly!"

Oliver introduced himself and then told her, "These are letterbooks and business papers for the Longstreet family. We thought you would want them for your collection."

Ellen lifted a top. "Where did you get these?"

Oliver looked to me and I shrugged. "In an attic on Bull Street," I explained. "I contacted the family and they granted permission to donate them to you. Here's the signed document. They have no interest in any of it. Honestly, they told me to toss the lot, but there's at least one important document in there."

Ellen raised her eyebrows.

"A firsthand, detailed account of the *Pulaski* explosion written twenty years later by a survivor, Augusta Longstreet, who married another survivor, Henry MacMillan."

"Are you serious?"

"I am. Gold, isn't it?"

"Pure gold." Ellen's face lit up like we'd brought her true buried treasure. She eyed us both with a grin. "Thank you."

"Do you have anything on the MacMillan family?" I asked. "Anything else of Augusta's we might be able to see?"

"A MacMillan box was donated last year, but we haven't curated it yet. Seems to be repeats of what we already have: business papers. I had no idea that was Augusta's married name or I would have given it to you. If you look around, you'll see why I haven't gotten to it yet."

The room was crammed end to end with boxes and folders, all waiting to be archived. "May I have a look at it?"

"If you want. It doesn't have anything to do with the wreck."

"If the papers have to do with Augusta, they have to do with the wreck. Everything . . ." I said.

"Is connected," Oliver finished for me with a grin.

Ellen disappeared and returned quickly with a small metal box. "This is it. Family artifacts from a house in New York. They donated it to us because he lived here part time and they didn't know what else to do with it."

Ellen scurried off to the sound of a bell, and Oliver lifted the lid of the metal box and reached inside. He withdrew a pile of papers and with a quick glance we both knew they were similar to what we'd already found evidence of: a family who kept meticulous business records. "Looks like her husband took over some of Lamar's business—it's all shipping and banking. I don't believe Henry would have had anything to do with cotton plantations."

I withdrew a thick leather-bound family Bible that lay at the bottom. Its gold-edged pages shimmered in the light. "My mom has one of these; it's five generations old. The entire family tree is in the front. As far as I can tell, that's mostly what these Bibles were used for."

Oliver opened the Bible and sure enough on the front page was a family tree for the Longstreets and another for the larger family Augusta had married into, her four children's branches that edged to the ends of the papers. But that wasn't what caught my eye; it was the stationery that poked out from the middle of the Bible. I flipped to where it lay between the pages of the Book of Ruth. Underlined in dark fountain pen was the verse, *"For whither thou goest, I will go; and where thou lodgest, I will lodge: thy people shall be my people, and thy God my God.*" I lifted a handwritten paper that was almost thin enough to see through, the script small and tight. I slowly unfolded the fragile vellum. The crease was so old the page almost ripped. The date on top stated *August 12th, 1858.*

"*My Dear Augusta,*" I read with a hitch in my voice.

Oliver stood behind me, placed a hand on my shoulder and squeezed. Our eyes scanned to the bottom.

Together we read out loud.

"*With all my love, Lilly.*"

47

AUGUSTA

December 1858
Twenty years later

A mild December descended on Savannah, the cerulean sky scattered with bloated clouds drifting toward the river. Augusta sat on the piazza wearing a light gray wool cape she'd brought from New York City, where she lived most of the year. Only in winter did she return to Savannah, as summer brought with it not only the deadly heat but also the malignant reminder of the journey that had destroyed her family. Yet despite everything, she still loved the city. Its slow ways and vibrant beauty eased her flesh and soothed her heart.

The breeze had died by midday and the soft clomp of horses' hooves along the dirt roads was all she heard. A white-winged bird swooped into the yard near the cistern and sat upon the chinaberry tree, eyeing Augusta before lifting off again.

She sat content as the *Daily Georgian* newspaper bled black print onto her fingers. A cold glass of water rested on the table next to her, and although it had been two decades since the *Pulaski* disaster Augusta was always grateful for a drink of water. She pressed the glass to her forehead and took a long sip before reading an article on the front page with the headline:

ILLEGAL HUMAN CARGO PUTS ASHORE AT HORSE CREEK

Augusta shivered and read on.

A ship carrying four hundred and eighty-seven enslaved Negroes illegally imported from Africa recently landed near Brunswick. The human cargo was offloaded to rivergoing vessels, brought up the Savannah River, and put ashore on Tuesday evening about three o'clock, at the mouth of Horse Creek, three miles south of Savannah on the Carolina side.

The *Wanderer*, transformed by its owner Charles Longstreet from a luxury yacht to a vessel for rudimentary slave transport, departed from Charleston with the New York Yacht Club pennant flying, and arrived on September 16, 1858, at the mouth of the Congo River. After negotiating and paying for almost 500 African souls, the schooner sailed to the South and landed on Jekyll Island on November 18th. Of the original four hundred and eighty-seven Africans on board, 79 perished during the journey.

Longstreet, a member of the controversial Fire-Eaters, a pro-slavery group that urges the separation of the Southern states from the Union and the creation of a new nation, has been accused of organizing the importing and holding of African Negroes, in contravention of the 1808 Act Prohibiting the Importation of Slaves.

The article continued to describe the deplorable conditions on Charles's schooner and speculate about the high mortality rate. The paper nearly tore as Augusta gripped it tightly in her fists.

She called out. "Henry!"

Her husband stepped onto the piazza and she felt his comforting presence before she twisted to see his beloved face. "Yes, darling?" he asked. She stood from the chair and held out the newspaper, tears falling unnoticed down her cheeks. "What has he done now?" her husband asked.

Henry stood partially dressed for his meeting at the bank in pleated gray pants and a white shirt as yet missing its starched collar. He eased the paper from her hands and wiped a tear from her face before he kissed her. His face had changed in the last years, as had hers. They were both in their forties now. In Henry's beard gray hairs were woven among the dark. Only six months after the *Pulaski* explosion, Augusta's hair had turned completely gray—a phenomenon, her doctor had explained, that sometimes followed great calamity. And yet, when she and Henry gazed upon each other, they saw their younger selves.

Even now a desire to touch Henry overwhelmed Augusta. She loved him with a fierceness that sometimes frightened her. Her need for him was as great as her blinding thirst on the wreckage all those years ago. He was her ballast. She encircled his arm with her hand and squeezed. "I knew those Fire-Eaters were dangerous. They are going to start a war. I can feel it in my very bones. Read it, darling."

Henry sank into a chair. The double doors to the house had been left open and Augusta shut them against the ever-present mosquitoes. She sank onto the chair next to him as he read, his forehead deeply etched above the reading glasses. The scars on his hands had healed in thick pearly lines that never tanned as the rest of him did.

Henry lifted his chin and faced his wife. "A horror."

"Why has he chosen this path? We were saved. We were the ones who walked onto dry land and were given another chance at life. Thomas . . ." Even after all these years, she still couldn't speak his name without a catch in her voice. "And his sisters and brother. His mother."

"My love, Charles has chosen to buttress his heart with forces that injure rather than heal. You tried to help him."

"It doesn't seem like I tried hard enough."

Henry folded her hand into his and the rough edges of his palm comforted her. "Yes. You did. He elected to become this man. There were other paths open to him just as there were for you and for me. Lamar deeded over to Charles so much money, his homes, and his business, but he could not leave him a kind heart."

"And off Lamar went and married another woman in just a year. One year." Augusta shook her head. "And he had six more children. He amassed a new fortune. Maybe his abandonment of Charles broke something inside him, I don't know, Henry. I had you to save me."

"And I had you to save me."

"If not for the tragedy, my love, do you think he would have become such a horror? Was hate already etched into his soul?"

"The tragedy did happen. There is no use in such questions . . ."

She interrupted her husband. "Do you think *we* would have come together if not for the tragedy? If we could do it over, would we give up those days and nights of terror if it meant not being together?"

"Oh, love, it's not a question we can answer. Please don't try."

"I'd like to think we'd have come together anyway." She touched his cheek.

"I'd like to believe the same." He kissed her lips and the passion he always lit took flame and she pulled him closer.

From inside the house a voice called out, "Mama," and they separated. Augusta adjusted the cape around her shoulders, folded it tighter as a cold breeze rustled the oak leaves.

"It's Eliza." She moved to stand and Henry placed his hand upon her leg.

"Stay here. I'll attend to her."

"She most likely wants a book she can't reach in the library."

He smiled and in that smile, Augusta saw his pure love for his daughters, all four of them. Augusta hadn't borne a son and yet Henry had not minded in the least. What did he care if his name did not continue into the next generation? His life had been spared that night and living the life after was enough for him.

As Henry carried the newspaper and strode through the doors into the house, Augusta's thoughts made the long, rambling journey they often took when she was left alone to grieve over her nephew Charles.

How had they come to this? The stepping-stones had been the same, hers and his, yet their destinations had grown far apart. Maybe it was Henry's love that prevented her from becoming as intransigent and cruel as Charles. Or maybe there was an inner moral compass that she possessed and Charles lacked. Yet how had he once been the child who wept with her upon the wreckage, who sacrificed his sip of wine for a suffering man—how had that boy become this man who brought such suffering to others?

Lamar had left Savannah—the memories there were too painful, he'd told her—and built a new homestead in Virginia. Augusta saw him on holidays and she did love his wife, although she seemed a child to Augusta, twenty years Lamar's junior and only six years older than Charles himself. Lamar had become a different man, altered by the misery he'd endured. He didn't take up so much space in the world; he was more humble, quieter. Who could blame him for leaving the remnants of his old life for a new one?

Augusta's thoughts turned to Lilly. Adam, gone mad and raging at the losses he'd suffered, had brought home a young woman he met in London and married her. Still he demanded the whereabouts of his first wife and child. He claimed someone was hiding her, that she was living nearby. He was often convinced he saw her turn a corner or appear in his bedroom—a ghost, he claimed, come to haunt him. The statue he had built on the river bank became an ever-present reminder of the *Pulaski* disaster.

In Savannah that year of 1858, unrest filled the air with nervous energy. With the Fire-Eaters fueling the anger, talk of secession was escalating. James Buchanan was president, but Abraham Lincoln was making noise enough to be heard. So much change in the world; so much altered in Augusta's life.

Over the last century and more, Savannah had survived fire, earthquake, pestilence and war. But would her citizens remember the *Pulaski*? Would someone in the far future walk along the river's edge and know about those who had boarded the polished decks of the steamboat? Would they have heard the harrowing stories of survival? Did it matter? The history of Savannah was full of such stories—of the hardships, the persistence and the bravery of so many.

Augusta was convinced her story *did* matter. The city stood both proud and broken; its people moved on, just as her brother had, just as Charles had, just as Augusta and Henry had. They had all built new lives, found what mattered most for them and lived for it. Charles's choices broke her heart and she thought often of the rough voice of the man who took the drop of wine upon his leather tongue—"You are a noble boy."

Charles had been a noble boy.

But he'd changed. They'd all changed. Could they choose by will alone how they were altered?

Augusta stood and went inside. At her mahogany desk facing a window that overlooked Bull Street, she gazed at the daguerreotype they had taken just last year, her four daughters posed around her in gauzy white dresses, with wide smiles. Henry's hand rested on her shoulder. Only she could see the ghosts that surrounded her family; only she could see those lost souls.

From a drawer she slipped out a letter, let it stay open on the leather blotter. It was the last from Lilly and she wanted to read it once more before she answered.

Two years after the wreck, through a discreet courier from New York, she'd received the first letter from Lilly. She'd prayed every day for news such as this. Lilly trusted Augusta never to speak a word of her survival. The life Lilly had chosen wasn't easy, but she had come to see the precious value of a life lived on her own terms—a life of freedom for herself, her daughter, and a nursemaid she now called by her given name, Chike. They had been reborn in that sea, made anew in that water. Their lives—for the best and for the horror—would be completely different if they had not boarded that ship, or more accurately, if the second engineer had not poured cold water into an empty, hot boiler. Such a small thing—pouring water—that rendered such a formidable rip in the fabric of their lives. It made no sense on the face of things, yet still it happened.

Lilly's letters had sustained Augusta through the worst of the heartache, and over the last twenty years. She had shared the knowledge of Lilly's survival only with Henry. The two women wrote about everything, returning again and again to how through anguish and heartache the explosion had come to shape and define who they were today.

From Wilmington, Lilly, Priscilla and Madeline had made their way north, often sleeping on the side of the road. Eventually they'd arrived in Michigan, in a small lakeside community in Ottawa County. Lilly had sold the jewelry for coin and had raised her daughter in a cabin at the water's edge where she'd learned to swim and then taught both Madeline and Priscilla.

Priscilla sewed for money, while Lilly taught school, seven-year-old children under her feet, and she'd never been happier. The three of them formed a family more so than some who were blood related. A deep bond born of tragedy and salvation awoke them both to their common zest for a new life. This year Lilly had fallen in love with a man from town who'd lost his wife, a kind man with soft hands and a gentle voice who treated her with love and respect. Priscilla herself had also found love, a minister in town who'd courted her for almost three years. Lilly wrote to Augusta of how she'd attended the first Seneca Falls Convention of the women's suffrage movement in 1848. Such changes were unfolding in the world.

Lilly used her life to help others. And Augusta thought again of her words—"If not for the accident . . ."

One day Augusta hoped to see her dearest friend, her niece, again, but for now their letters just had to be enough; Adam could not know her whereabouts. Their friendship endured the tragedy and the distance. She slipped Lilly's last letter back into the thick leather family Bible on her desk—the one place no one would ever look—and decided now was the time to write down what she remembered of that fateful night.

Augusta lifted her quill, dipped it into the dark ink, and took a thin sheet of valuable vellum from the drawer. To save space, she wrote in tight cursive, beginning . . .

"The steam packet Pulaski, *with Captain Dubois in charge, sailed from Savannah on Wednesday, June 13th, 1838 . . ."*

When she'd written the first sentence, she lifted her head to the sound of her children's laughter across the hallway. The youngest, ten-year-old Melody, cried out, "Give that back to me." Their bickering lifted her smile. She thought of the sheer miracle of her daughters' existence, made possible by her own survival. And then she thought of the generations that would come after her—all because she'd lived.

On her desk lay a rock her husband had brought her from London.

A trace fossil, it contained the imprint of a single fish skeleton, thousands of years old. Not the fish itself but the memory of it, forever indelible. She touched it with her finger and ran it over the indents.

Trace fossils had also been etched on her heart—the imprints left by those who suffered in those last days, those she loved, and those she barely knew. Her life was a living testament to survival, and to love.

48

EVERLY

Six months later

Let me tell you a story," I said. My voice echoed across the garden courtyard of the Rivers and Seas Museum of Savannah, and everyone ceased talking, champagne glasses perched in midair. As Pat Conroy once said, "'Tell me a story' are the most powerful words in the English language." I was using them now.

The models of the *Pulaski* and the *Wanderer* had been carefully moved outside to the middle of the cobblestone courtyard. I stood between the two ships and channeled Oliver's words, the phrases he'd used when he sent me off on a journey to discover the stories behind the tragedy, and therefore a different story of my own.

"This ship," I said, my hand wavering over the intricate model of the steamship, "the *Pulaski*, is the reason we are here tonight. This ship"—I pointed to the schooner in its case—"is the *Wanderer*, an illegal slave-importing vessel, which is also part of the bigger story. Now, let me tell you how the stories of these two ships intersect." I paused and the crowd grew quiet. I sought Oliver's gaze and found it. We'd practiced this speech together so many times I felt the words slipping easily from my lips.

"One breezy June morning in 1838, a family of twelve, plus a nursemaid, boarded the steamship *Pulaski*, intending to sail from Savannah to Baltimore before continuing by rail and coach to their seasonal stopping place of Saratoga Springs, New York, where they would escape the South's brutal summer. This was the Longstreet family, prominent in Savannah and a vital part of the city. Lamar, the father, was a banker, merchant, plantation owner and stockholder in the great ship he was boarding with his family. Together they climbed the gangplank that beautiful summer morning—Lamar; his wife, Melody; their six children; his sister, Augusta; and his niece Lilly Forsyth, whose statue even now looks over the Savannah River. Lilly traveled with her husband Adam, baby Madeline and nursemaid, an enslaved woman named Priscilla. Lamar Longstreet's children ranged in age from two to fourteen. Only seven of these thirteen people survived the devastating catastrophe that would follow."

I allowed the murmurs of the crowd to settle. They wanted to know what I had once wanted to know—who had survived? And how?

"I will tell you this—and the rest you will discover on your journey through the exhibit—the oldest child, Charles, survived the explosion and spent five harrowing days and nights at sea. He not only lived through the hell but also helped others to survive, earning him the name Noble Boy."

I stopped to take a breath and survey the crowd, which was nearly leaning into the story.

"Twenty years later, that same boy, now a man, Charles Longstreet, sent a reoutfitted luxury schooner, which was flying the New York Yacht Club pennant, to the Congo in Africa." I waved my hand over the model of the *Wanderer*. "From there, that ship returned with over four hundred enslaved Africans in bondage as human cargo, packed back to back on this ship, their hands and feet shackled. This, the penultimate illegal slave-trading ship. Charles was also part of the Fire-Eaters, a rebel group that agitated for the South's secession from the Union, knowing it would mean civil war. He was never convicted of a crime despite his evil acts. That and his flaming head of red hair earned Charles a new nickname: the Red Devil."

The crowd seemed rapt; I had them. "This same man was also the very last man to die in battle in the Civil War. He was shot through the heart on a battlefield in Columbus, Georgia, in 1865 while leading a charge against Union troops, six days after Lee had already surrendered to Grant in the famous Appomattox Accord and twenty-seven years after he survived the *Pulaski*. How could this be? How could a young boy once called a noble boy eventually earn a reputation for evil and die an unnecessary death at the end of a brutal conflict? Could it have gone any differently for him? Yes, I believe it could have.

"There were others who survived the great explosion of the steamship *Pulaski*. There were others who chose a different path. So, let us ask ourselves as we head into this exhibit: What happened on the night of June 14, 1838, when a boiler exploded at 11:04 p.m. and sank the luxury steamboat that has since been called the Southern *Titanic*? What happened to Charles Longstreet and his family to irrevocably alter their world and therefore ours? What happened to Lilly Forsyth and why has her legend continued to enthrall us? To answer some of that, we have found a treasured cache of Lilly's letters to her dearest friend, Augusta Longstreet, and you, too, can see portions of these letters and read her story and the choices she made. We have also found the written account of Augusta's travails. Would you have made the same choices some of these passengers made as they fought for their lives in a treacherous sea? And what about the choices they made with their lives afterward?"

I took a breath and leaned forward. "How did they survive the surviving?"

The crowd began to talk to each other, whispering. I raised my voice.

"When we open these doors in thirty minutes, you will journey through the night of the explosion and the terrible days that followed along with the passengers of the *Pulaski*, and especially with the Longstreet family. Maybe you will answer these questions for yourself. We are so thrilled you are the first to see it. Welcome."

I set the microphone into the stand and stood back. Applause filled the air and I looked for Oliver. His gaze caught mine and he mouthed, "Well done."

Music swelled and spilled from the front doors of the museum, composed to imitate the sounds of the sea's waves. The crowd gathered under tents in the garden. Magnolias in full bloom were dropping palm-sized, creamy blooms to the ground. Patrons lifted champagne glasses and grasped tickets bearing names they didn't recognize next to the sketch of the doomed steamship.

I walked away from the ship models and ambled through the crowd; I wanted to find my family.

The night sky shimmered, a violet dome, the air still warmly dense from last night's storm. A crescent moon seemed to swing over the oak trees. Twinkling lights stretched from branch to branch like fallen stars, and lanterns flickered on tabletops. Canapés were passed on silver trays by servers who wore the garb of 1838 passengers—the women in intricately sewn silk dresses with shirred sleeves and pleated bodices, the men in dark vested suits and top hats.

I spied Sophie across the garden and waved, thought of our conversations. The entire situation—from noble boy to slave trader—floundered for an explanation. How did it all happen and what do we do about it now? It felt like a poem without words, a drowning fish: it made no sense.

The devaluation of humanity was incomprehensible to me and those I loved. And yet so it continued even today in new and different ways. The intolerance and bias echoed. I had no real answers, but for now, what I could do was tell the truth in the artifacts, stories and curation of this exhibit.

I took small breaths in the tight blue silk dress that Allyn had insisted I wear, one she'd worn to a cotillion years before. "Both appropriate and sexy, with a dash of 1800s flavor. It is *your* night," she'd said. I even wore Mom's pearls.

The last nine months seemed to have slipped past in a rush. My passion for the project had consumed me. I'd been teaching a heavy load, and had eventually agreed to teach the next semester at SCAD's LaCoste abroad program. I'd finished my job here and wanted to find out who I was without Savannah, without the stories that I had lived with all my life.

Now, opening night glowed before me, and I was both nervous and excited, wired and alert. My high heel caught in a tuft of moss between the stepping-stones and I almost twisted my ankle as I spied my family huddled together at the far end of the patio.

"Here!" Allyn waved.

I reached them, hugged my sister and Mom, drew Hudson close and kissed the top of his head. "You look very handsome in your little suit."

"Mom made me wear it but I picked out the bow tie." He touched its edge carefully. "It's made of feathers."

"I see that." I smiled. "Where's your sister?"

Hudson pointed a few feet away where Merily stood with a friend by the fountain's edge, throwing in coins.

"How are you feeling?" Allyn asked. "You look simply amazing."

"It's your dress." I tugged at the snug waistline.

"I guess that's why you look amazing, then." Allyn leaned over and kissed my cheek.

Mom plucked a tube of lipstick from her purse and held it out. "A little of this will help, too."

I took the bright red lipstick and gave it a quick swipe across my lips, acquiescing with a smile. "Thank you, Mom."

"Keep it. If you're going to be at that lectern on that big stage, we need to see your lips." Mom nodded with certainty. "Now, how are you feeling? Are you nervous? It's all so glamorous."

"I'm nervous, but also glad opening night is finally here. We're ready."

"I can't wait to see it." Hudson stepped up. "I wonder if I live or die."

Allyn popped her son lightly on the shoulder.

"Hey. Isn't that the whole point? We get to find out?" He held up his ticket. Everly spied the name: First Mate Hibbert.

"Not the *whole* point," Allyn said. "You get to learn about the night and the ship and some of our city's history."

"And whether I live or die." He pulled at his mom's hand. "Let's go."

I leaned down and whispered, "You live, and you're a hero."

Hudson stood taller and I looked again to my sister. "I'll meet y'all inside. I have to sneak in the back and then open the front doors."

"Go get 'em," Mom said.

"I'll try." I walked away, rubbing the lipstick off with the back of my hand.

Slipping through the back door, I took a moment in the hallway to stand in the darkness and catch my breath near a container that held acquired artwork that needed to be acclimated to the humidity and temperature of the building before it could be displayed. My mind flipped through the contents of the notecards waiting for me on the lectern with words of welcome for the guests.

I'd practiced this second part of the speech at home, walking around the courtyard as I muttered it over and over until my neighbors were no doubt convinced I was mad. "What are you doing back here?" A voice startled me and I twisted to see Maddox coming down the darkened hallway, backlit by the ballroom. He wore a tuxedo and his hair was slicked back.

"Preparing myself," I said as he reached my side. "And you look mighty handsome."

"Thank you. You look absolutely stunning."

"Thank you, Maddox. Sometimes I do clean up."

He tossed his arm over my shoulder and squeezed. "It's time to join the party. What you don't know now you won't know." His laugh had become as familiar and warm to me as my own family. "We'll open the doors and go through with the first group as if we've never seen the exhibit before."

A tremor ran through me. I took a moment and paused to identify it—Fear? Thrill? Desire? No, it wasn't anything like that. It was relief.

"Let's go see the masterpiece you've created. They're waiting."

I stood on the tiptoes of my high heels to kiss his cheek. "I have grown to love you. You know that, don't you?"

"As I have you."

We linked arms and headed toward the light.

Oliver, Maddox and I stood at the blue front doors with the banner over them that read "Don't Give Up the Ship"—a motto of the U.S. Navy—and then opened the doors with a grand gesture as a hundred and ninety-two blue and white balloons floated out and up in the sky. One for each passenger and crew.

The crowd was queued up according to the numbers on their tickets, since we only allowed twenty people in at a time. They exclaimed and grabbed for the trailing balloons as they floated out.

The first thing visitors would see when they walked into the foyer was the anchor, rusty but whole, on a pedestal. The crowd separated around it, paused to stare and wonder and then entered the exhibit hallway. Children bounced on their toes; adults chatted.

My family oil painting of the *Pulaski* hung in the grand entrance as an overhead light shone down on the ship that had once been strong and proud. *Donated by the Winthrop Family*, a plaque read. I thought it should read, "The painting that led us to the true story of Augusta and Lilly," or "The painting that changed my life," but that wasn't quite the point for anyone but me.

First in the exhibit rooms came the history of Savannah in the early 1800s. Large images of the city as it would have appeared that fateful day—carriages and sandy roads; cotton bales hanging from hooks on a wharf and in hemp bags; park squares surrounded by stores and businesses on the east and west sides and homes on the north and south sides. Some of the sketches were in color, but most were black-and-white charcoal sketches done by a local artist. Over speakers echoed the sounds of horses' hooves on clay and dirt. Voices called in rich southern accents and metal clanged on metal at the riverside docks where a sketch showed the *Pulaski* tied to pilings next to other ships being loaded with bags of cotton.

The hallway then led to a room where a blown-up rendering of the ship's blueprint was projected on the floor. At the front end of the room was one mast and at the far end another. Jagged marks on the blueprint showed where the ship had come apart. Patrons read about the sequence of events on the night of the explosion on illustrated boards along the walls.

Also on the wall were illustrations of the lifeboats and ropes, of the promenade and aft decks. A picture of a watch face, made a hundred times larger than the real pocket watch, the glass shattered and the hands reading 11:04, hung high toward the ceiling and next to it a timeline of the remainder of the night's events, clocking each moment until the ship disappeared into the sea forty-five minutes later. The sounds in this room changed from the echoes of the dock to the splashing of waves lapping against the boat's wooden hull, and people's cries for help.

Then began the Longstreet family's journey. A painted family tree with sketches of each family member hung on the far wall. When patrons stood in front of it, they could push a button for each family member to discover what happened to them. They were then given numbers to follow into the next room where the means of survival were displayed.

Each Longstreet family member's name was placed on their means of rescue: Lilly, Priscilla and Madeline on a quarterboat; Augusta, Charles and Thomas on the floating piece of the promenade deck raft; Lamar also on a separate yawl that had been repaired and had left the promenade deck on the third day. Affixed to a linen backdrop and framed in gold, A. Longstreet's iron luggage label hung beneath a picture light. Whenever I saw it, I felt the initial thrill of knowing it had been discovered, that Augusta's story had wanted to be told as badly as I had wanted to tell it.

Lilly's enchanting story had been typed up on a huge plexiglass sheet. It filled a wall with a dotted trail across a map, showing her journey from Onslow County, up the coast and through small towns until she found the haven in Michigan where she settled with her daughter, and with Priscilla. Photos of her handwritten letters hung framed with the typed words below for those who wanted to linger and read the tales that Lilly wrote to Augusta. Their friendship, which endured for a lifetime, survived the surviving, lived through the tragedy and nourished both of them for all their life.

This full story of Lilly stood in sharp contrast next to the photos and story of Charles.

The Red Devil—the exhibit showed the verity of his life, who he had been and who he had become. There was no turning from this truth.

Oliver sidled up next to me in his tuxedo and bow tie. "If you wore a top hat you would look as if you just stepped off the ship," I said with a smile.

He ran his hand through his thick hair and nodded at Lilly's display. "A friendship that endured a lifetime. Long after tragedy."

"Yes." I nodded with a lump in my throat. "Even distance didn't let it suffer."

He shook his head. "No. That kind of friendship lasts even if . . ."

"Someone is gone . . ." I said. "I know what you're thinking."

"Oh, no you don't. Not really." He drew closer just as someone called his name and he turned.

I wandered away and noticed how the patrons grew more and more silent, as they read and became immersed in the experience, as they were drawn to the third area where there were four split sections separated by mirrored partitions. One area held the model of a lifeboat; another a broken piece of decking with the title Promenade Deck; and the third a larger piece of decking with a bench attached to it labeled Aft Deck. In each area was a framed poster with the names of those who were known to have found brief refuge on the pieces shown. The sounds of wind and waves simulated what it had been like for those struggling to survive. The visitors spoke in whispers punctuated by exclamations when they ran across a name or fact that jolted them.

In the last exhibit hall before the ballroom were artifacts protected in glass cases. The pocket watch was displayed front and center on a pedestal surrounded by thick glass. The brass plate beneath it read, "A pocket watch believed to belong to the Lamar Longstreet family, shattered at exactly the time of the explosion."

Crowds lingered at the display, prompting Maddox to gently encourage them to move on, as there were others who were waiting to get through.

I stood in a far back corner of the last room, marveling at what we had created. Here in this room were the chords of a symphony orchestra. Servers handed out food and drink until eventually everyone made their way to the ballroom. As they entered the large space, they were given a card listing their passenger's fate—whether he or she had survived or perished. Exclamations of dismay and rejoicing spread among the crowd, and then voices were lowered as they looked among the artifacts of another age, of lives long gone.

At the far end of the room stood a replica of the ship's gangplank with suitcases at the bottom where "passengers" could get their photo taken as if they were boarding the ship. When everyone had shuffled in, Oliver nodded at me that it was time.

I climbed to the lectern and tapped the microphone.

"Welcome to the Steamship *Pulaski* Exhibit—*Only One Night at Sea*." In a slow and modulated voice, I thanked all those who needed thanking, from the museum donors to Maddox's crew. I regaled the crowd with a history of the ship's discovery as told by Maddox. Then I moved on to the part where my voice might break, and I'd decided it would be okay if it did. This wasn't a story to enthrall—it was true and it was heartbreaking.

"Much of what we know about the tragedy of the *Pulaski* was lost to the dust of time, until now. History matters—what happened to our city in 1838 echoes today." I paused and cleared my throat. "Loss and devastation to our city and to our people still pulses through our history: lost families, lost fortunes and lost hope. Our city grieved then, as did the nation. But we, the citizens of Savannah, are formidable people and we've thrived in the years since the *Pulaski* sank. How did the city endure despite such loss? How did the individuals on that ship continue their lives? Here at the museum, we asked ourselves those questions numerous times as we studied the wreckage and learned about the loss."

I took a breath. "We want answers when tragedy strikes. We want to know why it happened. We want to cast blame, to discover what caused the *Pulaski* to explode. We know now that a second engineer let the hot boiler become dry and then poured cold water into it, and it exploded like a bomb, blowing the ship apart. As you saw in the exhibit, it took only forty-five minutes for the ship to sink to the bottom of the sea and lie scattered across the ocean floor. But we don't really have a deeper explanation for such a tragedy, only a cause.

"It took years to design and build this ship. It was a trusted, sturdy vessel. And beautiful to boot. But a mistake was made and the ship was destroyed. We can blame the engineer and we must. But what happened even before that? Was it the pressure to be the fastest and the best that forced him to act negligently? Why were there only four lifeboats, only two of which were seaworthy? Was negligence involved? We still search for the answers. We may never find them, yet some good came out of tragedy—maritime laws were changed dramatically, making steamboat travel safer in the years afterward."

Behind me a large sketch of the *Pulaski* appeared on a screen that covered the wall. The crowd let out an audible sigh, and I paused and scanned the crowd, my sight snagging on Oliver standing at the back of the room, the light falling around him. He stood next to a pillar we'd decorated to look like a smokestack, his left shoulder propped against it. He grinned and nodded at me.

I had paused too long. The crowd murmured. Was I done?

I brushed my hair back. "As we end this night, let me read from Augusta Longstreet's letter to Lilly. Augusta was the many-times-great-grandmother of my dear friend Mora Dunmore." I took a breath and read out loud Augusta's words from so very long ago.

"'Was it fate when the ship shattered and I lived while others died? I don't know. How can I? Unless fate can be defined as the seemingly minutest occurrences—a wave that lands at a different angle; a corset not undone; a basket of wine appearing as if by magic; a wound that festers or does not; a snagged shoe or jammed door. I don't believe fate chose who should live or perish according to their worthiness. I didn't deserve to live any more than my little two-year-old nephew deserved to die. The life we live is the life we choose with every decision of the heart, soul and mind. What do we do with our survival? Now what?'"

I glanced at the audience. "Augusta Longstreet leaves that question for us to answer. *Now what?*"

Applause filled the room, drowning out all doubt that I'd harbored about speaking the truth of my own heart through the words of another. I slowly descended the stairs from the stage, careful in the unaccustomed high heels, and found myself in the waiting arms of Maddox, Allyn and Mom. Hugs all around with murmurs of "That was beautiful."

I stepped back and glanced to the pillar-turned-smokestack where Oliver had stood. It was empty.

"See?" I said to Maddox as he handed me a glass of champagne. "One thing leads to another. It's all connected."

"A spider's web," he agreed softly as Oliver joined us, so handsome in his tuxedo.

A group of those I loved most fiercely surrounded me—Mom and Allyn, Maddox and Oliver. I was in the museum I loved with the passengers I'd researched and followed for a year filling my heart and mind. Oliver moved to my side and everything in the room faded but for him. Mom, Allyn and Maddox eased away as if a tide carried them.

"Up there, Ev, your speech, it was beautiful. Mora would have loved seeing you like that. Radiant, in your element. And how you ended it was perfect."

"You mean that last line?" I asked.

"Yes." He stepped closer and lowered his voice. "Ev, *now what?*"

"Well, next is LaCoste. I've got a lot to do to get ready."

I'd told myself it would be easier when I didn't have to see him every day; when my heart wasn't easing toward him even as I dragged it away. My life would be simpler when I had no daily reason to text or call. It would all be okay . . .

Oliver lowered his voice. "I don't want to let us go just because this project is over." He took another step closer.

"Let us go? That's ridiculous. We're friends and . . ."

"I've thought long and hard about how to say this, Ev." He took a breath and in that slice of time, my thoughts rattled through all he might say to me. But I didn't anticipate the one thing he did utter.

"Don't go to France."

I tried to read his familiar face, but his expression was one I'd never seen.

"Why not, Oliver?"

"Because Everly Winthrop, I love you."

His words so surprised me, I couldn't take them in. My body leaned toward him even as my words pushed him away. "Don't . . ."

"Because you don't feel the same way?"

"No. Not that at all."

"I know what you're going to say but this isn't *wrong*," he said. "For a long time I thought the same. But the way I feel is an honoring. We loved her. She loved us. It's the opposite of wrong."

"Do you think maybe you're in love with me because I remind you of those times with Mora? It's not . . . me."

"No, Ev. I'm in love with *you*. How else do I say it?"

"Why?" The need to know was vital.

He took my face in his hands and did not let me look away. "I love you because you are smart and wise, gentle and fiery. I love you because you never, ever back away from feelings; they are the fuel to your fire. I love you because you can laugh at yourself and laugh at me. I love you because you don't just love, Ev, you love with everything you've got. There is no halfway with you; there is no just a little bit. You don't just dive in, you dive to the bottom. I love you because you ask the questions that matter and you have no patience for the ones that don't." He dropped his hands to my shoulders and held me fast.

"Oliver . . ."

"I'm not done yet. I love you because you'll climb into a dusty attic just to find out what happened to a long-lost best friend of a woman you never knew. I love you because you're the kind of woman who will chase down a hit-and-run driver. I love you because you are Everly."

Something tight inside me let go, something I'd held locked in secret with white-knuckled determination—my love for him. "That's all?" I asked with a smile.

"Please give me time to tell you all the other reasons. This exhibit, this wreck, it shows us—life is such a quick thing. Please don't let us waste one more minute of it apart."

"Then come with me to France," I said.

Without a second of hesitation, he answered. "Okay. Yes. I will come with you." He smiled, so beautifully he smiled. "I'll take a leave of absence and—"

"You're serious?"

"Never been more serious in my life, love," he said in a terrible French accent. "LaCoste is tres magnificent."

I smiled at the silliness, at the simple joy between us. "Oliver." I lifted his hands to my lips, kissed the inside of his palm. "You must know I have loved you for so long."

He brought me closer; I washed ashore to the solid ground of his kiss, a home I'd wanted to find. His touch carried me to the bottom of the sea, to the moment when truth had rushed in, and I'd known that all of life is worth living; his touch resurrected love and hope and raised me back up to the sparkling sunlight.

He pulled me so close that with my lips next to his ear, I whispered, "So . . . this is what happens next."

AUTHOR'S NOTE

On a balmy summer morning in Savannah, Georgia, on June 13, 1838, a cotton merchant, shipper, financier and steamboat pioneer named Gazaway Bugg Lamar and his family boarded the gleaming new steamship *Pulaski*. It was the fourth voyage of the fine ship and she was headed north to Baltimore. This family—a husband and wife, their six children, and also Gazaway's sister and his niece (his brother's daughter), expected smooth sailing and only one night at sea before arriving in Baltimore to travel on to enjoy their summer holiday in Saratoga Springs, New York.

But what we expect and what we get are rarely the same things.

The sudden and unforeseen changes in our lives usually come in the middle of what we think is a normal day. I was curious about this turn of fortunes, not only in the matter of something so utterly tragic as a shipwreck, but also about how such sudden changes affect our daily lives. What do we do when tragedy bursts through the door trailing smoke and grief in its wake? For this novel, it all began in Savannah, Georgia—both in the modern-day story and in the historical story.

I am enamored and fascinated by Savannah and its rich history, as well as the town of Bluffton, South Carolina, just on the other side of the Savannah River. In Bluffton, on the May River, there is a memorial stone that reads "Samuel Parkman: Perished on the Steamboat *Pulaski* with his three daughters, Authexa, Caroline and Theresa Parkman." I had seen the white pillared stone, surrounded by a white-slat fence, a hundred times or more as I biked past it. But I hadn't given it much thought—it was so old and so very far away from my life. Until a dear friend, Boo Harrell, a Bluffton native who intimately knows the waters and stories around Savannah, Bluffton, and South Carolina, asked me, "Have you heard about the steamship *Pulaski*?"

Now, much in Georgia and South Carolina is named after Casimir Pulaski, a noble Polishman and military commander known as the "father of the cavalry," who fought for the United States in the Revolutionary War and was fatally shot in the Battle of Savannah. One of the twenty-two park squares in Savannah is called Pulaski Square, and there is a monument in Monterey Square. So yes, I'd heard of Pulaski, but not the steamship dubbed the Southern *Titanic*.

I headed straight for the Ships of the Sea Maritime Museum in Savannah, where a model of the *Pulaski* sits under protective glass. I also made my way to the stately home of the Georgia Historical Society facing Forsyth Park. Between these two extraordinary places, and with the help of the experts who work there, I found myself with a folder of copies of ancient newspaper articles, handwritten letters, and accounts and narratives of that disastrous night and its following days. The hunt for information was as fascinating as the stories. My immediate interest wasn't so much in the maritime disaster and its exact cause (the boiler room explosion is well documented) but in the stories of the families who boarded this ship in Savannah and then in Charleston. The "flowers of the South," these passengers were called, and they were all escaping the South's brutal heat, flying insects and possible malaria of summer. But instead of a cool summer and seasonal parties in the north, they found their lives tested to their limits.

Experts in the shipwreck field tell me they see over and over this fact: that we are who we truly are at our core in the midst of such a crisis as a sinking ship. Survival puts us to the test. When I learned of the fourteen-year-old child Charles Augustus Lafayette Lamar and the true story of how he'd been dubbed a "noble boy" during the days and nights at sea to then later become "the Red Devil," I looked much closer at our collective ideas that survival merits some kind of worthiness, that everything happens for a reason, and that our lives are destined to end up in certain ways. I still don't know the solid truth to any of those ideas (I leave that to the philosophers and theologians), but I do know that, for me, asking the bigger questions usually leads to a story.

Do we have a destiny? How do we survive the surviving? What happens to us after we live through tragedy both great and small? Is there such a thing as fate? Who do we become and why? Can we ignore our past if we are ashamed of it?

I set out to write a dual-timeline novel about a modern-day museum curator, Everly Winthrop, a Savannah woman who has suffered a great loss, alongside two historical women who boarded the *Pulaski* with their family that summer morning. I wanted Everly to research and discover what happened to the historical family. My office looked much like I describe Everly's living room in the novel—covered in charts, photos of artifacts, pieces of sketched broken ship, and lists of names.

A few weeks after the start of my research, I was searching for some of the ship's dimensions and facts when I stumbled on a piece of startling news—the Endurance Exploration Group along with their salvage partners Blue Water Ventures and Marex announced they'd found the steamship *Pulaski* thirty miles off the coast of Wilmington,

North Carolina, a hundred feet deep. I hadn't known anyone was looking for the doomed ship. When I read the news, the powerful chill of story-excitement ran up my spine.

This kind of synchronicity sometimes happens, and each time it does I am led again to the mystical knowing that we are all connected, that stories are our lifeline, and that they want to be told.

I immediately contacted Micah Eldred, the CEO and founder of Endurance Exploration Group, Inc., and from that moment he helped me tell the story in innumerable ways: he sent me the divers' photos of the artifacts retrieved from a hundred feet below. He answered questions about treasure hunting, diving and this ship's discovery. For almost two hundred years the keys, plates, silver flatware, pocket watches, jewelry, baby rattles and so much more have rested at the bottom of the sea as hidden secrets and stories of the *Pulaski* tragedy. Mr. Eldred partnered with Blue Water Ventures and its CEO, Keith Webb, known for their shallow-water salvage expertise, to perform physical salvage operations using its vessel, *Blue Water Rose*, and its divers. The other partner, Marex, originally founded by Herbert Humphreys and now run by Tim Hudson, offers the important IP work that must be done to bring us these fascinating artifacts.

Among the found artifacts there is a filigreed gold pocket watch. Its face has been shattered and its hands stopped at the time of the explosion. This single image of loss and horror lured me to the hidden life of the ship and its passengers like the songs of the Greek Sirens.

What do one-hundred-and-eighty-year-old artifacts have to tell us about the lives of the passengers? So very much. They hint at what the passengers valued; how they lived their daily lives; what they took with them on the journey; what belongings mattered the most to them. Of course this all changed with the fiery explosion. And that is what I meant to portray: how the very things we value ultimately change when our lives are shattered and the course of our days is utterly altered.

With historical fiction, the natural question always arises: What is real and what is fiction? The question I prefer is: What is *factual* and what is *inspired* or *imagined* in the historical parts of the story?

To that end, let's start here: Everything about the ship itself—its story, its demise, and its measurements and values—factually concurs with the literature. From the time of the explosion to how it broke in half and sank forty-five minutes later, to the lifeboats' journeys and the floating remnants of the decks, to the number of survivors and perished, it is all true, or as close as one can find with ancient and conflicting accounts.

Although there must be hundreds of tales that transpired on that night, I focused on the Longstreet and Forsyth families, who were inspired and informed by the real Lamar family. Lamar Longstreet's character is based on Gazaway Bugg Lamar (I gave him Gazaway's last name as a first name). Charles Longstreet is based on the historical figure Charles Augustus Lafayette Lamar. His role with *The Wanderer*, as a Fire-Eater, and his death in the Civil War are all accurate as documented best in the book *The Slave-Trader's Letter-Book* by James Jordan. Thomas Longstreet is inspired by the youngest Lamar son, Thomas. Adam Forsyth, on the other hand, is a completely imagined character inspired by a composite of other men on the journey.

Augusta Longstreet is modeled on a brave and fearless woman named Rebecca Lamar, Gazaway Lamar's real sister. In her tight and beautiful script handwriting, Rebecca left us a narrative of the night that begins with the words I rewrite in the novel, "The steam packet *Pulaski*, under Captain Dubois, sailed from Savannah on Wednesday, June 13th, 1838." This account can be found at the Georgia Historical Society and in their published journal the *Georgia Historical Quarterly*, written by Rebecca Lamar McCloud and published in June 1919, originally published in the Rev. George White's *Historical Collections of Georgia* in 1854. She wrote the accounting long after the actual event

(I imagine the horror of it prevented the recounting until later in her life). She consulted with two other men who had been on the ship—James Hamilton Couper and Major J. B. Heath—to give us as full an accounting as we can find. My imagining of her life after the ship-wreck sways far from the historical account, but the events of the explosion and the following days of horror and survival stick close to the facts she laid out in her narrative.

Lilly Forsyth is entirely imagined and is premised from the composite inspiration of numerous female passengers. Her slave, Priscilla, and her child, Madeline, are the same—a complicated and blended sketch of the enslaved people and the children of the ship. There was a real woman who was a niece to Gazaway; she was Gazaway's brother John's daughter, yet sadly she perished in the explosion. In my novel Lilly gives that woman, Eliza Lamar, a new life and a new story. Yet what happens to Lilly, and to the others on that lifeboat during those horrific twenty-four hours, is entirely accurate from the direct accounts of the brave men Mr. Hamilton Couper and First Mate Hibbert, who were on the lifeboats (once again, their accounts can be read at the Georgia Historical Society in Savannah where the documents are meticulously kept).

The remaining passengers on the ship are fictional but inspired by real passengers who both perished and survived. The accounts of that night and their brave and harrowing narratives have been saved through the years. If you, the reader, have any further interest in the accounts, the chapters about this disaster written in other books or in other stories of the *Pulaski*, I have a Resources section at the end of this novel.

The real list of passengers is inadequate as the enslaved and children weren't always included. In this novel, I have used a few real names to honor the passengers' lives: for example: Captain Dubois, First Mate Hibbert, Samuel Parkman, and Mr. Hamilton Couper, who all saved numerous lives and almost sacrificed their own.

To tell a historical story in a fictional narrative, there must exist both the facts and also the emotional truth, or as close as we can come. From the narratives and accounts written by those who survived, I have come as near as I know how on this side of history to the truth of how they felt, what they saw and how they survived in a very different South than we know today. My desire was to hold that old (and imperfect) South up to the light of our present (and imperfect) new south. They reflect on each other; they hold up as mirrors to the truth of who we were and who we are by setting our eyes clearly on the city of Savannah.

I hope I've treated the stories of those who both survived and perished on the steamship *Pulaski* with the utmost esteem and respect I feel, and that I have honored their families, their tragedies and their lost artifacts.

Just like Everly, I believe that the past echoes into our present time if only we turn our ear toward its stories.

RESOURCES AND FACTS

For those interested in the facts and figures of the ill-fated *Pulaski*, read on!

This section provides the timelines, facts, and resources used in the writing of this novel. If you'd like to dive deeper into the story of this beautiful (and tragic) steamship, books and articles are listed here.

The Facts and Timeline

Summers in Savannah were brutal. From the heat to the insects, malaria and general malaise, those who could leave for the north did so. In 1838, steam travel had become an alternative to the three-or-four-day journey by land, which was both arduous and tiring with very few places to stay along the way. And this is where Gazaway Bugg Lamar enters the picture with his newly outfitted luxury steamship, the SS *Pulaski*, that would ply between Savannah and Baltimore with a stop overnight in Charleston (Only One Night at Sea!). Tickets went fast and the ship was full for each journey.

In this novel, I follow a fictitious family inspired by the very real family of Mr. Gazaway Bugg Lamar, who was a financier, banker, shipper and much more. He was also one of the original founders of the Savannah and Charleston Steam Packet Company, eventually becoming the director. Just as in this novel, he indeed boarded with nine family members for the fourth journey of the *Pulaski*. Although I wandered a bit from the true story, there is plenty to read about this fascinating family, and you can find more in the resources that follow.

But there were of course many other families and many other stories of both horror and survival. Here, if you are interested, are the facts and numbers of what can be ascertained by research—the combination of articles, letters, books and accounts. There are, as would be expected in such chaos, disparate recollections. Sometimes the numbers don't match from account to account. But the main facts are solid.

On a balmy Wednesday morning, June 13, 1838, the Pulaski set sail on its fourth journey with ninety passengers and approximately thirty-seven crew from Savannah, Georgia, at eight a.m. under Captain Dubois and First Mate Hibbert. The passengers had paid thirty-five dollars each for the two-day journey (stopping in Charleston the first night and at sea the second night). Once the ship docked in Charleston, sixty-five more passengers joined at thirty dollars each, and they set sail at six a.m. on Thursday, June 14.

The numbers vary, but most agree that the *Pulaski* carried 187 to 192 people.

The trip went beautifully. The weather was lovely and the breezes refreshing. Nothing was expected to go wrong.

Until it did.

At 11:04 p.m. on Thursday, June 14, the second engineer poured cold water into a hot and empty copper boiler, causing it to transform from boiler to bomb, exploding through the starboard side of the ship. The ship was now forty-five miles south of Cape Lookout and approximately thirty miles from the shore of North Carolina.

The horror began. Some passengers were sitting on settees above the boiler room where steam rushed up and those people were killed or maimed. Some crew were killed instantly in the boiler room itself. Some passengers were injured while others rushed out of their cabins and climbed the companionways (stairways) toward the main deck.

This is where both the stories of passenger survival and also the horrific stories of those who perished began.

There were four lifeboats on the *Pulaski*: two tarp-covered quarter-boats hung from davits on the main deck, while the two yawls were stored upside down on the deck, exposed to the sun. The passengers who could rush for these boats did. But meanwhile the ship was suffering and sinking. Families were attempting to gather and find each other, since men and women bunked on separate levels. The starboard side had been blown apart and most of the wheelhouse was missing or fragmented. Captain Dubois was never seen again after the explosion, and First Mate Hibbert, who had been in the wheelhouse, was knocked unconscious. Eventually First Mate Hibbert regained consciousness and was instrumental in lowering the quarterboats from the davits to begin evacuation.

There weren't enough lifeboats for the passengers, and those who did find purchase in the two yawls found a new horror: the boats' seams were cracked from sun exposure and they began to sink immediately in the large sea swells. Some passengers made it back to deck and others drowned. In this novel, we follow the Longstreet family (inspired by the Lamar family) into these yawls to experience the well-documented events that followed.

Meanwhile, others—both passengers and crew—made it to the quarterboats, one holding eleven people and the other holding twelve. In this novel, we follow Lilly Forsyth, an imagined character who shows us the unfolding events of the lifeboats, which are also well documented (see the resources that follow).

At eleven forty-five p.m. these quarterboat passengers watched the

Pulaski break in half, tossing at least a hundred people into the sea. Some found flotage on the two pieces of ship that broke off in large chunks: the aft deck and the promenade deck, which acted as rafts. At the start, each raft held approximately twenty-three passengers. Other passengers lashed together settees or found floating trunks or whatever loose wreckage they could float upon.

In *Surviving Savannah*, we experience the harrowing days and nights of those on the piece of promenade deck fragment through the eyes of Augusta Longstreet, who is inspired by a woman named Rebecca Lamar (sister of Gazaway Bugg Lamar). Rebecca wrote a detailed and terror-filled description of those days (see the resources that follow).

The ill-fated night wore on until at approximately three a.m. on Friday, June 15, when the two quarterboats, with twenty-one passengers total, left the site of the vanquished *Pulaski* and began to row toward North Carolina. By necessity they had to abandon all those still floating at sea to go find help.

On Friday evening, June 15, the two lifeboats arrived near Wilmington, North Carolina. They rowed hard toward shore over harrowing breakers, losing five of their passengers to the sea. They landed on a small spit of land called the Bermudas. By ten p.m., those who did not drown in the landing were rescued by the kind citizens of Onslow County.

As for the two rafts of the aft and promenade deck fragments: the first day they floated at sea was Friday, June 15. During this time, some survivors were added to the two rafts when they floated up on debris. During this day not another vessel came in sight.

The rafts bobbed on the sea all day Saturday, June 16, and Sunday, June 17. Days passed in horror. Rain came and went. Four vessels were seen but without salvation. One of the cracked lifeboats had been found floating and the men on the promenade deck fixed it using rope and clothing as caulk. On Sunday, June 17, five men, including Gazaway Bugg Lamar, took the salvaged lifeboat and headed to shore to send help for the others. They made it to land safely, but through varying circumstances (weather and time), Gazaway could not convince anyone to go look for survivors, even with his offers of money. Another day and night passed for those floating at sea. Some died from drowning and others suffered and died with dehydration while others fought for survival.

On the fifth day, Tuesday, June 19, a schooner called the *Henry Camerdon*, under Captain Eli Davis, spied the aft deck fragment and saved the passengers afloat on it. Captain Davis, who has been lauded for his acumen and prayers, then spent hours searching for more survivors until he spied the promenade deck raft, which had now dwindled from twenty-three passengers to seven. Five (or maybe six) of them had left on the lifeboat with Gazaway.

On June 18, Wilmington knew of the wreck.

Savannah didn't hear the news until June 21 (eight days after the ship launched).

On June 23, the news was reported by the *Charleston Courier*.

On July 5, a day of mourning was designated for the City of Savannah.

On July 13, Savannah held a memorial at the Christ Episcopal Church on Bull Street for those who perished. Nearly every family in the city had been affected in some way.

Perished and Survived

Although the numbers of those who perished and survived vary slightly, the consensus according to the resources below mostly agree on the following:

187–192 passengers and crew
128–133 lost

Fifty-nine survived in this manner:

1. Lifeboat One with Couper: Eleven people aboard—all survived.

2. Lifeboat Two: Eleven people aboard—one died at sea (the ship's fireman); five perished at landing; five lived.

3. Salvaged lifeboat with Gazaway Bugg Lamar that set off from the promenade fragment on day three: Most accounts say five people survived (although Rebecca Lamar's account states six).

4. Two rafts rescued by the *Henry Camerdon*: Thirty survivors were rescued.

    a. The promenade raft began with twenty-three people aboard, and seven were rescued. This is the piece on which Rebecca Lamar and Charles Lamar survived (Gazaway's sister and son).

    b. The aft raft: Twenty-three people were saved.

5. Other flotage: Eight survived.

Accounts used from surviving passengers to piece together the story

J. H. Couper, Esq., from Glynn, Georgia—He was a lifeboat survivor and saved many other lives. His account is in the *Historical Collections of Georgia*, 3rd ed. (New York: Pudney and Russell), originally published in 1855 from a handwritten account that Couper wrote for his family, and also in *Narrative of the Loss of the Steam-packet Pulaski: Which Burst Her Boiler and Sank on the Coast of North Carolina, June 14, 1838* (see the resources that follow).

Rebecca Lamar (became Rebecca McCloud)—Her account on the promenade deck fragment appeared in the *Georgia Historical Quarterly* in June 1919 (see the resources that follow).

Major Heath on the aft deck fragment—The accounts of Couper and Heath are combined in *Narrative of the Loss of the Steam-packet Pulaski: Which Burst Her Boiler and Sank on the Coast of North Carolina, June, 14, 1838* (see the resources that follow). His statement was also published in the *Baltimore American*, June 25, 1838, and reprinted in the *Daily Georgian* on July 3, 1838, with a compilation of other accounts.

Mr. Fosdick from Boston—His account came from the *New York Journal of Commerce*, June 25, 1838, and was also published in the *Daily Georgian* on July 3, 1838.

Mr. Hibbert—His account appeared in a compilation titled "Narrative of the Lost Pulaski" in the Wilmington, North Carolina *Advertiser* (see the resources that follow).

Col. Robert Downie Walker, a passenger who survived on the aft deck fragment—A verbal history by his grandson, Robert Walker Groves, was read before the Cosmos Club of Savannah in 1955 (see the resources that follow).

Peter Lawson, the second mate—His account was published in the *Daily Georgian*, July 3, 1838; he survived on the promenade deck fragment and then in the third lifeboat with Gazaway Bugg Lamar.

Harmon Eldridge—His account was published in the *Daily Georgian*, July 3, 1838, in a letter written in Onslow County, North Carolina, on June 17, 1838; he survived on the promenade deck fragment and then the lifeboat with Gazaway Bugg Lamar.

Resources

"Awful Calamity," *Daily Georgian*, June 21, 1838. This article includes a document published in the Charleston *Office of the Courier*, June 19, 1838, 8 a.m., which lists passengers who left Charleston; and an extract of a letter from Col. W. Robertson of North Carolina, dated June 16, 1838, recounting his experience.

Jonathan M. Bryant, *Dark Places of the Earth: The Voyage of the Slave Ship* Antelope (Liveright, 2015).

William H. J. Bulloch, untitled article, *Daily Georgian*, July 3, 1838, which includes a copy of a letter from Harmon Eldridge, a survivor of the *Pulaski*, written in Onslow, North Carolina, dated June 17, 1838; a copy of an article from the *Baltimore American*, June 25, 1838, which provides an account given by Major Heath; a copy of an extract from "The Loss of the Pulaski," *Sentinel and Herald*, June 18, 1838, noting that their citizens Miss Heald and Mrs. Britt were missing; statements of Mr. Fosdick and Mr. Lawson given to the Chairman of the Committee of Investigation in Savannah on June 30, 1838; and Mr. Fosdick's statement to the *New York Journal of Commerce*, June 25, 1838, regarding the *Pulaski*.

Erik Calonius, *The Wanderer: The Last American Slave Ship and the Conspiracy That Set Its Sails* (St. Martin's Griffin, 2006).

William H. Ewen, *Days of the Steamboats* (Mystic Seaport Museum, 1988).

"Further Particulars of the Loss of the Steamboat Pulaski," *Wilmington Advertiser*, June 20, 1838 (extra, 1 p.m.).

Robert Walker Groves, "The Wreck of the Steam Packet 'Pulaski,'" verbal history, read before the Cosmos Club of Savannah, November 9, 1955. Georgia Historical Society.

Thomas Robson Hay, "Gazaway Bugg Lamar, Confederate Banker and Business Man," *Georgia Historical Quarterly*, Vol. 37, No. 2 (June 1953), 89–128.

S. A. Howland, *Steamboat Disasters and Railroad Accidents in the United States (To Which Is Appended Accounts of Recent Shipwrecks, Fires at Sea, Thrilling Incidents, Etc.)* (Dorr, Howland, 1840).

Jim Jordan, *The Slave-Trader's Letter-Book: Charles Lamar, The Wanderer, and Other Tales of the African Slave Trade* (University of Georgia Press, 2018).

"Joyful Intelligence," *Wilmington Advertiser*, June 20, 1838 (extra, 8 a.m.), about the thirty survivors rescued by the *Henry Camerdon*.

Frances Anne Kemble, *Journal of a Residence on a Georgian Plantation in 1838–1839*, edited with an introduction by John A. Scott (University of Georgia Press, 1984).

Mrs. Hugh McLeod (Miss Rebecca Lamar), "The Loss of the Steamer Pulaski," *Georgia Historical Quarterly*, Vol. 3, No. 2 (June 1919), 63–95.

Brenna Michaels and T. C. Michaels, *Hidden History of Savannah* (History Press, 2019).

Narrative of the Loss of the Steam-packet Pulaski: Which Burst Her Boiler and Sank on the Coast of North Carolina, June 14, 1838 (Harvard University, 1838).

Details of the Ship

Builder: John A. Robb, Baltimore, Maryland

Machinery: Watchman and Bratt, Baltimore, Maryland

Hull: 206 feet, 1 inch long

Beam: 25 feet, 2 inches wide

Depth: 13 feet, 7 inches

Weight: 685 tons

Engine: Vertical beam

Power: 225 horsepower (nominal)

Boilers: Two copper boilers, low pressure

Owners: Savannah and Charleston Steam Packet Co., 1837–1838

Salvage and Artifact Rescue Resources

Micah Eldred is the founder/CEO of Endurance Exploration Group, Inc. Endurance is the manager of the salvage partnership, which consists of Endurance, Blue Water Ventures and Marex. Together these three entities have formed a joint venture/partnership called Swordfish Partners, which is the entity that is salvaging the *Pulaski*.

Each partner has a role. Endurance organized the project, located and validated the wreck's identity, filed the admiralty claim, and manages the overall project.

Blue Water Ventures and its CEO, Keith Webb, were contracted by Endurance because of its shallow-water salvage expertise to perform physical salvage operations using its vessel, *Blue Water Rose*, and its divers in conjunction with Endurance personnel.

Marex has provided certain IP related to the wreck to the joint venture/partnership. Marex was originally formed by well-known salvage expert Herbert "Herbo" Humphreys and is now run by Herbo's nephew Tim Hudson and longtime Herbo lawyer Jerry Sklar.

ACKNOWLEDGMENTS

This fascinating story quite literally rose from the bottom of the ocean and wanted to be told. And yet it was also brought up by metaphorical fishermen with a huge net—by others who helped tell the story, rounded out its details and brought it to life with me. I wrote the words and dug deep for the story, but I could not have done it alone.

The hint of this story was first brought to me years ago by a Bluffton, South Carolina, native named Boo Harrel. He had printed out an article about the long-gone and doomed steamboat *Pulaski* and its sinking in 1838. I am grateful to Boo for being knowledgeable and persistent, as well as for his friendship and kindness.

There are loads of reasons why I put off working on this particular wreck's story, but lack of interest wasn't one of them. In hindsight, I wasn't ignoring the story but waiting for just the right time. About three weeks into my research and writing, the remains of the *Pulaski* were discovered by a company called the Endurance Exploration Group, under the guidance of CEO and founder Micah Eldred, and in a salvage partnership with Blue Water Ventures and Marex.

I am grateful for all of their work, and my absolute and deep gratitude goes to Micah Eldred, who has put up with my every question from how the coins are cleaned and sold to how the artifacts are logged and stored to technical terms like "admiralty" and so much more. With every artifact that rises from the sand a story rises also, and this story would not be nearly as fascinating without Micah's expertise and passion for the subject of shipwrecks and their discovery.

The Georgia Historical Society in Savannah stores a treasure trove of books, articles, papers, journals, family trees and so much more. As researchers know, not everything can be found on the Internet. And the days I spent sitting at those long tables in the historical house on Forsyth Park with the puddled light of a gooseneck lamp illuminating ancient newspapers and accounts were some of my favorite times writing this novel. I felt as if the passengers rose up to try to get my attention to tell their stories. If I could thank every one of the historians and librarians who keep these records in such immaculate order, I would.

If you've been to Savannah and haven't visited the Ships of the Sea Maritime Museum in the William Scarborough House and Gardens, you are missing out. This museum is as fascinating as it is educational. Just as in my novel, the *Wanderer* and the steamboat *Pulaski* ship models stand next to each other under protective cases. You can, just as I wrote, stand between them. It is enthralling to learn about how the young boy who survived the *Pulaski* disaster went on to finance the *Wanderer* for such horrific purposes. One would think that surviving a disaster would lead someone to want to do good in the world, not cause pain. But this isn't what happened. I learned of this story at the museum and I want to thank most notably Wendy Melton, Curator of Exhibits and Education. She was and is a fount of information and stories—is there anything better?

And speaking of museums, I want to thank the Telfair Museum's Owen-Thomas House and Slave Quarters of Savannah. When I wanted to identify the monogram of found silver, I turned to Cyndi Sommers. Her expertise was invaluable and her first hint—telling me that the silver's hallmark revealed the maker to be Nehemiah Dodge from Rhode Island—brought me closer to finding the owners (just as in the novel). I felt like a detective and Cyndi was my cohort in discovery. She was also extremely helpful in allowing me to see how the Telfair Museum does its absolute best to stay true to the facts of history and not merely the romantic notions of southern pride.

I interviewed the powerfully healing therapist Margarite Martino about the effects of trauma and PTSD in the body and mind of anyone who has survived a great tragedy. Her insight into how the body holds such memories allowed me to create more human and wounded characters than I would have otherwise. I thank you, Margarite, and your sister, Mary Alice Monroe, for connecting us!

I learned how to dive a long while ago, another lifetime ago, but it has been years and years, so for those details I turned to my author pal Joshilyn Jackson. She spent more time than she should have guiding me through the details of what would happen if Everly became narked. As always, for way more than just information, I am thankful for Joshilyn.

There is a bookstore in Savannah called E. Shavers. It is the oldest bookstore in the city and as charming and full of books and cats and tea as you'd dream about. The owner, Jessica Sognier Osborne, attended to all my questions about growing up in Savannah, about its history, its legends and its hidden traditions. I am grateful for her dedication to books, to Savannah, and to me.

Then as always there is the cadre of author friends who make sure I don't jump off the ledge of a story and into the abyss of blind alleyways and dead ends. More than once I almost gave up on this complicated story, and between the wisdom of Signe Pike, who said one sentence that changed everything; and Paula McLain, whose one-line truths often bring me to my senses, this book would still be languishing in my computer. I am profoundly blessed to have so many in my corner who would never allow me to "give up"—J. T. Ellison, Ariel Lawhon, Blake

Leyers (who read a few early pages), Lisa Patton, Kerry Madden, Lanier Isom, Barbara Cooney, Kate Phillips, Cassandra King, Lisa Wingate, Beth Howard, Tara Mahoney, and many more who encourage and cheer. To Sandee O, who always says just the right thing to keep me from despair and bring me back to what matters: the creativity that sustains us. And to Carol Carr, who said, "You must write this, and did you know there is a model in the Ships of the Sea in Savannah?"— thank you always! All of them, at one time or another, had to listen to me over the past years as I opined on and on about this story. To my Friends and Fiction Tribe, Mary Kay Andrews, Kristin Harmel, Kristy Woodson Harvey and Mary Alice Monroe, I am the luckiest. Your friendship and encouragement has changed my life and my writing in all the very best ways.

And to Berkley/Penguin Random House—what a team we have. I am so honored and pleased to work with you on this project. What a story it is. Claire Zion has been working on my tangled stories since my first book; I am deeply grateful for her honesty, ingenuity and stubborn belief. My editor, Danielle Perez, abided every little true-to-life detail I wanted to keep in the story; I am grateful for her keen eye! Thanks to Ellen Edwards, who was patient with me as I tried to figure out the door into this story, the opening and closing that would carry us along. To the art department for their innovative creativity. To all those whose names I do not know who touched this story to get it into the world. To the sales staff who love bookstores as much as I do—why else would we live this crazy life? Especially to Betty Lawson, who always listens with a smile. To Craig Burke, Danielle Keir, Fareeda Bullert and Jeanne-Marie Hudson—thank you! They listen to my crazy ideas and instead of talking me out of them, they try to figure out how to make it all happen. To Christine Ball and Ivan Held— thank you for your wise navigation of this ship that is our publishing world during some trying times.

To our bookstores—what would we do without you? You have been so supportive and wonderful and kind to my stories. You've been there for me and I am here for you. To our librarians—you are my heroes. Yes, I am talking to you, Ron Block, Carrie Steinmehl and Amanda Bonner Borden.

To the author James Jordan, whose book *The Slave-Trader's Letter-Book* opened my eyes to the real "story behind the story" of Charles Augustus Lafayette Lamar. James's meticulous research made my job a bit easier.

To my webmaster, Judy Collins, whose attention to detail is sharper than the eye of an eagle. She keeps me on the straight and narrow as much as she possibly can. To Meg Walker at Tandem Literary, whose constant upbeat enthusiasm is a balm to my anxious heart, and whose creative ideas are a force of nature.

To my agent, Marly Rusoff, who has willingly taken the roller-coaster ride that is my life from celebration to despair and everything in between, and never given up.

And always and always to my family—you have my heart and you know that. No way I could ever do this without your love, support and cheering. Pat, Thomas and Rusk Henry. Meagan, Evan and Bridgette Rock. Bonnie and George Callahan. Gwen and Chuck Henry. Barbi and Dan Burris, Jeannie and Mike Cunnion, Kirk and Anna Henry and Serena Henry have all kept me sane in so many different ways.

Although it might seem odd to actually thank a city, I must do so. It doesn't feel impersonal to me—I love, admire and honor the city of Savannah for its beauty and brokenness, for its past and its future. And to the now-named passengers and crew of the *Pulaski*—what an inspiration you have been to me. Your stories matter and I hope I have done them justice.

And not last and not least, you, my reader reading this: I am honored to be part of your life in story, and I do this for us.

DISCUSSION QUESTIONS

1. Did you know about the sinking of the *Pulaski* before you read this book? Why do you think that stories like this get lost to time? What surprised you most when you learned about this shipwreck?

2. The stories of the *Pulaski* sinking were part of Everly's childhood. Her grandfather told and retold the story—adding bits and pieces of mythology and lore. Do you have family stories that are part of your heritage that have changed over time?

3. The Longstreet family (inspired by the true Gazaway Bugg Lamar family) boarded the ship all together. In hindsight, knowing the dangers of steamboat travel, should they have traveled separately? Were they taking unnecessary risks? Did you ever blame Lamar Longstreet (Gazaway Lamar)?

4. Augusta writes "If not for the tragedy . . ." and then she lists the things in her life that she cherishes; this is how she makes meaning

out of something so awful. How do we make meaning of tragedy? How have you done this in your own life?

5. Much of this novel is about the kind of person someone becomes after a tragedy. We learn early on that Charles Longstreet (inspired by Charles Lamar, a real person) survived the explosion and the five days and five nights at sea. Twenty years later, he earned the nickname "the Red Devil." What did you make of this? Do you know anyone who survived something terrible only to become someone who did horrific harm to others? Why, or how, do you think that might happen?

6. Maddox Wagner tells Everly: "Not everyone who survives trauma becomes a better person. The idea that surviving brings everyone to a new and better place is a lie told by people who need the world to make sense." Do you agree with this? Have you or a loved one been through something that makes this statement ring true or false?

7. The city of Savannah is an integral part of the story—a character in its own right. Is there a city that is important to you? Do its tragedies and triumphs shape it? Do you believe that if you love a city, you must care about its complicated history?

8. Everly has been through her own loss and tragedy, and her grief has impacted her ability to engage or "thrive" in life. How do you think that working on the *Pulaski*'s curation and learning about the women who were on the ship affected her? Does learning about other people's stories help us to understand our own? Do you seek out stories that are similar to yours? Or ones that are different?

9. How does the time period (1838) affect the rescue of those who survived the explosion? How might this story be different today?

10. What do you think of the portrayal of enslaved people in this novel?

11. One of the most heartbreaking scenes in the novel is when Augusta must choose between Charles and Eliza. How did this affect Charles's story later in life? How did you feel when you read it? Did you wonder what you would have done?

12. Everly insisted on diving even though Maddox had a bad feeling about it. When Everly is narked on her dive, she hallucinates and sees her best friend. How does this impact her choices? Why do you think she felt she must see "what is below"? What is the difference between her desire to stay alive and her desire to live?

13. Everly blamed herself for Mora's death, believing that she caused Mora to stand in the path of the oncoming car. How does guilt impact grief? Why do you think we blame ourselves when we really had no control?

14. The shipwreck was found 180 years later, and divers brought up the artifacts—in both the real-life story of the *Pulaski* and in this novel. What was the most interesting artifact for you? What do almost-200-year-old artifacts tell us about the people who boarded that ship?

15. What did you think of the endings for the three women—Everly, Augusta and Lilly—who narrate the novel? Which of the three women do you identify the most with? Did you expect their endings? Would you change any of them? Which part of their stories touched you the most? Which part challenged you?

PATTI CALLAHAN is a *New York Times* bestselling author of both novels and short stories. She is the recipient of the Harper Lee Award for Distinguished Writer of the Year, the Alabama Library Association Fiction Award and The Christy Award for Book of the Year. Patti Callahan Henry is also the co-creator and co-host of the weekly web show and podcast *Friends and Fiction*. Patti has a graduate degree in pediatric nursing and is now a full-time writer living in both Mountain Brook, Alabama, and Bluffton, South Carolina.

CONNECT ONLINE

PattiCallahanHenry.com
AuthorPattiCallahanHenry
PCalHenry
PattiCHenry
PattiCalHenry